I0719190

CATSPAW

by

Nia Jean

Table of Contents

The Summons

"Why are there so many Zyphans?"

Aja snapped out of a daydream at the question, gazing across the garden she was seated in to where a young boy of eight or nine was gazing up at his mother. The two of them were walking down the path on the other side of the fence, over the cobblestone pathway that led through the village. She was glad the question hadn't been posed to her, not because she didn't know, but it was difficult to explain to a child. Carefully cutting two ripened squashes from their vines and placing them in her lap, she cast the boy's mother a curious glance.

"They're staying here with us right now," his mother said. She had her wicker basket of laundry held against her hip as she walked swiftly toward the Zyphan barracks. "Don't dawdle," she added, and the boy hurried his steps to keep up with her.

"I wish they would leave," the boy muttered unhappily. "I don't want to share our house."

"I know," his mother replied with a sigh.

They passed out of sight down the path as Aja finished gathering what she needed, and after rising to her feet, she brushed the dirt from her leggings and carried her armful of vegetables toward the General's house. *My house,* she corrected internally. *At least, it used to be.* Before the strangers known as Zyphans had come up the powerful current of the Uliah River on their steam-powered ships. That had been six months ago, and in that time, they had changed nearly everything about the quiet valley of Slyenials.

They had borne weapons when they came rushing in that day, expecting a fight as they marched into Aja's village of Northbank. What they found was a peaceful valley of dense woods, rich fields, and a community who lived in harmony with the land they cultivated. Wholly against any form of violence, Aja's people welcomed the strangers into their villages and homes. Aja's people, the Slyens, welcomed the strangers. They offered their surrender without being asked, choosing to work for them willingly so that they would not be treated harshly.

Now, their village had been transformed into the Zyphans' base of operations, as they prepared themselves for war against another nation to the southeast. Aja heard some of the soldiers talking about it from time to time, though she never caught many details.

"We won't have nearly enough soldiers if the ships don't arrive before winter," one would say.

"At least we won't run out of supplies," another would reply.

We were here first, Aja thought unhappily. She wished they would take their war back home with them. Or perhaps abandon it and live the way her people did.

She nearly stumbled on the two steps that led up to her front door, lost in her thoughts as she was. Catching herself just barely, she glanced up sheepishly at the marking carved over the entrance. It was of a sparrow surrounded by a wreath of pine branches, the Slyen symbol of peace. The carving had been made by her ancestors who first built the house, and she always glanced at it when she came home. Right now, it was a visible reminder that her careless thoughts had nearly caused her to lose her footing.

"Watch where you're going, Aja," she said, mimicking her mother's tone in amusement.

Her house was no larger than any other house in the village of Northbank, but it was the one the Zyphan General had chosen for himself. Aja and her mother Delia had become his housekeepers. Delia cooked, Aja gardened, and both of them kept the house clean. Her father had died when she was young, and her older sister had moved out when she got married, four years ago.

I'm glad we were worried for nothing, she thought, thinking back on the six months the Zyphans had been here as she pushed open the door and stepped inside. The strangers had been cold when they first arrived, suspicious of their tranquility and wary of their friendship. But it wasn't long before they found themselves trusting the Slyens as much as they trusted each other. They were friendlier now, familiar by name, encouraging when talking to them, and protective over the people they had once viewed with hostility. It didn't change the fact that the Zyphans were now their overseers. But because they had accepted them in that role, the Zyphans' hostility had faded.

Aja slipped off her canvas shoes just inside the entrance, pausing when she caught a flash of her reflection to her left. The General had hung a large mirror on the wall beside the door, as he liked to look at himself and adjust his uniform each time he left or arrived at the house. He was so fond of his own reflection that sometimes he would smirk at himself as he twisted the ends of his mustache with his fingers and tell himself he was "looking sharp." She stared at herself with far less enthusiasm. Her long brown hair, tied in a loose braid, had several wispy strands escaping from her hempen tie. Her warm tan skin, as well as the simple linen clothes she wore, were dotted by spots of moist dirt from the garden.

She scrunched up her nose at herself, her loam-colored eyes squinting. She wasn't fond of her own reflection, thinking her eyes too dark and her hair too straight. It didn't have the lovely waves her sister's hair had, or the hint of green in her irises. Yet every time she entered the house, she found herself stopping to look at herself in the mirror.

The sound of boots thudding on cobblestones outside snapped her out of her thoughts. Soldiers always walked loudly, so it was sometimes hard to tell if it was simply a Zyphan walking by, or if it was the General returning. She focused, straining her ears and sensing with her feet on the tile floor. Hearing things with sharper focus, listening with more than just her ears—this was something she had practiced since she was young. In her mind, she called it *Listening*, putting an emphasis on the word that meant so much more than its letters spelled. A puzzle, to see what she could discern with her senses alone. It was a game she still played, even though she was no longer a child.

The rhythm of the steps was familiar. *The General,* she decided, and swiftly stepped away from the door, heading across the sitting room for the kitchen. She didn't quite make it before the door was flung open, startling her with the sound.

General Ryder was whistling to himself as he paused by the mirror, brushing nonexistent dust from his ochre and white uniform. "Looking fine," he praised, his trademark smirk curling the corner of his lips. He brushed his hand over his groomed, black hair, smoothing back stray hairs only he could see.

It was comical to watch, though Aja didn't want to be caught. She slipped into the kitchen, setting the vegetables she'd gathered onto the counter. "Is this enough?" she asked.

Delia stood beside the brick stove, cutting pieces of dough and rolling them into circles for flatbread that she would roll out after the dough had rested a while. "That's plenty," she replied. "Thank you."

"Do you want help?" Aja asked. She pulled a knife from the knife block, testing its sharpness carefully with her thumb.

"Not with this," her mother said, glancing over her shoulder at the doorway. "I haven't beaten the rugs yet today, and with autumn here, more dirt gets tracked into the house than usual." She didn't say it, but Aja understood what she meant. The two of them never wore their shoes in the house; only the General tracked mud or dirt from the outside.

"Alright, I'll go," Aja nodded. The idea of going outside again was appealing to her. She loved being out in the garden, and she missed taking walks down to the river cliffs to watch birds and fish. She used to go down there and stare across the water for hours, imagining what wilderness might exist on the distant shore. The Uliah's current was treacherous, and no one dared to swim or boat across it. Trying would put them at the mercy of the river, and who knew where it would sweep them off to as it carried them far to the west?

"Aja, the rugs," Delia said, interrupting her thoughts with a mothering tone that was hard to ignore. "Bring your head out of the clouds."

"Yes, yes," Aja assured her, amused. Giving her mother a kiss on the cheek, she slipped out of the kitchen once more, making her way to the sitting room. They only had two rugs in their house, one in the sitting area outside the kitchen, and the other in the General's room. It was probably safer to start with the closest one and do the bedroom rug while he was sitting down to eat.

General Ryder was still gazing at himself in the mirror when she came out, but when he saw her go to the rug and begin to roll it up, he smiled at her with a sort of pleased, patient expression on his face. "Ah, Aja," he said, almost proudly. "Today is a good day. Do you know why?"

She hesitated, unsure whether he wanted her to stop what she was doing to listen or continue working. "Why?" she asked, choosing to return to her task. He liked the sound of his own voice, and she was sure he would continue to talk to himself even if she used her chores as an excuse to leave.

"Because, my simple girl," he announced, gazing at himself in the mirror again. "We are bringing you the secrets of technology! You've been living all this time with simple tools and primitive buildings. You don't have electricity like we have in Zypha, or even running water. Tell me, do you enjoy going out to the well to get water, every day? Wouldn't you like it if the water came directly to your kitchen? That's what we're bringing to you."

She listened, familiar with this particular speech. It was one he often gave, whenever they started some new project in the village. First, it had been the barracks they built, then it was the training grounds, a wide space that had once been a flourishing field. Each new thing they started building was more distressing than the last, and Aja wasn't the only one who was upset. *He still thinks us primitive, but we don't need more than this,* she thought, struggling to disguise her melancholy. *We have never lacked anything, and all our needs are met in this valley. Why can't the Zyphans be content with what they have, like us?*

"I sent word to Zypha today," Ryder continued, adjusting his sleeves, now. "They'll be sending architects and plumbers, city planners. We'll turn this valley into a thriving city, and we'll create schools so your people can be educated. You're a part of Zypha, now. And Zypha looks out for its own."

"We have no need for a school," Aja said, compelled by frustration to speak, though she hadn't intended to. "The children are taught by their mothers until they are old enough to be apprenticed."

"What can uneducated mothers teach their children?" Ryder shook his head, and his tone was pitying. "Gardening? The history of trees? We can teach you math, science, and all about the world outside this valley!"

A world where people wage war against each other, Aja thought grimly. She rose to her feet, lifting the rolled-up rug and draping it over her shoulder. "I need to take this outside," she said.

"You don't know what we're giving you, none of you," he sighed. He turned from the mirror, observing her carefully composed face with compassion. "But that's not your fault. When you've seen what we can bring you and teach you, then you will understand."

"We are happy as we are," Aja said. She didn't know why she was still talking, why she hadn't stepped past him toward the door. But her stomach felt tight while she was listening to him, and she *wanted* to voice the words that were bubbling up from her aching chest.

"You will be *happier* after we've helped you," he assured her. "And one day, you will thank us, just as we are thankful to you." He stepped toward the window that looked out into the garden, adopting a thoughtful expression. "Days like today, I find myself thinking back to when we first arrived in Slyenials," he said, and his tone betrayed he was prepared to continue speaking for some time.

Aja shifted the rug on her shoulder, scowling as she glanced toward the door. Maybe if she was very quiet, he wouldn't notice her slip out.

"Our maps didn't show the valley, you see," he continued, lifting his chin as he spoke, swelling with pride at his own words. "It was my decision to make landfall and climb the cliffs, and it was my decision to listen when your elders spoke to us. We expected to lose half our force in battle, yet we were welcomed warmly instead. If I had not stopped to listen, if I had not chosen to trust your people, think of what could have been lost! Instead, here we stand—fellow peoples of Zypha."

Walking quietly in her bare feet, Aja reached her shoes and slipped them on one foot at a time. She made no comment on his soliloquy, but none was expected. He just wanted to talk, and Aja was good at listening. *But we are not Zyphans,* she thought. *We are Slyens, and you are trying to change everything we love.*

"The Slyens have shown us kindness and given us their trust," Ryder nodded sagely to himself. "They offered their homes and chose to work for us. No one else would have done the same. It's unthinkable! It defies common sense! Yet here we are, thriving together without violence. Yes… the Slyens have welcomed us freely. And *I* will see to it that the people of Slyenials are treated as Zyphan citizens; with honor, with respect, and with kindness." He smiled, clasping his hands behind his back as he gazed out the window.

This was the moment Aja had been waiting for. She could tell that he was no longer talking to her, that he didn't care if she stayed to hear his words. And if she waited, she knew he would continue on as before, talking to himself about his lofty goals, needing only himself to appreciate his speeches. Quietly opening the door, she hurried outside with the rug and went around the house to the back, where the taut clotheslines stretched between wooden poles. She flung the rug over the nearest line in agitation, letting out all her frustration.

"It's not better," she said, taking up the rake and using it to beat dust from the rug. It fell to the ground in a shower, some of the finer particles filling the air and getting in her mouth and nose. "We don't need their schools or their architects. We *have* architects, and they know how to build houses that last even through earthquakes and storms! We know how to manage waste so that it doesn't contaminate the land or the water, to turn it into compost for the forest and gardens. We already have everything we need! Why can't they see that? Why can't they just be more like us?"

She kept beating the rug as she complained, relying on the sound to cover her muttered words, fearful of the General overhearing her. By the time she finished one side, she was breathing heavily, her forehead and lower back damp with sweat. But she was feeling better. It helped, being able to vent.

"Why are there so many Zyphans?"

The boy's question echoed in her mind, and she found herself upset once again. Even greater changes were coming than the ones already occurring all across Slyenials. More and more Zyphans would come in on their ships, planning for war and changing the valley to suit their needs. Rapidly and thoroughly, the Slyens were losing their way of life.

The approach of sunset was always beautiful in the valley. Aja liked to make excuses to slip outside and watch the sky, though she hardly needed to. She had nowhere to be but her own house, and the Zyphans didn't enforce curfews on them. When she was younger, she used to slip out through her window and sit on the fence, watching the sky change colors as the light faded behind the mountains, and the expanse became filled with stars. Now at nineteen, she no longer fit through the window, but she still liked to come out here without mentioning her intention, as though it were still something secret and private.

Her mind was troubled after Ryder's speech this afternoon, and she dreaded falling asleep and facing her dreams with her thoughts burdened. Despite the cool autumn air, she went out to the fence and leaned against it, studying the mountain range that circled the valley on three sides. *We used to be safe within these mountains,* she thought. *None of us would have ever dreamed of ships being able to sail up the river. Has the world outside our valley really changed that much?*

Filled with unease, and too restless to remain still, she walked through the garden and opened the wooden gate, stepping out onto the cobblestone road. She hardly paid attention to where she was going, drifting from house to house, fearing the day when more of them would be torn down to make way for new, larger buildings. Her eyes strayed toward the garrison, the large ochre tents and the hard-packed dirt and clay where the soldiers practiced their drills. Once it had been a field full of grass and flowers, where bees played and pollinated, little animals dug safe burrows, and pheasants made nests in the tall grass. Now she doubted the field would ever be green again.

At length, she realized that her walk was taking her out of the village toward the dense line of trees that marked the beginning of Slyenwood. It was dangerous to enter the forest, especially at night, so she turned around to head back. *Mother will probably scold me for staying out late,* she thought, glancing at the sky. There was still a line of color above the mountains, purple and orange bleeding into blues and blacks. Enough light to get home, and enough darkness to worry about predators from the trees. She'd never encountered a forest jaguar before, but she'd heard enough stories to have a healthy fear of them. Northbank was so close to the wood that the danger of dusk was too real to ignore.

Aja stiffened, growing alarmed as her attempts to move forward failed. Each time she tried to take a step, she felt as if her whole body went rigid, ignoring her efforts to move as though she were paralyzed. *Something's wrong,* she thought, her heart racing as fear began to creep into her mind. *Why can't I move?* She tried to walk, and her legs refused to budge. She urged her body forward, yet it remained still. Behind her back, her awareness of the forest pressed against her like a heavy weight, and all the hairs on her body stood on end.

The forest was watching her.

Swallowing with apprehension, she closed her eyes and *Listened.* If her body would not move, then it was sensing something. Without knowing what it was, how would she know what to do? At first, all she could hear was the pounding of her own blood in her ears, and the sound her throat made when she swallowed and found her mouth dry. *What is it?* she thought, drawing herself deeper into calm. It helped to press her hand to her chest and slow her breathing when she was feeling anxious. To open her ears and listen with her bones. Her pulse calmed with each breath, awareness spreading across her skin.

Something was calling to her, urging her to turn around. Aja opened her eyes, turning to face the dense line of trees behind her back with wonder. *The trees?* she thought. Her eyes lifted to the sky, to the deepening purple hues, and she knew that she shouldn't stay out past dusk. Yet for some reason, her legs wouldn't move when she wanted them to, and her heart echoed with longing to answer the call. She felt as though she must be out of her mind as she faced the trees fully and took a step towards them.

It should have scared her, leaving safety and common sense behind her as she walked first slowly, then swiftly into the forest. Instead, she felt her heart racing with anticipation, excited the way she used to be when she was younger. She *wanted* to see what was in there, to find out what compelled her to enter a place she knew better than to go. Feeling reckless, she slipped quietly between the trees, following whatever force was drawing her closer.

The sky was soon fully dark, yet the trees were not so dense that she couldn't see the sky above her. The Slyens cared for the forest as much as the fields, cutting down trees that needed to be cut, lighting controlled fires to help the ecosystem thrive, so it wasn't dangerously overgrown. As she made her way deeper, towards the foothills to the south, she found herself studying the woods with caretaker eyes. Here was a cluster of young trees that would need to be thinned, and over there were several mushrooms that could be harvested. She passed a tree that had split down the middle, paused to consider it, and saw that it had continued growing upward again as two trees connected at their base. It was thriving and would not need to be cut down. The night was quiet, and though she listened intently for signs of danger, she felt only peace around her.

She walked for two hours, growing more excited as she went. Something *was* calling to her, something that seemed to grow stronger the closer she got. When she stepped out from between the trees into a wide clearing she had never seen before, she let out a gasp of surprise. The clearing was covered in moss instead of grass, so lush that she wanted nothing more than to lie down upon it and stare at the endless sky full of many stars. Tiny little white flowers dotted the clearing, poking up through the moss, and occasionally there were patches of larger purple ones, too. Just as she was about to step forward and lay herself down in the center of it, she became aware of something she hadn't seen until that moment.

It was a cat, as large as a person. She knew it was a cat because it was covered in fur, its ears rounded like those of the forest jaguars, its eyes a pale yellow with pointed oval pupils. It was sitting in the center of the clearing with a relaxed expression, eyes gentle and curious as it—watching her as she stared back at it. She almost thought that it was seated the way a person might sit, legs crossed and elbows resting on its knees. But cats were not shaped like people, so she knew her eyes must be playing tricks on her.

I should not turn and run, she remembered, her heart racing with the danger she faced. *I must back away slowly, and if it follows me, I should speak loudly and firmly as I tell it to go away.* These were things her mother had taught her when she was young. Jaguars were terrifying creatures, unafraid of humans, though they could be dissuaded from attacking if she kept her cool and did not show weakness. Even knowing all this, she couldn't seem to get over her terror enough to move, and she was finding it difficult to breathe. *I'm afraid,* she admitted inwardly.

Watching her with interest, the cat's eyes half-closed with a sort of pleased expression. "You needn't be afraid," it said, its voice surprisingly masculine and human sounding. "I will not harm you."

Aja blinked her eyes several times, but no matter how many times she blinked, the cat was still there. Her chest felt tight when she realized what must be happening. *None of it is real,* she thought. *I'm already asleep.* She'd hoped to avoid lucid dreams tonight. They always left her with an ominous feeling when next she woke. She had gone five nights without having one and had been hoping the trend would continue.

If only I knew how to wake up, she thought. "Are you real?" she asked, her voice flat. It was a pointless question to ask in a lucid dream, but it usually had interesting responses.

"Certainly, as real as you," he replied evenly.

"What are you? You don't look like a jaguar." She glanced upward, marking the stars, and was surprised by how crisp the sky looked. Most lucid dreams were vague when she sought details, and places she had observed once always looked different the next time she studied them. She dropped her eyes to him once more.

At her comment, the cat turned his nose up with displeasure. "I am no mere jaguar," he declared unhappily. "But I suppose you wouldn't be familiar with my kind by sight. Come closer, sit down." He gestured to the moss in front of him, and she saw that while his arm was covered in fur, the shape of his arms and shoulders was closer to her own than a jaguar's. Only his hand was more like a cat's paw than a human hand.

A cat person? she thought, impressed at her own imagination. *I think that's a first.* She didn't want to get closer to him, but she was fairly sure he meant her no harm. Despite how real things sometimes seemed in dreams, she was never in any real danger. She stepped cautiously toward him, walking across moss so thick her steps made no sound as they sank into the carpet of greenery. Just past an arm's length from him, she stopped, sinking down to sit on her legs across from him.

Now that she was closer, she could see that he looked very much like a person, and he even seemed to be wearing some form of clothing. His chest was bare apart from his fur, which was a mottled gray with faint patterns of dots and lines in black. But his legs, which were shaped like a cat's despite being as long as a human's, were wrapped in loose-fitting leggings made of undyed plant fibers, stopping at the knee. They seemed too long for him to walk on all fours, indicating he must walk upright and use his front paws as hands. She found the level of detail she saw unnerving; it was so crystal clear.

Dreams this sharp always came true.

Aja's shoulders tensed, fear trickling into her mind as she forced herself not to recall those nightmares. This dream wasn't about someone's death. It wasn't about a storm, a flood, or a premonition of something terrible. And a cat-person did not exist in real life. *Nothing terrible is going to happen,* she told herself, holding her breath until her lungs hurt. She exhaled when dots darkened her vision.

"There, that's better," he said, his expression relaxed once she was seated. "You certainly took your time getting here, didn't you? The night will be over before you get home at this rate. Didn't you hear the urgency in my call?"

"Your call, was it?" Aja asked. She looked up at the sky. The same stars hung across the black, same as the last time she had observed them. Sweat beaded on her brow despite the autumn chill. *It's too real.* "Who are you?" She wasn't sure she wanted to find out what her dream wanted to tell her. *Don't tell me someone's going to die. I don't want to hear it.* Against her will, flashes of memory shot through her mind as she recalled the first time she had ever dreamed of the future. Her father walking by the cliffs, searching for a daughter who had run away in anger to hide, despite the storm.

If only she had listened to that dream. If only she had stayed inside.

"My name is Slyen," the cat said proudly. There was a rumble in his chest as he said his name, almost like a cat's purr, but it didn't last long enough for her to be sure. "These are my lands, and you are one of my people."

Aja drew herself from her thoughts with interest. "Your people?" she asked wryly. Her people were certainly called Slyens, and they lived in the valley of Slyenials, but they had named themselves after the mountain range. Not some mysterious cat who could speak and sit like a person.

"It doesn't matter if you believe me," he waved his paw-like hand dismissively. "It only matters that you *listen* to me. There is something that I need you to, and there isn't much time left to do it."

Listen. A word that had a special meaning to her. Aja pressed her lips together as she considered what her dream was trying to tell her, thinking of how often she was asked to do things she wasn't fond of. Gardening was something she loved, and she enjoyed the time she spent outdoors. But she detested being confined to the house to clean, or being asked to stand straight and silent as the General invited his squadron leaders to the house, just in case they requested something to eat or drink. It was true that her people had willingly invited the Zyphans into their homes and pledged to serve them, but it wasn't what they *wanted*. They were against violence, and that was all.

I love to Listen, she thought, growing frustrated with her dream. *But I shouldn't have to listen to a strange cat in my dreams. And anyway, I get the sense he's going to tell me something I don't want to hear.*

The cat who called himself Slyen seemed unaware of her inner thoughts and didn't pay attention to her frown. He continued on with what he wanted to say, not unlike the General when he wanted to hear himself speak. "As guardian and steward over my territory, I care a great deal about who I allow to live here. These Zyphans that you have welcomed in are troublesome, and I'm certain that only disaster can come of their being here. That is why they must be driven out." He looked at her pointedly, expecting a reply.

"We are not overly fond of them either, but we won't drive them out," she replied evenly, more honest in dreams than when she was awake. "They don't intend to harm us, even though they don't understand us."

"And that is exactly the problem," Slyen scowled. "They are not villains, and certainly they have more care for the natural resources of the land than the Querians, but the fact remains that they were *not* invited, and the war they intend to start threatens the precarious peace of our land!"

Aja straightened, curiosity rising despite her misgivings. She knew about the war they wanted to start, but not who they intended to fight. "Querians?" she asked. It was a word that had no meaning to her, perhaps no meaning at all. The subconscious invented things like this when she asked questions, and not all of the answers she received while sleeping made sense upon waking.

Slyen continued as though he hadn't heard her. "I do recognize that it's my fault it's gotten this bad," he sighed, leaning forward with his elbows on his knees and clasping his paws together. "The only reason your people didn't try to resist when they arrived is because of my Influence over this valley. I was arrogant in my protection of my lands—I believed that the mountains would protect you, that the current of the Uliah was too strong for ships to manage any sort of landing. The shore is a cliff as tall as these trees, for Mog's sake!" He waved his arm toward the evergreens that circled the clearing.

"It's easy to pin the blame for our own actions on someone else, is that what you're trying to say?" Aja wondered out loud. She leaned back until she was lying on the moss, staring up at the stars that remained the same no matter how many times she glanced at them. They an indication that this was more vision than dream. "Even in my sleep I try to find excuses to take refuge in, because I hate that they're here. I don't hate *them*, most of them are very nice. They are kind to us, even when they think themselves better than us. But I still…" she closed her hands into fists, frustration filling her heart so much that her chest hurt. "I hate the *change*. Cutting down trees that don't need to be felled, destroying our houses to make bigger ones, full of space they don't need. But what can I do? What can any of us *do*?"

This was what burdened her heart the most. The fact that none of them were doing anything to stop it, too afraid of what might happen if they tried. *It doesn't surprise me that I'd be as distressed in my sleep as when I'm awake,* she admitted to herself. *But why can't my nights be like anyone else's? Imagine going to sleep and waking up rested. I haven't felt that in years.*

"The fault is not yours, human child," the cat called Slyen replied. His voice was surprisingly soft and echoed the same distress she felt in her heart. "It is mine, and I regret that I cannot solve it by myself. That is why I called you here."

"I can't imagine what you expect me to do about it," she replied. She lifted her hand, tracing the shapes of constellations she knew in the sky, unnerved by their accuracy. In most dreams, constellations were indistinct and mercurial.

But these ones were right where they were supposed to be. "I *won't* fight." These words were spoken in a whisper, a promise in her heart that gave her peace. She was proud of the Tenets of her people, the code they had created when her ancestors first escaped into this valley from a world full of strife. Repeating them to herself often gave her a sense of comfort even in the face of grief.

"This land is our home, we will care for it," Slyen said, quoting the Tenets with a melancholy tone as though he understood her heart. "These mountains are our name; we will honor them. The beasts are our brothers, we will not harm them. Nature is our treasure; we will protect it. And peace is our heart, we will never turn from it." He sighed when he finished. "I remember when your people first wrote the Tenets. I was there when they vowed to teach them to their children. It made me proud, because their desire was the same as mine. That is why my Influence became unbreakable."

"How can a cat influence the forming of a nation?" Aja asked, smiling wryly. She dropped her arm to her side, growing sleepy as she stared at the stars. The wind had died down, and though the moss was damp, she was so comfortable she almost felt as though she could drop off. *Falling asleep in a dream. I wonder if such a thing is possible? Perhaps that is the answer to waking up.*

"I am no mere cat," Slyen insisted. "I am a Moglian. The magic of my people is called Influence, and it is far more powerful than you can comprehend. Powerful enough to shape the nature of this very valley. These evergreens grow taller than most, because I like them tall. The clearing is covered in moss because I desired it to be so. And your people, once a fearful and weary group of survivors escaping a war of genocide, became a nation of caretakers for the land that is mine. You protect what I love, and for that I protect you." He paused, a sort of rumbled growl rolling in his chest. "It is why I *must* send the Zyphans away before it is too late."

Aja rolled onto her side, turning her body so she could stare at the cat with curiosity. "Can you?" she murmured. "Can you really send them away?" The question was bitter, filled with doubt. Was this her mind's way of telling her this was what she wished? *I don't want them to change our valley,* she admitted to herself. *But I don't necessarily want them all to leave. I just want them to live more like us.* Things had certainly become livelier with their arrival. But sometimes, that was nice, too.

Slyen's pale eyes reflected the moonlight as he met her gaze. Once more, he seemed completely unaware of her inner thoughts, contrary to most of her dream visitors. "I can," he said gravely. "And I must. But I'm afraid I can't do it alone. That is why I need *you.*"

Red Skies

Dreams were funny things. Sometimes they were stressful, filled with ridiculous situations and many problems, where each problem Aja solved only spawned more. Other times, she felt as though she understood the secrets of life, learned things that were new and invigorating, only to be forgotten when the light of day drew her from slumber. It was not uncommon to find her subconscious creating solutions for things that were weighing her down. That was why she felt neither hopeful nor surprised at Slyen's promise to send the Zyphans away.

Her comfort was that this was no omen of death that would haunt her when the sun rose.

"The Zyphans have spent too long in the valley already," Slyen said, seeming to enjoy her rapt silence as she waited to hear what else he would say. She decided he was a character she had based on General Ryder and found the thought amusing. "They have not made vows of peace, so they won't abandon their war even under the weight of my Influence. Instead, they'll become attached to the tranquility of my lands and bring more and more of their kind to stay here. Then it will not be Slyenials, but Zyphanials."

A laugh escaped Aja's mouth, and when he looked at her with a sharp scowl, she pointed at him with one finger. "It's funny," she commended. "Zyphanials. But come on, you can do better than that. Why not Zyphanian? Zyphantopia? Or perhaps Zyphan's Reach?"

"You think yourself clever without understanding anything," Slyen sniffed, turning up his nose. "The words *ials* is from the Moglian tongue; it means 'lands', which is why this valley is called Slyenials. They are *my* lands."

"I'm sure it does mean 'lands'," Aja allowed her dream companion. "But they belong to the mountains, not to us. We are only their keepers." Her smile faded as she pictured the loss of the field, now covered in ochre tents and packed dirt. She thought of the woods that had been cleared, and the winding stairs now carved into the cliffs which banked the river. "Keepers," she murmured miserably. "Can I even call us that, anymore?"

Slyen watched her, his expression turning thoughtful. After a moment, he spoke again. "My Influence is the reason they did not attack your people when they landed," he said gravely. "And it is my Influence that keeps them from turning hostile against you now and does not allow them to suspect you of plots and secrecy. They trust you because I tell them to, and because you *are* trustworthy. But I'm afraid it's not enough."

"I can't help you," she told him. "I don't have Influence." She shivered when the breeze picked up, rubbing her arms with her hands. *I can't do anything,* she added internally. *Even to stand up to the Zyphans to stop them from changing the valley.*

"Luckily, that's not required," the cat responded. "It *will* take Influence to drive them out, especially since I desire to send them away without violence. But my Influence alone cannot accomplish it. That's why I'm sending you south, to find my brother. It should only take you a few weeks, I think. And once you bring him back here, our combined strength can compel the Zyphans to pack up and return to their own lands."

"Weeks?" Aja laughed again. There was nowhere in the valley that could not be reached in a few days. They had five villages, each with their own section of land to care for. Northbank was half a day's walk to the river. "Why should I travel to Nettledown to find your brother? He should come here." Nettledown was the southernmost village, high on the foothills among the trees. She couldn't picture any further south than that, apart from the mountains themselves.

"He's not in Nettledown," Slyen declared, growing exasperated. "His lands are much further, past desert and mountains, on the southern peninsula called Mettain."

"Why don't you call him the same way you called me?" Aja suggested.

"My Influence can't reach that far," he grumbled. "Otherwise, I'd have done that already. No, the only way is for *you* to go and fetch him. I can't risk leaving the valley, or I'd return to find my lands in ruin and my people in peril."

"Well, I can't go," Aja said. She closed her eyes, yawning as sleepiness weighed heavily on her. "I have work to do, and a garden to keep."

"It must be you, there's no one else who can," Slyen argued.

His words caused a twist of anxiety in her chest. Was this her subconscious's way of telling her she needed to overcome her fear and stand up to the Zyphans? *No, I can't do it,* she thought with a shudder. *If I start telling them off, they won't see us as friends anymore. They'll think that we've turned against them, and they'll be harsh with us.* "I can't," she said out loud.

"You can, and you must."

"No, I can't," she insisted, opening her eyes. Her heart started pounding, and her pulse racing so much it drove all her sleepiness away. Yet when she sat up and looked around her, she found herself still in the clearing, the cat called Slyen sitting across from her.

The idea began to grow in her mind that this moment, this conversation, might be real after all. As soon as she thought it, she became terrified. But it wasn't possible. This *had* to be a dream.

"Those old enough to go have become locked into their ways," Slyen told her, the yellow in his eyes seeming sharp to her. "After a certain point, my Influence becomes unbreakable, and not even I could compel them to go. And those young enough to be willing are too young to send. The world is too dangerous for me to send a child who cannot take care of themselves. They would die from hunger or wild animals before they ever reached my brother. You are the *only* one of my people who is old enough to go, and young enough at heart to be changeable."

"There are plenty of people my age," she pleaded, wrapping her arms around herself. The wind felt cold, and her back was damp from lying on the moss so long. She shivered, dread growing in her heart. "I'm nineteen… but Seila is seventeen, and she's more reckless than I am."

"I'm not looking for reckless, I need someone sensible," Slyen frowned. He crossed his arms too, eyeing her gravely. "I would have expected you to *jump* at the chance. You are filled with unrest, aren't you?"

"Of course I am!" she blurted. "I hate to even imagine what my home will look like, years from now. But what can I do about it? Certainly not leave, I haven't even gone as far south as Nettledown." She looked over her shoulder at the trees, uncomfortable when she realized she didn't know where she was and had no idea how to get back. "Besides," she added, "I'm definitely not *sensible*."

"In that, I suppose I agree," Slyen muttered. "A *sensible* person would go."

"A sensible person would go home and get back to work," Aja declared, rising to her feet. She intended to march away, following the dents of her footsteps back the way she came, but when she looked around, she could see no sign of them. The moss was healthy, and it had sprung back up after she had passed over it.

The cat sighed, clearly frustrated. Then, he too rose to his feet. He stood only to Aja's shoulders, which was not very high, but that didn't make him any less intimidating. "Perhaps you'd like some time to think it over," he suggested. "I can force you to go if I must, but I'd rather not. That defeats the purpose of sending someone who is willing." He grimaced, his whiskers spreading wider with the motion of his facial muscles. "If I have to, I will wait until your friend Seila is a little bit older. But I would rather not delay. Once the Zyphans have waited through winter, they *will* send their soldiers out for war. And by the time Seila is old enough, the war will have already started. By then, it might be too late to drive them out."

Aja looked down, her shoulders trembling faintly with a shiver, though it wasn't from the cold. She couldn't get over the dread in her heart, and the horrible premonition that something terrible would come to the valley if the Zyphans went to war. *It is an omen,* she decided. *I only have dreams this sharp when something terrible is going to happen.*

"Go home," Slyen said. "Sleep. And think on what I've said. If you decide to go, I will give you what you need so that you can make the journey. Just remember... once winter rolls in, it will be too late. The Zyphan army will march with the spring."

She didn't know when she walked away from him and didn't remember making the trip through the trees. But when she looked up again, she found that she was standing at the edge of her own village, the sky growing lighter as dawn crept up behind the mountains. Her legs were aching from her walk, her clothes were wet with dew, and she felt exhausted from head to toe. *It wasn't real,* she reassured herself, making her way toward her house with unfocused eyes. *It was a dream, nothing more.*

When she crept into the house and left her shoes by the door, she was utterly relieved to make it to the room she shared with her mother, crawling into her bed without changing clothes.

The sky was red, not with sunset or storm, but with a portent of wounds and loss of life. She saw it from the ground, staring upwards from where she knelt in the garden, vegetables in her lap and her shears in her fingers. The sight of red spreading across the sky made her ears ache, though she didn't understand what she was hearing. *I need to see,* she thought anxiously. *I need to know.*

The moment the desire took root inside her, she found herself rising upward, higher and higher, as though taking flight like a bird. She flew for the mountains, desperate to see what was behind them, as a chill wrapped around her tightly. Just when she thought she might crest the peaks, the sound she could not hear crashed into her. Her bones rattled, her ears bled, and she screamed as she plummeted down to the valley once more. She lay broken on the ground, gazing up as red stretched across the sky until all trace of blue was gone.

A whimper reached her ear, a whimper of pain and despair that she could not ignore. Turning her head, she saw numerous people lying motionless on the ground around her. Some of them were Zyphan, some of them were Slyen, and all of them were vacant of life. *We're too late,* she thought, reaching her hand toward the body of her sister, too far away for her to reach. *They have come.*

"Aja!"

At the feeling of hands grabbing her shoulders, shaking her awake, Aja screamed. But as she fought to free herself from their grip, she found herself in her own room. The hands belonged to her mother, whose face was pale as she shook Aja awake.

"It was a dream," Delia murmured, worry creasing her forehead as she gazed into her daughter's eyes. "Just a dream."

Something dripped down Aja's cheek, hanging at the edge of her jaw, and she wiped it with one hand. It was a tear. "What… what time is it?" she asked, swallowing. *A dream,* she thought miserably. *More like a nightmare. That's two dreams in one night.* After what she had just seen, she found herself wishing she could have continued talking to the cat-person instead. At least that dream had been harmless.

"It's still morning," her mother frowned. "You didn't wake at first, so I let you sleep." She glanced to her left, toward the window that looked out over to the yard. "You should go out to the garden. The sunlight will help."

It usually did. Sometimes, sunlight was the only thing that could chase away the chill of bad dreams. When she left, Aja rose and dressed in clean clothes—sturdy leggings under a woven tunic that would keep her warm—combing her hair before tying it into a simple braid that hung over her left shoulder. When she came out, she saw her mother kneading dough in the kitchen. *I should eat,* she thought, but the memory of unmoving bodies strewn around her made her stomach clench, and immediately she dispelled the thought. Hurrying to her shoes, she slipped them on and was surprised to find that they were damp. Had she stepped in something wet yesterday?

Unsettled, she pushed open the door without glancing at her reflection in the mirror. She didn't want to see what expression lingered in her own eyes.

Spending time in the garden was soothing. She didn't have anything she *had* to do, and no urgency of time compelled her to hurry her work. Unlike the soldiers who had to spend their day training and building, the Slyens were free to do whatever they normally did. Caring for the land, working at their crafts, keeping house and making food. The Zyphans seemed perfectly content to let them set the pace for their own lives, only giving them orders when they couldn't send one of their own. Slyens were not being forced to build new buildings, join the drills, or do things they weren't accustomed to. They were treated more like servants than workers, expected to cook and clean, and not much else.

They are kind to us, she admitted to herself, leaning over the garden bed as she weeded. *Even if they don't understand us. I just wish they would stop trying to change things. I wish I was brave enough to tell them.*

"Seems like I always find you in the garden," a playful, familiar voice declared. Aja lifted her head to see one of the soldiers leaning against the fence, grinning down at her. His name was Emrin, and he was one of the engineers, a term that meant nothing to her, though he had no small amount of pride in the title. He was often sneaking away from work and spent a great deal of time talking with the Slyens.

She liked Emrin better than most because he was more like them. He liked to take it easy, appreciating the little things and finding beauty in anything he looked at. Sometimes he'd find a place to sit down away from prying eyes and draw in his sketchbook, always pictures of things that Aja had never seen. He called them machines, which was a common enough word, but she supposed they were far more complicated than the type of machine she was familiar with. Slyens called the oil press a machine, but Emrin's drawings showed gears and crystals, beams he called "refracted light" and elegant designs.

"Are you daydreaming again, Aja?" Emrin teased.

"Are you skipping work again, Emrin?" she threw back. She liked how curly his hair was and thought the color of his skin was as appealing as dusk. All of the Zyphans were darker than the Slyens, which Emrin claimed was due to how hot Zypha was. But he was darker and more interesting than the rest of them, with greenish-brown eyes that looked like the depths of the forest. If she could paint like her sister, she would have tried to capture his unique colors that made her own brown eyes and brown hair seem flat and boring by comparison.

"Ah, ah," he scolded, wagging a finger at her disapprovingly. "We don't talk about work, remember?"

"Yes, we wouldn't want General Ryder figuring out you like to sneak away to his house to do your slacking," Aja smirked. She carefully pulled a weed out by the roots, running her hands through the soil to see if she missed any bits of it.

"Your house," Emrin corrected.

Aja's head snapped up to study him, and she was surprised to see a strange look in his eyes. Like he was bothered and trying not to show it. Her chest felt tight, and for some reason she recalled her dream of the cat named Slyen. "Why are you going to war?" she asked. The question seemed to come out by itself, before she could censor it.

He sighed, looking away with a grimace. "It's a whole lot of politics I don't really want to get into. None of us *want* to go to war, you know. Sometimes being here, in this valley… you forget why we're even bothering. But the world is much bigger than you can possibly know. There are other people, other nations out there. Not all of them are as kind and gentle as your people are."

"Other people," Aja said softly, grasping for anything she could remember. A word popped into her mind. "Querians?"

Emrin started, looking down at her with raised eyebrows. "Where'd you hear that?" he asked. He frowned, glancing over his shoulder briefly. "I wouldn't repeat that where anyone else can hear you. We're not supposed to talk about it."

"Why not?" Aja asked.

"Some of the higher-ups think that you'll try to go to our enemies with information, if you knew who they were," he said sourly. "A bunch of…" he paused, glancing at her, before changing his mind about his words. "Of nonsense," he finally said, seeming to struggle to find the word.

She wondered what he would have said if he was talking to his friends in the garrison instead of her. "Especially since I don't know what Querians—" she saw him tense and glance around and lowered her voice. "What that *word* even means."

"Probably better you don't," he said gravely. "If they'd been the ones to find this valley, I doubt they would have listened when your elders offered a peaceful surrender. We thought they were our allies, once. A lot of things happened to change that, and the only way we can make things right is by showing them we won't back down. That's why this place is so crucial. It's right in the middle of everything, a hidden haven that no one but us knows about."

It was clear he believed his own words, even though she could see doubt in his eyes. She thought of what Slyen had said in her dream, goosebumps spreading across her arms. "After the winter is over, you're going to fight?" she asked.

"I should probably stop being surprised," he rubbed his forehead with one hand, chuckling under his breath. "The General lives in your house. You probably heard it from him during one of his meetings."

She didn't know how to put into words how much it meant to her, hearing him call the house hers and not Ryder's.

"Yes, that's the plan," he lowered his voice and continued softly, "We're hoping more ships arrive before winter, and then in the spring, we'll set out for Queria. We'd have a much harder time if we had to take the port on the west coast and march across the desert, so it's truly a miracle we can advance from this valley. Sure, we'll have to make our way through the mountains, but…"

"Daly!" A sharp yell sounded from down the path, and Emrin Daly whirled and saluted, his face sheepish. It was one of the sergeants heading for the barracks, and he'd seen Emrin slacking off by the fence. "Stop flirting and get your ass back to base!"

"Sir!" Emrin yelled back at once. He shot Aja a grin and ran off before he could get scolded again.

Aja's eyes dropped to the soil, at her hands stained by dirt. Her arms were trembling. *Two dreams, too crystal clear to be anything but omens,* she thought. *It's true, isn't it? We're running out of time.* She didn't know what she was supposed to do about it. It wasn't like she could just walk up to the General and ask him to take his men and leave. "Go home," she whispered. If only they would. If only they had never found this place. And yet… she thought of Emrin and the general, and her heart ached. She didn't truly want them to leave, she just wanted them not to change everything.

She wanted them to not go to war.

"He spends more time here than anywhere else," Delia's voice broke through Aja's musing. She turned to see her mother standing by the door, glancing down the path toward the garrison. Her eyes were calculating. "He probably likes you."

A grimace twisted Aja's mouth. "Can we not do this?" she asked tiredly. She focused on looking for weeds, but there weren't any left in this bed.

"You could do much worse."

"Is that all you can think about?" Aja asked, sharper than she intended. "Emrin is a friend, that's all."

"He's more like us than he is like them," Delia said. She gave her daughter a look that seemed as weary as it was scolding. "You're nearly twenty. Kyra got married at eighteen."

"Which is *barely* old enough," Aja argued. She stood, moved to the next vegetable bed, and dropped down to her knees.

"And twenty seems just about right," her mother countered.

Aja sighed. She didn't want to have this conversation again. She knew that seeing her daughters married would give Delia comfort; that she wanted to see them both loved and cared for. But it was not something Aja wanted, at least right now.

Desperate for a change in conversation, she said the first thing that came into her head. "I had a dream that a cat could speak," she said. She plucked a tiny weed from the edge of the garden bed. "He said his name was Slyen, and that we were named after him."

She had expected her mother to say something about her head always being in the clouds, but she was strangely quiet. Aja glanced up at her to see her face blank, her eyes staring distantly at nothing, as though she was trying to recall something she had forgotten.

"Naturally, I told him that we took our name from the mountains," she continued. She waited, unsure why her stomach clenched with anxiety.

Delia's eyes focused again. "Perhaps you were remembering something from your childhood," she remarked. "Sorin liked to tell you and your sister old fairy tales. He was fond of one in particular. Do you remember?"

Aja usually tried *not* to remember her father, never able to get over the guilt of what had happened. She was only a child when he died, and though her family never blamed her, she knew in her heart it was her fault. She had dreamed what would happen the night before, but when the moment came, she ignored the dream's warning. It was the first of many dreams of the future, and by far the worst of them.

"No," Aja said, her face falling.

Her mother's gaze softened with sadness. She came and sat down in the garden, her hands lightly brushing the soil as she helped search for weeds to pull. "A long time ago, we were called by a different name, one that is now forgotten. We did not have the care for our lands that we do now, and exploited our resources for higher gain, not caring what effect it had on the world. We grew too large for our cities, and when there wasn't enough space, we cut down forests to make room for more. Our expansion and our greed were harmful, but we wouldn't see it."

This part of the story, Aja had heard many times, not just from Sorin, when he had still been alive to hold his daughters on his knees and tell them tall tales, it was recorded in their history, so their people would never forget where they had come from, and what they had left behind.

"And then, when our nation was at its greatest, the price for our greed fell upon us," Delia continued. "Beasts of terrible power and anger destroyed all that we had built, killing everyone young and old. We were all guilty, in their eyes. They say that the sky was red with their wrath, and the ground was red with our blood."

Aja felt sick to her stomach. She tried to shove the image of the red sky from her mind as quickly as possible. *It was a dream,* she thought. Except that it wasn't. It wasn't the past, or a legend. Her dream had been an omen of something that hadn't happened yet.

"Precious few escaped, and those that did managed to flee before the beasts came," Delia said. She watched Aja out of the corner of her eyes, gauging her expression. "The man who led our people to this valley saw what would happen in a vision, and he saw that we would be safe in this valley. He led anyone who would believe him over the mountains, and as far as he knew, they were the only ones to survive. After many hard days of travel and near starvation, they finally found this place—but the valley was not empty. It already belonged to someone else."

"There were other people here before us?" Aja straightened. She didn't remember reading anything about that in their history. All it said was that their ancestors founded the five villages after they wrote the Tenets, so that they would never over-populate the area, and so that they could care for nature across the whole valley.

"Not people," her mother smiled faintly. "A single person—a Guardian. His name was Slyen, and when our ancestors asked him for refuge in his lands, he welcomed them. The mountains were named after him, and like the mountains, we took his name too." She laughed under her breath. "Or so, Sorin would have said. The legend is nothing more than fairy tale, but it's near and dear to our hearts. It's the reason we welcomed the Zyphans when they came, because Slyen welcomed us. Slyen the Guardian, or Slyen the mountains. Either way, I think the lesson is still the same."

"What if Slyen were real?" Aja asked.

"Your father would have believed he was," Delia said softly. "He would have tried to get you and your sister to believe it, too. Even though there's never been any facts to support it." Her smile turned sad, as it often did when she thought of Sorin. "I don't suppose it matters whether Slyen the Guardian is real, or whether it's a colorful legend to help us remember our past. But the story teaches us an important lesson about welcoming peace and abandoning strife."

Aja nodded, recalling listening to her father tell her stories when she was little. She no longer remembered the stories he told, but she would never forget how special it had been to listen to them. Thinking back on it now made her heart ache. "What if Slyen came to us today and told us he didn't want us to welcome the Zyphans the way we did?"

"Welcoming others with kindness is our way," Delia shook her head. "If he were real, then we learned that from him. I don't think he would disapprove."

"But he would disapprove of war," Aja insisted. "Nothing good can come of letting the Zyphans go to war. I can *feel* it. I just wish I knew what to do about it."

"I don't think there's anything we can do," Delia said. "Maybe things will work out just by letting time pass. It's been six months since they landed here, and much has changed since then. They are calmer and gentler than they used to be. Perhaps after the winter, they will have no more desire to fight."

"And perhaps their war will bring wrath to the world," Aja lamented. "And red will darken the sky with a horrible sound." She shuddered, eyes slipping closed. The image of her sister's lifeless eyes terrified her. "I'm scared," she whispered.

"There's no need for fear," Delia said, wrapping her arm around her shoulders and squeezing her comfortingly. "It will be alright, you'll see."

It won't, Aja thought. But she didn't voice her fear out loud.

Listening

That night, she dreamt of red skies again and was awoken by a scream. It was her own, and while her mother was trying to calm her, the door burst open and the General came through. His eyes were wide, his pistol drawn, as he stared around the room for a sign of attack. When he saw Aja crying and Delia hugging her, telling her it was just a dream, he lowered his weapon and backed out, grimacing as he closed the door. Aja couldn't hear what he muttered under his breath, but it surprised her that she felt comforted by his appearance.

He had come in wanting to protect them.

She was unable to get back to sleep after that and sat up till the morning with her thoughts troubled. When the sun crossed the mountain peaks, she came out to find General Ryder was standing in the sitting room, gazing out the window at the garden. He had his hands clasped behind his back, and when he sensed she was there, he turned to face her with a serious expression on his face.

"They're getting worse, these dreams of yours," the General said. "Aren't they?"

Aja's eyes were tired from staying up half the night, and she found herself too weary to disguise her fear with a smile. "I'm sorry for waking you," she said quietly. Her gaze strayed toward the door, where the quiet of her garden beckoned to her. All she wanted was to distract herself with something she loved and erase the urgency of her nightmare from her mind.

General Ryder sighed. "I know you have difficult dreams sometimes—have known since I first began to stay here. I'm a light sleeper, and I've come to recognize familiar sounds in the house at night." He offered what he might have thought a compassionate expression, though it looked more like a grimace. "I think that's the first time you screamed. Is there…" he hesitated, searching for the right words with some awkwardness, "something you're… worried about?"

Is he trying to console me? Aja wondered with surprise. She hadn't expected that, though now that she was faced with it, she found herself grieved even more by her vision. Her dream of red skies and the consequences of war weighed heavily on her. She didn't want to see something terrible happen to General Ryder, the Zyphans, or her people.

But it would, if something didn't change.

"Don't go to war," she pleaded, the words seeming to bubble out of her. "Please don't go. Something terrible will happen if you do." She had nothing to back up what she was saying but dreams—of cat people named Slyen, of red skies and violence wiping them out—but it was important to her that she try. She had been given visions of the future before, and not listening to them caused her to lose people she cared about. That was how she lost her father. She couldn't bear the consequences of not acting this time.

It was the General's turn to be surprised. His eyebrows shot up at her plea and he looked at her in astonishment for a moment. Then his worry evaporated, and a kind, almost pitying smile spread across his face. "Are you that worried about us?" he asked with a soft chuckle. "You needn't be so concerned, my dear. We are taking all the precautions we need, and more. We won't lose."

"But how many of you will die?" Aja insisted, walking a step forward in her urgency. "How many of your enemies? I *know* something terrible will happen if you go to war, something none of us can predict. Can't you sense that?"

"It's true that many of us will die," the General agreed, and his eyes were filled with grim determination. "But none of our soldiers were drafted. We volunteered to fight, and we're prepared to surrender our lives to see tyranny and trickery defeated. There are some things *worth* fighting for, Aja. Worth dying for, too. This is one of them."

"How can we know that?" Aja argued. She could see that her words weren't getting through to him, but she didn't know what else to say, or how she could reason with him. "You don't tell us who you're fighting, why you're fighting them, or even what you want to accomplish. But you'll throw your own lives away, and change everything we love about our valley, to do it!"

"I understand that change is hard," he said with a sympathetic tone. He came toward her and placed a hand on her shoulder, patting it twice with an awkward motion as though trying to comfort her. "But change is also good. And you must trust me, even though I can't tell you about the war or why it's important. Trust in us, Aja. Trust in Zypha. We will protect you."

The surging emotion in Aja's chest was not comfort, but grief. *I can't change his mind,* she thought, her shoulders trembling with the effort it took to keep herself from crying. There would be no point in showing him her tears. He might misinterpret them and not take her words seriously. Instead, she forced herself to nod, hanging her head until he patted her shoulder once more and headed for the door.

"I'll be at the barracks," he said, clearing his throat. He stopped beside the mirror, adjusting his uniform, before looking towards her again. She sensed this but did not look up to meet his expression. "Your worry is touching," he said kindly. "And we will treasure it when we march. Victory will be ours, Aja. For both Zypha and Slyenials." As he stepped out and headed swiftly down the path, he let the door swing heavily back, making a loud sound as it closed.

"There will be no victory," Aja replied quietly, lifting her head to stare at the door. Now that he had left, her tears finally came. They slid down her cheeks freely, her heart aching in her chest. "Only death and red skies."

"Is that what you dreamt?"

Hearing her mother's voice behind her, Aja turned swiftly, startled. She hadn't sensed her, or realized she was there. Hastily, she wiped her face with both hands to dry her tears. "I didn't hear you," she said quickly.

"Then you weren't listening," Delia replied softly. She stood in the mouth of the short hallway to the bedrooms, concern in her eyes. "Is that what you saw, last night? Red skies?"

Aja grimaced. Suddenly, she didn't feel like a sensible, nineteen-year-old woman. She felt like a child who wanted only to be comforted by her mother. Rushing forward, she threw her arms around her mother's waist and leaned her face into her shoulder, a sob shaking her body. "Yes," she cried. "The sky was red. We were all dead, all of us! The Zyphans, the Slyens… it was so terrible. I could hear this *horrible* sound of anger in my bones."

Delia wrapped her arms around her daughter's shoulders, rubbing her back with her nails. "It was only a dream," she murmured. "Dreams are not real."

"Sometimes they *are* real," Aja insisted. She pulled back, gazing into her mother's worried eyes intently. "The dream that brought our people to this valley was real. The dream about the storm that took father's life was real. And *this* dream is real too. I saw what would happen if they were to go to war. They're going to awaken *something* out there. Something that is angry, that hasn't forgiven us. And this time, they won't let any of us survive!"

Her mother didn't offer words of comfort, looking shaken as she gently tried to calm her daughter by stroking her hair with one hand. Aja realized, seeing her mother's fear, that she had *wanted* to be soothed. To be told that everything would work out, somehow. Now, the fear she felt seemed to solidify into a block of ice in her stomach, and goosebumps spread across her arms.

Delia saw Aja's face go pale, and she pulled her close in a tight hug again. "We'll be alright," she said softly. "If Sorin were here, he would say that the Guardian will take care of us. If… if you need something to believe in, then believe in your father."

"What will you believe in?" Aja whispered. She was stiff as her mother hugged her, all her limbs going rigid as her dread settled into realization. No one else was having dreams of the future. No one else was trying to convince the Zyphans not to go to war.

If something was going to be done, *she* would have to do it. *"It has to be you,"* Slyen had said in her dream. And in her heart, she finally understood that he was right.

"I believe in our Tenets," Delia said, breathing deeply. "This land is our home; we will care for it. These mountains are our name, we will honor them. The beasts are our brothers, we will not harm them. Nature is our treasure; we will protect it. And peace is our heart, we will never turn from it." She kissed her daughter on the head and released her, stepping back. "We will live by example, and I believe the hearts of the Zyphans will change. When spring comes, they will not go to war. They will join us."

Aja wanted to believe that too, more than anything. But she couldn't. *I have to believe my dreams,* she thought, as her heart found resolution. *My mother trusted my father, and he believed in Slyen. That's why she told me I could believe in him, even if I don't feel the same way she does.* "Do you trust me?" she asked. "Like you trusted my father?"

Delia released her, studying her face with surprise. "Of course I trust you," she said. "I have *always* trusted you. And I know that you take your dreams to heart." She tucked a loose strand of hair behind Aja's ear, smiling warmly. "I am with you, Aja. I always have been."

"I know," Aja said, relief filling her at her mother's words. "I am with you, too," she promised. *And I will do anything to protect you. To protect our home.* She knew that she would have to go and knew that leaving would be difficult. But her mother's faith in her gave her the courage she needed. "There's something I have to do," she said quietly. "My heart is burdened and I'm afraid of what will happen if I don't listen to the warning of my dreams."

For a moment, her mother studied her face, searching her expression carefully. But then she nodded, a sad smile on her face. "If you feel like it's something you need to do, then you should do it," she said. "You are old enough to make choices for yourself." She looked over Aja's shoulder toward the door, nodding toward it. "If you are burdened, then go to the garden. It has always brought you peace." Delia turned and walked softly toward the kitchen, offering her one last glance before she stepped out of sight.

Her expression said that she knew Aja was leaving.

But neither of us can bring ourselves to say the words "goodbye," can we? Aja thought. *That's alright. It isn't goodbye, because I'm coming back. I'll come back and save all of us.*

Slipping on her canvas shoes, she walked out of the house and headed down the path for the trees. She did not look back as she left her village behind. There could be no hesitation, not when so much was at stake. As the shade of the trees fell over her, and the sounds of people talking, soldiers training, and Zyphan architects building grew distant, she finally allowed herself to slow down.

She had come into the woods without a plan and had no idea what she would need. It was only two nights ago that she had dreamt of Slyen, but it was still crystal clear in her mind. He had said he would call her out to the clearing again to ask for her help. It hadn't happened yet, but she was sure it would. Dreams that vivid were always visions of the future. But while she knew he would send her south to find his brother, she wasn't sure how long it would take or if she was prepared for it.

She glanced down at her clothing, simple and sturdy— undyed hempen leggings, a blue, long-sleeved, woven tunic, and a belt around her waist. It was the fashion to wear intricately patterned   with brightly-colored belts, which were long enough to be wrapped twice around the waist before it was tied. It hung down in two strips over her left hip. One of the tails was always longer than the other, because asymmetry was artistic. And while the fashionable knot was difficult to tie, it laid flat so cleanly that she preferred it to other, simpler knots. Her sturdy canvas shoes were well-worn, fitting snuggly to her feet after months of use. The tread was thick and weather-treated so they could be worn in the garden or the forest without concern, though they were starting to wear out. She would have to replace them soon.

In my dream, he said his brother is further south than Nettledown, she thought, lifting one foot and then the other, contemplating the soles of her shoes. *But I think these will do fine. It would be worse in new shoes that have to be broken in.* Deciding her clothing was perfectly suited for a journey, she continued walking until she had come so far into the woods that she could no longer hear or see her village behind her. Then she stopped beside a large tree, placing a hand on its trunk as she considered her surroundings.

Now that she was out here in the light of day, without a dream calling her through the woods, she was forced to realize that she had no idea where to go. Should she have headed straight south to Nettledown and entered the woods there? Or was it better to search for the clearing in her dream and go south through the woods?

How do I find the clearing? she wondered, biting her lower lip with worry. How did someone follow a dream, even one that might be true? Her eyes scanned the trees around her, searching for anything familiar. She placed a hand over her heart, willing it to calm down, and opened her senses to the sounds of the forest. *Listening* with her eyes closed was easier; trying to *Listen* with her eyes wide and searching was distracting. Each time the wind blew the leaves, her gaze went there. Each chirp of a bird drew her focus.

Stop, she thought, growing frustrated. *Listen, Aja. Open your ears and Listen!*

The forest seemed to grow louder the longer she *Listened.* Birds called to one another as they flew north in preparation for winter. The wind changed directions as it pleased, creating music through the leaves and pine needles above her. A branch cracked far in the distance. Insects buzzed as they sometimes flew past her, and other times circled her to investigate. She knew that none of these would tell her which direction to go, but the more she heard, the more confident she felt. She was awake. And she was focused.

Then, like a faint echo, she heard the sound of quiet footsteps treading through the forest.

She turned, looking for a person, but she was utterly alone in the woods. The footsteps continued, faintly echoing through the trees, until they vanished. But her eyes snapped in the direction she'd heard them, and to her surprise, she saw something she recognized.

There was a young evergreen a short distance ahead of her. It began at its base with one thick trunk, but a branch from a nearby tree had fallen on it, causing it to split. The split trunk then became two, growing upwards around the branch as though it had only been a minor inconvenience, and now the tree stretched high into the sky, each thin trunk laden with many branches. "I saw it when I was dreaming," she whispered, walking towards it, placing her hand on the leftmost trunk above the split. She had passed it on her journey toward the clearing, and with a secret thrill thrumming through her, she realized what she had heard.

The echoes of footsteps had been her own.

Her heart skipping a beat in excitement, Aja turned her head, making a mental note of the direction she had walked that night. With renewed determination, she began to walk as straight a line as she could through the forest. Without deviating to the right or left, she walked steadily forward, recalling that it had taken her hours to reach the clearing. Yet even with a long distance to go, she was encouraged. She *knew* which way to go, and if she became lost, she could stop and *Listen* again to find her bearing.

It was less than an hour before she remembered that she had not eaten before venturing in here. So, when she spied a cluster of mushrooms growing on a fallen log—the very same she had seen in her dream—she stopped to harvest a few of them to eat while she walked. They were a woodsy brownish-orange color with wide caps that were turned upwards, mushrooms that grew somewhat close together. They had a very delicate flavor that she was fond of, especially roasted with oil and seasoned with salt and herbs. But they were tasty raw, too, especially on an empty stomach.

The mushroom find brightened her outlook, and she was in much better spirits as she continued her walk. She passed the time *Listening*, playing a game of trying to identify the birds and sounds she was hearing. Were those the calls of geese high above her? Yes, of course. Geese were easily distinguishable. Was that a branch creaking from the wind, or was there some silent creature climbing in the trees? She certainly hoped it was just the wind. Encountering a jaguar now would very likely end in her death.

When she stepped out into a wide, moss-covered clearing, it was completely unexpected. It seemed to just appear out of nowhere, as though the trees had been disguising its location with their trunks, despite the brightness of the low, autumn sun. She was three steps into it when she came to an abrupt halt, surprise and delight shooting through her. *I found it!* She thought with a shiver. *It's really...*

Her thoughts blanked when she saw a great cat lying on its side in the center of the clearing, and she was gripped with a sudden sense of danger. But when it turned its head toward her sharply, she saw that it was not a jaguar. It was Slyen, exactly as she remembered him from her dream. His eyes were filled with astonishment when he saw her, and at once he pulled himself to his feet.

"You're here?" he asked, his words as easily understood as they had been when she dreamt him. "But I didn't..." he stopped himself, shaking his head. "Never mind that, I suppose it doesn't matter. You're here, and that's significant." He stretched out his paw toward her, beckoning her to come to him, and he offered her a smile that seemed full of pride. "That was very well done," he praised.

Aja came towards him, her steps silent across the moss. "Do you know me?" she asked curiously. *It almost feels as though we've already met. I know I dreamt that he was going to call me out here, so I suspect he didn't expect me to come out by myself.* It filled her were a strange sense of elation when he praised her, and in her heart, she was encouraged. *I did the right thing by coming,* she thought.

"Of course I know you, Aja," he said, chuckling with some amusement. When she stopped directly across from him, she was momentarily distracted by his height—his head was no taller than her shoulder. "I know all of my people by name, and I'm quite proud of that. Even Seila, who you asked me to consider instead."

At this, Aja's calm evaporated, overtaken by a strange feeling in her stomach. "Pardon?" she asked. *He mentioned Seila. Why would he mention her if... if we hadn't already...* The realization that her conversation with Slyen had not been a dream struck her like a blow to the stomach. She staggered backwards dizzily, her mouth falling open as she inhaled a sharp breath of air. "Not a dream?" she blurted.

Slyen gazed at her in growing confusion, his whiskers shifting as a scowl settled on his face. "A dream?" he demanded. "You think our conversation that night was a…" he sighed, shaking his head. "No, I suppose I'm not overly surprised to hear that. Humanity has always been skilled at ignoring the things they see in front of their own eyes. It's one reason why Influence is so effective with them. But if you thought I was a dream, why in Mog's name would you come all the way out here on your own?"

Aja swallowed, recalling her precious time in this clearing as carefully as she could. *It really happened,* she thought with a shiver. *That night, he called me out here to talk to me. Then my vision of red skies is because of the conversation we had?* The solid chill in her stomach from this morning seemed to grow colder, and any doubt she'd previously clung to faded away.

The red sky dream was an omen, and if she didn't listen to its warning, then it would come true.

"You wanted me to go find your brother," Aja said, drawing herself out of her thoughts and staring down into Slyen's pale eyes. "I'm willing to go."

His scowl faded, and she saw concern fill his eyes that reminded her of the General's expression, this morning. "What changed your mind?" he asked. "I had thought…" He glanced up at the sky as a flock of birds flew north in a V, its leader changing places with one of the birds further back. Slyen's expression turned grim. "I suppose it doesn't matter. I need your help, Aja. And I'm convinced you're the only one I can send."

"I'll go," Aja said again. "You don't have to persuade me." She had already persuaded herself this morning, after speaking with her mother. Two nights of dreaming the same omen were enough.

"Well," he replied with some surprise, blinking his eyes a few times as he considered the serious expression on her face. Then he relaxed, relief in his smile. "That's reassuring. Are you ready to go now, or would you like to return to your village and wish your family and friends farewell?"

As much as she longed to, she was afraid of losing her nerve. It seemed much easier to face the journey now that she was here. "If I go back, I might not return," she admitted quietly. "Let's go now. Will you teach me how to find your brother?"

"Naturally," Slyen said, his voice cheerful now that he had Aja's promise to go. He began to walk out of the clearing, and as Aja kept pace beside him, he continued talking. "I'll take you through my forest to a secret exit out of the valley," he explained. "You won't have to risk crossing the mountains, and it will bring you out into the arid lands of Scoria. From there, all you have to do is head southward until you reach Mettain."

The names Scoria and Mettain held no meaning for Aja, but she tried to assign them to memory as best she could. "And what was your brother's name again?" she asked. As they moved through the trees, she was surprised at how peaceful it felt to walk among them. More than usual, as though Slyen himself warded away any of the dangers that could have harmed her. *He exudes peace,* she thought, studying him thoughtfully. *I feel calm around him.*

It was different, seeing him in daylight. Now that she could study him more closely, she could see that he was well-groomed and unassuming. He was refined when he spoke, a sort of proud tone to his words that reminded her a little of General Ryder. And despite his humble appearance, he was effortlessly regal in a way that filled her with a sense of awe. Slyen was special. He was a living embodiment of everything her people loved, and everything they had tried to live by.

"My brother's name is Vedlyr," Slyen said. "He lives in hiding amongst his people, just as I have done among my people. It's easier that way, you see. We have no intention of interfering in the lives of our people, but it is important for us to protect them. That is the Moglian way."

The way he spoke—with his chest puffed up with pride, trilling his r's with his tongue and letting his eyes half-close leisurely—reminded her so much of the General that she laughed. She could just picture him, dressed up in one of those white and ochre uniforms, posing in front of the mirror as he relayed his pride in caring for his lands and his people.

"What's funny about that?" Slyen said, his fur bristling with offense. "It's very serious for us, I'll have you know!"

"No, that's not it," Aja said, stifling her laugh with a hand over her mouth. "You just remind me of someone I know." It took some effort to stop picturing the comparison, and she had to work to redirect her focus. "Tell me about your brother," she suggested. "It seems strange that his lands are named Mettain if his name is Vedlyr. Why not Vedlyrials?"

Slyen's scowl remained on his face, his gaze somewhat suspicious as he studied her out of the corner of his eye. "They certainly used to be called Vedlyrials. Moglians are not overly creative when naming. We name ourselves, and then everything we own becomes named after us. Only humanity has different names for every single thing in the world." His scowl faded, his expression becoming thoughtful. "Vedlyr and I were always fascinated with the way humanity names things. The people who moved to Vedlyrials named it Mettain, which means 'protected within,' because Vedlyr gave them refuge. He was flattered."

"If we had chosen a different name for Slyenials, would you have been flattered, too?" Aja wondered. She tried to think of what her ancestors would have called it, though it was difficult to think of any name besides the one she had grown up knowing. Slyenials seemed so… perfect.

"I suppose it would depend on what name they chose," Slyen admitted, idly scratching under his chin with one claw. "But I doubt it would have upset me. Humanity gives names to everything, from people, to objects, to places. It would have… fascinated me." He turned his head, observing her. "What would you have called it?"

"How about Zyphanian?" she said innocently.

Another scowl darkened his face. "You are treading a very dangerous edge," he warned.

She chuckled, not threatened in the slightest. "Alright then, let me give it some thought." She lifted her head, gazing up at the sky she could see through the deciduous leaves, and the coniferous branches higher up. She *Listened* to the sounds of the forest thriving around her, the crunch of their footsteps on fallen leaves and branches and thought of their five villages that each had a role in caring for the different parts of the valley.

They existed within a shield of mountains that surrounded them on three sides, banked on the fourth by the fast-moving river at the bottom of the cliffs. Their valley was protected, safe, and beautiful. It was a refuge and a gift, a place that she was willing to leave just to protect, and longed more than anything to return to, safe and sound. They had come here, not just to escape strife, but to live in a way that would protect the land, rather than exploit it. And because of their Tenets, of their desires and of Slyen's welcome, it had become a place of peace.

Slyenials was precious. It embodied everything she loved.

"If I could give this place a name," she said softly, "I would call it, A Place Where Peace Remains."

Slyen stopped walking. Aja paused when he did, turning slightly to face him, and was surprised when she saw the expression on his face. There was moisture in his eyes, and he seemed to struggle to breathe for a moment.

"What is it?" she asked, worried. *Did I say something wrong?*

His fur ruffled, standing on end for a moment before it settled. Like the hairs on her skin would when she got goosebumps. "That's..." he said, his voice rough. He cleared his throat, turning away from her and blinking his eyes rapidly. "That's my name," he finished quietly. "Slyen. It means 'remain in peace' in the Moglian tongue. It has always been my heart, since I was young. That's why I chose that name for myself."

"I didn't know," Aja said. *It makes sense,* she thought with a smile. *Why this place has always been one of peace, and why it matters so much to us. His heart and our hearts are the same.* She reached out a hand, setting it on his head gently. "There, you see?" she said warmly. "Slyenials is a perfect name. It doesn't need another one."

"I'm not a child," he bristled, though it seemed more with awkwardness than with anger. He brushed her hand off, clearing his throat again as he continued walking. "We're wasting daylight. There's many hours to walk if we want to reach the canyon by nightfall. This valley is not overly large, but it will take two days to walk through the canyon to Scoria."

"Yes of course," Aja replied placatingly. She smiled to herself as she followed him, keeping a few steps behind him. From here, she could see that like most cats, he had a tail. But unlike the jaguars, his was quite short. It was a fluffy, bobbed tail with a tuft of white on the underside, and the back of his leggings had been cleverly designed to wrap around the tail without restricting it, fastening with two buttons at the waist.

"I'll take you as far as the entrance to Scoria," Slyen continued. "From there, you will be on your own. So do try and pay attention while I explain everything you need to know." He paused, waiting for her to come beside him once more. When he looked up into her face, his expression was grim. "It will not be the same, out there. This valley is protected by my Influence, and reinforced by the Tenets you live by. But once you step foot into the world outside these mountains, everything you have been accustomed to will be gone. You *must* stay on guard. And you must *not* let anyone know where you come from."

The gravity of his words weighed heavily on her, and she felt her mood darken with apprehension. She didn't know what to expect when she stepped out of Slyenials. The Zyphans had come from outside the valley, and they had insisted that their fight was against treachery and tyranny. She knew the definitions of the words but had no experience with them to allow her to picture them. If other people learned where she came from—people like the Querians, whom the Zyphans were preparing to fight—then she could unwittingly bring disaster home with her that not even Slyen and his brother may be able to drive away.

"I will prepare you as best I can," Slyen promised. "But the rest will be up to you, Aja. So, keep your wits about you."

"I will try," Aja said, though her courage seemed to crumble inside her. The confidence and determination that had brought her out into the forest this morning grew fainter in the face of what was to come.

The Door

————————⊛————————

The journey through Slyenwood passed quickly. Slyen did his best to explain things he felt Aja should know, but he followed up each bit of knowledge with the warning that he had not been outside his valley in three hundred years and had no way of knowing how much things had changed. By the time they reached the canyon that would take them to Scoria, Aja felt sure than none of his knowledge would be helpful.

The Querians, he told her, were people who had once lived across the entire continent. But after incurring the wrath of the Moglians, their nation had been greatly reduced. How they had survived, he wasn't sure. He had not joined his people to fight against humanity and he had just taken in Aja's people. The Zyphans were preparing to fight the Querians, but that was all he could say about them.

Scoria was the rocky desert south of the Slyen Range and north of Mettain. She would have to cross through it to reach Vedlyr, though he could tell her nothing of what it would be like. All she knew about deserts was how dry they were, and how little water and vegetation could be found. She couldn't imagine what such a place would look like and wasn't sure how she would manage to survive it. But Slyen assured her that the desert was not large, and that it did have water in some places. Where those places were, he couldn't say. But she would be able to find them if she were clever.

I'm beginning to feel like I'm going to my death, she thought to herself as she considered the dangers ahead of her.

How am I supposed to survive a desert when all I've known is forests and fields? But despite her growing concerns, she tried only to voice questions and not complaints. They had but a short time together before she was on her own, and she was afraid of wasting time.

They reached the canyon that evening and slept under the trees before venturing into it. Aja was so exhausted from walking all day—something that she was not accustomed to— that she fell asleep right away. When she woke the next morning, she was chilled and sore, and just the thought of pulling herself to her feet seemed too much to bear.

"Oh, you're finally awake?" Slyen asked, as she sat up and leaned her back against a tree, wrapping her arms around herself. "We have precious little time, you know. The sooner you reach Mettain, the sooner we can send the Zyphans safely on their way. Winter will come before you know it."

She was too tired to reply to him, but she offered him a pointed glare that said plenty of how she felt. He made a chiding noise, clicking his tongue against his teeth, and offered her a large pinecone. She took it in hand, staring down at it blankly. "What is this?" she asked.

"Breakfast," he said. "I've kept the squirrels from eating all the pine nuts inside, so there will be plenty there. Break it open, you'll see."

Well familiar with pine nuts, as they often used them in their own cooking, she lethargically twisted the cone, her hands too chilled to do it swiftly. Soon, she had extracted all there was to eat, bits of cone and several large pine nuts resting on her thigh. She ate them one at a time. Pine nuts were rich and flavorful, a good source of protein, oil, and some carbohydrates, which she desperately needed after traveling all day yesterday. Still hungry, she glanced around the forest for signs of other food she could forage.

"I'll take you to the other side of the canyon," Slyen said, gazing out towards it with a concerned expression on his face. "But I dare not go further. It might be wise to gather food you can take with you. Do you have a bag?"

"I didn't think to bring one," she admitted. She caught sight of several ferns clustered around the base of the trees and though not all of them were the edible kind, she noticed a few that were safe to eat. She rose to her feet with a grunt, her body stiff and her feet aching. *I don't like traveling,* she decided. *I think I already regret agreeing to this.* Moving toward the edible ferns, she searched for the small fiddleheads that grew in the center, plucking a few and munching on them. They were bitter and not overly tasty, but they were a good source of fiber. *What should I bring with me? Pinecones? Mushrooms?* She looked around for any fungi that were edible.

"I suppose I can fashion one for you," Slyen murmured, scratching thoughtfully under his chin with one claw. He walked towards the ferns, took a seat beside them, and closed his eyes. Aja was busy searching for things she could eat and didn't pay much attention to him until she had gathered an armful of pinecones, a few clusters of mushrooms, and several fiddleheads. But when she brought them back to where they had slept, she froze in awe.

The ferns in front of him were moving, growing longer and tougher, and weaving themselves together. Their little leaves trembled as they moved, adjusting themselves as frond after frond crossed over each other. What they were forming, she wasn't sure at first. But after several minutes of growth, she recognized the shape they were creating.

It was a satchel, the type with a long strap that was worn on one shoulder and crossed over the body to rest against one's hip. The fern fronds wove themselves so tightly that she doubted anything would fall through them once placed inside. And it was beautiful, artistically crafted. When it finished growing, the fern shivered and went still, and the satchel sagged until it was resting on the ground. Slyen let out a breath of air he had been holding, reached out with his claws, and carefully cut it free from the rest of the fern.

He rose to his feet, handing it over to her. "This should do nicely," he said.

She took it with both hands, gazing first at the bag and then at his face, awed. "How did you do it?" she breathed. "This is incredible!"

Slyen's fur seemed to fluff up with pride, though he waved his paw dismissively. "Influence, of course," he said.

"This forest is mine, and everything that lives here belongs to me. If it is my will for the ferns to grow a bag, they will do so."

"That's… still incredible," she insisted. *And somewhat terrifying,* she admitted to herself. *If Influence can do things like make plants grow strange and cause soldiers not to fight, I shudder to think what else can it do.* She carefully draped the satchel over her neck, setting the strap to her right shoulder and letting the bag rest against her left hip. It was a perfect fit. "Thank you, Slyen," she said, her voice soft. "It's lovely."

He blinked his eyes, his whiskers spreading as he smiled. "Well, I couldn't just send you out ill-prepared," he cleared his throat somewhat awkwardly. "Come, let's fill it with food." He helped gather several more pinecones for her, lecturing her on which mushrooms were safe to eat as he observed each item she placed in her bag. Though she knew these things well enough on her own, she let him advise her without complaining.

At last, they were ready to go, and he led the way into the canyon. "We have many paces to walk before we reach the end," Slyen explained. "Let's make good use of the sunlight."

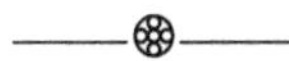

It took two days to travel the length of the canyon. The nights were cold, and the ground was rocky, which made sleeping difficult. Slyen Influenced grass to grow for her to sleep on, but there wasn't enough foliage for him to weave a blanket for her. They slept back to back, and the warmth of his fur was the only thing that kept her from freezing.

Midway through the third day, they stopped at the opening of the canyon's far end. The air felt dry and the wind hot, and as far as Aja could see, there was only brown sand with juts of rock sticking up here and there. Each day that had passed during their trek, she had felt a growing sense of heaviness, one she was only dimly aware of at the back of her mind. But now, with the desert in front of her and the forest two days behind her, she felt the weight of it keenly.

The peace and safety that she had always lived with did not exist out here. She had left it behind in Slyenials, and her heart dreaded what kind of world she would face outside of that valley.

"This is where I must leave you," Slyen said. He gazed out at the sands, his face twisted into a grimace as he considered the desert. "I wish that you didn't have to go, I really do. But without my brother's help…" he sighed, shaking his head. "It still doesn't feel right to send you away with only a few pinecones. Perhaps there is something else I can do for you." He considered her a moment, his mouth pursed and his brow furrowed. Then with a nod, he drew himself up to his full height—small though it was. "Aja, look at me," he urged.

She was already looking at him, as she was reluctant to face the desert that waited for her. *I don't want to go,* she thought, though she kept her mouth tightly shut so that she didn't admit it aloud. She had *promised* to go. Her own conviction had brought her here, and if she turned back now, she wouldn't be able to stop disaster from coming to their valley. So, she did her best to keep her worry from showing on her face.

As Slyen placed his paws on her shoulder, gazing into her eyes intently, she began to feel a strange pressure building around her. She found herself unable to blink or look away, as his pupils narrowed to mere slits. The sight of his pale, yellow eyes focused like the gaze of a hunting jaguar instilled an almost instinctual sense of terror in her. Her skin prickled as every hair on her body stood on end. She found herself unable to breathe, unable to hear anything but the hammering of her own heart. It was like the tightness of the air before a storm.

And then, Slyen blinked, and the pressure faded as though it had never been there. He dropped his arms, stepping back with a sigh, exhaustion filling his eyes. "There," he murmured. "I believe… yes, that should help."

Aja shivered, her heart still racing as she tried to sense what he had done. She couldn't place what had changed, but *something* had. "What did you do?" she whispered. Her ears popped, and for a moment she heard a faint ringing sound that slowly faded away.

"I have placed a ward on you with my Influence," Slyen explained. His voice was as weary as his face. "I might have used more than I can spare… but it was worth it. Yes, worth it to me." He rubbed his face with his paw, whiskers springing back up after he rubbed them. "If you should ever find yourself in danger from people or beasts, all you have to do is gaze into their eyes, and my Influence will keep them from killing you. It's the most that I can do, and I hope that it will be enough."

"Would people try to kill me?" she asked in disbelief. She couldn't imagine that. It was expected that a wild animal might try to hunt her, but she couldn't imagine someone trying to kill her when she had done nothing to them.

"Things are different outside my valley," Slyen warned her. "It's my Influence that keeps the Zyphans from turning hostile, or from cultivating suspicion in their hearts against you. Out here, people who are prone to violence will be violent. And some animals will kill even if they do not need to hunt. You must be clever, Aja. Clever enough to know when to trust someone and when to avoid them. And above all else, you must remember never to tell anyone where you come from. They *must not* learn about Slyenials. Do you understand?"

"I understand," Aja said, feeling less confident with each passing second. Could she really manage this? Even with his Influence protecting her? *I'm afraid,* she thought. *I don't want to go!*

"Go with my blessing," Slyen urged. "And my thanks. I will be counting the days until you return."

Her heart burdened with her task, Aja offered a nod. She couldn't bring herself to reply, so she turned and faced the desert, gripping the woven fern strap of her satchel. With as much courage as she could muster, she took a step towards the sands. Then another. She climbed out of the canyon and stood atop the edge, finding only sand and rocks as far as her eyes could see. Hesitantly, she turned to take one last look at Slyen.

He smiled reassuringly at her, offering her a wave. A lump formed in her throat, and tears formed in her eyes when she realized it might be the last time she ever saw him. *I will return,* she promised in her heart, lifting her arm to wave back at him. Facing the south once more, she forced herself to step out into the desert, and walked as swiftly as she could manage as her steps shifted unevenly on the sands.

The canyon's exit faced due south, and she walked in what she hoped was a straight line for over an hour. But her progress was slow, and it didn't take long for her to decide that she hated the desert. The sand was burning hot, and the soles of her canvas shoes were not quite thick enough to protect her from it. Her feet ached and burned with each step, and sand inside her shoes grated against her skin. She had to stop constantly and take her shoes off, shaking sand and pebbles out before sliding them back on again.

Worse, the wind was constantly blowing sand into her face. Her nose, mouth, and eyes were dried out and irritated, and strands of her hair escaped from her braid to blow in her face. She was parched for water yet could find none wherever she looked. All around her, there were only large, jagged rocks, coarse sand, and a few desert plants she had never seen before. Some of them were oddly endearing, little round bulbs with tufts of soft-looking fluff along vertical seams. She made the mistake of trying to touch one, and found that instead of being soft, the white fluff was a dense grouping of sharp needles. They became immediately stuck in her skin and were difficult to pull out.

Without knowing whether they were edible, there didn't seem much point in trying to mess with them further. But her one attempt had her thinking twice about messing with *any* of the plants she encountered on her trek.

The sun beat down cruelly as she walked. There were no clouds in the sky, and despite the sun hanging closer to the northern horizon this time of year, it seemed to be placed in just the right angle to reflect off of the sand directly into her eyes. It wasn't long before Aja was sure she couldn't go any further. It was too hot and dry, too much for her to bear without water. Desperate to get out of the wind and sun, she turned west and headed toward a large outcropping of stones that formed a sort of barrier. It took her a while to reach them, but she was relieved to find that they provided more than just a basic protection from the wind. They towered over her, leaning over her just enough to provide shade from the burning sunlight.

Tucking herself up in the corner of the largest of the rocks, she sat down on the shade-cooled sand and let out a groan, setting her satchel in her lap and digging through it for something to eat. She chose the fiddleheads since they had some moisture to them. And after eating them, the headache she'd been enduring finally began to let up a little.

This is too much for me, she thought, closing her eyes and leaning her head back, resting it against the rocks. The wind howled through cracks in the stones, and listening to it made her feel unsettled. Everything about this place was foreign to her. There weren't any people out here, so Slyen's ward did little good to protect her. Nor were there animals to avoid or to study to see how they survived. It was barren and miserable, and she'd wind up dead if she wasn't careful.

Slyen had told her to be clever. She didn't have the knowledge or skills she needed out here, and she was so miserable she wanted to cry. Except that she was so dehydrated that tears were impossible. Maybe cleverness was all she had to work with.

Think, she told herself, taking a mushroom from her bag and chewing on it. It had been sweating some of its moisture in the bag, so it tasted more rubbery than it normally would. *What can I do to survive?* She gazed out at the sand, watching it move as the wind blew. The eerie whistling through the cracks over her head seemed like a sad song, as melancholy as she felt. *Listen,* she thought, closing her eyes. Even if it was only to calm and center herself, *Listening* had always helped her.

At first, all she could hear was the wind, blowing noisily through the cracks. Then the sand moving across the dunes and driven against the rocks. She almost thought she could hear the sound of sizzling, as the sun baked the sands and cooked the dry, brittle tufts of grass scattered around the rocks. She fell into a sort of trance, her mind empty. She *Listened* and rested.

Until a new sound reached her. It was like rocks being ground together, a deep rumble that she could feel through her bones. It was coming from deep below her.

Startled, her eyes snapped open, and she saw that the sun was hanging low. Hours had passed while she was resting, and with the sun, the heat was swiftly reducing. It almost seemed cool enough to travel without being too miserable. *But what was that sound?* She thought, unnerved, though she couldn't say why. She pulled herself reluctantly to her feet, gazing around and trying to determine which way was south.

The Slyen Range was easily visible on the horizon, and she knew that it lay north of the desert. Turning her back to the mountains, she forced herself to move her feet, one weary step at a time. The sand shifted under her weight, the rocks dug into her soles, and the wind continued to lash her with loose, coarse grains. *I have to keep going,* she thought drearily. *If I can just make it to Mettain, I can find Vedlyr and come home.*

It got easier to walk as the sun set. She was so relieved to be free from the heat that her energy lifted somewhat. She munched on a few mushrooms as she walked, looking up at the sky as it darkened and became covered with a multitude of stars. Out here, there were no mountains around her to block half the sky, and no lampposts to obscure all but the brightest of the night lights. She felt hopeful again, and marveled that she might never have seen this sky if she hadn't decided to come on this journey.

All of that changed when the bitter cold closed around her. Without the sun's heat, the desert became a freezing wasteland. The wind, still a constant nuisance that threw sand into her face, now seemed to pierce through her clothing and chill her to the bone. The sand, which had once burned her feet, now felt like it was made of ice. She rubbed her arms with her hands, shivering as she walked, but could get no relief.

Autumn had always been temperate in the valley. But out here in Scoria, it seemed as though winter had already come. Why hadn't Slyen warned her about this? He had told her the desert was hot. He hadn't mentioned anything about freezing to death at night!

Eventually she became too miserable to continue on, and she decided she would rather brave the heat of the day than suffer the chill of night now that she had experienced both. Desperate for relief, she headed for the largest outcropping of rocks she could find.

There weren't a lot of options to choose from. Most were too small and scattered to offer any sort of shelter. So, she was forced to keep walking in search of something suitable. At last, she spied an odd shape in the distance, a cluster of stones that seemed large enough to huddle beneath. Her hope renewed, she found the strength to keep going for several long minutes before she reached them.

The stones, she noticed as she approached, formed a wide semi-circle, their jagged points curved toward each other like a sort of dome. She was so hurried to get out of the wind that she didn't pay much attention to them until she had dropped to her knees beneath them, pressing her back up against one of the spires. But as she wrapped her arms around herself and shivered, her eyes lifted upwards to study them.

There were five in total, stretching over her like claws. *Are they natural?* she wondered, feeling unnerved by their shape. *Or did someone carve them this way?* The longer she stared at them, the more uncomfortable they made her. So, she dropped her gaze and tried to pretend she hadn't seen them. For now, she was safe from the wind, and that was all that mattered.

Sleeping was impossible, and even when she closed her eyes and tried *Listening,* she was unable to rest. Danger seemed to press around her, as though the claw-like rocks were a large hand that was slowly drawing closed around her. *I should go somewhere else,* she thought, her heart racing anxiously. But the thought of going back out into the freezing sandy wind was so distressing that she ignored the urge. They were just rocks.

Then she heard the sound of stone groaning and grinding against itself, rumbling so deeply that her bones seemed to vibrate with the sound. It was not below her this time. The sound came from directly behind her, so loud that alarm shot through her body. She jolted, scrambling to her feet and falling over herself as she backed away from the spires.

In the center of the semi-circle, a section of rock began to withdraw into itself, a doorway opening as a slab of stone recessed into the ground. It looked like a mouth, opening up to swallow her, and a bright blue light was flickering within the opening, getting brighter. Aja stumbled and fell onto the sand, scooting backwards with frantic motions, too panicked to get back up. *I'll be swallowed,* she thought in horror.

The flickering blue light grew brighter, and up from the mouth that had opened, a person stepped out. He was tall, wearing a gray cape that obscured most of his body. He held a long staff in one hand, and from the end of it, a lantern hung from a swooping hook, flickering with a bright blue flame. When she realized that he was human, she stopped trying to withdraw, and relief surged through her. Suddenly, she was aware of how utterly alone she felt in the desert, how scared and unprepared, and she thought she might cry in relief.

"Halt!" the man declared, pointing his lantern at her. She couldn't see his face past the bright glow, but she was surprised by the hostility in his tone. A hand that had previously been hidden behind his cloak now came free, and she saw that he bore a strange weapon. It had a long handle, and its blade was curved like a sickle, yet sharp on both its sides. He spun the weapon expertly, and she got the distinct impression that he did it to be threatening.

Slyen's words came to her, then. That there would be people who might attack her, even if she had never done anything to them. So, she gazed at his face with wide eyes, afraid to blink even once. "Peace," she pleaded, fumbling a common greeting from her home. The Slyens often greeted one another with a friendly, "Peace and sunlight," during the day, or "Peace and moonlight," during the night. But she was too alarmed to manage more than one word.

He stormed toward her swiftly, thrusting his lantern close to her face so that he could get a better view of her. And then he brought his weapon around, the point of the curved blade aimed at her throat. "Trespasser," he declared, his voice deep and harsh. It was only now that she could see his features, and she was surprised by how pale his skin was, as though he had never spent a day in the sun. "We tolerate none to linger on our doorstep. The penalty for treading these sands is death!"

How was I to know? Aja thought, her arms trembling as her fear surged higher. She didn't know what to do in this situation, and the only protection she had was Slyen's promise that no one would kill her so long as they looked in her eyes. "I'm sorry," she said, her voice wavering. "Please… I was only trying to get out of the wind."

The man's eyes narrowed as he gazed at her, his expression as fierce as the sword he bore. Muscles tensed in his neck, and a vein bulged on his forehead. Seconds took ages to pass, before at last he swept his sword-hand back toward the secret doorway behind him. "Get up," he ordered, his voice as cold as the wind.

Aja didn't dare question him, though she was trembling so much that she could barely manage to get to her feet. Her heart raced, her blood pounding so hard that her ears ached and her chest felt tight. When she was standing, the man sheathed his sword under his cloak and grabbed hold of her arm so tightly that it hurt. He marched toward the doorway, dragging her with him. "Wait," she blurted, terror sweeping over her as she stared at the yawning mouth in the center of the jagged rocks. "Where are you taking me?"

"None may tread on the sands at the Door," the man said harshly, forcing her to walk beside him as he entered the cave. There was a narrow, steep staircase that curved down into darkness, and down these steps he pulled her. "You will come, or you will die."

Swallowing, Aja found that she was too frightened to reply. All she could do was try to keep her footing as she descended into the cave. The sound of rocks grinding against each other rumbled all around her once more, and she looked over her shoulder to see the stone slab rising back into place, sealing the doorway and locking her inside. Pitch blackness closed around her, their path lit only by the blue light of the man's swinging lantern.

I knew, she thought, as she was led deeper and deeper down the winding stair. *I knew that I shouldn't have stayed at the stone claws.*

Garnet Eagle

At the base of the stair, Aja found herself surrounded by several other people. Like the man who held her by the elbow with bruising force, all of them were shockingly pale and wore long cloaks that covered them in front and behind, with openings on the sides so that they could move their arms freely. But she could hardly focus on the people when her eyes kept straying to all she could see around her.

The stranger had brought her down into what appeared to be a large, underground city. Glittering cobblestone roads wound their way through buildings with many stories, and great pillars had been carved into the stone. Tall lampposts on the street corners flickered with bright blue flames, and behind circular windows in the buildings were round bulbs that glowed with some sort of phosphorous chemical. On the cave walls and stalagmites, occasional flashes of blue light were reflected in glittering flecks in the rock. The roof of the cavern was so high above her that she couldn't see it, and some of the stalactites that hung down from it were as thick as the evergreen trunks in Slyenwood.

She had never seen anything like it, and she was staggered by how expansive it was. Everywhere she looked, there were multitudes of buildings, and more people walked the streets than she had ever seen in her life.

Where am I? she thought, stunned. She didn't realize that she was being spoken to until the man shook her roughly, and she let out a faint gasp at how painfully tight his grip was. "You're hurting me," she exclaimed.

"Why did you come?" the man snapped. "What are you planning?"

"I was cold," Aja said, turning her head so that she could look directly into his eyes. She felt keenly aware that Slyen's Influence might be the only hope she had of protecting herself. "I was just trying to get out of the wind. I didn't mean to trespass; I never knew there was a door, there!"

"Lies," declared one of the others. "You came to scout out our city. We know better than to trust a Querian."

Aja almost insisted that she wasn't Querian, but she recalled Slyen's urgent instruction that she must not reveal where she had come from. "I'm not lying," she pleaded. "You must believe me."

"Was she alone?" asked a tall woman to Aja's left. She had pale blonde hair that was tied in three looped buns on her head.

The man holding Aja's arm nodded. "The stones detected only one at the doorway, but we should still kill her. She must be a spy for the Querians."

"There's no need to be hasty," a man to Aja's left countered, stretching out his hand in a calming gesture to his comrades. A calculating look spread over his face as he studied Aja, and when she turned her head to meet his gaze, she saw that his eyes were almost pink, they were so pale. "Perhaps she speaks the truth. Are we so suspicious of the overdwellers that we have forgotten how to show hospitality?"

"It's too convenient," Aja's captor argued.

"Relax," the pink-eyed man shook his head. "We hardly need to fear one Querian woman who got lost from her caravan, and it does little harm to care for her as a guest. Should we discover her to be our enemy, we can always kill her later."

The tall woman touched a hand to her chin, a strange look sweeping over her face. "The Garnet Oblation draws near," she said slowly. "We could at least keep her until then."

Aja could see a swiftly growing agreement in the eyes of everyone who stood around her. There were six of them, all cloaked and pale, nodding sagely to one another as they decided what to do with her. She wasn't sure what the Garnet Oblation was, but for now it provided a chance for her to avoid death. "I never meant to trespass," she tried pleading with them once more. "Please, if you return me to the desert, I will leave and never come back."

"I'm afraid we can't do that," the man with pink eyes offered her a smile, though it seemed more placating than comforting. He placed a hand on her shoulder, glaring at the man who gripped Aja's elbow until he released her. "We take the safety of our people very seriously, and that means investigating everyone who trespasses on our doorstep, even unwittingly. For now, we'll give you a place to stay while we investigate the situation. You should be thankful we have a ceremony coming up. It's because of that you have a few more days to convince us you aren't a threat."

He began to lead her down a street of glittering cobblestones, lined on either side by tall lampposts with burning blue flames encased in glass. The others remained behind her, standing at the winding stair and whispering to each other words she could not hear. "I'm not a threat," she said, her distress growing, the further away from the stair she was led. She couldn't shake the awareness that she was hedged in on all sides, and she was finding it difficult to breathe.

"Perhaps you aren't," the pink eyed man sighed, "but we can't afford to take chances. Can you blame us for being wary, while your people are brewing war above us?" He kept a firm hand on her shoulder, walking with swift steps that were difficult for her to keep up with.

But the Querians are not my people, she wanted to argue, biting her lip to keep the words from escaping. She couldn't say she was from Slyenials, so what else could she say? That she was Zyphan? *The Zyphans are just as involved in the war as the Querians and naming them won't prove my innocence. But what else am I supposed to do?*

"What is your name?" he asked, watching her face. He could see that she was in distress, and it seemed that he wanted to help her calm down. His tone was gentle, though he never slowed as he brought her through a section of the underground city.

"Aja," she replied, grateful for a question she could answer. As they passed people walking on the streets, she saw that many of them stopped to stare at her as though she were as strange and frightening to them as they were to her. "What is your name?"

"Cairon," he said, and he offered her a warm smile. "Are you thirsty, Aja? The desert can be a very miserable place to travel, even this time of year."

At the mention of thirst, Aja found herself suddenly so parched that it was almost unbearable. She'd been thirsty from the moment she had left the canyon and eating ferns and mushrooms had done nothing to soothe it. "Yes," she admitted.

Cairon led her into a stone building not far from the stair, pushing open a shuttered door made of rock. He kept a tight grip on her shoulder as he guided her through a narrow hall toward a room in the back. The moment they entered, the feeling of breathlessness in her grew, and she was gripped with a sense of distress she didn't know how to withstand. It was too enclosed. Just a short time ago, she had been so burdened by the wind that she ignored her instincts to keep moving. And now, imprisoned underground, she was deeply disturbed by the lack of wind.

I can't bear it, she thought with a shudder, feeling as though the walls were drawing closer around her. *I don't want to be here!*

"It's late," Cairon said gently. "Just past the twenty-third tone, I believe. We'll have some water and something to eat brought to your room, but you should get some rest while you can." He seemed aware of her sluggish steps and frantic breathing, though he kept pulling her along firmly but gently. As they stepped through another shuttered door, she found that he had brought her to a simple bedroom.

There was a bed against the wall, a lantern with blue light hanging from a hook beside the door, and a small table with a single chair beside it. The furniture was all carved from stone, with a mattress and cushions that were quite thick and soft-looking. On the floor was a grey and red rug, woven with geometric patterns like prisms spreading outward from the center. And on the far wall there was a glass window overlooking the glittering cobblestone streets, framed by a deep red curtain that was drawn up on one side by a golden cord.

"I know it's difficult for overdwellers to get used to being underground," he reassured her, "but those feelings will pass. Breathe deeply, Aja. You are safe here."

He closed the door as he slipped out, leaving her alone in the room. But when she tried to open the door to go out, she found that it would not move. *I'm trapped,* she realized, her vision darkening as it grew more and more difficult to breathe. "Let me out. Please… let me out!" She pushed on the door, pounded on it with her fist, and pleaded for him to come back. But it wouldn't budge, and no one came to answer her calls for help. Aja sank to her knees, pressing a hand to her chest as she struggled for air.

I'm suffocating! she thought. They were the last words in her mind before she succumbed to blackness.

Aja was lost. All around her was darkness and shadow, save for a few glimmers of light reflecting off the walls. She couldn't remember how long she had been walking, but it seemed like forever to her. "How do I get out?" she called. "I don't like this!"

A sound hummed in her bones, one that she couldn't hear with her ears, yet felt familiar to her. At once, she closed her eyes and *Listened,* trying to find where it was coming from. Wind blew on her face, and when she opened her eyes again, she found herself standing in a narrow hallway carved in stone. A cage was beside her, and turning to look inside, she stiffened in fear. A large jaguar bound in chains gazed out at her with wide eyes and bared teeth.

"You're making that sound?" she asked. The jaguar opened its mouth, and she had the strangest feeling like it would speak to her.

She never got to hear what it said. At that moment, something cold touched her face, and with a gasp, she bolted upright to find herself waking out of the dream. She was lying on the bed in the room Cairon had brought her to, and a young woman sat on a chair beside the bed. The woman was holding a cold cloth, damp with water, to her cheek.

"I'm sorry," the woman said, jolting slightly when Aja sat upright with a start. Her expression was nervous, but her pinkish-brown eyes were kind. Like the other people Aja had seen down here, she was pale in skin and hair. Her clothes were more colorful than the gray cloaks the others had worn. She was dressed in a long, slender dress that came down to her ankles, with long sleeves that had bare shoulders. It was a warm grey with deep red accents, in a style that was so unlike Slyenials clothing that Aja was impressed by it.

I've never seen a dress like that, she thought. But then the coldness against her cheek drew her out of her thoughts. "What's this?" she asked, reaching up a hand to take the cloth from the woman.

With an embarrassed expression, the woman pulled her hand back at once. "You came from the desert, didn't you?" she blurted, speaking quickly and nervously. "I brought you something to eat and drink, but you didn't wake up. So, I thought you might be hot, so I... I'm sorry. Are you hot or cold?"

The earnest concern in the woman's tone helped Aja to calm down, and she found herself smiling faintly. "I'm a little cold," she admitted. "I didn't know the desert got so cold at night, so I wasn't prepared." She paused, glancing down at the cloth in her hands. It was very finely woven, though the fabric was somewhat brittle and coarse. "My name is Aja," she continued, glancing up again. "What's your name?"

"Leyla," the woman said, rising to her feet. She went to the small circular table which sat beside the window, picking up a ceramic cup with an ornate, circular handle. When she brought it over, Aja saw steam rising from it. "Here's something warm to drink," she said. "I'm sorry it isn't much, I put it together in a hurry when I heard you were brought here."

"Where is... here?" Aja asked, taking the cup she offered. It warmed her cold hands, and for a moment, she simply held it and inhaled the warm beverage inside. *It smells earthy and sweet,* she decided. Taking a sip, she found that it was sweet at first, then had a slightly bitter aftertaste. It was pleasant though, immediately soothing. Even the prospect of being trapped underground felt less daunting now that she had something comforting to drink and someone kind to talk to.

Maybe they'll believe this is all a misunderstanding and will let me go, she thought hopefully.

"Oh, right," Leyla said, fidgeting nervously as she sat down on the chair once more. "Our city is called Garnet Eagle. There aren't any birds down here, of course, but there's a great rock in the center of the city, I'm told, that looks just like an eagle. So that's why they named it that when they carved the city. The eagle was made first, and the city came after. Have you ever seen an eagle? Are they very large?" Her words were quick and eager, running together in a way that made her somewhat difficult to understand. But her curiosity was refreshingly sincere.

She reminds me of Tula, Aja thought, recalling her neighbor fondly. Tula was several years older than Aja, a chatty and friendly person with an insatiable curiosity that had often gotten her into trouble when she was younger.

A pang of homesickness shot through Aja's heart when she realized she might never see Tula, her mother, or anyone else from home again if she couldn't convince these people she meant no harm. "I've seen eagles," she answered. "They can get pretty large. Some of them have wingspans longer than my arm." She held out her arm for reference.

"I've never been to the surface," Leyla said, her eyes wide with fascination. "They say all the people from there are violent and cruel. They say a war is going to start soon, and if they find out about us down here, they'll try to take our cities and precious gems for themselves."

"I don't think that's what they're fighting for," Aja said carefully, thinking back on what Emrin and Ryder had told her. *They said some fights are worth fighting, and that they're standing up against tyranny. That sounds admirable, if it's true, but I still don't think war is a good thing.* "But speaking of the war, that's why I have to leave here as soon as possible. I'm supposed to stop the war."

"Oh, I don't think that will happen," Leyla said, averting her eyes. Her posture and expression became nervous again. "Too dangerous. But…" she glanced back at Aja, almost hopefully. "But if they decide you're not a threat to us, you might be able to live here."

"Live here?" Aja blurted, shuddering with horror at the idea. Stuck underground in a dark city where she couldn't see the sky? Couldn't smell the trees or tend her garden? Couldn't see her family and friends that she'd left behind? "No, you don't understand," she begged. "I *have* to go. If I don't, the war *will* start, and terrible things will happen!"

"War is terrible, yes," Leyla said, shaking her head. "But it's already started. No helping that. Don't you want to live? It's really so very nice here."

"I don't want to live here," Aja insisted, growing frustrated. "I want to go home."

"I'm sorry," Leyla said, flinching back from Aja as though she expected her to hurt her. It was such an unexpected reaction that Aja felt distressed by it. Did she really think Aja would cause her harm? "I brought you food, too," Leyla said, hastily changing the subject. When she got up and retrieved a tray from the table, her arms were shaking as she offered it to Aja.

Why is she so scared of me? Aja thought, crestfallen. Taking the tray from her hands, she looked down to see that there was a bowl of soup and a ceramic spoon beside it. "Thank you," she said quietly. "I'm sorry for raising my voice."

"Oh," Leyla said meekly. "Alright." She returned to her chair, watching and fidgeting while Aja tasted a spoonful of soup. As soon as had it passed her lips, Leyla spoke again with the same hurried pace as before. "Do you like it? I made it yesterday, so these are just the leftovers, but I think soups tend to taste better the next day. Don't you? Unless you've never had soup. Do overdwellers eat soup?"

Swallowing the spoonful quickly, Aja found herself cracking a smile once more. *I can't decide if she's afraid of me or fascinated by me,* she thought, *but she seems nice.* If she could make Leyla grow more comfortable around her, maybe she could convince her to help her leave. "It's very good," she praised honestly. "And yes, we eat soup, too."

"Are you Querian?" Leyla asked, growing bolder at Aja's willingness to answer her questions. "That's what the Guards are saying. I guess you must be if you're trying to stop the war. How do you plan to stop it? You only had plants in your bag—and that's made of plants, too. How did you make it? What kind of plants are they? Do you have to water your bag to keep it alive?"

With each question Leyla asked, Aja merely listened and continued eating, feeling unsettled as she debated on how to reply. She wasn't Querian, but she couldn't tell anyone she was from Slyenials. So how was she supposed to answer without telling a blatant lie? But at this last question about her bag, she dropped her spoon into her bowl and looked around the room for the bag in question. She caught sight of it hanging from a peg in the wall, looking as vibrant and green as it had when Slyen first made it.

"I don't know," she said honestly. "I never asked when it was given to me."

"Oh, I see," Leyla said, following her gaze. "It's a very peculiar bag, isn't it? What kind of plant is it made from?"

"A fern," Aja responded. "They grow up from the ground, each frond like a long stem with many leaves sprouting along its length." She scooted to the edge of the bed, rose to her feet, and fetched the bag from its peg. When she came back to the bed, she opened it and showed Leyla the fiddleheads she had left. They were very wilted and limp now. "This is what they look like when they're still growing."

"We have some plants in our gardens," Leyla said, taking one and inspecting it curiously. "But they're mostly fungi and algae since we don't get sunlight. There are some foods we get by trading with overdwellers, but they're harder to come by so they are rationed sparingly."

Rationed? Aja wondered. She had no concept of what the word might mean in this context, though instead of revealing her ignorance, she merely nodded thoughtfully. The general had used the word once or twice, but never explained what it meant. "What is algae?" she asked. The only unfamiliar plants were the strange, spiked ones in the desert, so that was what came to mind.

"It's a living organism that grows in water," Leyla explained. "We can't eat it by itself, but since there isn't much else we can get naturally in the caves, we had to invent ways of using it. There's algae in your soup, too. That's what gives it the unique flavor it has."

"So, you trade with people like me for foods you don't have?" Aja wondered. She finished her bowl of soup, feeling relieved to have eaten. This time, when she left this place, she would make sure to take some proper food with her. Definitely some water, too, provided she could find a way to carry it.

"Yes, that's right," Leyla said, fidgeting with her hands in her lap. "But overdwellers are dangerous, so we can't let them know where we come from. We travel in secret to their cities and trade gemstones for their food."

This is an opportunity I can take, Aja thought, her heart quickening as an idea came to her. "I'd like to speak to the people who make the trades, if I can," she said earnestly. "Maybe they can help prove that I don't mean any harm. I was cold and took refuge under the stone spires to get out of the wind. I wasn't even aware that this place existed."

"I'll tell Cairon," Leyla said with a nod. "I'm to watch over you until the Garnet Oblation, so if there's anything you need, just let me know."

"Thank you, Leyla," Aja said warmly. She glanced at the door, remembering how it had been locked from the outside. "Being underground is hard for me," she said. "I'd like it if I could walk around."

"Oh," Leyla said nervously. "Well… that's not such a good idea right now. People are very scared of overdwellers, so it's better for you to remain here until we can warn the city about you."

"I don't mean any harm," Aja insisted, her voice pleading. "You must believe me."

"If you say so," Leyla said, flinching slightly. She rose to her feet and stepped backwards toward the door. By her tone and words, it seemed as if she wanted to believe her, but she was instinctively wary all the same. "If you need anything, just knock on the door and ask for me," she said. "Someone will let me know."

Before Aja could say anything else, Leyla slipped through the door and closed it firmly behind her. Aja heard a bar being laid across it on the other side, locking her in, and she shuddered with great unease. Once more, she was trapped and alone in this strange, underground city.

The people who trade with the overdwellers are my best chance of getting out of here, she thought, trying not to let misery claim her thoughts. *If I can convince them I mean no harm, maybe they will take me with them when they next go trading.*

With nothing else to do with her time, Aja took the ceramic cup into her hands once more, closing her eyes and *Listening* to the city around her as best she could. There were so many strange sounds she wasn't used to, murmurs of voices, footsteps in the streets, stones grinding as doors opened or closed. It was overwhelming, but she didn't have anything else she could do. At the very least, it calmed the anxiety that was swelling in her chest. *Listening* had always helped her feel calm. It gave her answers when she faced the unknown. Maybe it would help her gain a better understanding of this strange, wary city deep under the desert of Scoria.

It didn't surprise her that the first thing she heard were voices outside the door. Leyla was speaking quietly, her voice nervous and low. With her eyes closed and her senses focused, Aja noticed things she hadn't picked up on before. Like the way Leyla's tone seemed almost regretful, and how she swallowed often.

"I did what you asked, brother," Leyla said, almost stressing the word "asked" with a worried tone. "What more do you want from me? I need to go to the market now that I have a *guest* to take care of—not that you warned me about it first."

"Sorry, Ley," her brother responded. Aja recognized it as the voice of Cairon, who had brought her here. He sounded worried, too. She could almost hear the frown on his face as he spoke. "I had to act swiftly, and this was the first place I thought of. You've always had a good grasp on people. What did you make of her?"

Leyla hesitated, swallowing as she considered. Aja thought she could hear her fidgeting with her dress, twisting the fabric between her fingers. "I almost think she means what she says, that she doesn't intend any harm," she said at length. "I don't know. When I looked in her eyes, I thought she seemed sincere. Is she really dangerous?"

"Any Querian is dangerous," Cairon sighed. "But I know what you mean. I felt it too. Why do you think I brought her here to begin with?"

"Maybe she did get lost from a caravan," Leyla said, speaking in her quick, nervous way. "Maybe she was only getting out of the wind, like she said. How would she know about the door?"

"There was no sign of anyone else with her," Cairon responded. "I believe her story too."

"Then talk to the Council," Leyla urged. "Why should she have to die when she's no threat to us?"

"If we spare her, she will have to become a citizen," Cairon said, his voice edged with warning. "Overdwellers don't like living underground. She may refuse outright. And anyway, where will she stay if we let her? Will *you* take her in?"

"Maybe I will," Leyla said, with more defiance than Aja would have expected from the timid young woman. "You brought her to our house and put her in *my* room, anyway. And you didn't ask."

"I don't expect her to stay long," Cairon sighed. "The Garnet Oblation—"

"We already have someone for that," Leyla cut him off, and swallowed again. "And I think she's telling the truth. I don't *want* to see someone innocent get killed for trespassing."

"Neither do I," Cairon admitted. He hesitated, and in the silence, Leyla swallowed twice more. It made Aja swallow unconsciously, herself. "I'll talk to the Council. In the meantime, she'll be under your care, and my watch. That's all I can promise."

"Okay," Leyla said, her voice relieved. "Thank you, Cai." She stepped past him, her steps taking her somewhere Aja could no longer hear. Cairon followed her.

When she was truly alone in the house, apart from a guard posted outside, Aja opened her eyes and looked toward the shuttered window. The conversation she'd overheard gave her hope. There was a chance she could become a citizen, and a citizen would not be killed. Perhaps once she had their trust, they would let her leave once more. Or perhaps being a citizen would mean she was trapped down here forever.

"I don't want to stay," she whispered, wishing someone she knew was here to talk to her. She thought of her mother, her sister, her fiery friend Seila. She even found herself missing the General. "But I don't want to die, either. What is the right thing to do? How do I get out of here?"

Without anyone to offer counsel, she had to contend with imagining their advice herself. Her mother might tell her to trust her instincts. Or maybe she'd scold her for getting caught and not listening to her instincts out in the desert. The General... he would probably tell her to stand up for herself. Don't take no for an answer, and demand they take her to the surface. But that was something she could never do.

"Seila would just escape," Aja said to herself, smiling faintly as tears slipped down her cheeks. Her chest ached with homesickness, and her hands felt cold and numb. "If only I were as bold as she." At least she had Slyen's protection. It was the reason she was still alive, and the one thing that might give her a chance to get out of here.

All she could do was hope that Cairon could convince the Council—whoever they were—to let her go in the end.

Council

Being underground did get easier, though it caused Aja a constant unease that followed her into her sleep. Dreaming of red skies again the first night, she woke up with a scream and found herself alone in Leyla's bedroom. After calming herself down by huddling up under the covers on the bed, she heard Leyla and Cairon's whispered voices from outside.

"Overdwellers always have nightmares the first few nights," Cairon said. "Don't be alarmed."

"Is being down here where it's safe really so terrible for them?" Leyla whispered back. "I just can't understand it."

And you likely never will, Aja thought to herself. She didn't go back to sleep after that.

In the morning, Leyla came into the room with a breakfast of baked eggs, a spicy green algae sauce drizzled over them, paired with a round flat bread. Leyla showed her how to eat it, breaking off bits of the bread and scooping up eggs, then taking a bite right from her fingers. Aja found the meal enjoyable, and it helped her to feel more hopeful for the day ahead of her.

"Will I be able to look around your city?" Aja asked. "You told me this city was named for the large rock shaped like an eagle. I would like to see it."

"Oh," Leyla said, glancing toward the door nervously. "Well, I don't think that's possible. At least for right now."

"When would it be possible?" Aja pressed gently, offering what she hoped was a friendly smile.

"Trespassers can't wander the city," Leyla shook her head. She hesitated, meeting Aja's eyes and chewing on her lower lip. "You said you aren't a trespasser, didn't you?"

"I was lost," Aja said truthfully. "I never knew this place was here, and I'm sorry my taking refuge by the stones caused so much trouble. I promise, if you let me go, I will leave and never tell a soul about this place."

"Oh, I don't think that's possible," Leyla shook her head. "But… if you're telling the truth, there may be other options for you than a trespasser's sentence."

Aja noticed that she didn't say the word "death," as though she meant to keep it a secret. "What sort of options?" she asked. Her thoughts went to their talk about citizenship, and to the people who went to trade on the surface.

"Not for me to say," Leyla insisted. She was happy to talk about other things, like clothes, Aja's fern bag, food they liked to eat, and what surface animals looked like. But she would not talk about citizenship, about the Council, or anything else regarding Aja's imprisonment in her house.

The next night Aja didn't dream of red skies, but she did see the forest jaguar again. Like before, it was bound in chains, crouched in its cage and glaring at her with brown eyes that reflected the light, and when they shone, they almost looked yellow. "What is a jaguar doing down here?" she asked it, touching the bars with her fingers. Once more she felt a deep humming vibration run through her, a sound she felt in her bones but could not place with her ears.

"Come to gawk at an animal?" the jaguar replied.

She was surprised by the cynicism in its voice, a voice that sounded too human to be an animal's. It reminded her of Slyen, and she tightened her fingers around the bars. "You don't belong here," she said. The vibration ran up her arm into her chest, making her breath shallow. She yanked on the bars, trying to open the door. A jaguar did not belong in a cage. She did not belong in a cave.

They both needed to be free.

She woke to find herself on the floor, tugging at the bed frame with her fingers. No wonder the cage felt so unmovable in her dream. *The jaguar is me,* she thought miserably. *I'm trapped down here, and I may never get out. Everything I love will come to ruin.*

She was quiet and dour the whole day, and nothing Leyla tried to distract her with would lift her spirits. The nervous woman showed her lots of dresses, all with garnet-colored accents on grey fabric. She taught her a board game that was popular in Scoria, where they rolled a die and moved their pieces across a board, avoiding hazards and sometimes drawing cards that sent them back several paces, made them lose a turn, or gave them a lucky short cut.

Near the end of the day, when Aja showed no signs of cheering, Leyla bade her an early goodnight and went out to find her brother. Aja *Listened* to hear what they would say, but they were too far for her hearing to reach. She went to bed with a heavy heart, and to her relief, she had no dreams that night.

On the third day, when Leyla brought her the same breakfast as before, flatbread and eggs with algae and pepper sauce, Aja noticed a change in Leyla's demeanor. She seemed brighter, smiling more easily and talking even more rapidly than before.

"I brought you a dress to wear," Leyla said. "You'll need one, you see. If you *look* like you fit in down here, it will be so much better."

"What will?" Aja asked, eating lethargically. Her eyes strayed to the garment Leyla had brought in with her, a grey dress with geometric patterns of garnet hexagons sewn into the fabric. It was a striking design, fancier than the ones Leyla had worn before.

"They're having a hearing about you," Leyla said, "to discuss what's to be done with you. Cai says that if you can present yourself well, they might let you stay here as a citizen. And that would be *so* much better than a trespasser's sentence. You'd be able to walk around the city—I could show you the eagle, and you can tell me if it looks like one!"

At these words, hope stirred in Aja's chest. She straightened, taking a deep breath and filling her lungs, holding it for a moment as she considered what to say. When she exhaled, she smiled. "I would like that," she said, and she was surprised to see a bright smile spread across Leyla's face.

"I would too," she insisted. "There's a dress shop in town I would love to take you to. I think the seamstress would just *love* your long belt you wear. Can you imagine a pretty belt like that around a dress like this?" She lifted the dress she had brought for Aja, holding it against her chest and showing how lovely it looked. It was sleeveless with a high neck and a short skirt that came to her knees, and the patterns on it were flattering against her figure.

"Do you want to try my belt on?" Aja asked. She set aside her breakfast and rose to her feet, untying the belt from around her waist. When it was free, she came toward Leyla and carefully wrapped it around her, tying the knot her favorite way so that it could lie flat against her dress.

"You should make it so both ends are even length," Leyla said, pursing her lips at Aja's way of tying it asymmetrically. "It would look better."

"This way is fashionable where I come from," Aja explained.

"Is it?" Leyla raised her eyebrows, looking surprised. "Well…" she looked down at herself, admiring the belt, and then nodded. "I suppose it has its own charm."

Aja wasn't sure why the comment sent a pang through her chest. Perhaps it just made her more aware of how much she missed home.

"But you're the one who needs to get dressed," Leyla insisted. "The hearing will be in half an hour, and it's a fair distance to walk." Handing her the gown she'd brought, Leyla stepped out of the room, still wearing the belt and looking pleased with it as the straps swished by her side. She tugged on the shorter of the two ends, trying to even out the lengths of the straps. "Let me know if you need help," she called over her shoulder.

The door was left unbarred for the first time, and Aja felt a shiver travel down her arms. *This is it,* she thought. *My chance for freedom.* She changed into the dress, feeling strange and uncomfortable, but forced herself to calm her breathing. The hearing had to go well. And if she had to, she'd make eye contact with every single person in the room to convince them not to kill her.

A knock on the door drew her from her thoughts, and Leyla opened it shortly after. She gasped when she saw Aja, her eyes shining with delight. "It looks so lovely on you!" she exclaimed. "I just knew it would!"

"Thank you," Aja replied, feeling uncomfortable despite her praise. She said nothing as Leyla picked out shoes for her to wear, adorned her with a bracelet of raw garnet beads, and garnet dewdrop earrings. Then, when her caretaker beckoned for her to follow, Aja made her way out of the room she'd been locked in for three days.

No one looked at her as she walked down the cobblestone streets, accompanied by Cairon and Leyla on one side, and another guard on the other. On her previous walk from the Door to Leyla's house, everyone had stared at her with fear and alarm. But this time they hardly noticed her. Perhaps it was the clothing she wore that made her seem less alarming. *It's the gray fabric,* Aja decided. *I think it marks them as citizens, and they feel safe around their own people.*

The walk did not take as long as Leyla implied, as the streets were narrow and the blocks were tightly packed together. The city was tall rather than wide, with buildings carved into the rocks with narrow stairs leading up to the higher stories. Shops were all located on the ground level with dwellings situated above them. The cobblestone streets were well lit, and it appeared the people walked everywhere instead of taking steam-powered vehicles like the Zyphans used.

Aja liked walking. That was how her people had always gotten around before the Zyphans arrived. They had widened all the pathways between the villages and laid down stones lined with mortar to make them into roads. It used to take a couple days to reach the other villages. Now on the new roads, the Zyphans could reach them in half a day using their large moving vehicles.

Finding another place that had no steam and electric powered machines was comforting in a way Aja did not expect. Here, there was no sign of war, no strange machines, and no disharmony between the people and their environment. They sculpted their city out of living rock according to its natural contours, instead of cutting away the stone and building new houses on flat ground. Aja thought she wouldn't mind coming to visit a place like this, to see it and experience it when she had time to enjoy it. But this was not that time. Winter was fast approaching, and she needed to find Slyen's brother before time ran out.

The building they brought her to was larger than the others and appeared to be some kind of gathering hall for the people. Stone pews were carved into the sidelines, and in the center of the room was a circular platform that was in view for everyone in the room. Seated in a semi-circle in front of the platform were seven men and women, all regally dressed in gray with garnet accents. Unlike the average citizen, they each wore a wide collar of woven garnet beads that rested over their shoulders and chest, and bore a crown with a single large garnet upon their heads.

Cairon and the other guard brought Aja to the circular platform, and they halted in the center of it before the Council. Leyla slipped into one of the pews, which were beginning to fill with people as the townsfolk came to witness the hearing. With so many eyes on her, Aja's nerves began to feel strained, and she had to remind herself not to fidget.

I don't know what to expect, she thought anxiously, looking at each Council member in turn. Their eyes met, and she held their gaze steadily for a few seconds before turning to the next one. Several moments of awkward silence passed as people came and took a seat in the pews, and then the Council members rose to their feet. A woman in the very center of the semi-circle stepped forward and cleared her throat.

"This hearing on Cabochon the 3rd for the Citizens versus the Trespasser, Aja, is now called to order," the woman declared. She had perfectly white hair, even whiter than her pale skin, and her eyes were a ruby red. They seemed to shift back and forth with a very subtle vibration, and Aja found it difficult to make eye contact with her. "We, the Council of Garnet Eagle, will hear the testimony of the Trespasser, and before the people of Garnet Eagle, we will pronounce a sentence." The woman and the other members of the Council returned to their seats.

A man beside her, with graying hair and wrinkled skin, coughed to clear his throat. "First, the testimony of the Guard."

Cairon stepped forward, his back straight and his chin high and proud. "Four nights ago, the stones detected a trespasser at the Northern Gate. Upon coming to the surface, we found only a single Querian woman with no belongings other than a simple bag with plants inside. The guard on duty decided to bring her down for questioning."

"And where is the guard who found her?" the woman with ruby eyes asked.

"Here, your Honor," a man called from the back of the gathering hall. He stepped forward to the platform and stopped beside Cairon.

"Why did you bring her down instead of killing her on the spot?" the councilwoman asked.

He kept a perfectly composed, expressionless face as he replied. "I did not judge her to be a threat. I believed she got lost from a caravan and did not know she was on our doorstep."

"Proceed," the councilwoman nodded. He stepped off the platform and returned to his spot. "Was there any sign of a search party on the surface?"

"None," Cairon responded. "These past three days, we have been watching to see if anyone would come looking for her, but there has been no sign of a search party. We spied one caravan making its way to the east coast across the desert road, but they must have given her up for dead."

Aja focused on breathing in and out, steadying her nerves and trying not to shift her weight from foot to foot too often. Despite her nervousness, every word she heard was hopeful to her. *They don't think I'm a threat,* she realized, watching Cairon as he spoke. *That's why we are having a hearing at all. They've already decided that I'm no threat, and now they are making it official.*

"Trespasser," the councilwoman said. "Your name is Aja, I understand?"

"Yes, your Honor," Aja said, including the title the guard had used before.

"What brought you to our doorstep that night?"

"I was lost," Aja said, meeting her eyes as best she could, and trying not to be discouraged by the way they vibrated. "And I was cold. I didn't know it was a door, I just went there to get out of the wind."

"Were you trying to find your caravan?" the woman asked.

Aja didn't want to lie, but she knew she couldn't tell them the truth of where she had come from. Swallowing nervously, she offered the most careful reply she could think of. "I wasn't. I don't think I could have found the caravan, so I wasn't looking. I was just trying to find my way when the wind became too much for me."

"And where were you headed?" the councilman beside the woman asked.

"To Mettain," Aja answered. This was the truth, and since she didn't think she could stretch the truth successfully, it was all she could say. To her relief, no one seemed alarmed by her destination.

"Do you know the penalty for trespassing or espionage?" the councilman asked. When Aja shook her head, he offered an almost pitying smile. "It is death," he intoned. "A sentence we were prepared to give you on the day of Garnet Oblation."

Were, Aja thought without replying. *Meaning they no longer intend to kill me.* Hope surged inside her.

"You have stumbled upon our city by accident, this much we agree on," the councilwoman said with a firm tone. "Overdwellers who come to our city are never allowed to leave, except in death. Therefore, you have two choices. You can offer your life in the Garnet Oblation, or you can stay forever in Scoria as a citizen of Garnet Eagle."

Forever? Aja thought, momentarily stiffening with alarm. *I can't stay here forever. I can't!* She kept her mouth firmly shut as she inhaled through her nose, then exhaled slowly to calm herself down. "I don't want to die," she said honestly. "And I think Garnet Eagle is a lovely city. I would rather be a citizen, given those two choices." A pleading expression filled her face as she met the councilwoman's ever-shifting ruby eyes. "Is there no way I can earn your trust so that I can see the surface again?"

"At this present time, no," the woman shook her head. "But there have been cases where a citizen has proven their loyalty and been allowed to venture onto the surface, helping with trade between other nations. If you prove yourself similarly, you may apply for a visa to the surface at a later date."

So, it's not hopeless, she thought, still anxious about how long that might take. *But it's not soon enough. I'll have to escape out the door, somehow.* "I would like to become a citizen," she said. "Please."

To her surprise, the councilwoman smiled in amusement. "Then, with the testimony of the trespasser verified by the Guard, and her character vouched for by one of our own, this council is in agreement. State your full name, please."

It took Aja a moment to realize she was talking to her. "Ah… Ajana Sorinsa, your Honor."

"Ajana Sorinsa, formerly of Queria, this council grants you citizenship to Garnet Eagle. You will be issued an identification number, please keep it on your person at all times." The Council all rose to their feet as one. "This hearing is adjourned."

A buzz of voices broke out around them as people began to discuss the hearing amongst themselves. Cairon guided Aja off the platform toward the door, and Leyla came up to her at once as they left the building. "I just knew they would let you stay," Leyla said, speaking so swiftly that it took a second for Aja to distinguish the words. "I think they'd already decided. After all, we already have someone for the Oblation, and Cai verified your story himself."

"This is your number," Cairon added, handing her a thin slab made of stone with an eight-digit number engraved on it. There was a hole drilled in one side, and a woven cord tied through it. "Most of us wear our numbers attached to our belts, I suggest you do the same. Since you are a new citizen, you'll be asked for your number a lot."

"By whom?" Aja asked. She was looking at Leyla, going over her words in her mind. *They already have someone for "the Oblation?" What does that mean?*

"Businesses," Cairon explained. "You can't buy anything without it, until you're a known customer, that is."

"We'll definitely go clothes shopping," Leyla beamed. "You look so pretty in our colors."

"What is the Garnet Oblation?" Aja asked. She was being swiftly ushered away from the gathering hall by Cairon and Leyla, who seemed to want to keep her from getting overwhelmed. There were a lot of citizens staring at her and talking about her now that the hearing was over.

"A ceremony," Leyla said. Where previously, she had been hesitant to tell Aja anything about their city, she was practically bursting at the seams to tell her things now that she was a citizen. "It's to honor the Guardian of Scoria. These are his caves, and we make an offering to him every year so that we can continue to live under his protection."

"And I would have been that offering?" Aja asked, bewildered. Would she have become his servant? *No, they said that the oblation means death. I would have died as that offering.* "I don't understand. Who is he? Why does he want a sacrifice?"

"He is our great protector," Cairon said gravely. "And it was he who decided you could stay. The hearing we just had was only a formality."

After walking very swiftly through the city, Aja found that they had brought her back to their house. This time, though, they ascended the steps one more floor to the next story and opened the door to a small living space. A sitting area with a kitchen attached, a toilet room, and a small bedroom. Cairon handed her a large metal key, smiling widely. "Welcome to your new home," he said.

"We'll be neighbors," Leyla added. "They thought it best, since we've been watching you so we're the only ones you know right now."

"So be sure to let us know if you have any questions," Cairon agreed.

Aja held the metal key in her hand, blinking as she tried to assess her situation. Everything was happening so fast she could barely keep up. She was a citizen now… and it was the mysterious Guardian who would have killed her that decided she could live. She had even been given a place to live. *From prisoner to welcomed in the space of an hour,* she thought in disbelief.

But the relief she felt was short-lived. It had not escaped her that someone *else* was going to die. Someone else would be offered up to the Guardian for the Garnet Oblation.

"Who is the Guardian?" she asked.

"That's something you don't need to concern yourself with," Cairon said, a little more firmly than Aja expected. There were some things, it seemed, that she still wasn't allowed to know.

"I'm just worried," she explained, wondering how she could ask what she wanted to know without making them suspicious of her. She couldn't get the thought of that other person out of her mind. "Are you sure I don't have to be offered up to the Guardian? He won't change his mind?"

"Don't worry," Cairon smiled again, seeming to relax at this question. "He's the one who gave permission for you to become a citizen. Besides, we have the oblation taken care of this year."

"Who is it?" Aja asked. "Is it… someone from the caravan?" She remembered them saying they had seen one.

"Ah, you're worried it's one of your friends!" Leyla exclaimed. "Well don't worry, it's not even a real person. It's more like an animal, so there's no need to worry."

"Like an animal?" Aja asked, unsure why she felt such anxiety at these words. Slyen came to her mind—he was more like an animal than a person—and immediately she knew that she *had* to find out who it was. What if it was Slyen's brother? What if he had come looking for Slyen after all?" *I have to know. I have to see!* Turning to Cairon, Aja gazed into his eyes with what she hoped was a look of innocent curiosity. "May I see it?"

He hesitated. It almost seemed like he would deny her outright, but then he sighed and shrugged his shoulders. "Why not?" he said. "Leyla's been asking to see it too. I'll take you, but you both have to promise to stay by my side, alright?"

"Oh!" Leyla exclaimed, looking excited. "Aja, you got him to say, yes? I need to keep you around for these sorts of things! I've been trying for days, ever since they brought in that strange prisoner."

"Don't let her push you around," Cairon said, feigning a scowl. He walked down the stairs again and gestured for the two young women to follow him. "If you let her, she'll get you to do all sorts of things you don't want to do."

"I'm not *that* bad," Leyla insisted. "It's just that he never does anything I ask him to do. Must be because we're siblings. Brothers are like that, as you know."

"I wouldn't know," Aja replied, following the two of them as they left the house they had given her and began to head toward the edge of the city. "I don't have a brother." *But I have a sister,* she thought, emotion causing a pang to shoot through her. *I miss her. I miss everyone from back home. Do they miss me, too?*

The walk through town was swift, and unlike before, Aja felt several stares from passersby as she went. Talk of the hearing had spread, and now everyone in the city seemed to be aware of her. Out of habit, and perhaps nervousness, Aja *Listened* as she went, trying to pick out any possible danger to herself. She heard several people whispering about the "Querian Civilian" and questioning why it was allowed, but other than that, the conversations were more curious than negative.

Very shortly, they arrived at a large stone building that had four guards posted at the door, two outside and two inside. Cairon was known to them, so they didn't halt him as he entered the building with both women in tow.

"This is where I work," Cairon explained. "It's right near the Door, so that's how I came to be involved when you were brought down." He led them through a narrow stone hallway past two separate rooms. One was smaller, with a desk and a chair, and several shelves filled with papers and stone tablets. It was reminiscent of the room General Ryder worked in. He called it an office. The other room was larger, with a counter against the wall and two long tables lined with benches. It seemed to be some sort of dining area, and she saw a few of the Scorian Guard lounging and eating in there.

Past these rooms was a heavy stone door which made a grinding sound as it opened, and it was through this that Cairon took them. On the other side was another long hall, lined on either side by jail cells with metal bars. Aja shivered as they walked past them, her heart beginning to race. *I hear something,* she thought, instinctively quieting her footsteps to *Listen* more clearly.

Yes, she definitely could hear something, like a low rumble, or the unnerving sound of a forest jaguar's purr—not with her ears, it resonated through her bones with each step that she took. *Like my dream,* she thought. *It's vibrating through my skull.*

Cairon stopped beside a jail cell in the very back of the prison, rapping on the bars with his knuckles. "There it is," he said. "The one you wanted to see. Are you satisfied now, Ley?"

"Oh!" Leyla gasped, jolting in surprise when she looked inside the cell. Her eyes widened in disbelief, and her hand reached for Cairon's arm for reassurance. She seemed both fascinated and afraid at once.

Aja looked into the cell, her heart pounding uncomfortably as she studied the man inside. For it was a man, not an animal, that was locked up inside it, seated on the floor in chains with his back against the side wall. He was younger than Cairon, possibly closer to her own age, with sandy brown hair and yellow-brown eyes that seemed to catch the light and reflect them. Unlike a normal person, his ears were pointed and catlike, tan-colored with black tips, and they stuck upward out of his hair. One of them flicked—with irritation, Aja thought— and he turned to give them a sidelong glance. That was when she noticed his long tail, tan in color, with black stripes near the end of it.

The inaudible sound of rumbling grew louder in Aja's skull, and her back tensed as she met his sharp gaze. She had never seen him before, or anyone like him, for that matter. And yet as she stared at him without blinking, she couldn't shake the feeling that she *had* seen him somewhere.

His tail twitched and his ears angled backwards slightly. "Come to gawk at an animal?" he asked.

The Prisoner

Aja was usually unsurprised when she encountered something that she had seen previously in a dream. But as she stared at the stranger in the jail cell, she found herself taken back by how much everything lined up. Certainly, this man was no forest jaguar. But he *did* have catlike features, and his eyes were the same color as the jaguar's in her dream. And there was that low rumbling sound that hummed through her bones and rang through her skull, a sound that could not be heard, yet she *heard* it all the same. When he spoke the very same words that the jaguar had spoken in her dream, she felt as though something that had been bothering her finally clicked into place.

"You are not an animal," she said, surprising herself by the comment. For some reason she had never been able to explain, she was always bolder when she encountered things she had dreamt about. She half expected Cairon and Leyla to say something to her, perhaps to chide her for speaking to their prisoner, but they remained silent, staring at the man with confused and distracted expressions on their faces.

"And you are not from Scoria," the prisoner said, flicking his ear and focusing his attention on Aja. She felt the hairs on her skin stand up as he scrutinized her, and the deep purring vibration grew louder—something that didn't seem possible for an inaudible rumbling.

"What are you?" Aja asked. It wasn't the question she wanted to ask him, but she was afraid of saying anything that would make Cairon and Leyla mistrust her again.

"Not an animal," the prisoner responded dryly. He paused, tilting his head slightly and narrowing his eyes. "You don't know what I am? That's surprising for a Querian. Or am I wrong about your origin?"

"Does it matter?" Aja asked defensively, stiffening at his question. *I can't tell anyone where I'm from,* she thought. *Slyen told me I had to keep it a secret. If Cairon suspects I'm not from Queria...* she turned her head, glancing at Cairon. He had the same confused expression on his face, and he stared without blinking at the prisoner. Neither he nor Leyla had moved or spoken, as though they were locked in some sort of trance. "What did you do to them?" Aja blurted.

"Not so loud," the prisoner replied softly. "Or someone else might hear and come investigate. I can't keep this up for long."

"Keep what up?" Aja asked. Now she was curious. How did it work? Was it the inaudible purr that held them transfixed in place?

"Interesting," the prisoner remarked, crossing his arms and leaning back against the wall as he studied her. "Why aren't you affected?" It didn't seem like he was asking her, but rather talking to himself. He shrugged and rose to his feet, walking a couple steps forward. His steps came to a halt as the chains around his ankles prevented him from reaching the bars. "I suppose it doesn't matter. I can work with this. What's your name?"

"Tell me yours first," Aja shot back at him. Not because she wasn't planning on telling him her name, but she didn't like that he wasn't answering her questions. *For all I know, my time to talk to him before Cairon and Leyla snap out of this trance is short. I need to find out as much as I can about him. I dreamt about him for a reason, I'm sure of it.*

"Jaqlai," he responded, the corner of his mouth curling upward in an amused smile. "Now tell me yours, Querian."

"Aja," she replied, and didn't correct him about her origins. "What do you—" her question was cut short as the door at the far end of the hall opened, and a guard walked into the room. All at once, the vibration stopped. Jaqlai returned to his spot, sitting on the floor with his back against the wall, and beside Aja, Cairon and Leyla snapped out of the spell that held them.

"Fascinating creature, isn't it?" Cairon said, smiling at his sister as she shrank closer to him. "We caught it loitering outside the Door a few days before you chanced upon it, Aja. At first, we thought the two of you were working together."

"Is it dangerous?" Leyla asked.

"Of course," Cairon said gravely. "Wild animals always are."

Jaqlai exhaled sharply through his nose, a scoffing sort of sound, and his ears flicked backwards. Aja might have found it comical if she wasn't feeling so sick to her stomach.

Animal-like appearance or not, this is no animal, she thought with a shiver. *He's intelligent, and he has some sort of power he can use to put people in a trance. For whatever reason, it didn't work on me.* "And this prisoner is meant for the Garnet Oblation?" she asked, still looking into Jaqlai's face. Without being obvious, she wanted him to know that he was in danger of losing his life very soon. "It seems a pity to kill someone so interesting."

"Interesting, perhaps," Cairon shook his head. "But dangerous all the same. It's not an innocent traveler like you were, and we have reasons to believe it's a threat to our city." He did not elaborate on what those reasons might be.

"Did it hurt you when you captured it?" Leyla asked. "Does it have claws, too?"

Aja's nausea grew stronger, her stomach tying itself into knots. She didn't like that they were speaking about him like he wasn't right there, listening to them. Aja was sure her face reflected how grim she felt, but despite holding her gaze without blinking, Jaqlai kept his expression blank.

"We know how to take care of ourselves," Cairon assured his sister. "Now come, I've shown you the beast, and it's time for the two of you to return home." He started walking, guiding Leyla who held onto his arm, expecting Aja to follow.

Lingering for a breath, Aja's face twisted into a grimace as she held Jaqlai's gaze a moment longer. But the inaudible vibration had ended, and anything she said would be heard by the others. Exhaling through her mouth, she turned and made her way down the narrow hall after the other two. *We are both prisoners in this place,* she thought gravely, *but his situation is more dire than mine. He is going to be killed, and I am not.*

Her dream from the night before came to her mind, of how she had desperately tried to free the jaguar from his cage without success. She knew now that a decision had already been made in her heart. She would try to rescue the man just as fervently as she had tried to rescue the jaguar, especially knowing that he faced death. Was he a threat? Perhaps. And yet… she couldn't leave him to die.

Something about him reminded her of home.

I need to figure out a way to get in there again, she thought. *And that's just what I don't know how to do. I doubt they would let me just walk back in here without a good reason.*

"Oh Aja, are you scared?" Leyla's voice interrupted her thoughts, and she looked up to see the young woman had left her brother's side and was now taking Aja by the arm. "Don't worry, it can't hurt us. Cai and the Guard will take care of it, don't you worry."

"Take Aja home," Cairon instructed. "I'll stay here since I still have to work today."

"Alright," Leyla nodded. She pulled Aja out of the prison building onto the cobbled street. "I'll take you home," Leyla promised. "But! There's somewhere I'm just *dying* to take you, first."

Clearly not taking no for an answer, Leyla dragged Aja to the center of town to Market Street, bringing her from one shop to the next to look at pretty things like dresses and jewelry. She was unconcerned with the wariness of the townsfolk toward Aja, and talked about everything that came to mind with her fast, flighty way of speaking.

Aja tried to stay focused, but she was overwhelmed by the shops and the people who stared at her and whispered about her. And she couldn't get Jaqlai out of her mind.

The rest of the day was spent exploring the city with Leyla, who took her not just to the shops, but to landmarks around the city as well. There was a deep underground lake where the cave algae grew, rimmed with many crystals, stalagmites and stalactites. Leyla showed her the aqueducts that carried water from the lake to the city, explaining with pride the filters that made it safe to drink. Finally, she took Aja to see the great eagle carved into the rock. It was in the very center of the city, the solitary monument of a stone fountain.

The entire statue was one solid mass of garnet, which had been sculpted with extraordinary skill. The cuts in the stone caused the statue to shine with blue light from the city lanterns, and with the water trickling down its wings into the dark stone basin at its feet, the sight was beautiful.

"It does look like an eagle," Aja confirmed. "Whoever carved it must have been quite familiar with them, to have such accuracy."

Leyla beamed with pride, saying that it had been here as long as the city itself, carved when their people had first escaped the surface. "The Guardian gave us refuge when our people were being wiped out," she said, "and we've been safe ever since."

The story reminded Aja of home, and she almost said so, but Slyen's warning came to mind. So, she only nodded and told Leyla it was a beautiful story. *I think I understand,* she thought, as she gazed into the rippling waters in the stone basin. *Their people escaped the same great war my people did. But somehow, I don't think their Guardian is as kind as ours.*

She was conflicted when it came to their Guardian. He was the one who had allowed her to live, and yet he was planning on killing Jaqlai. She was against the idea of sacrificing anyone, finding it disturbing. Yet if she opposed the Garnet Oblation, Cairon and Leyla might consider it a betrayal.

Even if it's risky, she thought, her heart clenched by anxiety, *I have to try. I couldn't bear the guilt if I did nothing.* The problem was how she could do anything at all. Would they spare him if she begged them to? And would sparing him mean that someone else would have to die?

"Don't you think it's wrong to sacrifice someone?" she asked Leyla tentatively as they made their way at last back to their houses.

"Aja!" Leyla hissed under her breath, looking around them with wide eyes as though she expected people to jump out at them in anger. "You can't say things like that, it's blasphemy!"

Blasphemy? Aja wondered. *In what way?* "I only mean, perhaps the Guardian would accept another kind of offering. Rare items from the surface, food that he can't get anywhere else, that sort of thing." Aja offered a smile she didn't feel, her pulse racing despite her attempt to remain calm. She could sense she was treading a dangerous line, but it was a risk she had to take.

"I… don't think that's…" Leyla stammered, trying to find something to say in response. By the worried frown on her face, it was clear she'd had similar thoughts of her own that she dared not voice. "I don't know," she finally said, her voice small and quiet. "What kinds of things?"

"How about a bag made of ferns that never wilts?" Aja suggested. She didn't like the idea of parting with the gift Slyen had made for her, but the people of Scoria were definitely interested in it. Perhaps the Guardian might be, too. It had been four days since Aja was brought down here, but the bag showed no signs of wilting, and seemed to need no water or sunlight to survive. Some form of magic was keeping it fresh; she was sure of it. *Influence,* she recalled. *Slyen called it Influence.*

"I don't know," Leyla said carefully, glancing around her nervously. "I could always ask Cai about it. He knows more about these sorts of things than me."

"Would it be better coming from me?" Aja suggested. "I'm new here, so perhaps they would forgive me if the question causes offense. I don't know all the rules, after all."

Leyla seemed to perk up slightly at this. "I don't think it could hurt," she said quickly, "if you were the one to ask. But he's working right now, so this isn't the time. Let's ask him tomorrow."

Weary from being out on her feet with the stares of dozens of people on her, Aja was perfectly fine with waiting one more day. She longed to crawl into bed and shut her eyes, and having an idea on how to save Jaqlai was a relief. Maybe the Guardian would accept a different offering. Then, even if Jaqlai was released, or if he managed to escape, someone else wouldn't have to die in his place.

"Alright," Aja said. "I'll ask him tomorrow."

Leyla cheered up at this and steering the conversation back to frivolous things like clothing, jewelry, and the guards she found handsome, she brought Aja back to the small living space that had been given to her. They climbed the steps to the third floor, and there she stood in the doorway and waited for Aja to unlock it with the key.

"You're new here, so you won't know this," Leyla explained, watching Aja struggle with the lock. "But everyone in Garnet Eagle is expected to work. We're all provided with food and homes, and in return we are expected to contribute to the city with our skills. Don't worry about it for now, since you have a few days to get used to living here, but it's a good idea to think about what you'd like to do."

"I wouldn't know where to start," Aja said, finally succeeding in unlocking the heavy metal lock. She pushed the stone door open with a little bit of effort, frowning slightly at the grinding sound it made. There would be no silent sneaking out of her place. "What kinds of things does the city need?"

"I'm sure they have a list of jobs," Leyla said easily. "You can pick one from the list if you can't think of something. But it's best to start with your skills. What are you good at?"

"Gardening," Aja said quietly. She suddenly missed her garden back home so dearly that her heart ached. *Will I ever see my garden again?* "And cooking," she added, her throat tight from her attempt to keep tears from spilling down her face.

"You might like cultivating algae, then," Leyla said. "Or tending to the mushroom gardens. We can ask Cai if there are any openings tomorrow." She paused, tilting her head with a thoughtful look on her face. "You said cooking, too? What kinds of things can you make?"

"Nothing like the foods you've shared with me thus far," Aja admitted. She absently wiped the corner of her eyes with her thumb. She thought of the markets Leyla had shown her, of the food items that were sold there. Citizens would show their identification badges, and the shop owners would portion out what they wanted according to a list. No money was exchanged, and it seemed the amounts were based on the person who was shopping.

One of the items Aja had noticed was bi-sodium carbonate. Or "baking soda", as her people called it. *I could use that to make soda bread,* Aja thought. *Maybe it could be enticing to the Guardian.*

"Well, let's worry about it tomorrow," Leyla said, stretching her arms. "We've had a full day, and I'm tired. Think about it, alright?"

"Alright," Aja replied. She could tell that Leyla wasn't going to leave until Aja went inside, so she entered the dwelling and pushed the door closed, turning the latch to lock it. She heard Leyla's footsteps recede down the stairs and let out a heavy sigh.

She had a lot of planning to do. Slyen had told her to be clever, and that was all she had going for her. Tomorrow, she would make soda bread and take it to Cairon, suggest giving an offering of a different sort, and try to find a way to help Jaqlai escape. Then, perhaps he would take her with him to the surface.

It was the only plan she could come up with.

The moment Aja found herself in the prison once more, she knew that it was a dream. All around her, the walls vibrated with a deep, eerie, rumbling. Her head felt heavy from the inaudible purr that had held Cairon and Leyla in a spell hours before, as though it were assaulting her from all sides. She walked down the narrow hallway toward Jaqlai's cell, but it seemed to take ages to get there. The hallway just kept getting longer and longer. That was very much like a dream too, she reflected. Dreams couldn't recreate things perfectly, so details would change, movement seemed to take either too long, or she would get to her destination instantly. It was all subject to her subconscious and how it decided to portray things.

When she finally came upon the cell, she was surprised to see that it was the jaguar from her dream before, and not Jaqlai, who was chained inside it. Its eyes were fixed on Aja's face, changing from brown to yellow, and yellow to brown, never staying the same color.

"You want to come back," the jaguar said, and the deep rumble grew oppressively louder. Aja winced at its words. "You want to come back to see me. You want to get me out of here."

"What are you doing?" Aja demanded, holding a hand to her head. It was splitting now, a sharp pain piercing her skull. "Why are you trying to force me to come to you? I'm already planning on it!"

"You miss the surface," the jaguar replied, as though it couldn't hear her words at all. And unbidden, a memory of the surface swept over her. Blue skies, a valley circled by tall trees, the smell of the strong, salty river by the cliffs. And then, at last, she saw her garden waiting for her. "You desperately long to return to the world above," the jaguar continued.

Aja choked on a sob, now holding her face with both hands. "Why are you trying to convince me?" she asked, distressed. "Of course, I miss the surface! Of course, I long to go back there!"

Again, the jaguar showed no signs of hearing her. The incessant pressure of the inaudible rumble continued to push against her. It was suffocating. "I can help you return there," the jaguar said. "You believe this."

"Stop," Aja begged, her shoulders trembling. She was feeling anxious and trapped, the weight of his coercion too much for her to bear. "Stop trying to influence my thoughts!"

"You want to help me. You can't rest until you help me."

"Stop it," Aja cried out. Her anxiety was twisting into anger now, anger that he would try to push her to think something she had already decided for herself. Who was he to force this kind of burden on her? What gave him the authority to warp her mind to his desires? "Stop it," she called again. "Stop it. Stop! STOP!"

Abruptly, she found herself jolting upright in bed, screaming the word "STOP!" at the top of her lungs. Tears streamed down her face, and her arms were trembling from her anger and distress. Struggling to calm herself down, she forced herself to breathe deeply in and out, over and over.

Quiet steps hurried up the staircase outside her dwelling, and a knock rapped at the door. "Aja?" came Leyla's voice. "Aja, are you alright? It's me, Leyla."

Wiping her face, Aja slid out from under the blankets onto the cold stone floor, walking on the tips of her toes toward the door. She turned the lock and pulled it open, gazing out to see Leyla in a nightgown and robe, looking at her worriedly. "I'm sorry," she said. "I was dreaming."

Leyla's face was filled with compassion. "Cai says overdwellers get nightmares for a while when they first come down here," she said. "It won't last, I promise."

Aja didn't have the energy or the desire to explain her dreams were not like everyone else's. Instead, she nodded and attempted a smile. "Thank you, Leyla," she said softly. "And I'm sorry for waking you."

"Do you want me to stay up here with you?" Leyla asked. She peered past Aja into the apartment, as though checking to see if anyone else was inside.

"No, thank you," Aja shook her head. It took a bit more convincing to assure Leyla she was alright before the young woman returned to her own home, but at length she left Aja on her own. Closing and locking the door once more, Aja returned to the bed and crawled into it, already knowing she wouldn't get any more sleep.

The oppressive rumble was still there, and if she closed her eyes, she knew that she would find herself right back inside that prison, with that jaguar telling her what to think.

"I *will* rescue you," she whispered angrily, shivering under her blankets. "But not because you told me to."

The inaudible rumble continued all through the night, following her into the next day. Of course, Aja couldn't tell intuitively whether it was day or night because they were underground. Instead, the time was dictated by a large clock tower above the city hall where her hearing had taken place. It chimed the hours with a gentle tone, and Aja unexpectedly found the sound of it soothing.

She went down to Leyla's house before she had a chance to come up to Aja's, and when she knocked on the door wearing her own Slyenial clothing, Leyla gasped in disapproval.

"We're buying you new clothes at once," she insisted, and wouldn't take no for an answer. With Aja offering no resistance, she brought her to the market once more.

They spent a few hours picking out clothes, but Aja was weary and distracted the whole time, simply agreeing with whatever Leyla decided. Everywhere she went, the unbearable vibration followed her. She couldn't hear the words she had heard in her dream, but the *feeling* of them was present at the back of her mind.

Soon, it became too much for Aja to endure. She was angry at the pressure he was exerting over her, bothered by his attempts to warp her thoughts to his benefit. What could she do about it? It wasn't like she had some kind of magical ability to pressure people. All she had was Slyen's blessing, her dreams, and her ability to *Listen*.

Aja paused, her eyes unfocused as she stood in the latest clothing shop, letting Leyla pick out yet another dress. *I've always used Listening to understand my surroundings more,* she thought, a curiosity growing in her mind. *But I've never tried to turn it around. What if, instead of me being the one who Listens, I try to make* him *Listen instead?*

She inhaled deeply, held the breath, and stretched out her senses as she exhaled. The sounds of the market filled her ears, the rumble from Jaqlai grew stronger, and Leyla's cheerful voice seemed to grow too loud. But Aja focused inward, quieting her thoughts and trying not to get distracted. She imagined an invisible bubble around herself, blocking out the sounds she didn't want to hear, and eventually the murmur of voices in the city diminished. Leyla's voice didn't seem quite as loud.

Yet the rumbling continued, and her head was splitting from the force of it. Frustration surging up inside her, she stretched out her senses as far as she could, beckoning with all her might for him to *Listen* to her. *STOP,* she urged. *Leave me alone!*

She staggered as exhaustion suddenly washed over her, and when Leyla caught her by the arm to hold her up, she turned to face her in surprise. Drawn back to her present surroundings, Aja realized that Leyla and the dress designer were both looking at her with worried faces. "I'm sorry," Aja said, confused when she found herself short of breath. She felt as tired as she might have after running a great distance. "I don't know what just happened."

"Come here, sit down a minute," the designer insisted. She led Aja to a bench inside the store, patting her shoulder. "It's not uncommon for overdwellers to grow dizzy down here. You'll get used to the lower elevation in time, I promise."

Aja nodded, grateful to be seated. Was it the elevation that had caused her dizziness? Or was it her attempt to turn her *Listening* around?

"Why don't we go home for now," Leyla suggested. "We've picked out plenty of outfits for you, although it's a pity we can only get four at this time. Why don't you decide which ones you like best, and then we can leave?"

Looking over the outfits Leyla had selected for her, Aja remained seated as she picked out the ones she liked best. One gray dress with long sleeves and a garnet belt cinched around the waist, a gray tunic and leggings with garnet trims, a pair of gray trousers and a garnet blouse, and a fancy dress similar to the one she had worn to the hearing, sleeveless with geometric patterns. The designer folded and wrapped them up into a fabric bag, which Leyla insisted on carrying as they exited the shop.

"Wait," Aja said, pausing in the street and looking toward the food stalls. "I want to buy some baking soda."

"Baking soda?" Leyla asked. "What's that?"

"Bi-sodium carbonate," Aja explained. "I saw them selling it yesterday." Suddenly she found herself recalling a conversation she'd had with General Ryder about education. He was so sure that her people were uneducated, yet they were taught plenty of useful things growing up. She knew of more than one use for bi-sodium carbonate, and baking was just one.

"Oh, that! We use it for cleaning and for body odors," Leyla chuckled. "Whatever would you bake with it?"

"Bread," Aja smiled, pushing aside her thoughts of home. "Help me buy some ingredients, and I'll make something tasty for you and your brother as a thank you for all you've done for me. And who knows? Maybe the Guardian would like it, too."

Understanding filled Leyla's eyes as she remembered their discussion from the day before. "Oh," she remarked. "Oh! Well… I suppose… why not? Let's get some. What do you need?" Looping her arm around Aja's, she pulled her toward the food stalls with curiosity shining in her eyes.

It wasn't until after they finished shopping for the ingredients Aja needed and were on the return home that Aja realized something had changed. Her headache had improved, her strength was returning, and the anxiety she had been feeling had finally faded away.

The unbearable vibration that had been assaulting her was gone.

Influence

———————⊕———————

"What do you want?" one of the guards outside the prison demanded. He held his lantern staff in one hand and glared at Aja and Leyla with an imposing scowl on his pale face. "Office Iolite is working. You should go home."

"Don't be unreasonable, Gillain," Leyla scolded, lifting up a covered ceramic bowl in her hands. "We're bringing lunch to Cai. Aja made one of her overdweller recipes, and it's *amazing*."

Aja had made a simple vegetable stew, which had used up almost all of her allotted rations, since vegetables were so rare. Alongside it was a loaf of soda bread, which was designed to be dipped in the stew. *Now I understand what "rations" means,* she thought. She was holding her round loaf of bread in her hands, wrapped up in a simple, undyed towel. Each citizen had a certain amount of food and ingredients they were allowed to buy a week, and each type of ingredient had a value that took up "ration points." Aja's vegetable stew had taken up 75 of her 100 points.

It was worth it, she reminded herself. Making the stew and the soda bread was the first part of her plan, the bribe that she would use to convince Cairon to offer something other than Jaqlai's life for the Garnet Oblation. Now, she just needed to get in to speak with him. It had been Leyla's plan for Aja to bring him lunch, and she had promised to distract the guards in the front room so Aja could talk to Cairon alone.

Gillain, the guard, let out an irritated sigh. "Stop being pushy, Leyla. Just because you're the officer's sister doesn't mean you can come and go as you please—especially with the *overdweller*."

"She's a citizen now, remember?" Leyla insisted. "And anyway, she did this to *thank* Cai for his help. He's working until the twentieth tone, so this is our only chance to see him today."

Aja looked into Gillain's face, wearing what she hoped was a convincing smile. "I'm sorry to be a bother," she said gently. "It's just that, I'd never have gotten this opportunity without his help, so I thought I could thank him with a meal."

The other guard at the door leaned towards Gillain, whispering something under his breath that Aja couldn't hear. Then, Gillain's face transformed into a look of surprise and understanding. "Oh!" he said, and he cracked an amused smile. "You want to thank Officer Iolite personally, I get it." He shared a glance with his fellow guard and nodded. "Alright, we'll let you in. But make it quick."

After thanking him, Leyla and Aja slipped through to the other side, heading towards the room Aja thought of as an office. "They think you're interested in my brother," Leyla giggled under her breath, leaning over to say this directly into Aja's ear. "Not that I would blame you if you were, he's very handsome."

With an embarrassed blush, Aja decided not to protest that she felt nothing of the sort. Something she had learned from her neighbor, Tula, back home, was that it was easier to just go along with things like this rather than argue.

"Alright, you go on ahead," Leyla said, stopping beside the office. She passed the bowl to Aja, helping her balance both the bowl and the loaf of soda bread. "I'll stay and talk to the others. Good luck!" Winking playfully, she went back into the main area to talk with the guards at the door.

Aja shifted her grip so that she was balancing the bowl in one hand, the wrapped loaf sitting on top of the covered bowl. She found herself feeling unexpectedly nervous as she knocked on the office door. "Cairon?" she called. "Ah... I mean... Officer Iolite?"

The door was pulled open, and Cairon stood in the entrance with a look of surprise on his face. "Aja?" he asked. He looked over her head toward the main room, and seeing his sister, let out a sigh. "Did Leyla put you up to this?" he asked. He gestured for her to come in, his gaze falling on the food she had brought.

"Actually, I was the one who wanted to talk to you," Aja explained, entering the room. "To thank you, and to talk to you about something, if you have time."

"Why not?" Cairon said. "Here, let me take those." He took the food from her and set it on the table, raising his eyebrows as he opened the lid and looked inside. "Is that a vegetable stew?" he asked in disbelief. "That can't have been cheap." He closed the office door before gesturing to the chair opposite his desk. He didn't sit down until Aja did. "I should be thanking you," he chuckled.

Her nervousness growing, Aja tried not to fidget as she took a seat. *There's really no way to gracefully broach the subject, is there?* She thought, aware that her pulse was racing. *I suppose I just have to go for it.* She cleared her throat and began. "I wanted to thank you," she said. "Your kindness when I was brought down here was very comforting to me, and you believed in me when no one else did. It's no exaggeration to say that you're the reason I'm alive." She paused, wondering why her mouth had gone dry. "And it's thanks to the Guardian, as well."

Cairon's face softened as he listened to her, and he folded his hands together on his desk as he answered. "I like to think I am a good judge of character," he said. "Both my sister and I have always had a knack for judging whether someone is trustworthy, and we both took a liking to you at once. Your caravan left you for dead, and you would have surely died on your own up there. I'm glad that you can live down here with us, where it's safe."

I don't want to live down here, Aja thought, but didn't voice it. She offered a faint smile instead. "I made this stew for two reasons," she explained. "First, because I wanted to thank you. But second, because I wanted to thank the Guardian. It was his decision to let me live, wasn't it?"

"That's… not untrue," Cairon said carefully. "But I think it's too soon for me to discuss the Guardian with you. Maybe after a year or two—"

"Actually," Aja interrupted. Her pulse was racing from the stress it took to work up the courage, and she was beginning to feel sick to her stomach. "Would you hear me out a bit, before you answer me? I have something I want to propose."

He closed his mouth, leaning back in his chair and observing her thoughtfully. After a moment, he nodded. "Go ahead," he said, gesturing with his hand.

"Thank you." Aja took a deep breath, steadying herself. "I understand that the Garnet Oblation is almost here, and that you intend to offer the prisoner to the Guardian. But I was hoping you would let me offer something instead. You see, I want to personally thank the Guardian for his kindness by offering him things from my home. I have a magical bag made of plants that doesn't wilt, and I can make food from my homeland that he's never tried before. I don't know why he requires a sacrifice of a life, but mine was spared because of him so I want to personally pay him back."

Cairon let out a sigh, an almost pitying expression on his face. "You're a very generous person, Aja," he remarked. "I can tell. It speaks well of you that you would offer something like that. But I'm afraid that simply can't happen. The Guardian has only ever accepted a sacrifice, and we already have one."

"Couldn't you just ask him?" Aja pleaded, leaning forward and staring into his eyes. If Slyen's blessing could help her be more persuasive, then she would use it. "If the answer is no, I'll understand. But please at least let me make this offer." She slid her fern bag off her shoulder, which she had brought on purpose, and set it on the desk in front of him. "Take him this bag and taste the food for yourself. Ask him if there isn't something he would accept as a gift from me, in thanks for his kindness. If he says no, I'll understand, but I won't be satisfied until you at least ask."

"You've obviously been spending too much time with my sister," Cairon remarked with a wry smile. He shook his head, almost as if he would say no, but he didn't. Instead, he opened the towel to see the bread she had baked, broke off a piece of it, and dipped it in the soup. His first bite, he made an approving expression with his eyebrows raised, then immediately he took another. "This is quite good," he praised. "A better lunch than I normally have, that's for sure."

Aja was glad her bribe was working. "It's a recipe of my mother's, back home," she said. "I can make other dishes too, but I wasn't able to buy the ingredients with my rations. The soda bread wasn't hard to make, at least."

"The bread is delicious," Cairon agreed. He continued eating both the soup and the bread together, until he had finished the portion she'd brought him. Then, closing the lid over the empty bowl, he leaned back in his chair. "It probably won't make a difference, but I'll bring your bag and your request to my superiors. That's all I can promise, and after that, it's up to the Guardian whether he will accept."

"Would you ask right now?" Aja blurted, her eagerness betraying itself on her face. "Leyla said the Garnet Oblation is soon."

"Three days from now," Cairon nodded. He smiled in amusement as he rose to his feet. "Alright, Aja. It's not far, so why don't you stay here until I get back? That way I can give you the answer right away."

"I'd appreciate it," Aja said, relief surging through her. *It's working,* she thought. *This is my chance.*

Cairon took her bag off his desk and moved to the door, leaving it open behind him when he exited, and Aja stood up swiftly once his steps were far enough away. Her heart beating rapidly, she stretched out her senses and tried to *Listen* for any sounds of footsteps coming toward her.

Good, they're all up front talking with Leyla, Aja thought, hearing Leyla's rapid and energetic voice from the front of the building. She was telling a story about Cairon when he was younger, and for a moment Aja was tempted to listen to it as well. But with a firm shake of her head, she slipped quietly from the office and made her way to the prison area.

The door was not locked, but it was heavy. When Aja pushed it open, she moved it slowly so that it didn't make much noise, until it was wide enough for her to slip through. Then, cautiously, she closed the door behind her. Nervousness bloomed in her chest, her nerves squirming uncomfortably. If she was caught, she could just say she was curious about the prisoner while she was waiting for Cairon. Everything would be fine. At least, that was what she repeated to herself over and over as she walked down the narrow hallway for Jaqlai's cell.

The moment the deep, inaudible rumble began, she heard it. But unlike before, she was glad it had returned. It meant she had a chance to talk to him without being overheard, at least for a short while. Still, just to be safe, she kept her senses alert, *Listening* for any sound of footsteps.

When she reached the cell, Jaqlai was sitting forward with his legs crossed, a curious expression on his face. "So, you returned," he said. "I sort of thought you wouldn't, after…" a bewildered look crossed his face. "What did you do, earlier?"

She could only assume he was talking about this morning, when she'd used her *Listening* to make the vibration stop. "What did *I* do?" she demanded, crossing her arms. "What were *you* doing? Who gave you any right to try and mess with my thoughts? How on earth were you doing something like that, anyway?"

His bewilderment became astonishment, and his ears flicked forward curiously. "You could tell what I was doing?" he asked.

"Of course I could tell," Aja scolded. "Anyone would be able to feel an awful pressure like that, especially with the headache it causes. I didn't sleep last night thanks to you."

Jaqlai blinked, processing her words with a look of disbelief. Suddenly, he jumped to his feet and tried to walk forward, scowling when the chains kept him from reaching the bars. "Are you telling me," he demanded, "that you can not only feel my Influence, but it *hurts* you, too?"

Aja's rebuke died on her tongue, her stomach jumping inside her. "Influence?" she murmured. She thought of her dream, of how he had appeared as a forest jaguar, and suddenly understood why. There was something familiar about him that she hadn't been able to place, something that reminded her of home. That was why he was a jaguar in her dreams.

He, like Slyen, could use Influence.

Stepping forward, she took hold of the bars and stared earnestly up into his face, which was several inches higher than her own. "You can use Influence?" she asked. "How is that possible? Are you… the one I've been looking for?"

"Who are you looking for?" he asked. "No, wait, of course I can use Influence. I'm a Vedlyran."

Vedlyran. Vedlyr. The person she was trying to find.

"I'm looking for Vedlyr," she said urgently. "Do you know where I can find him?"

Jaqlai looked baffled, and he hesitated as though he didn't understand what she was asking him. "Forget that for now," he shook his head. "We don't have time. Look, I need to get out of here, and I can't do it by myself. If you help me, I'll help you."

"I'd already decided to help you," Aja frowned, remembering her headache from this morning. "*Before* you tried to manipulate me with that awful sound."

"We're going to revisit that," he said, pointing at her with one finger. "But alright, I get it. I'm sorry my Influence caused you pain, it doesn't normally do that. I just wanted you to help me."

"I'm already helping you," Aja insisted. "By giving them another offering for the Garnet Oblation."

"Right," Jaqlai's mouth twisted into a grimace. "The sacrifice they're intending to make of me to their villain of a Guardian. I highly doubt they'll just let me go, even if you do offer them something else. No, I need to get out of this cell. Once I'm free, I'll be able to make it to the surface without anyone even knowing I'm there."

"How?" Aja asked. She didn't doubt him, for she had seen what he could do when he put Cairon and Leyla in a trance.

"Influence," Jaqlai said. He glanced down the hallway, tensing, and Aja turned her head to look, too. No one was coming, at least not yet. "Aja," he said urgently. "If I shield you with my Influence, can you sneak into the jailer's office and find the keys to this cell? I recall it being a large metal ring with several keys hanging from it."

Despite the fear she felt at sneaking and stealing, she offered a hesitant nod. "I can try," she said. "When will you shield me?"

"Right now," Jaqlai said. And sure enough, Aja could sense the vibration of his Influence all around her, not oppressing her like before, but cocooning her in an orb of tense air. It reminded her of the tension one could feel just before lightning struck.

Exhaling a nervous breath, Aja walked as quietly as she could down the hallway for the door once more. It was a struggle to open it silently, but to her relief she heard Leyla still talking to the guards on the other side. Her story had ended, and she had begun another one. Leaving the door cracked, Aja slipped back into Cairon's office and began to search around.

There weren't a lot of places to look, so perhaps that was why she was able to find them so quickly. In the top left drawer of his desk, she found the large ring of keys, which she hastily picked up and wrapped up in the white towel that had been wrapped around the bread. This would muffle their sound, in case they jingled while she was walking. She hesitated by the door to *Listen*, checking if it was safe to return to the prison cells, when suddenly she heard Leyla's voice from the front of the building.

"Oh Cai, you're back," Leyla chuckled. "Don't you know you shouldn't keep a lady waiting?"

What rotten timing, Aja thought, her hands shaking as she quickly darted back to the chair opposite the desk and sat down at once. She bundled the towel in her lap, pressing her hands on top of it to diminish its size so it wouldn't look obvious anything was in there. When Cairon came back to the office, she forced a smile she didn't feel. "Well?" she asked.

He wore a baffled smile on his face as he came in—without her bag, she noticed at once. "I wouldn't have believed it if I hadn't heard it with my own ears," he said, shaking his head. "But the Guardian accepted your offer! He even went so far as to say he was touched by your generosity."

"He wanted my bag?" Aja asked. She couldn't help but feel a pang of loss, thinking she would never see it again. Slyen had made that bag for her, woven it with Influence from a living plant. *I think he wouldn't be displeased,* she tried to reason with herself, *if he knew it was traded to save a life.*

"Apparently," Cairon returned to his chair, chuckling, "it contains quite a lot of magic—and our Guardian can put that magic to good use protecting us. We'll still have our ceremony, but instead of a life, we will be presenting your bag. He said he can hardly wait to claim it."

"That's a great relief!" Aja said, forcing herself to be cheerful. "I confess, I'll miss it dearly, but I'm glad it can be put to good use."

"It makes it a more meaningful gift when something precious is offered," Cairon said gently, smiling at her. "You've done a generous thing, Aja. I'm glad you were found on our doorstep, and I think Garnet Eagle is a better place for your company."

Aja felt a twinge of guilt at his words, knowing she was planning on escaping as soon as she could, but she appreciated them, nonetheless. She was just considering how to ask to see Jaqlai again when Leyla poked her head through the door.

"Aja, we need to get going now," she said. "I hope you were able to have a good talk with Cai?"

"Oh," Aja said, her pulse racing. Now? They had to leave now? She rose to her feet, gripping the towel in her hands and hoping desperately the keys could not be heard or seen. "I did have a good talk, but... do we have to leave right now?"

"I'm afraid so," Cairon said. He handed his empty bowl and lid to his sister, who took them at once. "I have work to do, and the guards can't afford to be distracted, no matter how good the company. I'll be off duty tomorrow, so we can talk more then."

"Thanks, Cai," Leyla smiled. She looped her arm around Aja's elbow and pulled her out the door. There was no chance for Aja to protest without looking suspicious, so all she could do was follow along as she was guided out the door into the city, back toward their houses. "Well?" Leyla demanded, speaking under her breath. "Your bag is missing. Does that mean it went well?"

"Yes," Aja said, trying not to sound dejected. She could no longer feel Jaqlai's Influence on her, and she knew that he had been unsuccessful at hiding her presence. *He calls it Influence, but it's really different from Slyen's. When Slyen used it, there was no uncomfortable pressure.*

"Wait, the Guardian accepted your *bag*?" Leyla exclaimed, before lowering her voice again. "That's incredible! Do you know what this means?" her eyes were shining with hope. "No one has ever tried to give him anything other than a sacrifice. They said to question it was blasphemy. But if he'll accept something else, then maybe… maybe we never have to give him a life ever again!"

"I would hope so," Aja agreed, feeling disturbed by the idea of sacrificing lives to the Guardian. It was almost more upsetting that no one had ever tried to question the practice before now. She shivered, chilled by both the prospect and from how cold it was underground. She had not gotten used to the temperature yet, which wasn't as chilly as the desert at night, but wasn't as warm as her temperate valley back home. The long-sleeved dress she wore today was not quite warm enough for her.

"You poor thing," Leyla patted her arm. "You were shivering this morning, too. Let's go back to town and get you a cloak. They're really nice—Cai says they are warm enough to wear up in the desert even in winter."

"I could use a cloak like that," Aja admitted, her hands tightening around the towel which held the ring of keys. "But I'm much too tired to go back to Market Street."

"Then you should go home and rest, and I'll go buy you a cloak," Leyla insisted.

They parted ways at the foot of the stairs of their building, and Aja waited until Leyla was out of sight before she walked up to her house and entered. After locking the door, she ran to her bed and hid the towel and the keys underneath the mattress. She was shaking when she finished, terrified of what might happen when Cai saw his keys were missing.

What should she have done? How could she get back there to let Jaqlai out? Would they kill her if they found the keys in her bedroom?

"I feel sick," she whispered, lying down on her side on the mattress. Cold, sick to her stomach, and anxious for the future. She had done something she couldn't take back, and whatever consequences came from it, she would have to face. "What would you do?" she asked, wishing she could talk to Slyen, her mother, or anyone she trusted. "What should I do?"

She wasn't planning on falling asleep, but her weariness from not sleeping well the night before took its toll on her. Before she knew it, her eyes were closed, and she was drifting away from reality.

Aja wandered the market, looking for something she couldn't find without knowing what it was. She felt like a pair of eyes were watching her from somewhere far away, but she couldn't tell who or from where. It was uncomfortable. Stifling. She felt unsafe and didn't know why.

When she decided to *Listen*, it was out of habit. *Listening* brought clarity when nothing else did, and it was to this clarity she turned for comfort. Sounds stretched out around her, eerie and distant, yet at the same time she was soothed by them.

There was the clock tower, sounding out the nineteenth tone. Throughout the streets there was the murmur of voices and conversation. A slow, constant *drip, drip, drip* of water could be heard splashing into a puddle somewhere. Footsteps were sounding all around her, people walking through the city on the cobbled streets.

And then came the rapid *tap, tap, tap* of Leyla's light footsteps scurrying up the stairs to Aja's dwelling, followed by a rapping of knuckles on the door. "Aja?" Leyla called. "Aja, are you awake?"

Aja bolted upright, surprised to find that she wasn't out at the market at all. She was back in her own room, and all was quiet around her. *The door,* she realized, jumping to her feet and hurrying toward it. *Leyla is at the door.* She almost forgot to turn the lock before she pulled it open in her haste, and then she stood frozen in place in confusion.

No one was there.

Hesitantly, Aja closed the door once more, leaning against it with a frown. *I was dreaming,* she reminded herself. *Dreams don't always come true.*

It was at this moment that the clock began to chime, ringing out its pleasant tones one after the other. Aja counted them, and when the count ended at nineteen, she suddenly understood.

"It hasn't happened yet," she said, stepping back from the door. She closed her eyes, *Listening* to see if she could pick out the sound of Leyla's footsteps. After several minutes, she heard the soft *tap, tap, tap* of her footsteps coming up the stairs. Leyla stopped at the door, knocking lightly with her knuckles.

"Aja?" she called, "Are you awake?"

My dreams are becoming oddly specific, Aja thought, pulling the door open. She didn't even have a chance to say anything before Leyla was pushing a thick gray cloak into her arms.

"Have you eaten?" Leyla asked. "No, of course not. You spent all your rations on ingredients for Cai's lunch. Are you hungry? It's late, but I brought you something from downstairs." She lifted a wide bowl in her left hand, which was filled with a sort of thick green paste. "It's hummus," Leyla smiled widely. "This one has fresh herbs in it from the surface, I thought you might like that."

"Hummus?" Aja asked in surprise. It was a dish she was well familiar with, though the kind she made back home was never green. "Do you eat hummus here?"

"It's adapted from a Querian dish on the surface," Leyla admitted. "It's easy to make and the beans aren't too expensive to trade for. It's become one of our staples, and since it's originally from Queria, I thought I would surprise you. Sorry it took me so long to finish!"

"Don't be sorry," Aja insisted, stepping aside so Leyla could enter. "I'm comforted to eat something so familiar." *Although I didn't know it was a Querian dish,* she reflected. Was that something her people had brought with them when they escaped to the valley? *It's strange to think of how different and how similar places can be.*

Leyla shook her head, passing the bowl to Aja along with a round of Scorian flatbread. "It's late, I just stopped by to give you the cloak and to make sure you had something to eat. Rest well, Aja. And let's talk to my brother tomorrow about what jobs are available."

"Alright," Aja smiled. "Thank you, Leyla." She felt a warmth in her heart towards her, as well as a twinge of sadness. If she ever got out of this place, she would miss Leyla. She had never expected to find a such a good friend in her.

When Leyla descended the steps to her own dwelling, Aja closed and locked the door, sitting down at her table to eat. The hummus was more herbaceous than she was used to, but the beans were similar. *They put algae in it, too,* Aja thought, recognizing the unique flavor. It was pleasant to eat, but the differences from her mother's hummus made her homesick.

Humm.

A low rumble seemed to creep through the rock, vibrating through her bones in silent pressure. Aja stiffened with recognition, turning her head toward the door. *Jaqlai?* She thought, her muscles tense. *Is he calling for me?*

The vibration seemed to grow stronger, as if to say, "I found you!"

The hair stood up on Aja's skin, and she closed her eyes and focused her senses, reaching them out and following the rumble to its source. It seemed so distant, almost too far for her to reach. *What is it?* She called, trying to turn her *Listening* outward just as she had done this morning.

There was no audible response, no words formed in her mind, like her dream. And yet, she felt as though she understood what he was trying to say. He wanted her to come back.

I can't, she called, shaking her head. *I will be turned away at the door!*

The pressure for her to return grew stronger, more urgent. It was painfully sharp, causing her to wince as she weathered it, but she didn't try to make him stop. Instead, she *Listened,* trying to understand what he was saying to her. It was so much easier in her dreams, where her subconscious put words to what she was sensing.

Come back, the pressure seemed to say. *Come back, before it's too late.*

An image came to her mind, like a dream despite her being wide awake. She saw Jaqlai, and not the jaguar, staring at her from his cell. "My Influence can shield you," the dream said. "But only if you come right now."

It was absurd for her to risk everything on a dream that very well could be her own imagination. She could end up in that very prison herself, or worse! Yet Aja was gripped with a sense of urgency she couldn't shake, and without allowing herself to doubt, she rose to her feet at once.

She didn't have her fern bag anymore, but she had the cloak Leyla had given her. With hurried motions, she laid it out on her bed and placed all of her clothes in the center of it—the ones she had purchased in the market, and her original outfit from home. Then she wrapped up the loaf of soda bread she had made for herself in a towel and placed it with her clothes, before hastily folding up the cloak around them. At last, slipping on her shoes, she took up the bundled cloak in her arms, retrieved the towel-wrapped ring of keys from under her bed, and made her way to the door.

I'm coming, she called, stretching her senses as far as she could. She hoped that her trust was not placed in vain.

The door made a grinding sound as she opened it, swinging slowly on its hinges. She winced at the sound, closing it carefully and *Listening* to see if Leyla or anyone else took notice of it. No sound of steps came her way, so she took a shaky breath and descended the steps as quietly as she could. The air felt tight around her, and the soundless vibration hummed through her bones as she walked nervously down the cobbled street for the prison.

It wasn't far. Leyla's house was near both the prison and the winding stair that led up to the Door, and Aja knew both would be guarded carefully. What was she doing, trusting the magic of a man she didn't even know? What would she do if she were caught? It wasn't like she could pretend she was out for a stroll, with all her belongings wrapped up tightly in her arms, and the keys to the cells in her hands.

She passed by a pair of citizens walking the other direction, speaking to one another. Neither looked her direction, and she grew bolder. Her steps quickened, as she worried that Jaqlai would not be able to keep up his Influence for long. When she heard rapid footsteps coming up from behind her, she flinched and shrank to the side, fearing at once that she had been caught. But the stranger—a guard wearing a thick gray cloak—walked past her without so much as a glance.

I can't believe it, she thought, swallowing. Her mouth was suddenly dry, and her pulse raced so hard she could feel it thumping in her neck. Her ears ached from the pressure. Not daring to waste a moment, she pushed herself to keep walking. When she approached the prison building, she saw that the two guards posted out front were different from the two who had been there earlier. They stared straight outward, their expressions watchful, yet their eyes seemed to pass right over her as though she wasn't there.

It felt eerie, walking right up between them and pushing the door open. Aja couldn't say what courage prompted her to try, but the moment she sensed they couldn't see her, she found herself acting. The doors opened easily, both of them unlocked, their hinges well-greased. When she slipped through them, their own weight pulled them closed again.

She was inside.

The guards inside near the entrance were held in the same sort of trance Cairon and Leyla had been, the first time Aja had seen Jaqlai. Recognizing their blank, frozen expressions, she hurried forward and slipped down the hallway toward the prison area. Her steps were light in her canvas shoes. When she slipped through the next door into the narrow hall, she let out a shaky sigh of relief. After all of that, she was finally here.

Aja quickened her pace as she hurried to Jaqlai's cell, and after setting down her bundle of clothes, she unwrapped the keys and began trying each one in the lock. Her hands were shaking, and adrenaline surged through her veins. *I'm scared,* she thought, frustrated as key after key refused to fit. *What if I get caught?*

"Relax," Jaqlai murmured, his voice gentle. He stood a few paces away, unable to reach the door for his chains. "Just breathe steady and try the keys one by one. You'll find it."

"Easy for you to say," Aja mumbled. "You don't know how terrifying it was stealing them."

He smiled faintly. "You did well. Even without my help, you managed to hang onto them this long." He paused, tilting his head. "Try the last one again. It seems right, but your hands are shaking."

Aja forced herself to slow down, taking a deep breath before she tried the last key again. It fit, and with a gasp of relief, she turned the lock and pushed the cell door open. "How did you know?" she asked, hurrying into the cell and handing him the ring of keys. He didn't have to ask her to hand them over, she could just sense that he wanted them.

"I can sense a trace of memory on objects, sometimes," Jaqlai murmured. He flipped through the keys until he found the one he wanted and began to unlock his chains. "It's not something every Vedlyran can do, but scouts are trained to do it."

"Scouts?" Aja asked. She was relieved when he finally freed himself from his chains, and scooping up her belongings, she followed him out the cell door.

"Yes," Jaqlai responded. He did not elaborate. Instead, he locked the cell once more and slid the keys into his tunic pocket. "Come with me, and stay silent," he urged quietly. "I'm going to head for the exit, and I'll be using Influence to turn away the eyes of everyone around us. It won't work for people far away, and it won't work if people are alert and searching for us specifically. So long as you stay close, you'll be shielded too."

"How close?" Aja asked, shrinking toward him until she was nearly close enough to brush his side with her arm.

He smiled crookedly. "That's plenty close. Come on."

He began to lead the way down the narrow hall, knees bent and steps light. He was utterly silent, and there was a shimmering in the air around him that made Aja's eyes twist away from him. She followed him as quietly as she could until they reached the door, and then when it opened, she looked away from him just a second to see if anyone was in the other room. When she looked back, he was gone.

She couldn't see or sense him anywhere.

Frozen in terror, she stood there with her cloak wrapped tight in her arms, breathing shallowly as she tried to figure out what to do. Where did he go? When did she lose track of him? Would he just leave her behind?

"Closer," came his voice, whispered so close to her ear that she nearly jumped. She felt his hand at the small of her back, and when she turned her head, she suddenly saw him again. He was right beside her once more. "I forgot that you won't be able to see me either," he sighed. "I'll hold onto you, so just follow my lead even if you can't see me."

Aja nodded, swallowing around the anxious lump in her throat. Her adrenaline was rushing so fiercely that she felt sick to her stomach, but she did as she was told. Putting one foot in front of the other, she walked forward as Jaqlai guided her, his hand pressing on her back and directing her which way to go. At the exit, she felt his other arm reach past her to push the doors open, though she couldn't see it. Somehow, it was like he was utterly invisible. Her senses unable to pinpoint exactly where he was.

Out on the street, she walked toward the winding stair without having to be guided, though Jaqlai never took his hand away. Her heart was racing the closer they came to it, and with her fears heightened, she did the only thing she could think of to calm herself. She forced herself to breathe deeply and quietly, opening her ears to *Listen*.

People were winding down for the day. The clock was ticking in the center of the city. Snoring could be heard in the house directly to her left. And somewhere behind them, she heard the grinding of stone doors as they moved on their hinges. No one was alarmed. No one was searching for them. Yet.

At the stair, she paused in fear when she found herself face to face with the steps. But with Jaqlai's pressure at her back, she was forced to continue onward and upward. It was utterly black in the stairwell, as neither of them had a lantern to light their way. Twice she tripped and caught herself, but then she forced herself to slow down and feel her way forward.

Jaqlai didn't rush her, though she got the feeling he could find his way just fine, even in the pitch black.

"Wait a moment," he whispered. "We're at the top. Get ready to run once we're out there, since I don't know how long my Influence will last. Someone will come to check on the Door after it's opened."

She heard the jingle of keys as Jaqlai pulled them from his pocket, and *Listening* as he slid one of them into a lock she couldn't see. Above their heads, stone ground against stone as a great black slab descended downward into a carved crevice. As it lowered, the staircase was filled with faint moonlight, and Aja could see stars spread across an indigo sky.

The sky, she thought, tears filling her eyes as she gazed at it. *I feared I would never be able to see it again!*

"Now," Jaqlai hissed in her ear. He pulled her up through the doorway out into the desert, where the sharp, bitter wind cut at their faces and swept sand into their eyes. He began to sprint, holding her hand tightly in his own. And stumbling as she went, Aja ran as fast as she could behind him.

Sand, wind, the freezing cold of a desert night. All of it was nearly unbearable, and yet Aja was overjoyed to feel them. *I'll never take the wind for granted ever again,* she thought. *No matter how miserable I may feel.*

She could hardly believe that they were here. Against all odds, she had freed Jaqlai from his cell, and he had brought her to the surface, just as he'd promised.

The Dunes

They ran until Aja couldn't run any more, but Jaqlai would not let her rest. He slowed his pace to a brisk walk and kept going, keeping a tight hold of her hand. Each time she begged for a respite, he warned her that they were still too close to the door. And with terror at the idea of being trapped underground once more, Aja would push herself to continue. It was a painful and unpleasant experience, wading through unsteady sand, her arms full and her body battered by wind so cold, it blew right through her clothes.

Her lungs were aching, her side had a sharp pain stabbing through it, and she could hardly keep her eyes open to see where she was going. The bits of sand blown into her eyes were painful, and Aja remembered now how much she had hated the desert.

"I can't go on," she pleaded, slowing to a stop and collapsing to her knees. She was breathing hard, and she was so cold she was shaking. "Let me put on my cloak, please."

Jaqlai let go of her hand, moving to stand behind her. "Hurry," he said quietly, his words almost eaten by the wind. "They'll be searching for us soon, and their searches range much farther than this. That's how they caught me."

Her hands trembling, Aja unwrapped her clothes and donned her cloak, immediately relieved by its warmth. The fabric was thicker than her clothing, made from wool and well designed to block the piercing wind. *It was designed for coming to the surface,* she thought, wrapping up her clothes and the now smashed loaf of soda bread in a bundle and tying them together with her long belt. She forced herself to stand up again, taking the bundle in one hand. Jaqlai took her other one.

"Ready?" he asked. She nodded, and he began to run again. It took all of Aja's determination to keep up.

Eventually, much sooner than Jaqlai would have liked, her strength gave out. She had never been much of a runner, never had any reason to be. Seila used to enjoy running, and she was brazen enough to run along the edge of the cliffs in the mornings. She had invited Aja to join her a few times, but Aja had always declined. She used to think she would never have any reason to run.

How she regretted it now!

With her strength gone and her lungs aching, she collapsed to the sand and lay there on her back, gasping for each breath. "I can't!" she moaned. "Please… let me rest!"

Jaqlai paced back and forth beside her, his tail whipping agitatedly from one side to the other. "We don't have time," he urged. "We have to keep going."

"Then *you* keep going," Aja complained, too miserable to think her words through. She didn't want him to leave her behind, but she was hungry and weary, so she found herself saying things she didn't truly mean. "I'm just a gardener, I don't run. Let me rest for just five minutes!"

"We don't have that long," Jaqlai clicked his tongue in his teeth. He stiffened, looking out across the desert, then bent over and scooped Aja into his arms. "I'm not going to leave you behind," he said. And gripping her body tightly against his chest, he began to sprint across the sand, tail whipping in a circular motion behind him to improve his balance.

Aja was so surprised to be carried that she said nothing, clutching her belongings tightly. Now that she was being carried, she was surprised at how much faster Jaqlai was running. It was a speed she could never hope to reach, and she could barely look where they were going because of the wind.

"I'm a burden!" she blurted, looking over her shoulder behind them. Whatever had spurred his haste, she couldn't see it.

"It doesn't matter," Jaqlai insisted, his words nearly lost in the wind. "I won't leave you behind."

Aja shivered, relieved not to be on her feet any longer. "Thank you," she murmured, leaning her head against his shoulder.

"What?" Jaqlai called. "I couldn't hear you."

"I said thank you," she replied, louder. "And I'm sorry."

He cracked a wry smile. "Don't thank me yet," he said grimly. "We're not out of danger until we reach the dunes."

Instead of asking what the dunes were, Aja just nodded. *I meant thank you for carrying me,* she thought with a sigh. She closed her eyes to block out the sand and clutched her bundle of clothes tightly. Right now, she couldn't be much help to him. But if they managed to reach safety where they wouldn't be followed, she would do whatever she could to pay him back.

Aja wasn't aware of dozing off. She simply found herself back home, wandering through the forest looking for Slyen. He was waiting for her at the clearing, seated in the center with his paws resting on his knees. She ran to him when she reached the clearing, relief surging through her.

"Am I back?" she asked. "Is it over? Please tell me it's over!"

"Winter is coming," Slyen said, reaching out a paw. She sat down on the moss beside him, and he rested it on her head. "We're running out of time."

"Aja?"

Aja's eyes snapped open. She found herself looking up at a cold blue sky, bereft of clouds. The sun was rising, and she was lying on her back in the sand. Jaqlai stood over her. *I'm not home,* she thought, grief and longing weighing heavily on her heart. *And dream-Slyen is right. I'm running out of time.* Stiffly, she pulled herself to her feet and looked around. The sun was up, but it was still bitterly cold.

"We made it to the dunes," Jaqlai said. He had dark circles under his eyes, and he looked exhausted. Aja wondered if he had been running all night. "There are no rocks to take shelter under, so we're going to be miserable for a while. You'll want to take off your cloak."

"It's cold," Aja shook her head. She didn't want to take it off, even knowing that the sunlight would turn harsh soon.

"If you sweat, you'll lose precious hydration," Jaqlai urged. "I know which way to go as long as the sun is rising and setting, but at midday we'll have to take a break. I'll dig a shallow in the sand and then we can hide under your cloak until midday passes. We can sleep at night."

Aja shivered, not from the chill, but from the revelation of how little she knew about traveling through a desert. If Jaqlai had left her behind like she'd told him to, only one of two things would have happened; she would have been found by the Scorians, or she would have perished. "Alright," she said, and reluctantly took off her cloak.

"I'll carry it for you," he said, smiling gratefully. He already had her bundle of clothes under his arm. "You just focus on keeping up. This won't be easy, but we've got to do it. Understand? We'll die out here if we don't make our way through the desert as quickly as possible."

"I understand," she said, a little tersely. Her nerves were frayed from the adrenaline of last night's escape, but she didn't want to snap at him. She knew it wasn't *him* she was upset at; she was just worn out and stressed. Pulling herself to her feet, she gestured out at the dunes around them. "Lead the way."

He was quick to do just that. "See the direction the sun is rising from?" he asked, pointing at the horizon where the sun hung low in the sky. Despite how barren the desert was, it was a striking view to look at; the hills of sand and the glow of the morning sun rising behind them. "That's east. We need to head west to get out of the desert, and there will be two more doors down to the gemstone cities that we'll need to avoid. Thankfully, Scoria isn't a large desert. There's a Querian port city on the coast, and if we make good progress, we should reach it in four or five days."

"How do you know?" Aja asked, worried about going to a Querian port. She was pretending to be one of them but wasn't sure she could keep up the ruse in one of their cities. *And anyway, I have to head south to Mettain,* she thought, chewing her lower lip absently. It was chapped, and she was just now beginning to notice it. *What should I do? I can't go west; I have to go south. Do I part ways with him?*

Anxiety crawled through her stomach at the thought. There was no way she could survive the desert on her own. What should she do?

"I came from that direction initially," Jaqlai replied. He set the pace at a brisk walk, but when he saw that Aja was having trouble keeping up, he slowed down slightly.

"What were you doing in the desert?" Aja asked. As they walked, she began to understand why he had suggested taking her cloak off. The sun would only get hotter, and walking was warming her up as well. She still shivered every time the wind blew through her clothes, though.

"Looking for something," Jaqlai murmured. He didn't elaborate, and Aja got the sense he wouldn't even if she pressed him.

"What do you plan to do at the city?" she asked instead.

"I'm going to charter a spot on a ship," he replied. "I need to head back to Mettain."

"Mettain?" Aja perked up, so relieved to hear it that a smile spread over her face. "That's where I need to go, too! Can you take a ship there? I thought the only way was through the desert." She had seen the Zyphans' ships many times from the cliffs. They were steam-powered and sleek, able to cut their way through the powerful current of the Uliah with ease. Riding one of those would take no time at all!

"Why are you headed to Mettain?" Jaqlai frowned, looking at her with a scrutinizing expression in his eyes. He mistrusted her.

Because I want to go to Mettain? she wondered. *Or because I'm supposedly Querian, and the Zyphans are going to war against Queria?* She stared into his eyes evenly, her expression calm. "I'm looking for Vedlyr," she explained. "I'm supposed to find him so I can stop the war from happening."

Disbelief flashed across Jaqlai's face. "Ri-iight… you said something like that earlier. I think you have your information wrong—there is no person named 'Vedlyr,' there are only my people, the Vedlyrans. And we are in no position to stop the war from happening, we are only gathering intel so we can stay prepared. Either one of the Zyphans or the Querians might turn against Mettain and try to occupy it for its central location."

"The Zyphans wouldn't," Aja shook her head, thinking of the day they had come to the valley. They had only stopped there to refresh their water and look for supplies and found Aja's people by accident. And the people of Slyenials had *welcomed* them. "They are only going to war because they feel they need to stand up against Queria. But even so, I must stop them."

Jaqlai stopped walking, turning to face her with a strange look on his face. "What do you know about the war?" he asked. "Do you have personal information about it?"

"Not really," she shook her head, wondering what his expression meant. "I only know what the general told me."

"Which general?" Jaqlai asked, gently.

Aja hesitated, wondering if it was a good idea to tell him. *Maybe I need to,* she reasoned with herself. *He says his people are called Vedlyrans. That means they are Vedlyr's people just as much as we are Slyen's people. Perhaps he doesn't know about Vedlyr—I certainly didn't know about Slyen.* Her best bet was to have Jaqlai bring her to Mettain, where she could look for Vedlyr on her own. But to do that, she would need to gain his trust. "I will answer your questions on one condition," she said bravely.

He looked more curious than upset at this suggestion. "What's the condition?" he asked and began walking again. Aja followed after him.

"Take me to Mettain with you," she said. "And I'll tell you everything."

"Everything?" Jaqlai chuckled. He glanced at her over his shoulder, and she felt the uncomfortable pressure of his Influence around her once more.

"Stop that," Aja scowled. "If you try to manipulate my thoughts even once more, I'll tell you nothing."

He laughed, which surprised her. "So, you *can* feel it," he said, shaking his head. "Don't worry, I wasn't trying to do anything, I just wanted to see." He turned around, walking backwards so he could look at her face as they spoke, and using delicate movements of his tail to keep himself balanced. "Alright, I'll consider taking you to Mettain—*if* you can prove you're not a danger to me or my country." He observed her thoughtfully. "Let's start with who you are. You might look like one, but you're no Querian, are you?"

Aja stiffened nervously, afraid at first to answer him. But then she reasoned that if she wasn't truthful with him, she might never find Vedlyr. He was her best chance. "Is it that obvious?" she asked.

Jaqlai shook his head. "You could easily be mistaken for one. They're a very diverse group of people, and the largest nation on the continent. Some of them even have magic, like you do. But as far as I know, none of them can tell when they are being Influenced."

"I don't have magic," Aja insisted with a frown, thinking of Slyen and Jaqlai's Influence. She had nothing like that—couldn't make a bag grow out of ferns or convince a nation to forgo a war they were determined to wage. And yet… her thoughts turned to her dreams, many of them premonitions that had come true. Her face clouded with concern. "Although… I do have dreams."

"Dreams that come true?" Jaqlai asked. "That's similar to Querian magic. They have Seers who can predict things before they happen. Sometimes through dreams, and other times through cards and dice. It's a very fascinating practice." He tilted his head curiously. "How is it that you can sense my Influence? You mentioned that it was painful. I've never heard that before. Even when Vedlyrans use Influence on each other, it isn't painful."

"It feels like an unbearable pressure," Aja said, as curious about his people as he seemed about her. Could all of them use Influence? Or just some of them? "Like the tension before a lightning strike. And there's this deep vibration that you can't hear, but you can feel in your bones."

His ears perked up, his curiosity clearly growing. "Is that so?" he asked, adjusting the bundle of Aja's clothes under his arm. He checked the sky to make sure he was still leading them west, then focused back on Aja. "Actually, that's similar to how we sense Influence, though without the pain. It feels like the air is tight, and there's a subtle sensation I'm not sure how to describe."

"Like a rumble?" Aja proposed.

Jaqlai lifted and dropped his shoulders in a shrug. "Hard to say. Not all Vedlyrans can sense Influence being used on them, but when it's done poorly, it feels like a tense pressure in the air." He paused, grinning. "And no, I wasn't using it poorly on you. I'm considered highly gifted in Influence, so the fact you could sense it means there's something special about you. How *did* you sense it? Did you do anything in particular?"

"I felt it," Aja said. "I didn't try to, it just showed up and made me miserable."

His grin faded some. "I'm sorry about that," he said genuinely. "Still, you had to have done *something*. I was reaching out for you, trying to convince you to help me, and suddenly it felt like I'd been slapped in the face. I couldn't hear a voice, per se, but I definitely sensed you wanted me to stop."

At this, Aja perked up with interest. "So, it worked?" she asked, growing excited. *No wonder I felt so tired after attempting that.*

"What worked?" Jaqlai asked curiously.

"It's… hard to explain," Aja admitted, growing somewhat embarrassed. She'd never tried to explain *Listening* to anyone before—well, anyone besides her sister, and her sister had told her to stop playing games. Kyra had always been mature for her age, and stopped playing anything when she was thirteen. After her rebuke, Aja had never tried to explain *Listening* to anyone else.

"Start anywhere you like," Jaqlai gestured around the desert with his free hand. "We've got plenty of time, and *hopefully* no one following us."

That wasn't exactly comforting to hear, after their nerve-wracking escape, but Aja obliged him. In halting words and run-on sentences, she explained how Listening worked. Without going into too much detail, she recounted how it had helped her find a path through the forest by following the sound of footsteps she had taken in the past. Then, as an afterthought, she told him of her dream where she heard Leyla come up to her door on the night they escaped before it had happened. She wasn't sure if it was just a dream premonition, or if *Listening* had anything to do with it.

Jaqlai was silent through her explanation. He turned to face the west as they walked, nodding every once in a while with a thoughtful expression. When she finished, he was quiet for several more minutes before he responded. "I think," he said at length, touching his chin with one hand, "that *Listening* might be similar to Influence. At least, that's how I can wrap my head around it. It's human magic, for sure. There's your precognitive dreams and your ability to hear things before they happen or hear things that happened in the past. But the way you go about it is closer to Influence than it is to a Querian Seer's Clairvoyance."

"Is that what they call it?" Aja wondered. "The ability to see the future?"

"That's what it's called in Queria," Jaqlai nodded. "Though it covers a wider range of abilities, as I understand it. Some Seers can use Clairvoyance to tell if someone is lying or telling the truth, and some use it to sense the emotions people are experiencing. I have always found human magic to be fascinating."

"I didn't know it existed," Aja said, marveling at the very idea. Was it possible that she had Clairvoyance too? Was that where her dreams came from? She dropped her gaze to the sand below her feet. The sun was reflecting off the dunes ahead directly into her eyes, and she was growing tired and was afraid of losing her footing. She wasn't used to walking on sand for long distances.

"*Listening* is similar to Influence," Jaqlai continued, "because it is an extension of your senses. It allows you to be aware of your surroundings and use that awareness to your advantage.”

“It seems like Vedlyran Influence is different than Slyen’s Influence,” Aja offered with a wry smile. “His is more subtle and gentle than yours, and it can do things like make plants grow the way he wants them to or make people who would otherwise be violent more receptive to peace.”

“Is Slyen the name of that general you mentioned?” he asked with interest.

Aja had forgotten she’d mentioned him. “No, Slyen isn’t a Zyphan,” she corrected him. “He’s—”

“A Moglian?” Jaqlai finished for her, a knowing tone to his voice. He smiled wryly at her surprise, his ears flicking once. “I suspected as much. Moglians are the only ones besides Vedlyrans who can use Influence, but theirs is much more powerful than ours.”

“Then why did you ask if he was the general?” Aja frowned.

He shrugged one shoulder. “You mentioned a general, but not his name. Which general did you mean? I might know of them.”

“His name is Ryder,” Aja said, and though Jaqlai’s face was blank, his ears perked upwards slightly, a reaction that implied he recognized the name.

“This General Ryder is where you got your information about the war?” he asked, doubtfully.

Aja nodded, then shook her head. “Ah, not exactly. Some things, yes. But I learned the most from Slyen.” Her foot slipped on loose sand and she stumbled, catching herself before she fell, and she began to watch her feet more carefully as she went. It was then she began to notice more things about the desert than she had seen before. Insects skittered across the sand. A winding track showed evidence that a snake had slithered through recently. Tiny brown plants stuck up through the sand, indicating that there might have been rain at one point.

The desert was alive, despite how dead and dry it felt to her.

“The Moglian,” Jaqlai clarified. He furrowed his brow thoughtfully. “You’re *sure* he’s a Moglian? They don’t like humans, and normally keep to their forests in solitude. It's exceedingly rare for anyone to meet one."

"I'm sure he's Moglian," Aja nodded, shading her eyes with her hand so she could look at him without the sunlight glare in her eyes. "And so is Vedlyr."

Jaqlai sighed, shaking his head. "Vedlyrans are a people, not a Moglian," he insisted. A gust of wind blew past them, and a gnarled, round tumbleweed rolled across the sand. He watched it move with his eyes, not turning his head to follow it.

"How would you know?" Aja asked calmly. She placed a hand on her side, which was beginning to ache. She would have to take a break, soon. "I didn't know that Slyen was a person until he called me out to meet him and sent me to find his brother, Vedlyr. It makes plenty of sense that you wouldn't be aware of him. Nevertheless, he *is* real, and I *must* find him."

Abruptly, Jaqlai stopped walking and faced her. She nearly walked into him he stopped so fast. "Aja," he said, a calculating look on his face. "Where are you really from? How do you know about any of this?"

Even though Slyen had told her not to tell anyone about the valley, Aja knew that this was her best chance at finding Vedlyr. She had to get Jaqlai to understand, to believe her, or he would leave her behind in the Querian port city and go to Mettain by himself. She couldn't say how she knew this, but she felt it in her heart like a deep, inaudible sound.

For several minutes, she chose not to reply. He didn't press her, as though he could sense that she might, given enough time. And though she was almost resolved to tell him, she made him wait for it. Her gaze traveled out across the sands, looking for signs of trees or rocks that might provide shelter, but all she could see was pale brown sand piled up in dunes in all directions. To her left was a massive one, which might have provided shade if the sun were in the right place.

At length, her desire to win him over outweighed her caution.

"I'm from the hidden valley called Slyenials," she said gravely, hoping she wasn't making a mistake by telling him. "A place protected by the Moglian named Slyen. The Zyphans found our valley and are planning to launch their war from it, but if they do, something far more terrible than a war will take place—Red skies and violence. All of us will die, not just the Zyphans." She held his gaze as she spoke, a grimace crossing her face. "That is why I *must* find Vedlyr and bring him back to Slyen, so the two of them can stop the war with Influence before it begins."

Jaqlai said nothing. He stared at her face with an intent expression, brow furrowed and eyes piercing as they held Aja's gaze.

"I have until the end of winter," Aja said. "The Zyphans will go to war in the spring."

When she felt the pressure of Jaqlai's Influence around her, she did not resist it. She wanted him to see that she was telling the truth. After a moment the sensation faded, and Jaqlai rubbed his face with one hand. "Well," he said grimly.

Aja waited patiently, but he remained silent. She licked her dry lips and cleared her throat. "Well, what?"

Jaqlai grimaced. "Well, it's my turn to share. A truth for a truth." He inhaled deeply and let it out with a sigh. When he began to walk again, Aja dutifully followed. "My name is Jaqlai Videlle, of Armons Fief in Mettain. I'm a Scout for the military, and I was sent out here to find information about the war—routes the Zyphans and Querians might take, news of danger to Mettain, that sort of thing. I came to Scoria because I suspected they would use desert caravans to reach the west coast, strengthen their ports, and try to block Zypha from making landfall along the coastline."

"And are they?" Aja asked. Not knowing the geography of the continent, she felt extremely out of the loop. "I wish I could see a map," she sighed. "I have no knowledge about the lands outside my valley."

"I can show you one when we reach the city," Jaqlai suggested. He glanced out across the desert, ears turning side to side as he listened for sounds of danger. "But to answer your question, yes, Queria is well familiar with traversing the desert. They've been using it for trade for hundreds of years. I've seen them moving soldiers across the desert too, and I suspect that's why the Scorians were so wary when they captured us. Even just being near their doorstep is enough to warrant their hostility."

"I didn't know that when I took refuge under the stone spires," Aja said, thinking back on that cold night. It was her first night in the desert, and it was proof that she wasn't equipped to travel on her own at all. *I won't be able to make this journey without help. I hope Jaqlai will take me with him.*

"If the Zyphans have already made landfall, then Mettain is not in immediate danger," Jaqlai said, his tone serious. "This is the kind of information I need to bring back to my superiors, so that they will know how to act." He paused, frowning. "What did you mean about red skies? Where did you hear that?"

"It was a warning I was given," Aja said, not wanting to admit that it was a dream.

"From the Moglian?" Jaqlai stiffened, his eyes widening. "If what you say is true, then we'll need to be prepared for the worst. There is a legend in my country, a warning we have never forgotten, about red skies."

Aja straightened with curiosity, though part of her felt tense with dread. "What is it?" she asked.

Jaqlai looked uncomfortable, as though he were hesitant to share. Eventually he did, after walking in silence for a few more minutes. "They say," he said quietly, "that before the founding of our nation, the Moglians banded together to wipe out all of humanity. The skies were red with their anger, and many nations were destroyed by them. If they were ever to unify like that again…"

Aja felt sick to her stomach. Moglians like Slyen and Vedlyr? *They* were the ones who had caused the red skies? *Then the terror my people fled from was a genocide?* She shivered, rubbing her arms to get rid of her goosebumps.

"If the Moglians gather together to destroy humanity, as they tried to do once before," Jaqlai said gravely, "then no nation would be safe from their wrath. Except, perhaps, ours. We are not humans."

"They would wipe out all humanity because of one single war?" Aja asked, sick to her stomach. She couldn't picture Slyen going to war, not when he was so fond of peace.

And yet… hearing Jaqlai's words, all Aja could think about was her nightmare. Red skies, dead bodies, and that horrible, unbearable sound. *The sound of Influence,* she realized. *Influence and anger.* She shuddered, distressed by the thought. *That's what my dream was about? Moglians killing humans?*

It couldn't be true. Could it?

"They have more than enough justification in their minds," Jaqlai said, looking up at the sky to check his bearings. He turned slightly so that they were headed due west. "Humans are not from this world, originally. They came from a different one, and when they first arrived, they promised to respect the land and the original inhabitants—the Moglians. But they didn't do as they promised. They began cutting down the forests of the continent. Their factories began polluting the water sources. The nations they founded fought wars against each other, and their wars caused devastation to the land. The Moglians viewed humans as monsters, and they sought to wipe them out completely. That's what our history describes, and it goes back to the time the humans first arrived."

Aja felt nauseous, comparing what he said with the history of her own people. They had escaped to the valley because of their ancestor's dreams of red skies and bloodshed, and Slyen had given them refuge. "But they didn't wipe us out," Aja said, swallowing. She didn't want to think that something so horrible could happen a second time. "The Zyphans and Querians are still here, and so are the Scorians and my people."

"The war ended because the Moglians were not united about what should be done," Jaqlai nodded. "Not all of them wanted to fight, and so they stopped after driving out the humans to the coasts. Now, the Zyphans live on their island to the northwest, where the humans' spacecraft landed. And the Querians live spread out along the coasts on the west and southeast. The Scorians went underground to live in the caves." He turned his head, looking north in the direction of the Slyen mountain range. "And your people live there, I take it?"

Aja nodded gravely. "It's a secret," she said. "I'm not supposed to tell anyone, even you."

"Then why did you?" He looked bothered and wouldn't meet her eyes.

"I need you to trust me," she replied. "And we made an agreement. I would tell you everything if you took me to Mettain."

"We didn't make an agreement," Jaqlai corrected. "I said I would think about it. But Aja, I can't keep your valley a secret from my superiors. The fact that the Zyphans found a place to land in the center of the continent is an important detail that will enable us to better prepare for the war."

"You *can't* tell anyone about us!" Aja insisted, her stomach tightening anxiously. "Don't you understand? Our secrecy is our freedom! Slyen and Vedlyr are going to *stop* the war before it happens, and then the Zyphans are going to leave my valley. We don't *want* anyone else coming to our home!"

Jaqlai turned to give her a sympathetic glance, studying her urgent expression thoughtfully. "I believe you, you know," he said gently. "That you're from a hidden valley in the Slyen mountains. I believe you that they are inhabited by a Moglian that doesn't want anyone coming in. I'm sure that's why he sent you out here and told you to keep the valley a secret." He sighed, shaking his head. "But I don't believe that a Moglian named Vedlyr exists. If our lands were ruled by a Moglian, we wouldn't have a king. We wouldn't be divided into seven fiefs ruled by dukes and duchesses. Moglians want their lands to be exactly as they want them, and they don't like change."

"Make another deal with me," Aja said boldly. She *knew* she was right, that Slyen was right, but she just didn't know how to prove it without finding Vedlyr himself. "If I can prove that Vedlyr is real, you must promise not to reveal my people and our valley to your superiors. You can say that the Zyphans have made landfall, and you can say that they are traveling to war from the center of the continent, but don't say anything about us."

"Why should I agree to that?" Jaqlai demanded. "You don't know what's at stake for my nation."

"And you don't know what's at stake for mine!" Aja countered. "If Vedlyr is real, then the war *can* be stopped, and your nation will be safe. If he's not, then you are free to tell your superiors everything."

Jaqlai scowled, shielding his eyes from the glare of the sun off the dunes. "I'll think about it," he said. "No promises."

Aja let out a tired sigh and didn't argue. They still had four or five days before they reached the port.

She still had time to convince him.

Through The Sands

They walked for hours, taking frequent short stops so that Aja could catch her breath. Not being athletically inclined, she didn't have Jaqlai's stamina. Yet while it was clear he was impatient to get out of the dunes, he never rushed her. Instead, he gave her encouraging words. "The dunes won't last much longer, then we'll have more solid footing." "I know it's difficult, but you're doing great, just hang in there." "Once we reach the rocky area, I'll find us something to eat."

At first, these little encouragements were helpful, motivating Aja to keep pushing herself past her limits. Eventually, as her determination petered out and her weariness grew, her mood took a noticeable dive. After one such moment where Jaqlai tried to motivate her, she turned and snapped at him that he wasn't helping. He apologized and fell silent, and in the hours that followed, Aja realized that she missed his encouragement. The quiet was broken only by the wind, and the minutes seemed to take longer and longer.

When the sun was directly overhead, Jaqlai stopped and began to dig a wide and shallow hole, scooping sand away with his arms. After he had dug down a couple feet, he beckoned for Aja to join him, and they sat down in the hole together. Jaqlai unfolded Aja's cloak and spread it out over their heads.

"Lie down and get some rest," he said. "We'll sleep away the heat of the day and keep moving once the sun is lower. I'll stay awake and keep us hidden."

Too tired to argue with him, Aja scooted down until she was lying on her back, grateful that the cloak blocked the sun's unbearable rays. *I feel burnt,* she thought miserably. *My throat is parched, and I think I might faint.* It was hot under the cloak, but not as hot as it would be without it. The wind blew through the crack between the sand and the cloak, and though it was hot, it was a comfort. Aja fell into a light sleep, too shallow for dreams.

She woke to the feeling of Jaqlai shaking her arm and groaned at the prospect of more walking. "Thirsty," she said, her lips so chapped that she found herself licking them. It only made them hurt worse, and she regretted having done so.

"I don't have any water," Jaqlai lamented. "When we reach the rocks, there are cacti there. Some of them are safe to eat, and some of them have a healing salve inside them that will help our burns."

The prospect of something to soothe her sunburn was appealing to Aja. Sighing unhappily, she forced herself to sit up. "My clothes," she said tiredly. "There's a loaf of bread in there."

"Bread is dry," Jaqlai smiled wryly. "But I confess, I could use something in my stomach right now. We need the calories." He handed her the bundle of clothes, watching with interest as she untied her belt and searched through them for the soda bread.

What she found was a towel wrapped around a bundle of pure crumbs. "Oh," she said, disappointed. "It's broken."

"We can still eat it," Jaqlai chuckled, then coughed and cleared his throat. It sounded as dry as her own. "Let's each take a handful of crumbs and eat, then we'll save the rest."

Aja nodded, more thirsty than hungry. She scooped a handful, mashing the crumbs together in her hand before dumping them in her mouth. When she chewed, she felt a grinding sensation of sand along with the crumbs and nearly gagged. *Can't escape the sand,* she thought, forcing herself to swallow before she'd finished chewing. She didn't think she could stomach more of that grit.

Jaqlai scooped a small handful as well, trying to moisten his mouth with his tongue without much success.

When he swallowed, he laughed. "Apart from the sand, that was quite good. I haven't had bread in such a long time, I almost forgot what it tasted like." He stood up, still holding the cloak over his head with one hand. "Thank you for sharing with me."

Nodding, Aja stumbled to her feet unsteadily. She felt lightheaded and sick, and her desperation for water was all she could think about. "How long till we can start looking for cacti?" she asked.

"We'll reach the rocky area in another few hours," Jaqlai promised. "Thankfully, we're only in the northern tip of the dunes. If we were to head south, we would be stuck in them for a long time. Directly west leads toward the coast, and as we get closer to it, the desert has more life." He gestured to the cloak. "Let's each hold part of this over our heads as we walk, it could make travel more bearable. Wish I had thought of it before. The heat must be impacting my ability to think clearly."

Aja looked down at her clothes. "I don't want to leave these," she said.

Jaqlai nodded, bending down and tying them up into a bundle for her. He tucked it under his arm as he stood up again, then held his end of the cloak. "Ready?"

Nodding, Aja pulled the other corner of her cloak over her head and began to walk, Jaqlai leading the way ahead of her. He was right about it being easier to travel. It was tiring to keep holding it, but it was a relief not to have the sun beating down on her head anymore.

The walk during the second half of the day felt even harder than the first, and Aja was so worn down that she couldn't even be cranky. She felt sick and hot, and every time she opened her mouth, she found herself begging for water. "I know," Jaqlai would say every time, urging her to keep going. It eventually got easier when the sun began to hang low on the horizon, though by then Aja was so exhausted she could hardly place one foot in front of the other.

Hours ago, she had been sweating. Now, she had nothing left to sweat.

"Aja," Jaqlai called over his shoulder.

She caught herself from falling forward to the sand, lifting her head to look towards him. For the past hour, she had been staring at her own feet, willing herself to put one in front of the other with no other thought on her mind. "What?" she croaked.

"We made it," he smiled. "Come here."

Aja had stopped wondering if they would ever make it, because thinking about it had been causing her despair. Now, hearing his words, she felt like she might have cried if she had any tears to shed. Instead, she simply collapsed to her knees with a moan, her cloak fluttering down to the sand beside her. Now she could see it—the desert leveling out, broken by boulders and plants. She saw new signs of life in the sand, the evidence of tumbleweeds rolled by, and the tiny indents of a small critter's footsteps. Above her head, a bird of prey circled low, watching her. There was more life here than in the dunes.

Jaqlai set her bundle of clothes beside her, then straightened and looked around them for several minutes. At length he sighed and faced her. "I don't *think* we're anywhere near a Door. But try to lay low and quiet for a bit while I find us water. Can you do that?"

She nodded, not having the strength or the will to push herself any further. She wasn't going to move from this spot until she absolutely had to.

"I'll be right back," he promised. His yellow eyes fixed her brown ones with a calm gaze. "Don't move."

I couldn't if I wanted to, Aja thought, watching as he turned and walked further ahead. He was looking left and right, his tail twitching side to side. The air felt tight with his Influence. *In fact, I think I'm going to pass out.*

She wasn't aware of collapsing, only of her eyes closing.

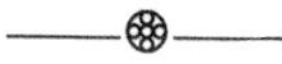

Aja thought at first she was back home, walking up the cobbled path to her house. But when she reached out for the garden gate, she couldn't see her hand. She could see the general pacing back and forth through the window, and the moment she wondered what he was saying, she found herself inside the house.

This is a dream, she thought. *I'm not really here.* Only she couldn't remember where she must be.

General Ryder was pacing the living area, his jacket off and tossed over the nearby arm of the sofa. He was speaking through his hand-held radio device, which he often used to communicate with the other officers. "Don't tell me there's no point, Gimloch. Even if we have to search the whole forest, I want her found. Over."

"Sir," came the voice of Sergeant James Gimloch. "You know how dangerous these woods are. She was probably eaten by jaguars. We've been searching for days, and we've found nothing! It's a waste of our time and resources. Over."

Ryder threw himself into the sofa, leaning over with his elbows on his knees. He rubbed his face with one hand. "Damn it," he muttered, without pressing the button on the side of the radio. "I'd cut the forest down if I wasn't so afraid of what might happen." He gritted his teeth in frustration. "There might still be hope. She might still be alive."

It was at this moment that Aja's mother came out from the kitchen, carrying a steaming ceramic mug of coffee for the general. It was his favorite beverage, brewed from the roasted beans that were imported from Zypha. "Please don't cut down the forest," she said. "It is a part of us, and wounding the forest would wound all of us."

"Why aren't you trying to find her?" Ryder snapped, taking the mug and staring morosely down into the dark liquid. "She's your *daughter.*"

"She's alive," Delia replied. "A mother always knows." She smiled faintly. "Though I appreciate how hard you're looking, I don't think you will find her."

"Because she ran away?" Ryder asked. For a moment suspicion washed over his face, but it passed and was replaced by grief. "She begged me not to go to war," he sighed. "And I didn't see how much it was bothering her. What was I supposed to say? We're going to war, that's the bitter truth. I don't want to go either!"

Aja could only listen and watch, unable to feel her own body as she observed the scene before her. She couldn't think of anything to say, even if she were able to. A heavy exhaustion was weighing on her, following her into her dreams.

"There are some decisions she must make for herself," Delia responded, taking a seat beside him. She stared at the window, her eyes unfocused as if gazing far into the distance. "Aja must come to understand in her own way."

"Where did she go?" the general asked, straightening. He turned to look at Delia with a frown. "You know something."

"I only know that she went somewhere," Delia shook her head. "That she was pondering over something deeply."

"Into the forest?" Ryder demanded. "Where jaguars could eat her?"

"She's not dead," Delia insisted. "A mother always knows."

Grimacing, Ryder lifted his radio and pressed on the button. "Sergeant, you're right. I know you are. Tell the lieutenant we're abandoning the search. Over."

"It's the right call, sir. Over."

"I know," Ryder said, his voice resigned. "If by chance we find *something*, tell me immediately. There's a chance she's still alive. Over."

"Sir, yes sir, over."

Ryder slid his handheld radio into his shirt pocket, leaned back in the sofa, and took a sip of his coffee. "I hope you're right," he said quietly. "It never occurred to me just how much your family meant to me, until she went missing. I feel like I lost my own daughter." He laughed wryly. "And I'm not even married."

"I believe in Aja," Delia responded, offering him a fond smile. "And I believe in her dreams. If she felt the need to pull away for a while, then I trust her. And I know that she will be back."

"I will be back," Aja called out, struck with such homesickness that her heart ached with longing. She tried to reach out for them, wanting to hug her mother, to thank Ryder for caring about her, but instead she found herself being pulled backwards. Her house vanished, her garden disappeared, and the lovely valley of Slyenials was left behind.

She woke to find herself coughing, her mouth wet.

"Easy," came Jaqlai's voice. "You're suffering heat stroke; you might be delirious."

"I was home," Aja moaned, struggling to sit up. Jaqlai helped her, and she found him pressing something into her hand. "What is this?"

"Water," Jaqlai said. "Just a little bit, for now. Drink slowly."

Aja blinked her eyes, rubbing sand from them and wincing when some of the grains remained in her eyes. Blinking rapidly, she looked down to see that he had given her a makeshift cup made from the husk of a dead plant. It might have been a cactus at one time, though it was shriveled and hollow now. Inside the cup was barely a mouthful of water, which was full of sand. She didn't care, lifting the cup to her lips and draining the liquid as quickly as she could.

It was sandy and stale tasting, but she was so desperate for it she could have wept. "More, please?" she gasped, stretching out the cup toward him.

"I'll get more," he promised. "But it would be better if you could come with me. The water I dug up is a bit of a ways that way," he pointed to his left, and Aja followed his hand.

What she saw was not water, but a man standing in the distance, watching them without moving. "Who is that?" she asked.

Jaqlai turned his head, stiffening, and then relaxed after a moment. "It's a rock," he said. "It almost looks like a person, so I can understand why you're confused. Come on," he stood up, pulling her to her feet beside him. "I already carried your belongings there, and now it's your turn."

"You'll carry me?" she asked. It was so difficult to think, and all she could concentrate on was how desperately she wanted water. *I feel sick,* she thought. *I'm going to throw up.*

"Do you need me to?" he asked. He leaned over, peering into her face, and she felt the pressure of his Influence around her. Without waiting for her answer, he lifted her into his arms and began to carry her. "Don't throw up," he said quietly. "Whatever you do, you must fight the urge as hard as you can. If you throw up here, you could die."

Why? she wanted to ask but couldn't seem to find her voice. The warning terrified her, and she struggled to keep her stomach calm. She breathed in and out of her nose slowly, trying to concentrate on anything she could think of to distract her. Water. Jaqlai carrying her. The chill of the wind. The last rays of the sun shining over the horizon. Ryder worrying about her.

"I was home," she said, wanting to cry. "They miss me. They were looking for me. And now they're not."

Jaqlai grimaced, hesitating as though he didn't know what to say. After a moment, he cleared his throat and began to speak. "Have you ever seen the ocean? It's an incredible sight—water as far as the eye can see. It's salt water, you know. You can't drink it, but it's still full of life. Have you eaten fish before? We could try some when we reach the port."

Aja recognized he was trying to distract her too, but she didn't like where the conversation had turned. "Please don't talk about fish," she begged. *Don't throw up. Don't throw up. Don't... please, don't!*

"Sorry," he replied quickly. He chewed his lip for a moment, then started again. "Why don't you tell me more about *Listening?*"

"I don't know what to say," Aja groaned. She lapsed into silence, thinking about *Listening* and how much it meant to her. She could hardly remember what she had already told him. "*Listening,*" she began, breathing shallowly, as her stomach turned uncomfortably, "is fun. I never know what I'm going to hear, but I always hear *something.*" She stopped, taking a deep breath through her nose. *My stomach hurts,* she thought.

Jaqlai seemed to sense she was having trouble, and he spoke up again. "Would you like to hear more about Influence?" he asked, gently.

At this, Aja lifted her gaze to stare at his face. He had a beard beginning to grow, a darker color than the brown of his hair. The beard hairs were almost black. "Yes," she said, her interest piqued.

He smiled at her before focusing on his footsteps over the rocky sand. "Alright," he said. "I'll tell you about it. Did Slyen mention how it works?" She shook her head, and he continued. "Influence is a very subtle kind of magic—the Vedlyran kind, anyway. It works best when it moves slowly."

"What does it do?" Aja asked. "Make you invisible?" She thought of when she'd lost track of him, down in the prison. It had seemed like he was suddenly not there.

"I suppose, in a way," he replied. "Influence deals with the senses. It can mute your ability to perceive me, so that I can't be seen or sensed. It can also be used to influence the internal perceptions of others."

"I don't understand," Aja closed her eyes wearily. But when the movement of being carried with her eyes closed made her more nauseous, she opened her eyes again to watch where they were going. Now she could see that the silhouette she thought was a man was only a rock, standing tall out in the sand.

Jaqlai smiled faintly as he explained. "In your mind, you perceive things about yourself like 'I am tired' or 'I like the rain.' Influence can make you question those, and in some cases, change your mind. You might find yourself thinking, 'maybe I don't like the rain today,' and not know that your change of mind came from Influence. The change doesn't always last, especially if I'm trying to change a deeply held belief. You probably have the internal perception that you are from the Slyen mountains. If I try to change your mind to think, 'maybe I'm not from Slyenials,' it would only work if you don't hold that perception as a *conviction*. Does that make sense?"

"Show me," Aja suggested. "I am from Slyenials."

Jaqlai concentrated, his ears angling sideways slightly, and soon she felt the recognizable pressure around her. Though she didn't hear him speak any words, she felt as though his Influence was telling her that she was from Scoria.

"I'm not from Scoria," Aja smiled. "And I can tell you're using it."

"That's because you're unique," Jaqlai stopped trying, and the pressure faded from the air. "No one *else* can tell it's been used on them, because Influence is subtle."

"How come you couldn't manipulate my mind, but you could make yourself invisible to me?" Aja asked curiously. The conversation was helping, and she wasn't thinking about her nausea anymore.

"When I was trying to change your internal perceptions," he explained, "it didn't work because you could feel it. And you used your *Listening* to tell me to stop. When I vanished from sight, it's because I was changing your external perceptions—your ability to see, sense, and hear what's right in front of you. Could you sense I was using Influence then?"

"I think so," she nodded. "The air felt tight, but I couldn't see you."

"That means Influence works around you, but you can tell when it's happening. It just might not work *on* you." He smiled wryly. "I guess I'll have to keep that in mind." He stopped walking, setting Aja down on the sand. "We're here."

He had brought her to an old waterbed which might have once been a pond, but it was completely dry now. The only evidence of water were the plants surrounding its edges, and the hole dug in the center of it. She could *smell* the water from the hole, and her thirst suddenly became unbearable. "Can I have some?" she asked.

Jaqlai nodded. "Tiny sips," he warned. "If you throw it all up, you risk losing more hydration than you can spare. That could easily kill you out here."

"I'll be careful," she promised, licking her dry lips.

"Sit here," he instructed, gesturing on the edge of the dry waterbed. "I'll bring you water."

Aja dropped down to the sand, touching her hot face with her hands, which were slightly cooler. It helped soothe some of her headache. "Where is my cloak?" she asked when the wind caused her to shiver. Was the heat of the daylight already evaporating? *Winter is coming,* she thought grimly. *I'm running out of time.*

"I brought it," Jaqlai called. "It should be beside you." He went to the hole he had made in the center of the oasis, dug a little more with his hand, then pressed his fist against the wet sand at the bottom of the hole. Then, lowering the fragile makeshift cup, he filled it with a tiny bit of water and brought it to Aja. "Drink slowly," he warned.

Aja tried to do that, but she couldn't help herself from gulping down all of the measly sips that were in it. "More," she pleaded when she finished, but Jaqlai made her wait several minutes before he let her have more. And then it was only a tiny bit once again. This continued over and over until the sun had fully set and the sky began to grow dark. Then, wrapping Aja in her cloak. Jaqlai bade her sleep.

She couldn't argue against him, though she wished he would give her more to drink. Lying on her side with her head on her bundle of clothes, she curled up inside her cloak and let herself drift off back to sleep. She was no longer delirious, and she didn't dream of home again.

The next morning, Aja felt better than the night before, but Jaqlai didn't let them continue walking until he was sure Aja recovered. He treated her burns with the viscous fluid inside some of the cactus bushes around the oasis. They had long, thick leaves growing up from the center of the plant like a flower—or like a fern, Aja thought. Jaqlai sliced one open with his nail along its length and had her rub the salve over her burns.

"The Zyphans call this plant 'aloe,' and the Moglians call it 'maova'," he explained.

"Can you Influence a bag to grow out of it?" she wondered, and he laughed.

"I'm not a Moglian," he replied, an amused grin on his face.

For food, after they finished eating all of the soda breadcrumbs, Jaqlai brought a cactus fruit for each of them. They looked just like cacti, except for their color. The edible parts were red rather than green. Aja found them slimy and odd to eat, but they were sweet and gave her a bit of much needed energy. And to her relief, Jaqlai let her drink as much water she wanted.

They remained at the oasis until after midday had passed. Jaqlai gathered several leaves of aloe, which he stuffed into the pockets of his trousers and button-up shirt. His clothes, like Aja's, were soiled with sweat and sand from their journey, except that he didn't have anything else to change into. Aja didn't change her dress, not feeling comfortable doing it out in the wilderness, so she pushed her long sleeves up as far as they would go and remained in the same dress as yesterday.

"Ready?" Jaqlai asked. "Let's go as far as we can today. It will be easier in this part of the desert, and it will get better the farther we go. We'll see more plants, we'll find more dry ponds, and we'll be able to catch something more substantial for dinner." He gazed out across the desert, his ears swiveling back and forth as he searched the horizon. "Maybe I can catch a rattlesnake," he murmured, more to himself than to Aja.

"I won't eat the snake," Aja said, holding her cloak over her head to protect her from the sun. Jaqlai grabbed the other end of it, hoisting it above his own so they were both covered.

"We can't afford to be picky in the desert," Jaqlai said wryly. "And anyway, snake meat is delicious."

"I don't eat meat," Aja said. She was tired and lightheaded, hungry and worn. But this was a conviction she would never back down on.

Jaqlai seemed to sense it, and he looked at her in surprise. After a moment, he nodded with resignation in his eyes. "I'll find us something," he promised. He began walking, and Aja followed dutifully behind him. "I take it that means you don't want fish when we reach the port?" he asked.

It took Aja a second to realize he was teasing her. "No fish," she affirmed, cracking a smile. Her lips were so chapped that it hurt, though the aloe she used earlier was helping soothe them. "The Zyphans eat it back home, and I can't stand the smell of it."

"You'll smell a lot of it at the port," he replied with a laugh. "Fish, seawater, salt, and seagull droppings. You won't be able to escape it in a port city."

"What is it called?" she asked, wanting the conversation, longing for something to distract her from the miserable chore of walking.

"The port is called Anatya," Jaqlai answered. "I've been there once before. A lot of merchant vessels make their way from Port Anatya down to Mettain, carrying spices that the Querians bring through the desert. They are famous for their spices."

"What is Zypha famous for?" Aja couldn't help being more curious about Zypha than Queria. She remembered her dream about the general and felt immediately homesick again. *I wonder if it was just a dream of my own making, or if that really happened,* she thought sadly. Would the general really send out search parties for her? Even knowing how dangerous the forest was?

The Zyphans never went into the forest, and never tried to expand the valley by cutting down its trees. None of them talked about it, but they didn't have to. Aja knew that they had an instinctual fear of it that kept them from touching it. She couldn't imagine them venturing into it to search for anyone, let alone a single woman they had known less than a year.

"Zypha is famous for its technology, and for the varieties of plants that aren't from this world," Jaqlai answered. "Coffee, for example, came from the human world. It's become very popular in Mettain." He exhaled a long sigh. "I could really go for some coffee, right now. Iced coffee with a bit of cream."

"I've never tried it," Aja admitted, again thinking of her dream. "But... the general is fond of it."

"General Ryder?" Jaqlai asked, almost offhandedly. He glanced over his shoulder at her with a curious look in his eyes, despite his tone.

"You do know him, don't you?" Aja said, scowling. "Don't pretend you don't, your ears give you away." They were currently swiveled towards her, slightly pointed upward.

Jaqlai looked away awkwardly, clearing his throat. "Not personally," he admitted after a moment. "But his name is familiar to me."

"Why?" Aja asked. "Is he famous?"

"Not famous, per se," Jaqlai shrugged one shoulder. "Just known. He is one of the top five generals of Zypha. He's got the authority to make judgement calls that can change the course of the whole nation." His face clouded with a grave look. "Such as choosing to invade Queria from a central location like your valley."

"Would he have the authority to stop the war altogether?" Aja wondered out loud. Was Slyen aware of that? Perhaps that was why he felt Influencing them would be successful.

"If not stop it, at least postpone it," Jaqlai admitted. "I'm curious what else you learned from him about the war."

"He never let anything slip about the war," Aja shook her head, then stumbled over a rock in the sand. She fell forward with a gasp, expecting to land on her face, but she managed to catch her footing again when Jaqlai's tail curved to catch her and push her back up. "Thank you," she breathed, relieved not to have injured herself. *His tail is stronger than I expected it to be,* she thought, watching it flick before it relaxed behind him once more. Not very much like a jaguar's tail, if it had the strength to catch her from falling. *Just what kind of people are Vedlyr's people? They aren't fully human, and they aren't fully cats, either.*

"No problem," Jaqlai smiled. "Then it was Slyen who told you about the war?"

Aja nodded, now watching her footing instead of her companion. "Yes," she said. "I didn't know what Querians were until Slyen mentioned them. Only then did I have the courage to ask the general not to go to war."

"I doubt he would stop simply because you asked," Jaqlai said wryly.

Aja thought of that last conversation with him, her heart aching. "No," she said. "He wouldn't."

They walked until the sun set, eating any edible cactus fruits they found along the way. And when night fell, Jaqlai made a fire out of dead plants. Aja was in much better spirits when she lay down to sleep that night. *I can make it through this desert,* she thought in relief, as her eyes closed and she huddled by the fire under her cloak. *Because I have Jaqlai with me.*

She was still getting comfortable when Jaqlai murmured he was off to hunt and wandered out into the night. He didn't even give her a chance to protest. Nervous at being alone, she wrapped her arms tightly around herself and stretched out her senses, *Listening* for any sound of danger. All she could hear was the wind, blowing through the plants and whipping sand against the rocks. She waited for nearly an hour before she finally heard the sound of footsteps.

At first, she froze in terror, remembering the night she'd been taken down into Scoria. Was it a guard out on patrol? Was it a caravan of Querians who would question where she was from?

Just as she was beginning to panic, she caught sight of Jaqlai walking proudly back into camp with his tail swishing and his ears high. Aja let out a shaky sigh of relief, relaxing muscles she hadn't realized she had tensed. Jaqlai was carrying what looked to be a dead rattler that was twice as long as his arm.

I'm glad he caught his snake, she thought with a shiver, *but gladder that he returned safely.* "Are we near a Door?" she asked. She didn't want to say that she was not okay when he was gone. And she needed the reassurance that they were safe.

He glanced toward her, surprised to hear her still awake. "I checked," he assured her. "And I can't sense a doorway anywhere near us. The reason I got caught before was because I wasn't looking for them." He offered her a wry look as he sat down to skin and cook his snake. "I won't make that mistake again."

"Don't leave me behind so long," she whispered, unable to make herself say it louder. She felt embarrassed for being scared, as though she was still a child needing protection. But he was the only one she could rely on out here, and he had proven himself with his kindness and dedication more than once.

If he heard her, he didn't respond. And Aja drifted to sleep before his snake finished roasting over the fire.

Port Anatya

The desert had become rocky and uneven, filled with swooped slopes of sand-hills and tall spires of sandstone. And the further west they traveled, the more the landscape began to change. Plants became more abundant, the rocks became more prominent, and there were gnarled trees with fraying bark and spindly branches that reached up into flat canopies. There were even birds nesting in the branches of the trees, hunting for insects in the sandy clefts between the rocks. And in the distance, the horizon became a perfectly flat line.

Aja found the flat horizon to be eerie and uncomfortable, though she couldn't explain why. She had always been able to see *something* in the distance, be it mountains, trees, or sand dunes. The existence of a flat horizon was unfamiliar to her. And the closer they got to it, the more things changed around them. The sand became grassy, the rocks became hardier chunks of different colors, instead of just brown sandstone, and the sky became filled with clouds. Even the smell of the air was different, sort of salty and wet, reminding Aja of the salty shores of the Uliah.

"Look," Jaqlai said, on the fifth day of travel. "Do you see it? We'll reach the ocean tonight."

In Aja's mind, the Ocean was the name of a great, expansive river, like the Uliah. She had no concept of the sea, or how large it was. "The land on the other side of it must be very flat," she ventured, peering at the horizon with squinted eyes.

"Not likely," Jaqlai chuckled. "You won't be able to see it, anyway. The ocean is so large, there is only water as far as the eye can see."

The scope of his words had little meaning to Aja until they reached the shore. There, the wind changed directions so that it was coming towards them from the water, and though the desert had ended, the ground was still covered in sand. It was bitterly cold by the ocean, and gazing out across the turbulent waves, Aja was astounded by how vast the water was. They hadn't gone down to the water's edge, but the wind was wet and Aja was grateful to be wearing her cloak. She found herself pitying Jaqlai, who had nothing but a long-sleeved shirt with a tan tunic over it.

"It's so much water," she said, and felt that her words were a pitiful description that barely touched the enormity that was the Ocean.

Jaqlai gazed out across the water, a contemplative expression on his face. "All that water, and none of it drinkable," he said, his words barely audible over the sound of the wind. "The ocean is a desert of water."

Having just come through a desert herself, Aja felt a shiver at his words. Would crossing the ocean be just as miserable? Or would it be much worse? There would be no plants or insects or rocks they could take refuge by. *I'm glad we'll be able to cross it by ship,* she thought with a shiver. "Where is the city?" she asked, gazing left and right along the horizon.

"I don't know," Jaqlai admitted. "Not yet, anyway." He knelt and picked up several stones, then began to create a circle in the sand with them.

"What are you doing?" Aja asked, taking a seat on a boulder beside the circle he'd made.

Jaqlai didn't answer until he had finished crafting it, then he took up a final stone that was sort of long and tubular. He placed it in the very center of the circle and knelt down in the damp sand. "The Scorians have a method for detecting people," he explained, rubbing his hands together to warm them. "They call it Stone Dowsing. We make a circle like a compass and choose one longer stone for the center, then we pour our energy into the stone while holding it up like this." He stood the stone on end, in the very center of his compass. "When the stone is full, we let it fall and see where it lands. That direction should have people."

"I thought dowsing was a way to find water," Aja pointed out. She had read about it before, when she was still in school. Dowsing rods made of copper could be used to determine the direction of water and had been used by her people to dig wells.

"Normal dowsing, sure," Jaqlai said. He concentrated on the rock in his hands, positioned it carefully, and let it fall. It flopped directly toward the ocean. He frowned, shivering when a gust of wind blew hard against them. "Maybe I'm not doing it right," he sighed.

"How do you pour your energy into the stone?" Aja asked, curious. She remembered the Scorians saying that "the stones" had detected one person at the door, and that person was Aja.

Jaqlai's ears swiveled toward Aja, and he lifted his head sharply in her direction. "You're human," he said, a curious expression on his face. "Maybe you should be the one to try it. Perhaps only humans can do it."

"I still don't know how to put my energy in the stone," Aja said, though she herself was curious to try. Scooting forward from her perch, she knelt on the sand beside him and picked up the tubular rock. It was cold to the touch, crusted with wet grains of sand. Brushing these off, she closed her hands around it and shut her eyes. *Pour my energy into it,* she thought, trying to do just that. It was difficult to envision, and she had no way to determine if she was successful or not. Should she try *Listening*?

Aja opened her senses, spreading them around her. The sound of the waves was reminiscent of home, of the great river Uliah, and she found herself soothed by it. The wind was familiar, cold, and incessant, and never ceased its blowing. She could hear the beating of her own heart, her own breathing, as close and as loud as the wind. And then, distractedly, she realized she could hear Jaqlai's breathing, too. She could hear the swish of his tail across the sand, the rubbing of his hands as he tried to warm himself up. *I'm getting sidetracked,* she thought, and focused her senses on the sensation of the cold rock in her hands. *Focus,* she told herself. *Listen to the stone.*

There was nothing for her to *Listen* to, but she could feel the temperature of the rock changing the longer she held onto it. Slowly but surely, it was warming to match the temperature of her hands. Was that how she could pour energy into it? By focusing on the warmth she was sharing with it? Curiously, she adjusted her grip and tried to imagine pouring her body temperature into the rock until she began to feel a tingling sensation in her palms.

"Okay," Jaqlai's voice startled her from the focus of her thoughts. "Let go."

Opening her eyes, Aja let go of the rock carefully, trying not to influence which way it fell. It teetered on its end for a second or two, swayed, and fell in a slight curve, its angle changing halfway down. It landed on the sand, pointing nearly due south.

"Did it work?" she asked, curious. Jaqlai was right beside her, and the rock hadn't fallen in either of their directions.

"Only one way to find out," Jaqlai grinned, rising to his feet. "Let's head south and see if we find the city."

"And if we don't?" she asked, shivering at another gust of wind. Her hands felt ice cold, and her palms were still tingling.

"Port Anatya isn't the only city on the coast," Jaqlai reassured her. "It's just the closest and the largest. We'll find civilization one way or another." Gesturing for her to follow, he started heading south, putting the ocean to their right.

"How did you learn about stone dowsing?" Aja asked, hurrying her pace so she was walking beside him. She rubbed her hands together, blowing on them to heat them up again.

"I had the opportunity to see it in action when I was captured," he explained with a wry smile. "They were trying to determine if there were any others with me. I thought it was fascinating and wanted to give it a try." He sighed, shaking his head in disappointment. "Turns out, it might be something only humans can do."

"Glad I could at least be of some help," Aja admitted, wrapping her arms around herself under her cloak. She was grateful for how warm it was, and she wished she had given Leyla a more proper thanks for it.

"You're plenty of help," Jaqlai assured her. "I never would have escaped without you." He had a strange expression on his face, as though his thoughts were conflicted. "I'm glad you came with me on this journey."

"You say that like we're about to part ways," Aja commented, watching his face. He showed no reaction, either on his face or with his ears and tail. *Am I imagining it?* she thought. *It feels like he's about to tell me 'Goodbye'.*

"I hope we reach the port by nightfall," Jaqlai said. "It will be hard to start a fire on a beach this wet."

The sky was still light, despite the sun having set, when they caught sight of the city in the distance. They were so heartened by the sight of it that they picked up their pace and pushed themselves to get there faster. Even after darkness fell, they continued on, determined to reach it before stopping for the night. Luckily, the city was lit by lanterns, standing out like a beacon in the night for them to follow.

When they arrived at the port, Aja was too weary to get a good look at it. They were met at the gates by a sour-faced guard wearing a thick felt jacket. Jaqlai introduced himself and said he found Aja separated from her caravan in the desert, and the two were looking for a place to stay the night.

"Do you have identification?" the guard at the door demanded.

"Not with me," Jaqlai said calmly. "It's at the embassy."

"Not you," the man scowled, eyeing Aja with a narrowed gaze. "You. Where's your identification?"

Aja was stunned in place for a moment, until she recalled the only identification she had on her person. The stone card with her Scorian ID number carved into it. Even now, after their long trek through the desert, it was still fastened to her belt. She pulled it out and handed it to him, looking him in the eyes without a word.

He studied it briefly before shooting her a look up and down. He saw her gray cloak and seemed to recognize it at once. "What city are you from?" he asked.

"Garnet Eagle," Aja said.

He handed her ID badge back to her with a nod. "Your caravan's already left, but I'm sure you can wait for the next one. Good night."

Aja and Jaqlai were quiet after they passed through, until they had gotten a safe distance away. Then Jaqlai let out a relieved sigh.

"Well, that was lucky," he said, looking at her approvingly. "I almost said you were Querian. Glad I didn't."

"He didn't give you as much trouble as he gave me," Aja said, also relieved. She was certainly glad that in her hasty escape, she hadn't thought to take the badge off.

"It's because I'm a Vedlyran," Jaqlai said, leading the way through the city. "This *is* Port Anatya, just as I'd hoped, and there's an embassy here in the city we can rest at. They can't give me too much of a hard time because of it."

"Embassy?" Aja asked, not familiar with the word.

"A building owned by my people," he said, clearly not wanting to go into much detail. "We'll be able to rest there, if I tell them you're with me. I'll be able to charter a ship through them, or at the very least, use them to get a message to Mettain."

Aja wasn't sure why she felt worried about this, but she didn't voice her concerns. Instead, she walked by his side quietly, *Listening*. The city was still active, even this late. It was larger than Garnet Eagle by a long shot, though she was too weary to pay much attention to her surroundings now.

Eventually arriving at a building with white plaster walls and a ceramic-tiled roof, Jaqlai entered and held the door open for her. There was a desk in the entrance of the building, where a young Vedlyran woman was seated. She rose to her feet when they entered, a look of surprise on her face.

"Jaqlai!" she blurted. "When you didn't check in…" her words trailed off as she looked at Aja, a slight scowl furrowing her brow. "Who's this?"

"A friend," Jaqlai said, offering a smile at the woman. "I was in a tricky situation, and only got out of it thanks to her help. Can we spare a room for her?"

"We only have one room available at the moment," the woman said quickly, now scowling at Aja fully.

What did I do to her? Aja wondered, brushing strands of her hair out of her face. Now that she was no longer in the wind, she was conscious of how she looked to other people.

"That works fine," Jaqlai responded. "Thank you, Cait."

Cait's eyes widened at his words, darting from his face to Aja's. Clearly upset, she pursed her mouth without a reply, taking a seat behind the desk once more. She dipped a feather quill into a pot of ink and began to fill out a ledger in front of her. "And how long are you staying?" she asked.

"Not sure," Jaqlai yawned, equally as exhausted as Aja, though this was the first time he had shown it. "Can I discuss it in the morning? It's late."

"Fine," Cait responded testily. She finished filling in her ledger and stuck the quill in its holder, rising to her feet. "This way, please." She shot Aja a glare before walking down the hallway to her right, and Aja and Jaqlai's left. The building wasn't very large, but it was more spacious than the buildings in Garnet Eagle had been. In a short time, they made it through the hall, up the stairs, and down another hallway to the room Cait was leading them to. "This is the room you stayed in last," Cait said. "I kept it open for you, just in case. When we didn't hear from you, we feared the worst."

"I was delayed," Jaqlai answered, without giving her any details to work with. "Thank you, Cait." He opened the door and held it for Aja to enter.

Are we staying in the same room? Aja wondered. Out in the wild, it wasn't strange to spend all her time with the only traveling companion she had. But now that they were in a city, she felt suddenly uncomfortable with the arrangement. "You should take it," she said, looking up at him with an awkward smile.

"I'll sleep in the break room," he said, a wry smile on his face. "I'd have rented you an inn room, but I don't have any money right now. We both need a good rest, so please take the room."

Realizing that she was making things more awkward by refusing to go in, Aja nodded and moved past him into the room. She was conscious of Cait's sharp glare on her and didn't want to weather it much longer. When she had entered, she saw that it was a simply decorated, with one bed, a chest of drawers, and a small, attached bathroom. Larger than her room had been in Garnet Eagle, but with fewer pieces of furniture.

Jaqlai closed the door after he entered, letting out a sigh. When Aja glanced at him, she thought the angle of his ears made him look irritated. "Do you know how showers work?" he asked, walking toward the bathroom. "There's a handle you turn for water, to adjust the temperature. Why don't you take the first one and get settled, and I'll go speak with the embassy employees. There are a few arrangements I need to make."

"Such as?" Aja found herself asking. She didn't like how vague he was being but couldn't place why.

"I'm hoping they can issue my two-week pay," he said, yawning. "Once I have money, it will be easier to do things like eat, get a ship, get a decent inn room. That sort of thing."

Aja's anxiety faded into relief. "Alright," she said. "Thank you." She glanced toward the door, *Listening*, and was sure she could hear Cait still lingering outside. Was she trying to eavesdrop? "I guess I'll just..." Aja gestured toward the bathroom.

Jaqlai handed her the bundle of clothes he had been carrying for her and went back to the door. "Right," he said, his expression awkward. "I'll be back later to grab one of the blankets." He slipped out hurriedly and closed the door behind him.

Just outside, Aja could hear Cait ambush him the second he exited. "Who is she? Where did she come from? Why did you bring her here? Are you two dating?"

Dating? Aja wanted to sigh, understanding now washing over her. So *that* was why Cait was so negative toward Aja. *She clearly likes him,* she thought, setting her clothes on the chest of drawers. She picked out her outfit from Slyenials and carried it into the bathroom with her. *Well, she has nothing to fear from me. I'm not interested.*

The bathroom had a mirror hanging over the sink, and when Aja looked into it, she was appalled and how ragged, thin, and disheveled she looked. Her hair was knotted and frazzled, her skin was dark from the sun, her lips were badly chapped and she had dark circles under her eyes. She scrunched up her nose at her appearance, making a face at herself, and suddenly was reminded of home.

Reminded of the general, looking in the mirror and calling himself a "dashing figure."

She felt a dry ache in her eyes but was too dehydrated for tears. Now, more than ever, she missed home. The days kept passing, but she was still so far from returning. She hadn't even reached Mettain. And what if she couldn't find Vedlyr? What if she never saw her home again?

"I miss you," she whispered, hanging her head as she pictured the ones she missed. Her mother Delia and her sister Kyra. Seila, her best friend. Emrin and his creative drawings and playful personality. Tula, the neighbor next door. Even General Ryder.

She couldn't bear the thought of never seeing them again.

Her thoughts were heavy as she showered and changed her clothes, and she felt like she must have taken a long time figuring out the controls. The Zyphans had installed showers in the new houses they had been building, but Aja's people used baths to get clean. She wasn't used to the mechanism, and the water kept shifting between too hot and too cold until the very end. But now she was clean, feeling far better than she had felt in six days.

After stepping out and drying off with a towel that had been provided for her, she tried brushing her hair with her fingers without success, so she did it up in a braid to hide the knots. When she finished, she was so tired she felt she might pass out at any moment, but Jaqlai had not returned. Too weary to wait for him, she pulled off one of the blankets from the bed and took one of the pillows, setting both on the chest of drawers. Then, climbing into the bed, she left the oil lamp on and closed her eyes.

She could hear the gentle rolling of the waves outside, a never-ending noise that was surprisingly soothing. Before she knew it, she was lost to her dreams.

Aja woke up slowly, so comfortable that she didn't want to wake up at all. The sound of the ocean made her want to sleep longer, and after waking up briefly, she let herself fall right back asleep.

The next time she woke up, she felt much more rested than before. She sat up and looked around, noticing that the oil lamp had been turned off, and the pillow and blanket were now resting on the foot of the bed. Jaqlai was not in the room, but she was sure he had been here at least briefly.

Reluctantly pulling herself out of the comfortable bed, she slipped on her canvas shoes and changed into another of her Scorian outfits. It was probably best to keep up appearances while she was here, after all. She stopped by the mirror to check on her hair and redid her braid to hide the snarls. Then, making a playful face at herself, she turned and made her way for the door.

It wasn't difficult to find her way back to the front office, and when she got there, she saw that a different Vedlyran was sitting at the desk. He was a man with a large mustache and a very short haircut, and one of his ears had a notch in it as though it had once been injured.

"Ah, there you are," the man said. He rose to his feet and leaned over the counter toward her. "I have something I'm supposed to give you." He set a small pouch on the counter, along with a sealed letter.

Aja couldn't explain the sinking feeling in her gut when she saw them. Nervously, she reached out and took both into her hands. The pouch was full of coins and folded paper bills, and the letter had her name written on it. "Where is Jaqlai?" she asked.

"By now, he's probably on his way to Mettain," the man shrugged both shoulders. "He went out to charter passage with a ship this morning before the tide went out."

The sinking feeling was now a leaden weight in her gut. *He left me,* she thought, dread and despair washing over her. *He left me without saying goodbye. Taking the knowledge of my valley with him.*

"Everything should be in that letter," the Vedlyran said, offering a sympathetic smile. "And you are welcome to stay here as long as you need. Please let me know if I can help in anyway."

Aja tore open the letter, pulling out the single slip of paper with trembling hands.

Aja,

I'm sorry that we have to part ways like this, but there wasn't time. I've left this money for you, which should be enough either to help you get home or to buy passage anywhere you'd like. I have to get the information I've learned to my superiors as quickly as possible, and I can't afford to wait. You're welcome to stay at the embassy as long as you need, so please take your time to rest and recover. They'll take care of you here.

I sincerely wish you the best. Thank you for rescuing me, and I hope this makes us even.

Jaqlai.

"Makes us even?" she whispered, now feeling angry as well as distressed. That was what he was worried about? What about their deal? She had told him everything he asked, even things she probably shouldn't, and he was supposed to take her with him! Couldn't he have woken her up? Was it because she slept in? Crunching the note up in her hands, she looked toward the Vedlyran clerk defiantly. "Which way did he go?" she demanded.

"I'm afraid he's long gone by now," the Vedlyran shook his head. "Why don't you stay and get something to eat?

You came from the desert, I understand. Jaqlai made sure we would take care of you in his place."

"Oh, did he?" Aja asked bitterly. *That wasn't our deal.* She stuck her pouch of coins in the pocket of her dress with the crumbled letter. "I'll eat later. Just tell me which way he went."

"I'm afraid I couldn't say," the man sighed. "I didn't see."

Aja chewed on her lower lip, which was still chapped and flaky with dried skin, as she considered what she should do next. On the one hand, she *was* hungry. But on the other, Jaqlai might still be out there somewhere. *I once heard footsteps I'd taken in the past,* she recalled, *when I made my way through the forest to Slyen. Maybe I could hear his footsteps, too.*

Closing her eyes, she stretched out her senses and quieted her mind. *Listen,* she told herself. *Listen for Jaqlai.*

At first, all she could hear was the ocean, the people out in the city, and the birds cawing in the air as they hunted for food. But the longer she focused, the more those sounds seemed to fade into the background. Now she could hear her own heartbeat, her breathing, the breathing of the Vedlyran clerk who watched her with interest. And then, voices. Voices she recognized.

"What do you mean?" came Jaqlai's voice, so faint she could barely hear it. "I'm clearly *not* dead, so why can't you issue my paycheck?"

"You were pronounced dead four days ago," Cait's voice answered. "My hands are tied."

"Cait, give me *something* to work with," Jaqlai pleaded. "I'm *not* dead, and I'm going back to Mettain anyway. I'll get the matter figured out there, and I'll show them a receipt of my payment."

"Well…" Cait hesitated. "Alright. Since it's you, I'll make an exception."

"Thank you," Jaqlai exhaled in relief.

Aja's eyes snapped open, scanning the room in confusion. The voices seemed to be coming from this very room, yet when she looked around, all she could see was the one Vedlyran watching her curiously. What did it mean? *Am I hearing voices from the past?* she thought, inhaling sharply with excitement. It wasn't what she had expected to hear, but it might be even better. This was a full conversation! Closing her eyes once more, she *Listened* with anticipation to hear more.

"Jaqlai!" she heard Cait's voice blurt in surprise. "When you didn't check in…" her words trailed off briefly. "Who's this?"

"A friend," Jaqlai replied. "I was in a tricky situation, and only got out of it thanks to her help. Can we spare a room for her?"

"We only have one room available at the moment," Cait said, with a clear tone of irritation.

Aja opened her eyes again, discouraged. Now she was hearing the conversation she had just experienced last night. That was too far back. *If only I could control exactly what I want to hear,* she thought, sighing.

"Miss," the Vedlyran at the counter said, with no small amount of compassion. "Please come get something to eat, you were out in the desert without supplies. You look as though you might keel over at any moment."

"Keel?" Aja asked, having never heard the word before.

He seemed to think she was making a joke, and only chuckled. "Come into the back, we have a break room where you can eat something, and there are pastries and tea, and some fruit as well." He began to lead the way, gesturing toward the hall with his hand. "My name is Mikail," he added. "What do I call you?"

"Aja," she answered. As they got closer to the break room, she could smell the fresh fruit and pastries, and her stomach grumbled loudly. *Well, I do need to eat,* she thought. She had eaten so little in the desert that she had lost weight. Burning more calories than they consumed, Jaqlai had said. Aja wondered if her stomach could even handle a normal sized meal.

"I'm afraid we don't have any coffee," Mikail added, his tone regretful. "The Zyphans have stopped trading with Queria, so it's exceedingly hard to come by. I hope you like tea."

"Yes," Aja said. She thought of the General and his morning cup of coffee and felt homesick once again. It reminded her all too keenly that she needed to get to Mettain. *As soon as I eat, I'll go down to the docks,* she thought. *There might be another ship that can take me.*

Mikail showed her to the back room, and after making sure she was situated with a plate of sliced fruit and fresh cream-cheese pastries, he returned to the front desk once more. The fruit was light and sweet, deliciously juicy and tart at the same time. Aja had never seen orange fruit quite like it and had no idea what it was called. It wasn't a citrus fruit, more like an oblong melon with seeds inside that had to be scraped out before they cut it. She finished what was on her plate and ended up going back to get the rest of it, she enjoyed it so much.

Even though she had served herself so little, she wasn't able to finish her plate. Regretfully leaving the rest of the delicious food behind, she left the break room and made her way back to the entrance to speak to Mikail.

"Excuse me," she said, walking up to his desk. He looked up from a ledger he was writing in, expectant. "Can you tell me which way to go to get to the ships?"

He smiled graciously. "Once you exit the door, turn right and head down the hill toward the ocean. Then, when you come to the water, turn left. The docks will be all along the shore, and they will be busy with merchants. Be careful not to get drawn in by them, some of them won't leave you alone till you buy something."

"I'll keep that in mind," Aja said. That didn't sound like a situation she wanted to deal with.

"If people talk to you and try to get your attention, just ignore them and keep walking," Mikail instructed. "That's the only way to avoid getting sucked in."

"Alright, thank you Mikail." The thought that Jaqlai might still be around was making her feel pressured for time, so she offered a parting smile and went right out the door. The less time she wasted, the sooner she might either find Jaqlai, or find another ship that could take her.

As soon as she was outside, she was buffeted by a strong gust of wind coming up from the water. Last night, she hadn't been able to see very much of the city because it was dark and she was tired. But today, she found herself marveling at how large and beautiful it was. All of the buildings were made of white terracotta walls and shingled in red ceramic tiles that were curved in shape. It gave the roofs of the houses and shops a very charming look, and it was a style she had never seen before. All of the windows had arched tops and flat sills, and the streets were paved with reddish brown bricks in intricate argyle patterns.

The Vedlyran Embassy was near the top of the hill, and the rest of the city stretched out across the hill down to the sea, where several long wooden docks were built out into the water. The bay was deep enough that the few ships she could see were anchored directly at the docks. She could count four from here, and a few other smaller boats that had large nets being folded up by fishermen. As soon as Aja caught sight of the ships, she felt an urgency come upon her to get down to them as fast as possible. There were four docked there now, but by the time she walked through the whole city, those four might leave, too.

They don't look like the Zyphan ships I'm used to seeing, she thought, picking up her pace as she hurried down the hill on a cobbled brick sidewalk. *These ones have tall masts with sails, and the Zyphan ships are steam powered. Does that mean these ones don't move as fast through the water?*

The city was alive with people all manner of colors from pale to dark, and the diversity was comfortably normal. Unlike Garnet Eagle, it didn't seem to matter that Aja was an outsider. Port Anatya was so large it would be impossible for everyone to know each other, and not a single person appeared alarmed by her presence. In a strange way, she felt invisible. At the very least, she didn't stand out like a sore thumb.

It took her the better part of an hour to reach the docks, and by then her feet hurt and she was tired again. But at last, she made it to the first pier where one of the ships were docked. She could see that all four were still anchored, which was a relief.

She had four chances to find a ride to Mettain.

Along the pier, there were several fishermen yelling at people that passed by, demanding people buy their fresh fish that had been caught this morning. Some stopped, but most just walked by without even looking at them. Aja followed their example, and though it made her nervous, she hurried passed the fishermen shouting at her and went right up to the first large ship.

Burly workers in rough clothing were busy unloading cargo with long ropes and pulleys, and stepping around them so she wasn't in their way, she went up to a tall man who was standing on the dock observing his crew. "Excuse me?" she asked. He didn't look at her, and her face flushed with embarrassment. "Is this your ship?" she tried again. "I'm trying to—"

"No passengers," the man snapped, shooting her an irritated glare. "Fly off, chickie, you're interrupting our work."

This isn't going well, Aja thought, anxious at how abrasive he was. She didn't know if she should keep trying, or if she should just move on to the next one. Thinking of the pouch of money Jaqlai had left for her, she decided to try again. "It's very urgent that I make it to Mettain," she said, aware that her hands were fidgeting from her nervousness, but she couldn't seem to stop. "I can pay."

"I don't care if you have a pile of gold," the man's scowl deepened, and he waved a hand vigorously at her to back away. "We don't take passengers. Be off or I'll call the dockmaster and have you escorted away!"

Aja turned and walked swiftly away, too uncomfortable to even utter a goodbye. There was no way that ship would take her, and she didn't think she had the courage to try and bargain with a man that stern anyway. Slipping past the merchants, she walked up the pier and continued on to the next ship.

The second one was no better than the first, only this time the crew laughed at her for even asking for a spot on their ship. They didn't even give her a chance to offer money, just jeered at her for trying to book passage while "looking like that." She wasn't sure how she looked in their eyes. Was it because her hair was tangled and they could tell? Or were they laughing at her Scorian clothing? It didn't matter what their reasons were, Aja left feeling humiliated and discouraged. She didn't even want to go to the next two, now.

Slyen sent me on a mission that's too hard for me, she thought miserably, moving slowly on toward the next ship. *How am I supposed to manage this by myself? It's not fair.* She was tired, cold, and her feet ached. And now she was hungry again. Maybe she should just turn around and go back to the embassy and give up on this whole venture. Maybe there was another way to get to Mettain.

She came to a stop on the third pier, watching the crew unload their cargo onto the dock. It was another crew of vastly diverse people, working hard and yelling at each other over the din of the fish merchants. The man directing them had very dark skin and short curly hair, a gold earring in one ear, and a voice that was so familiar that she found herself rooted in place, trying to recall where she heard it. Then he turned, and she caught sight of his face.

It was Emrin.

Andrus

Seeing the face of someone so familiar was astounding to Aja, considering how far away from home she was. Of all people to run into, it was Emrin! Her friend, the Zyphan engineer who was always drawing in his sketchbook, shirking his duties so he could come to Aja's garden to talk to her.

How was he here? *Why* was he here?

All her discouragement and humiliation were forgotten as she rushed toward him, and with her heart full of longing, she reached out a hand and touched his arm. "Emrin?" she asked. "Is it really you?"

The man turned in surprise when she touched him, and suddenly she saw that although he looked nearly exactly like him, this man could not be Emrin. Emrin had green-brown eyes that always caught the light and reminded Aja of the forest. This man's eyes were a dark, deep brown. No green.

Aja pulled her hand back, suddenly embarrassed as he stared her up and down without recognition. "I'm sorry," she said quickly. "I thought…"

"Wait!" the man blurted, reaching out and snatching her hand in his. His palm was heavily calloused, another indicator that this was not Emrin. As he stared at her face, his eyes were wide and intense, and his expression was almost anxious. "Don't go. You called me Emrin, didn't you?"

"It was a mistake, I'm sorry," she insisted, growing alarmed. *He won't let go of my hand.*

He tightened his grip, a strange look crossing his face. "Come with me a moment," he urged. "I want to talk to you." He began to pull her toward the ship.

"I really should go," Aja tried to say, but they were already down the dock toward the plank that bridged the gap between the dock and his ship. At first, she thought that she was in danger, and she almost screamed for help. But when she caught sight of his profile, of the worry in his eyes and the tension in his jaw, she was reminded so much of Emrin that she couldn't bring herself to resist. He led her so swiftly that all it took was a few seconds for her to find herself up on the deck of the ship, through a door with a round window, into the captain's cabin.

The man closed the door behind him, standing between it and her as though to block her way. It was then that Aja realized she probably *should* be afraid.

"You know Emrin," the man accused, his eyes just as wide as when she put her hand on his arm. "How? How do you know my brother?"

"Your brother?" Aja asked, shrinking back from him. She was contemplating how to escape such a small room with only one door, when his words finally made sense in her mind. "Wait," she blurted, "Emrin is your brother?"

"My twin brother," the man scowled. "And you haven't answered me. How do you know my brother?"

To Aja's bafflement, tears suddenly sprang to her eyes. She couldn't understand where they came from, or why her heart felt so tight. And then it hit her.

Home. Emrin reminded her of home.

"He is my friend," she said, emotion making her throat tight, and her words strained. "He comes to my garden to talk, and to show me his drawings." She was surprised when her eyes filled up with tears, and her shoulders shook with a small sob. *Why are you crying?* she thought in frustration. *This man isn't Emrin, you're embarrassing yourself.*

Emrin's brother seemed to grow anxious at her tears, and he reached a hand awkwardly toward her as if to console her, only to drop it by his side again. "Don't cry," he urged, clearing his throat. "I wasn't… I didn't mean to scare you. It's just that you *can't* know Emrin, not unless…" he straightened with a jolt, eyes going wide again. "Garden?" he blurted. "You—what's your name?"

"Aja," she answered, wiping her eyes with her long sleeve. "What is yours?" *Can I trust you?* she wondered, and her heart ached again. *Is it wrong for me to feel glad to see you in this unfamiliar place?*

Amazement filled his face, and exhaling a long breath, he said, "So *you're* Aja. How the blazes did you get all the way over here? What are you *doing* here?"

He says that like he knows who I am, but how can that be possible? she thought, frowning at his words. "You didn't tell me your name," she accused. "How do you know me?"

"Sorry," he said quickly, looking embarrassed. "My name is Andrus. Please, come sit down and let me get you something to eat. Do you like wine? We don't have anything fancy to offer you, just wine, bread, and some cheese. Well, and meat. But if you're from *there*, you don't eat meat, do you?"

He walked past her into the center of the room, gesturing toward an oval table that had four chairs bolted to the floor around it. He gestured to one, smiling somewhat nervously. His smile was so much like Emrin's, only without the dimple on his left cheek. "You didn't say how you knew me," Aja reminded him. She *was* hungry, and the prospect of eating something a bit more substantial than fruit and pastries appealed to her. Stiff with wariness, she made her way to the table and sat in the chair he offered her. *At least I have access to the door again,* she thought.

Andrus went around to the other side of the room. He stopped at a cabinet built into the wall and pulled out a square loaf of bread wrapped in a towel, as well as a round of cheese. When he set them on the table, he went to the other side of the room to take a bottle of wine from a secure rack. "I'll tell you everything," he reassured her, "but a story is best accompanied by wine."

Perhaps to some people, Aja thought. She wouldn't refuse the wine, but she wouldn't drink much of it. The kind that her people made was rich and bitter, made from the bitter plums that grew in the valley. She had learned from Emrin that Zyphans drank wine made from grapes.

When he had finished uncorking the bottle and pouring them both a half-glass in silver goblets, he handed one to her and went to take a seat on the opposite side of the table. "A toast," he said, lifting his goblet. "To meeting new friends."

Is that what we are? Aja wondered, though she lifted her own glass accordingly.

"Cheers," Andrus said, clanking his goblet against hers. He downed a large swallow and set it on the table with a satisfied sigh. "Good stuff," he commented. "Querian wine is some of the best you can get."

Taking a much smaller sip, Aja was surprised by how different it tasted from the wine she was used to. Light and sweet, with a mellow flavor of fruit blended with an almost oaky finish. She liked it much better than she expected to, but she knew how alcohol could mute one's senses. It was best not to drink too much. After another small sip, she set her silver glass down. "How do you know who I am?" she asked.

"Well," Andrus said, taking a deep breath. He unwrapped the bread and began to cut two rather thin slices. "Emrin is my twin, younger by seven minutes. We both entered the military after school, though in different departments. He became an engineer, and I joined the navy. Both of us got assigned to posts that require a lot of secrecy, things we can't even tell each other. All the same, there are *some* things we are allowed to say, and we write to each other all the time."

Aja listened with a divided focus, so hungry at the smell of the bread that she was finding it difficult to pay attention. Andrus paused his story to place the bread on wooden plates, then began to cut thick slices of cheese from the round. "You write to each other?" she asked.

"Often, yes," Andrus nodded. He dropped the slices of cheese on their plates and pushed one across the table to Aja. "We can send messages every 90 minutes if we choose to, though it's better if we don't. I'd say we write about once a month these days. Anyway," he paused to put the cheese on the bread and took a large bite. "Emrin's told me a few things about where he's stationed. How beautiful it is, how peaceful it is, and how his work is going. But the thing he writes the most about," he pointed at her with his bread and cheese, cracking an amused smile, "is a pretty, young gardener named Aja."

"He writes about me?" Aja asked, baffled. "I can't imagine there's even anything to write about." Her cheeks flushed as she said this, and she wondered why she felt embarrassed. Why did her heart skip a beat in happiness when she heard that? *Does Emrin really write about me that much?* A nervous thought crossed her mind. What exactly did he say about her?

Andrus stared at her with a skeptical look, only to shake his head and sigh a moment after. "Clueless," he muttered. "Poor Emrin."

Aja flushed deeper, suddenly recalling her mother's words. *"He spends more time here than anywhere else. He probably likes you."* Hastily picking up her food, Aja took a bite in an attempt to disguise her embarrassment. She found that the bread was quite tough, which must be why he cut it so thin. The cheese was wonderful though, and it paired surprisingly well with the wine.

"So, you know my side of the story," Andrus cleared his throat after another swallow from his goblet. "I know of you from my brother. My question is, what are you doing way out here looking like you're starved half to death?"

Is that how I look? She wondered, not surprised but still disappointed. *More importantly, what am I supposed to say?* "I can't tell you," she answered hesitantly. "Only that it's important, and it's… about the war." Was that saying too much?

Andrus raised an eyebrow, scrutinizing her carefully. "You're the one who lives with General Ryder," he said. It was not a question.

"Yes," Aja answered, her expression gravely serious. "And you can't tell anyone that I'm here—not even Emrin."

Andrus nodded, understanding crossing his face. "And you can't tell me anything else," he concluded, more to himself than to her.

"Only this," Aja set her food down and stared into his face with an earnest expression. "I *have* to go to Mettain. It's imperative I get there as soon as possible, so that I can return home before winter."

"Before?" Andrus laughed. "Winter is just about here! And this is no steam vessel," he gestured about the ship with his hand. "It's a Querian style, for reasons I can't get into. But while we're on the subject, there are things I can't talk about. Things *you* can't mention, either. You can't tell *anyone* how you know me or mention my brother outside of this cabin."

Aja got the sense that his secrets were related to the war, too. "I won't say anything," she assured him, a wry expression crossing her face. "I have no one to tell."

Andrus seemed satisfied with this, and he leaned back in his chair with a nod. "You're out of luck if you want to get to Mettain," he told her gravely. "They've closed their borders to all but their own ships. You can ask every captain that docks ship in Anatya for passage, but not a single one will take you."

"Can *you* take me?" Aja asked. Finding Andrus was a stroke of luck she could hardly believe. If he didn't take her, no one would.

"Did you hear what I just said?" Andrus scowled. "They've closed their borders. We wouldn't even be allowed to dock, not without a letter from the embassy at the very least!"

"The Vedlyran Embassy?" Aja asked. She straightened as an idea came to her. "What if… I could get one?"

"One what?" Andrus devoured the rest of his bread and cheese, chasing it down with the last of his wine.

"A letter," Aja said. "From the embassy, with permission to dock in Mettain."

Andrus laughed again. He wiped his mouth, slammed his goblet on the table, and leaned forward over his arm. "Alright I'll bite," he said with a grin. "Just how do you think you'll swing that?"

Aja threw on a brave smile, feigning confidence she didn't quite feel. "Humor me a moment," she said. "If I were in a position to get such a letter from the embassy, would you be willing to take me to Mettain? I can pay you." She pulled out the pouch of coins and bills that Jaqlai had left for her, setting it on the table.

Andrus's smile turned skeptical as he swiped the pouch and opened it. His eyebrows lifted in surprise. "Do you even know how much this is?" he demanded. He sighed and closed it, shaking his head before Aja could answer. "Your people don't even use currency; they barter goods and services with each other. Did you think I wasn't aware? Emrin may not be able to tell me too many details about his work, but he *does* tell me about the valley."

Aja felt a little like a child being scolded by an adult, and she scowled at him in response. "Would you be willing or not?" she demanded. "Remember, it's imperative that I get to Mettain by whatever means necessary."

"It's not hard to guess why," Andrus replied wryly. He slid the pouch across the table at her, grabbed the bottle of wine, and refilled his goblet. "The Vedlyrans believe what the Querians told them, that Zypha is at fault for certain trade disputes. They believe that *we're* the ones instigating a war out of greed. Utter bilge—" he cut himself off abruptly, clearing his throat. "Er... I mean... utter nonsense."

It reminded Aja of Emrin, and his way of checking his language around her. She couldn't imagine what else Andrus would have said, but she got the sense it was the kind of colorful wording she wouldn't much appreciate. *More importantly,* she thought, crossing her arms as curiosity grew inside her. *This is probably my best chance at learning more about the war and why it's happening. If I know more, maybe I'll be more effective at stopping it.* "But that's not the real reason, is it?" she asked.

"Of course not!" Andrus declared, taking a swig of wine and slamming the goblet on the table a second time. "Their ships have been pirating in our waters, stealing our cargos and sinking our vessels to make us more vulnerable, all while saying 'oh, it isn't us. These pirates aren't sanctioned.' When we've found letters of authorization on the ships we've managed to capture! They've already launched a war against *us*, and we're just making it official. It's unscrupulous, underhanded *bullying* and they've been getting away with it for years."

"Why would Mettain believe Queria over Zypha?" Aja asked. If they had proof of Queria's falsehood, why didn't they make it public? *Amazing how much I can learn now that I've left the valley,* she thought. It didn't make sense to her that the Zyphans would want to keep it secret, if they were only defending themselves. Did they trust the Slyens so little? *I know we've only known them almost seven months, but it still makes me feel a little sad,* she thought.

Ever since she had left the valley, people had been calling her Querian. Now, she wished they would think of her as Zyphan, instead.

"That's because of our history," Andrus crossed his arms, leaning back in his chair. "Because Mettain sided with the Kirilians when they were at war with us decades ago. Of course, that war is long over, and we're on good terms with Kirilian now. But that doesn't change how Mettain views us, if Queria, their ally, is whispering lies in their ear."

"So, let's say I can get a letter from the embassy," Aja said, folding her hands and leaning across the table to meet his eyes. "Would that be of use to you? Would you bring me to Mettain?"

Andrus mirrored her movements, smiling crookedly. "*If* you could pull something like that off—and let's be honest, there's no way you can—then sure. I'll take you to Mettain free of charge."

"Are you a man of your word, Andrus?" Aja demanded. She thought of the deal she had supposedly made with Jaqlai, and only now recalled that he had never agreed to it. "I'll think about it," he had said. She wasn't going to accept a half-hearted answer like *that* again.

"A Zyphan always is," Andrus said seriously. He held out his hand. "I'll shake on it."

Aja looked at his hand, then back at him. "Shake what?" she asked, confused. Did he want her pouch of coins, again?

To her surprise, Andrus laughed. He reached across the table and grabbed her hand, shaking it up and down twice. "Like this," he said with a grin. "It's how we make an agreement."

"Oh," she said, flushing. *I didn't know that,* she thought. "Then, alright," she lifted her chin with determination. "I'll head to the embassy right now and get that letter. So don't leave the port without me."

"Better get it before tomorrow morning," he snickered. "We prefer to leave with the tide."

Aja didn't understand what that meant and had no idea what time that would be. *But they can tell me at the embassy,* she thought. "Okay," she replied. "I'll be back."

"Good luck, Aja," he said, releasing her hand. "And take my advice… if you truly have the means to get a letter like that, then you ought to spend some of that money on some decent clothes. It will be windy and cold at sea, and wet, too. The Querians sell rain jackets in town. Ask for one." He reached out and snatched up her coin pouch, dug through it, and dropped four copper-colored coins on the table. "Don't spend over this much. If they act offended and say they won't sell to you, take the coins up and walk out."

"What, just walk out?" Aja asked, baffled.

Andrus grinned. "They'll stop you, don't worry. And you'll walk out with a nice new raincoat." He rose from the table and walked to the door, opening it for her. "Better get started. The shops don't stay open much longer."

"Alright," she answered, sliding out from the bolted-down chair and standing up swiftly. She walked out onto the deck, blinking when a gust of wet wind seemed to slap her in the face. It was nice and warm in the cabin, compared to the chill outside. "And thank you," she added, turning back. "I won't forget what we talked about."

"Neither will I," Andrus nodded. "Now get going. I don't have all day, either." He glanced over her head toward his crew, scowling. "HEY!" he yelled. "Don't think I don't have eyes and ears on every splinter of this ship. You think I don't know you're slacking?"

Aja left him to his work and carefully crossed the gangplank onto the dock again. It was strange how different her outlook was now, compared to when she first crossed it onto the ship. She had been nervous, scared, and disheartened. Now, she felt as though anything was possible, even getting a letter from the embassy. *I can do it,* she decided determinedly, her steps light as she walked swiftly up the dock towards the market. *I know I can.*

She saw two women walking on the street beside the docks, and hurried up to them and matched her pace to theirs. She knew that she would never find the shop she needed by herself and felt safer talking to them than one of the fishermen hawking their catches. "Excuse me," she said quickly. "I need to buy a rain jacket. Where do I go for that?"

Both women were surprised when she spoke to them, but after they looked her up and down and noticed her Scorian clothing, they relaxed at once. "You'll want the shopping district," one replied with a smile. "That's up the hill four blocks, and then take a right. There's a whole street lined with clothing shops there."

"Up this street, then take a right?" Aja clarified, gesturing toward the one beside her. It wasn't the one she had come down on, so she didn't want to get lost. *I wonder what a block is,* she thought, her confidence faltering somewhat. *Do I ask?*

"Yes, this one," the woman nodded. "When you reach the fourth intersection, take a right. You can't miss it." Excusing herself with a smile, she and her companion kept walking.

"That surprised me," the second woman said, her voice hushed. She whispered something else, but by then she was too far away for Aja to overhear.

I surprised myself, Aja admitted, turning down the road they had indicated and walking up the hill. *Talking to strangers is difficult, but it was the best idea I could come up with.* She turned around, glancing back at the water and the ships with tall sails. It was hard to believe she would be riding on one of those, tomorrow. What would it be like? Should she worry about food and water? Jaqlai had called the ocean a desert of water. *And I suppose that's why I need the rain jacket.*

Facing the hill once more, she counted each time the road intersected with another, and turned at the fourth one.

Finding the shops was easier than Aja had expected. They had large windows opening out to the streets, and featured their items in window displays to catch the eyes of passersby. She didn't spend long looking around, although many shops had stunning dresses she had never seen anything like before. And after choosing a shop with cloaks and jackets in their window, she walked in and asked for a rain jacket. Just as Andrus had warned her, they tried to sell it to her for nine sterling, an amount that had little meaning to her. She took out the four coins he had shown her, set them on the counter, and said she wouldn't pay more than that.

The shopkeeper loudly complained he couldn't possibly sell it for less than six, so she took up her coins and walked for the door. "Now hold on a moment," he called, "there's no need to get hasty!" He beckoned her back in with a friendly smile. "Let's talk." A few minutes later, she ended up walking out with a brand-new coat, sold for four sterling.

It was evening when she finally made her way back to the embassy. She had gotten lost trying to find her way, and in the end, one of the city guards found her wandering and offered to lead her to an inn. "I'm trying to find the Vedlyran Embassy," she said, shivering slightly. Now that the sun had set, the wind was bitterly cold and wet, and she missed the warm cloak that she had left behind at the embassy.

"The embassy?" the guard frowned, glancing to the north. Aja could only assume the embassy was in that direction. "Why do you want to go there? Aren't you with the Scorian caravan that stopped in this morning?"

"No, I'm from Garnet Eagle," Aja answered hastily, not wanting to explain more than that. She hoped he would just accept the response and not ask further. "Actually, I'm supposed to meet someone at the embassy, but I got lost after shopping. Can you show me there?"

"This is the residential district," the guard offered a wry smile. "Is this your first time in Port Anatya?"

"Yes," Aja offered a nervous laugh. "Is it that obvious?" *Please just show me the way.*

To her great relief, he began to walk north and gestured with his hand. "I'll show you to the embassy. It's near the gate, in the business district."

Residential, business, shopping... the city seems to be divided into sections based on themes, she thought, fascinated. *It makes sense in a place as large as this. If only there were signs posted that told me how to find things.* She fell into step beside him, wishing she had thought to buy herself new shoes while she was at the shops. Her canvas ones were worn from all the walking she had done, and they did little to protect her feet from the cold autumn air.

"Garnet Eagle," the guard said after a moment, stroking his beard with one hand. "Didn't your caravan already come through, last month?"

"Yes, of course," Aja replied, her heart beginning to race. What would she say if he questioned her further? Would he realize she wasn't from Scoria? What would she say if he kept asking her questions? Anxious to change the subject, she asked him the first thing that came to mind. "How long have you lived in Port Anatya? Do you like it here?"

"I was born and raised here," he answered, his tone proud. "Seen it grow, ever since they changed the seaborne trade routes. Used to be, Port Cheris was the major hub for trade and licensing. But all that changed when the earthquake happened. They've had to shift a lot of things up here to Anatya, so the city has grown a lot larger in just ten years."

"Do you miss when it was smaller?" Aja asked, thinking of home. She couldn't imagine living in a place like this, full of people and shops and buildings separated into districts. It was intriguing to visit for a while, but she wouldn't want to live here. "It's smaller where I live," she said without thinking. "I miss that when I'm away."

"Scorians don't normally talk about their home to others," the guard replied, giving her a slightly narrowed look.

"Maybe I just miss home," Aja threw on a smile, meeting his eyes. It was true, if misleading.

He shrugged and turned back to watching the road, taking a left when they reached the next intersection. "I suppose I do miss it," he admitted. "But it's nice to see our city flourish. Ah, turn again here," he gestured toward the street up ahead, and turned right so they were heading north again. "So, who were you meeting at the embassy?"

His question seemed innocent enough, but his eyes were narrowed. Aja tried to reply as naturally as she could, unable to shake how nervous she felt. "I know a Vedlyran who is staying there," she said. "His name is Jaqlai. I hope he hasn't gotten worried about my being late and come out to look for me."

"There is a Vedlyran named Jaqlai in the city," the guard answered, nodding to himself. "Didn't know the Vedlyrans were on good terms with the Scorians."

Aja didn't answer, not knowing what to say to that. *I could cause suspicion if I say the wrong thing.* She glanced at him, trying to keep her face free from her worry. "Are we nearly there?"

"Just about," the guard nodded. He gestured ahead, and Aja looked forward at once. She caught sight of the embassy, a building that looked like all the others except for a sign hanging out front with a peculiar design painted on the weather-worn wood. It looked like a wreath of vines around a shield, emblazoned with the symbol of a crown. There were seven roses on the thorny vines.

Aja turned and placed her hand on the guard's arm, offering him her brightest smile. "Thank you so much," she said genuinely. "If you hadn't come along, I don't know what I might have done!"

"If you don't mind, I'll come in with you just to make sure you're alright," the guard replied, offering her a smile in return. Although Aja wasn't sure whether he was doing it because he was worried about her, or if he wanted to verify her story.

"That's just fine," Aja answered right away. And it was. They were probably expecting her. *Unless Cait is there instead of Mikail,* she thought, recalling how jealous Cait had acted around her.

They walked up to the door together, and the guard opened it for her so she could walk through, letting it close on its own behind them. Aja shivered when she stepped in, adjusting to the much warmer temperature inside, and then came to a stop in the entryway, astounded.

There, leaning against the desk with his tail jerking side to side in frustration, was Jaqlai.

"What do you mean *you don't know where she is?*" Jaqlai demanded. He was standing with his back toward the door, and hadn't seemed to notice the two of them coming in. "You were supposed to be taking care of her! Has she eaten anything? Did you tell her where to go? She's probably lost out there right now!"

Mikail stood on the other side of the desk, a patient expression on his face, though his ears were angled backwards slightly, showing his irritation. He glanced over Jaqlai's shoulder and saw Aja standing there with a dumbfounded expression and cleared his throat.

Jaqlai turned angrily, only to freeze when he caught sight of her. Relief flashed across his face as he walked toward her. "Aja!" he blurted, placing his hands on her shoulders and studying her, as though he was looking for something. "Are you alright? Where have you been?"

The guard came up from behind her, stroking his beard. "Seems your friend was waiting for you after all," he remarked. He bowed his head slightly and gestured toward the door. "I should get back to my route. Good evening."

"Thank you," Aja said again, trying to smile and finding it difficult. She was too stunned to know what to do with herself. Part of her was filled with relief to see Jaqlai standing there like he hadn't left her behind this morning. Then it occurred to her that she was angry. She waited until the guard had left and the door swung closed behind him before she spoke. "You left me," she accused.

Jaqlai grimaced apologetically. "I had to leave extremely early if I was going to catch a ship, and I didn't want to wake you," he said. "Did you get my note?"

Aja still had it in the pocket of her long-sleeved dress. "You mean this letter?" she demanded, pulling it out. She draped her new rain jacket over one arm so she could easily reach it and scowled at him. "Oh, I got it, after you were long gone. Why wouldn't you just wake me up if you were going to leave? I thought we had an agreement."

He sighed, his ears flicking to the sides once. She wasn't sure what emotion that signified. "Can we talk in private?" he asked.

"Fine," Aja replied icily. When Jaqlai turned and headed for the hallway, she followed him. They made their way silently to the room Cait had shown them to last night, and after entering, Aja went to stand by the window with her arms still crossed. *He's here,* she thought, relieved despite her anger. *He didn't leave. He was worried about me. But why? Did he change his mind?*

Jaqlai closed the door. "Aja," he said seriously. "I'm sorry I left without waking you up. I was worried about your health after being in the desert so long, and I thought taking you on a ship with me might kill you. It would be better for you to rest and regain your strength, and I was afraid you wouldn't take no for an answer. I didn't have time to discuss it, so I left quietly. Just as I said in my letter, I left the money with you so that you wouldn't be stranded here."

Aja remembered what Andrus had said earlier, how she looked starved. Her stomach grumbled to emphasize the point. *He left because he was worried?* she thought, chewing her bottom lip without replying. *Still, that doesn't change what we discussed.* "What about our deal?" she asked. She opened the letter in her hand, reading through it again. *So that's what he meant by rest and recover?* she thought, her anger dissipating. He hadn't been abandoning her. He was worried about her.

"I didn't think I was breaking it," Jaqlai insisted. "You would have had time to rest and recover your strength, and money to get where you wanted to go. Meanwhile, I don't have time to waste. I have to get to Mettain *now*. That's why I left early this morning to try and catch one of the ships before they left."

"So?" Aja asked, lifting her chin. "What changed your mind?"

Sighing, Jaqlai walked toward the bed and sat down at the edge of the mattress. "I didn't change my mind," he admitted wryly. "None of the ships would take me. It's safe to say, no ship is going to risk going to Mettain, even with a Vedlyran on board." He rubbed his face with his hand. "Mettain has closed its borders, and the Querians are preparing for war. That's why I came back here to talk to you."

I know a ship that will take us, she thought, though she didn't say it out loud. A plan was forming in her mind, an agreement she hoped she would have better luck with this time. "I have to go to Mettain," she said.

"So do I," Jaqlai shot her a regretful look. "But I'm afraid I can't wait for a Vedlyran ship to make port. I have to leave now." He glanced out the window toward the sea, his eyes grim. "That's why I'm going to head there along the coast on foot. There's a chance I can meet up with a Vedlyran ship in Port Cheris, if I get there quick enough. And that means I *can't* take you with me. I'm sorry, but your best bet is to wait here and recover and take a Vedlyran ship when one arrives. I think one is scheduled to arrive in three weeks."

"I can't wait that long," Aja shook her head.

"And I can't take you with me," Jaqlai insisted. "Look, Aja I understand what you're trying to do, but I'm afraid I can't help you any more than I already have."

Aja turned to look out the window, unable to tell which ship was Andrus's from here. "Let's make another deal," she said. "If you promise me not to tell your superiors about my island, I'll find us a ship that can take us both out tomorrow morning."

"That's literally impossible," Jaqlai made a face. "What would be the point of that deal?"

"It's important to me, Jaqlai," Aja insisted, walking towards him. She sat down on the other side of the bed, leaning on the mattress with her hand. "I understand you have to tell your superiors about the war, but you don't have to tell them about my valley. Tell them the Zyphans plan to attack from the Uliah River with their steam ships. Leave my valley out of it. If you do that, I swear to you that I'll find us a ship. All I need is your word." She paused, then added, "and a letter of permission to dock in Mettain, from the embassy."

"I already got a letter of permission," Jaqlai said, shaking his head. "It meant very little. Mettain won't let them land, and the Querians won't risk their ships being fired on by our navy."

"Just trust me," Aja pleaded. "Or don't, it doesn't matter. If it really is impossible, you have nothing to lose by making this deal with me. If I can't get a ship, then you can walk to Mettain or Port Cheris or wherever you want and leave me behind. And if I can get one, then you get there faster, and all you have to do is leave my valley out of your report."

"Aja," Jaqlai sighed. "I can't make that deal."

"Why not?" Aja demanded. "What do you have to lose?"

He frowned, his ear flicking once. For a moment he just stared at her, thinking in silence. Then his eyes strayed toward the window, gazing out at the sea. "IF you can get a ship tomorrow morning at dawn," he said. "And that's a very big if—then I'll make that deal with you."

Aja held out her hand the same way Andrus did on the ship. "Shake on it," she said. "Bring that letter of permission down to the dock, promise you won't mention Slyenials to your superiors, and I give you my word that I'll get us a ship."

Rubbing his face once more with his hand, Jaqlai struggled internally with his thoughts. At last, he shook his head and grasped her hand. "Fine, it's a deal," he said. "I'll wake you up before dawn to get down to the docks, so you'd better eat and sleep now while you can."

Her stomach grumbled in agreement, and she flushed. She shook his hand awkwardly up and down twice, then rose from the bed. "It's a deal," she agreed. "Don't you dare break it."

"I won't," he said, grimacing slightly. "I know it's impossible, anyway. I'd rather you didn't get your hopes up, but if this is the only way to convince you, then I'll play along." He blinked when Aja's stomach grumbled again. "Let's… go get something to eat."

"Yes," Aja agreed, pressing a hand to her stomach, laughing nervously. She tossed her rain jacket onto the bed, not wanting to carry it down with her while she was eating.

"Did you buy that today?" he asked, glancing at it. "Not a bad purchase in this area." He hesitated, glancing at her nervously. "How much did you pay for it?"

"Four sterling," she said. She pulled out the pouch of money and handed it back to him.

He shook his head and wouldn't take it. "You're still going to need that, after I leave tomorrow."

"And you're going to need it after I get us that ship," she quipped back at him.

Jaqlai cracked a wry smile as he headed for the door. "We will see," he answered.

Aja nodded with a smile. "We will," she agreed.

The *North Wind*

It was dark and cold, and everywhere Aja looked there was only the deep black of night and a perfectly flat horizon in all directions. The sight of it was unnerving, enough to drive her anxiety to all new heights. But the worst part wasn't the darkness, the cold, or even the flat horizon. It was the horrible feeling of being watched, as though a great lidless eye had turned toward her from somewhere deep below. Her ears ached with pressure reminiscent of Jaqlai's Influence, and a gust of wet wind blew on her face.

"I don't want to be here," Aja said, trying to withdraw from the utterly black emptiness around her. "Stop watching me. Stop!"

And yet the more the watching darkness pressed in, the greater her urgency to be free of it. She must overcome her fear. Everything depended on it.

"Aja," Jaqlai's voice whispered, and she felt a warm hand touch her shoulder. Turning, she suddenly found herself lying in bed, gazing upward to see Jaqlai leaning over her. "It's time," he said. "We have to be at the docks before dawn."

I'm at the embassy, Aja thought, relief washing over her so strongly that she shuddered. She sat up and looked around her, noticing that outside the window it was still completely dark. *The sun is still far from rising. Is that why I dreamt about darkness and water?*

"You need to hurry," Jaqlai urged. He handed her a satchel; one she had bought from the embassy at his suggestion and stored all of her belongings in. He had his own bag over his shoulder, which she had seen him packing a fresh set of clothes and a packet of bound notes. She was curious about what was written in them but hadn't had the courage to ask.

"You have the letter?" Aja inquired, rising to her feet. She had gone to bed in her clothes so she would be ready to leave the moment she woke up. Taking up her rain jacket, she slipped her arms through the sleeves and fastened the clever zipper in the front. It was much easier than buttons would have been, and the shop owner had assured her it would keep out the rain much better. Not having seen a zipping garment before, Aja was fascinated by it.

Jaqlai handed her a cloth napkin wrapped around something, nodding. "The letter is in my bag," he answered. "Here, eat this while we walk. I had Cait prepare them for us."

At the mention of Cait, Aja wondered to herself if the woman had been upset to learn Aja was going with Jaqlai to Mettain. Perhaps Jaqlai hadn't told her, since he didn't believe it was possible. Hanging her bag on her shoulder, she opened the napkin to find a thick puffed pastry stuffed with cheese. It smelled heavenly, and her mouth was watering the moment she saw it. "Thank you," she said, and took a bite.

"I made sure yours doesn't have meat in it," Jaqlai said with a smile. He headed for the door and gestured for her to follow, and then led the way quietly down the stairs. Aja was amazed at how his steps were perfectly soundless, while hers made the floorboards creak. How could he manage that, when he was taller and heavier than she was?

They were too tired for conversation, so they munched on their breakfast as they headed down the hill for the docks. The air was damp and cold, and Aja found herself wishing she was wearing her cloak under the rain jacket. It was so much warmer than the lightweight fabric her jacket was made from.

After they had been walking for several minutes, Aja realized the sky was beginning to grow lighter. The stars were still visible high in the sky, but closer to the horizon they became fainter until they couldn't be seen at all. Now that dawn was approaching, she could see that there were only three ships docked at the port; one of them had already set sail. Even though she knew it shouldn't be Andrus's ship, she still felt an unsettled feeling in her stomach. He wouldn't leave her behind, would he?

"Looks like we only have three chances," Jaqlai said, breaking the quiet of the early morning. He nodded toward the ship sailing out of the bay.

"I only need one," Aja said, folding her empty napkin up and sticking it into her jacket pocket.

"I wish I had your confidence," Jaqlai chuckled. He was quiet for a little while longer, and then turned to glance at her with a worried expression on his face. "You need rest," he said. "And food. The desert was hard on you."

It was hard, she thought, and for some reason it filled her with relief to have it acknowledged. "Can I rest on the ship?" she asked. "You said the ocean is a desert, too. Will it be just as difficult?"

"*If* we get a ship," Jaqlai said cautiously, "then you must try to rest as much as you can. It won't be as hard physically, since we won't have to walk long distances, but there are other factors that will make it difficult. Some people can't stand being cooped up in a small space for a long time, and they go stir crazy. It might be hard mentally for you." He paused, glancing over his shoulder up the hill. "And when we don't get one," he added, his voice quiet, "please stay and rest at the embassy."

"If we don't get a ship, I promise," Aja said. His words about the ocean reminded her of her dream, of the flat horizon all around her, and she shivered. "Well, at least I'll have a friend to talk to," she ventured, glancing up at him. Even though the light was dim, she could see his face well enough to tell that he had shaved. When had he done that? While she was sleeping? *Did he even sleep at all?*

Jaqlai laughed under his breath. "You're more optimistic than I am. I'm just sorry your hopes are in vain. We won't find a ship that will take us, and that's a fact."

Soon they arrived at the docks, and Aja walked right past the first ship without stopping to look at it. Jaqlai kept pace with her, looking at her curiously. "I don't like the look of that one," she said, smiling faintly. The next dock was empty, and at last she came to Andrus's ship. Here, she turned, walking right up to the gangplank. Several sailors were loading cargo using a pully system, preparing the vessel to cast off.

"Don't you think we should ask for the captain before we trespass on their ship?" Jaqlai asked under his breath, frowning and looking around himself defensively. He stayed close by Aja's side, his tail twitching as it swished from side to side. When the sailors lifted the gangplank and stowed it, his ears shot up in alarm. "Wait," he said. "What's…"

Aja didn't have time to reply, for at that moment Andrus walked up to them. "Look at you, right on time. I hope you brought a letter," he grinned, raising his eyebrows when he saw she was not alone. "I didn't know you'd be bringing a Vedlyran *with* you."

"You need a letter of permission, right?" Aja asked, her tone confident. She could feel Jaqlai gazing at her in amazement, but she didn't look his direction. "We'll need to take him if we want it." She presented him with her hand. "This is Jaqlai, my travel companion. Jaqlai, this is Captain Andrus."

Andrus shook his head with a sigh. "I guess I can't argue with that. Hmm." He crossed his arms and glanced over his shoulder, looking towards the cabin. "Well, I fixed up a private cabin for you just in case you pulled this off, but I don't have anywhere for your buddy to stay." He looked at Jaqlai with a firm stare. "You'll be bunking with the crew, and I expect you to pull your weight. I've budgeted enough for *one* extra mouth to feed, but not two. Think you can handle that?"

"I can handle it," Jaqlai answered. He shot Aja a sidelong glance, ears still lifted in surprise. "So… you'll take us to Mettain?"

Behind them, the sailors were already raising the anchor and unfurling the sails. Andrus slapped Jaqlai's shoulder twice, hard enough to make him wince. "Do you have that letter?" he shot back. "I'll take that now so I can keep it with my docking license."

Jaqlai fished through his pack and pulled it out, handing it over at once.

Andrus snatched the letter, grinning with a pleased look. He gestured to them both, walking toward the cabin.

"Come on, I'll show you the bunks. Hope you have everything you need, because we're leaving with the tide. Welcome aboard the *North Wind*."

The ship rocked on the water as they pushed off from the pier, and Aja swayed unsteadily. *Is this what it feels like to float on water?* she thought, stretching out her arms to catch her balance. Jaqlai caught her hand and held her up, then let go when she was steady. As the two of them followed him, he leaned over and murmured in a low voice in Aja's ear. "How'd you do it? How did you convince them, when they wouldn't even meet with me, yesterday?"

Grateful for his help, Aja righted herself and walked more carefully, trying to get used to the swaying back and forth. "I guess I'm just lucky," she responded, and she didn't feel like that was an exaggeration. Finding Andrus was a stroke of luck she would never even think to ask for. It almost felt like Slyen was still looking out for her, even this far away from her valley. "Remember," she added, scowling up at him. "We had a deal."

Jaqlai smiled back at her wryly. "We have a deal," he agreed. "This is a whole lot better than having to walk to Mettain, and I don't go back on my word."

"This is the captain's cabin," Andrus said, coming to a halt by the door he took Aja through when they first met. "Any time you need, you are welcome to take refuge here for a spell." He looked only at Aja when he said this. "Your cabin is back this way." He walked down a flight of stairs opposite his cabin, into the hold of the ship. "The mess is in there," he pointed, indicating a long narrow room along the side of the ship with several tables built into the curved wall, and benches lining their sides. "Your cabin is here."

Aja's room was small enough to have been a closet, with a single bunk attached to the wall beside a circular window, a short cupboard with a mirror hung over it, and a lantern hanging from the ceiling. It didn't look like the kind with oil or candles; it had a strange bulb of glass in the center of it. "How does that work?" she asked, pointing at it. It was unlit, and she didn't know how to turn it on.

"You hang it in your window during the day so it can charge in the sunlight," Andrus answered, taking it down and showing her a switch on the bottom of it. "Then if you need it at night, you push this sideways to turn it on. The light isn't very strong, and it doesn't last very long, but it doesn't cause fires. Standard practice in Queria."

She nodded, wondering how different the Zyphan steam ships would be. She slid her bag off her shoulder and set it on the bed, glancing curiously at the captain as he hung the lantern back in its spot. "Where will Jaqlai be staying?"

"With the crew, down below," Andrus said. "I'll show you that next." He walked swiftly down the narrow hallway to the stairs which were so steep it was almost more of a ladder than a stair. Down in the belly of the ship, there were several bunks along the walls and hammocks in the center hanging from the ceiling. "This is where you're staying," he said, gesturing vaguely with his hand. "Ask someone in the crew which bunk to take. I think we have one or two spares, last I checked."

"I appreciate it," Jaqlai said. "I have a cousin in the navy, and I've been on a few ships. If you need me to work, I won't be a burden." He glanced at Aja briefly with a curious look. "Ah, I didn't discuss the trip fee…"

"Made a deal with the lady," Andrus jerked his head in her direction. "Said I'd take her for free if she could actually get a letter."

"Does that make my journey free as well?" Jaqlai's face was matter-of-fact, but his ears perked upwards with interest.

"If you're working, that isn't free," Andrus snickered. "I won't be paying you, but I expect you to pull your weight. Understand?"

"Easily," Jaqlai nodded. "Where should I go?"

"See the first mate on deck," Andrus said. "He'll know what to do with you. And you," he turned to Aja, eyeing her thoughtfully. He smirked when he saw the rain jacket, nodding his head in approval. "You still look like a starved rat. Get up to the cabin, I'll give you something to munch on."

Aja lost her balance when a large wave slapped the side of the ship, rocking it heavily. Catching herself against the wall with her hand, she offered a nervous smile. "Thanks," she said.

She couldn't help noticing that neither Andrus nor Jaqlai had any trouble keeping their balance. *Well, he's got that tail,* she thought, watching it shift and flick every now and then with each sway.

Andrus led them back upstairs, and Aja found herself breathing a little easier. It was stuffy down in the hold and smelled like salt and wet wood. Despite the wind being cold, and the spray of water on her face from the waves, she was grateful for the wind.

"Jerid!" Andrus yelled, startling her. "Got you a fresh new pair of hands!" he grinned, slapping Jaqlai's back and shoving him toward the deck where several sailors were pulling ropes and adjusting sails. "Put 'em to work, will you?"

"Sir," the first mate, Jerid, called back dryly.

Jaqlai shot Aja a slightly worried glance, then turned and headed for the first mate. She felt the briefest pressure from his Influence and got the feeling he was trying to tell her something. But she found herself led by the hand to Andrus's cabin before she could decipher what it was.

"Can I talk to you?" Andrus asked under his voice, glancing over his shoulder before ushering her through the door. When it was closed, he marched right to the cupboard and pulled out his round of cheese.

"Yes," Aja answered. The ship rocked while she was trying to walk toward the table, and she nearly fell against it. Wincing slightly, she slid into the closest chair and took a seat. *This is going to take some getting used to.*

Andrus plopped down across from her, cutting off a chunk of cheese with a dagger and handing it over. "Eat that," he ordered with a scowl. He didn't say anything else until she had taken a bite. "About the Vedlyran," he said, eyeing the door suspiciously. "It's risky bringing him on board. I understand it's the only way you could get a letter from the embassy, but I need to lay down a few rules."

Aja nibbled her cheese, feeling slightly sick to her stomach by the swaying of the ship. "Such as?" she wondered.

"As far as he can know, we're a Querian ship, with a Querian crew. You got that?" Andrus demanded. He pointed at her with his dagger, almost threateningly. "If you so much as mention Zypha, I'll consider it a breach of trust."

"I won't say anything," Aja assured him. *I've already told him more than enough,* she reminded herself. *And look where that got me? I believe that he is a friend to me, and that he plans to honor our bargain, but there's no reason to tell him Andrus is Zyphan.*

"Secondly," he continued, "I need you to watch your back on this trip. You're one woman on a ship full of men, and I expect that can make tensions a bit tight. My men will follow my orders, but I don't plan on taking chances. If you so much as feel nervous, just come to my cabin and hide out in here. Understand? I've got your back."

Aja wasn't sure whether she felt relieved at his offer, or nervous about something happening now that he'd brought it up. "I'll do that," she said, glancing toward the door. *At least I feel safe around Jaqlai, too,* she thought. "How long will it take to get to Mettain?"

"Less than two weeks, anywhere between ten and twelve days," Andrus answered, beginning to clean his dagger with a cloth napkin. "The current runs south along the coast, though it's a bit far from land. You won't be able to see anything but open sea as far as your eyes can see." He frowned, giving her a thoughtful look. "You've probably never been on the ocean before, have you? The valley is up in the mountains, off the Uliah River, isn't it?"

"Yes," Aja nodded, nibbling another bite of cheese. "You can see the land on the other side of it, though it's too far away to make out any details. Could be mountains or trees along the shore, I don't know."

"The Uliah will become an ocean someday," Andrus predicted, cracking a half smile. "It's not a true river, after all."

"What do you mean?" Aja asked. It was no sea, it followed a curved path from east to west along the cliff's edge, with a current so powerful that no one could swim in it without drowning. The fact that Zyphan ships could sail *up* the river was nothing short of incredible.

"You ever seen a map of the continents?" Andrus asked. He jumped up from his chair and walked toward a cupboard with many narrow, square shelves. In each shelf was a rolled-up scroll of weather-proofed paper, and he pulled one out and brought it back. Rolling it out across the table, he stabbed his knife down on one corner to hold it in place and held the other end down with his hand. "This is your continent, Moglia. Here are the Slyen mountains, and the Uliah River—as it's called, though technically, it's not a river—just north of them. And beyond the river lies Silvanus, which used to be part of Moglia. See how it cuts the land in half?"

Aja did see, and she traced her fingers across the paper with awe. *This is where I live. Where I traveled. I can see everything.* There was Queria, to the southeast of Slyenials. Just south of the mountains was the narrow desert of Scoria, which was shaped like a crescent. And south of that, in a peninsula protected by a winding trail of mountains, were the Mettain Isles. *Where is Zypha?* she wondered, gazing left and right at the places she didn't know. North of Queria was a massive stretch of land called "Moglia," the same name as the continent. She didn't see Zypha anywhere on the map, until she began to look along the outer edges, in the water.

Then she found it. Far to the northwest was the island of Zypha.

"This river," Andrus continued, tapping the Uliah with his finger, "is actually the line between two tectonic plates." Aja's face must have shown her confusion, because he laughed and tried to explain. "Every part of the world is divided into sections called plates, and they move very slowly over time. This continent broke apart because two of those plates are moving away from each other, and what you call the River Uliah is just the sea rushing through the space left behind. Every year, Silvanus grows farther and farther away, though it's slow enough that we won't see any major changes in our lifetimes. Eventually, the current of the river will slow down, until only an ocean lies between Moglia and Silvanus."

"I didn't know," Aja murmured. She pointed at the edge of the map, which showed the beginnings of a land mass that wasn't named. "What is this area, here?"

"That's Kirilian," Andrus said. "Another continent to the south. It's a much colder land than ours, with snow all year long in some places."

She remembered him mentioning Kirilian, something about a conflict with Zypha. "That reminds me," she said, looking up at him. "Are you going to try to tell the Vedlyrans the truth about the war? Since we have a letter from the embassy?"

"That's the plan," Andrus yanked his dagger out of the map, sliding it into its holster on his belt. He rolled up the map tightly and returned it to its cubby. "I've been sanctioned to attempt it, if only so we can give Mettain our side of the story. They'll probably still choose to remain neutral in the conflict, but it's worth it for us to share the truth. It may change how Mettain handles things if Queria calls for their aid."

Aja didn't say that she hoped the war didn't start at all, because she didn't want to admit why she was really on her way to Mettain. Andrus would probably just try to convince her to go home. "I hope it goes well," she said honestly.

Andrus smiled wryly. "So do I." He jerked his head toward the door. "Why don't you go out and watch the sun rise? It's always a neat experience. This time of year, the sun rises in the northeast and sets in the northwest, which gives the sunrise some unique colors. It's a pretty sight to see; worth rising early for. Unless you'd rather go to your cabin and take a nap? You did wake up pretty early."

"I'll watch the sunrise," Aja said. She followed him to the door. "What will you be doing?"

"What I always do," he cracked a grin. "Captain the ship."

They walked out onto the deck, which was wet and slippery from the spray of the waves. The sky was a mix of blue and orange, with a line of yellow along the horizon. The sun had yet to rise, but Aja could tell that it was close. *He's right,* she thought, carefully walking to the edge of the ship and leaning against the railing. *It is a pretty sight to see.*

Salty water misted against her face, the breeze tousled her hair, and her rain jacket made a flapping noise against her body in the wind. The flat horizon was eerie all around her, but the deep blue of the ocean shining with the reflection of the sky was beautiful.

She could hardly believe that she was here, sailing south toward Mettain against the odds. *I did it,* she thought proudly. *I did this, all by myself.*

It felt good.

Patrel

Every day on the ship seemed exactly the same as the last. The sailors were always working, divided into night and day shifts. The wind was always blowing, and the waves were always rolling. And very quickly, Aja realized that as a passenger, she had absolutely nothing to do. Most of her time was spent either in the captain's cabin or her own, since it was cold on deck, and she always felt like she was in the way. Thankfully she grew used to the rocking side to side, so she was no longer falling over when she walked. But she was growing more miserable each day.

The food was unpleasant to eat—hard oat bread and pickles, for the most part—but between Jaqlai and Andrus, she was forced to eat her fill at every meal. "You look like a starved rat," Andrus would say. While Jaqlai went for a different approach. "You need to regain your strength," he would plead. She didn't like the "tack," the oat bread with dried nuts and fruit, and she tolerated the pickled vegetables. But by far, the worst was the soup. It was watery and flavorless, with only two major ingredients—potatoes and beans.

It was the fourth day since they set out, and Aja had had her fill of wandering along the deck, pouring over maps in Andrus's cabin, or sleeping in her bunk. She was bored and restless, and she felt unsettled by the water surrounding them on all sides. She had to do *something*.

"But what?" she asked herself. She was alone in her cabin, lying on her back in bed and staring up at the wood ceiling. As boring as it was to be in here, she felt safer surrounded by walls than by water. *Ironic,* she thought with a grimace, *because my cabin is in a part of the ship that is nearly under water.* She could always hear it, sloshing against the side of the ship, and see it splashing against her window. Most of the time this section of the ship was above the water line, but whenever large waves slapped against the side, her window would show her cabin fully submerged.

There was absolutely nothing to see in the water. Nothing but deep blue leading down into black, and the white froth of saltwater in the waves.

"It is a desert, I understand that now," she sighed. "A desert, not because it's hot, but because there is nothing. No fresh water, no animals or birds, not even insects." The way the rationed water tasted was the hardest part. It was always stale, like the barrels it was stored in, but she craved each cup she was given. *I should stop thinking about water, or I'll make myself thirsty,* she thought. She rolled onto her side, staring out the window.

Splash, slosh. Splash, slosh. The waves rolled against the side of the ship. It had been difficult to sleep the first couple nights, but now she found it soothing to listen to.

Abruptly, Aja sat up. *Listening!* she thought. *Why didn't I think of that before?*

It had always been something to do, when she was daydreaming in her garden at home. Something that gave her peace and a sense of security, because it allowed her to be more aware of her surroundings. Baffled at herself for not remembering it till now, she closed her eyes and lay back down on her bed, opening her ears and senses to everything around her.

The waves. The sound of ropes being pulled, orders being yelled across the wind, and sailors singing shanties. The longer she *Listened,* the more she could hear. The cook was in the mess, cutting potatoes for their nightly soup. Andrus was on the deck, pacing back and forth with a loud stomp that reminded her of General Ryder.

And somewhere far away, she heard the sounds of whistles and clicks. Bizarre sounds she had no name for, as though someone were calling out through the water in a language she couldn't understand.

What is it? she thought, baffled. *Where is it coming from?* She tried to reach out further and was astounded at all the sounds coming from below her. *In the water?* Aja's breath quickened with excitement. The ocean wasn't empty at all—there were living things in the water! Fish and creatures she had never seen were calling out to one another with joyful sounds.

"Look larboard!" one of the sailors called overhead. "Dolphins!"

The clicks and whistles intensified, and Aja opened her eyes to look out the window. She could see several gray fish, larger than a person, playfully swimming alongside the ship. She didn't know what larboard meant, but she could understand that these strange creatures were called dolphins. *They look friendly,* she thought, watching them jump up out of the water and marveling at the sounds they made. It almost seemed like they were communicating with one another, like people having conversations. *Are we as fascinating to them as they are to us?* she wondered with a smile.

She was sad when the dolphins swam away, but when she closed her eyes and *Listened,* she was glad that she could still hear their animated clicks reverberating through the water in waves. Eventually the sound of them became distant, and longing to hear something else, she stretched her senses as far down as she could. Were there fish swimming below them? Would the dolphins return? *Where are you?* she queried, trying to turn her *Listening* inside out. She had done it once before with Jaqlai. Maybe the dolphins would hear her like he had.

Where are you? she called. And she *Listened,* lulled by the sound of water around her.

Here.

The word was not spoken by a mouth, carried to her by soundwaves. Instead, it seemed to slam into her senses as though she had collided with something hard. She shuddered at the feeling of its soundless voice, dwarfed by its strength and terrified at its depth. But then she felt it, like the swell of a wave looming over her. Whatever had answered her was coming.

It was coming fast.

Bolting upright in terror, Aja scrambled from her bed and threw open her door, dashing first down into the hold to see if Jaqlai was down below. He was not in any of the bunks or hammocks.

Where are you? the voice called out to her. Now it sounded taunting, and she trembled at the feeling of its words against her mind. She didn't know who it was or where it was coming from, but she knew one thing for sure—it was searching for *her*.

I need to find Jaqlai, she thought desperately, rushing up the steep, ladder-like stairs for the deck. She balked when she came up, seeing how the waves on either side of the ship were nearly as high as the masts. The wind was harsh and cold, and it blew right through her clothes. *Jaqlai,* she thought, urging herself to overcome her fear of the waves and venture onto the deck. She went to the center mast and hung onto it, her heart pounding so hard in her chest that her ears ached from the pressure.

She saw him leaning against the railing, talking to one of the sailors. At once she pushed away from the mast and began to hurry toward him.

Are you above or below? the voice asked mockingly. ***Do not think to hide. I will find you.***

"Jaqlai!" she screamed, her hands shaking as blood rushed from her extremities to her heart. Her chest felt tight and painful, and she was finding it difficult to breathe.

He heard her, his ears swiveling towards her voice, and when he saw her rushing toward him, he darted out to meet her, catching hold of her arm to steady her. "What's wrong?" he demanded, looking around. "Did someone hurt you?"

"Jaqlai," Aja gasped, shuddering. "I don't know what to do! It's coming. It's looking for me. I… I didn't mean to call it, but now—"

"Hold on," he frowned, heading toward the stairs. "Let's get out of the wind, I can't hear you very well."

"There's no time," Aja cried out. "It's *coming,* Jaqlai. It's coming for me!"

"What's coming?" Jaqlai demanded. He pulled her along with him, bringing her down off the deck into the hallway down below. "You're not making sense."

"I don't *know*!" Aja yelled. She felt near hysterics, she was so frightened. Deep below her, she could feel an overwhelming presence surging through the waters, drawing swiftly closer. "I was just *Listening*, trying to see if I could hear more dolphins. But then…"

A large wave rocked the ship, nearly knocking them sideways. And then a scream sounded out from above. "Patrel!" one of the sailors cried. "Patrel!"

Jaqlai's face went white. He gripped her shoulders with both hands, not breathing for a moment as chaos and yelling broke out on deck. Then, when Captain Andrus began yelling orders, he took a breath and began to move. "Stay in your room," he said gravely. "I'll do what I can with Influence."

"Jaqlai," Aja pleaded, wanting to beg him not to leave her. But before she could finish the words, he had shoved her back in her cabin and dashed up the stairs. She sank down to her bed, holding a hand to her chest. *I'm scared,* she thought. *What kind of being is a patrel?*

"Furl the sails!" Andrus called. "Fasten your lifelines!"

Aja dropped down to lay on her side, trembling with terror. *It's my fault,* she thought. *I called it here with my Listening. How could I have been so stupid?* Yet the more she berated herself, the more frustrated she felt. How was she supposed to know? It wasn't like she was trying to call a patrel, she was trying to speak to the dolphins!

"The Vedlyran's gone up the mast," Jerid yelled.

"Leave him!" Andrus shouted back. "Lie on deck; lie on deck! And *don't move!*"

Aja didn't want to know what was happening. She didn't want to hear the patrel's voice. But she couldn't help it. Without anything else she could do, she found herself *Listening* as the ship fell into a tense silence. Below them, the mountainous presence she had sensed was moving in a slow circle around the ship. And high above them, she felt the pressure of Jaqlai's Influence.

"There is nothing here," it seemed to say. *"Nothing but a cloud."*

You are no cloud, the cold voice sneered in return.

"You don't see anything interesting. There's no reason to stay."

Yet you have called me here yourself.

Aja swallowed, her throat unbearably dry. Jaqlai could use as much Influence as possible, but it still wouldn't do a thing. The patrel was not fooled. *I have to tell him,* she thought, shuddering. *I have to warn him.*

Above her, she heard a cry of dismay. "I can see its eye!" one of the sailors wailed. "Its great eye is watching us! We are doomed!"

Eye? Aja thought, her nerves suddenly electrified as an idea sprang into her mind. Abruptly she sat up in bed, staring at her door with trepidation. She knew what she had to do, but she didn't know if she could make herself do it.

"Its arms are above the ship!" a sailor cried.

"Be quiet!" Andrus snapped. "Let the Vedlyran handle it!"

"A Vedlyran is no Moglian," Jerid hissed. "Let's get out of here while we can."

"And go where?" Andrus demanded. "Do you see anyone else on board with Influence? He's our best shot."

No, he isn't, Aja thought. Her legs were shaking and weak, and she didn't think she could make herself stand. But she must. *She* was their best chance at surviving. "Move, Aja," she urged, fighting against the terror that arrested her limbs. "Move *now!*"

It took all her effort just to rise to her feet, but once she started moving, it began to get easier. She stumbled for the door and threw it open, crawled up the stairs, and came at last to stand on the deck overlooking the ship. All of the sailors had ropes tied about their waists that were fastened to the mast, and they were all lying on their stomachs. Rising up from the water on either side of the ship, Aja could see great, dark tentacles lined with circular suction cups. Her eyes lifted upward, to where Jaqlai was standing in the crow's nest gazing down at the water.

If she didn't act now, they would all die.

"Jaqlai!" she screamed. "Where is its eye?"

Andrus bolted upright when he heard her, a look of horror flashing across his face. "Get down below!" he called. "Aja!"

"Where is its eye?" Aja pleaded.

Will you not answer? the voice pressed against her mind, causing a shudder to snap down her spine. But to her relief, Jaqlai leaned over the nest and pointed to the left side of the ship.

She sprinted for the railing, stumbled over her own feet, and nearly fell into the water below. Wrapping her arms around the railing with all her strength, she hung nearly halfway over it to gaze down into the water, searching for the creature's eye.

It took her a minute to realize that she was already looking into it. The great eye was circular in shape, as large as the ship was long, with a great, inky, black center. She wasn't sure if it could see her eyes at all, but she knew that their only chance lay in her ability to meet its gaze. *Slyen said that not even beasts would kill me if they looked in my eyes,* she thought desperately. *So, look, patrel. Look at me!*

She called out to it, reversing her *Listening* into a soundless yell that carried all her strength. And with a great shudder, she felt the patrel's eye focus on her.

It was looking at her.

There you are, it responded, its voice haughty. *Not a cloud.*

"Not a cloud," Aja answered, too tired to call out with her *Listening* anymore. "But I wish you'd think of me as one."

The waters rippled and waves sloshed against the side of the ship. The patrel's arms began to wrap around the *North Wind* in a slow arch, as though it was taunting her. *I heard you,* the patrel said. *I heard your voice, little thing.*

Aja desperately hung on for dear life, her arms aching from how tightly she gripped the wooden railing. If her grip loosened even slightly, she would tumble right over into the water, onto the great eye that stared unblinking up at her. "I heard you, too," she said. Behind her, Jaqlai was rapidly climbing down the mast. She could hear him calling out her name.

"The arms!" Jerid yelled.

"There's no slipping by this one," Andrus answered. "To arms, everyone!"

"No, wait!" Jaqlai shouted back. "Not yet!"

I could crush you, the patrel said. It seemed proud of this feat, and Aja thought she could see blue light shining in the water, deeper down. As if the beast was lined with Scorian lanterns that could shine even underwater.

"Why would you?" Aja demanded. "We haven't done anything to you."

The patrel didn't answer. Instead, the eye seemed to change its focus from her face to the ship, and back to her face again. Waves rippled against the ship, and slowly, its arms began to withdraw. *Why would I?* it asked, as though confused by the question.

Aja could feel Jaqlai's Influence around her, bonding with her words. *It's working,* she thought, relief beginning to surge in her chest. Slyen's blessing and Jaqlai's Influence, working together with her voice. "Exactly," she said, growing bolder. "You wouldn't."

The beast rolled so that she could no longer see its eye looking at her, and she sensed it circling the ship underwater once again. *Then why else did I come?* it finally responded, almost as though it was asking itself more than her.

"To say hello?" Aja ventured. It was the first thing that came to her mind.

Suddenly, great waves began to splash and rock the ship so hard that Aja nearly screamed, but when she opened her mouth to breathe in, she found her mouth filled with saltwater. Desperately she continued to cling to the railing, and she felt Jaqlai dash up and wrap an arm around her waist. He too gripped the railing, with both his arm and his tail.

And deep below the water, the patrel was laughing.

To say hello! its voice battered against Aja's mind. *Why yes, I think you're right. I came to say hello.* It moved away from the ship, putting distance between them, before rising up to break the surface of the water. It had a strange, translucent body that she could only see part of, and a great many arms that writhed back and forth in the current. *Hello, little thing.*

"He-hello," Aja coughed, spitting seawater from her mouth. She was lucky it hadn't entered her lungs.

The patrel sank back into the water, its laugher causing more mountainous waves to lash against the ship. If Jaqlai had not been holding her in place, she might have slipped away from the force of them. *I have spent too long at the surface. So now, I'll say goodbye.*

"Good... goodbye," Aja gasped for air. She was thrashed and weary, soaked to the bone, and so cold she couldn't feel her hands or feet anymore. It wouldn't surprise her if her arms were frozen around the railing now.

To her great relief, she felt the presence of the patrel receding deep under water. It sucked water through its body and shot it out with great force, causing another swell of waves that sent the ship teetering sideways. She could hear Andrus yelling orders to the crew and sensed them rushing about to secure the ship as best they could, but all she could do was hang on as the ship sailed down a huge slope only to shoot upward again on the other side of a wave.

This went on for several minutes, until at last, the water evened out and the sea showed no signs of the monster. Aja could no longer feel its presence or hear its voice in her mind. The patrel was gone.

"Aja!" Jaqlai yelled. She turned her head to look at him with a dazed expression and realized he had been calling her name for some time. "Aja, say something!"

She shuddered, tears welling up in her eyes. "Hello," she said, her teeth chattering. She tried to let go of the railing and found that someone had lashed her to it with a rope. Had that been Jaqlai, too?

Captain Andrus came toward them, still yelling out commands to his crew, but he stopped beside them and lowered his voice. "Take her to my cabin," he said. "Wrap her up in as many blankets as you can find. I have some brandy that will warm her up—make sure she drinks some."

Jaqlai nodded, untying the rope hastily. He lifted Aja into his arms and began to carry her to Andrus's cabin. He didn't say anything while he got her wrapped up in blankets, and when he poured her a shot of brandy in one of Andrus's silver goblets, he poured another for himself and drank it. He made sure she was sitting down in one of the chairs before taking a seat beside her.

Aja shivered uncontrollably, though she wasn't sure if she was cold or shocked. *It worked,* she thought, squeezing her eyes shut. But when she saw the patrel's eye in her mind, she hastily opened them again.

"I would never have realized it," Jaqlai said, staring at nothing with a look of exhaustion on his face. "They look like Querians, they talk like Querians, their mannerisms and slang are Querian. Even the ship is perfectly Querian." He shifted his gaze, looking at Aja with an attempt at a smile that only managed to lift the corner of his mouth. "But they're not Querian, are they?"

Aja lifted the goblet, taking a sip of brandy. She was soothed by the warmth it gave her and the relief it provided her nerves. "Why do you say that?" she asked.

He looked toward the door. "Only the Zyphans call a kraken by its Kirilian name."

Patrel, Aja realized. *Is that all it takes to give away their secret?*

Jaqlai sighed, shaking his head. "It doesn't matter. They were the only ship willing to take us, and that's enough for me. More importantly…" he eyed her with a grave expression. "What *happened* back there?"

"I was *Listening,*" Aja said, guilt washing over her as heavily as the waves had. "I was trying to hear the dolphins. But then… the patrel heard *me.*"

Jaqlai shuddered, his ears sinking backwards. "I couldn't have Influenced it," he said. "I tried, but it was like trying to blow on a mountain to move it. Nothing worked until you…"

"It wouldn't have worked without your Influence," she cut in, shaking her head. "I could tell. Until you used it to strengthen my words—"

"And my Influence wouldn't have worked without you," he insisted. "We were incredibly lucky back there." He laughed, grabbed the bottle of brandy, and poured himself another shot. "But I'm beginning to think that's normal with you. You're lucky, Aja. Finding this ship, convincing the kraken to leave—even our escape from Scoria. Luck follows you, and I'm lucky to have met you."

"So am I," Aja said. Then hastily added, "lucky to meet you, too. I never would have made it through the desert without you. And back there, when the ship was tossing in the waves, I would have fallen overboard without your help."

"Then here's to us," Jaqlai lifted his goblet, clinking it with hers. "To a lucky friendship. May that luck follow us all the way to Mettain."

"And back again," Aja murmured. She drank the rest of her brandy, her thoughts turning once more to the narrow escape they had made. "If I had known that *Listening* for dolphins would call up that creature, I never would have tried," she said, her voice wry. "But as they say, by the time you see the spots."

Jaqlai recorked the bottle of brandy, standing up to return it to its place near the wine rack. "Who says what?" he asked, confused.

"You know the saying," Aja shrugged. "By the time you see the spots...you know, it's too late?"

"No, I really don't," Jaqlai said, tilting his head quizzically. He returned to his chair, reaching out to tug the blankets a little tighter around Aja's shivering body. "What does it mean?"

It never occurred to Aja that common sayings would not be so common, outside the valley. "It's something we say pretty often," she explained, and set her empty goblet on the table. The ship swayed to the side, and the goblet fell over. Jaqlai caught it before it could fall to the floor. "By the time you see the spots—meaning the spots on a jaguar—it's too late. You can only see a jaguar's spots if they're close, and they only get close when they're hunting you."

"That's actually pretty clever," Jaqlai said, cracking a smile. "Though I'd advise against using any expressions outside your valley. It could give away that you aren't Querian, or Zyphan, or even Scorian. You want to keep your valley a secret, right?"

"Right," Aja nodded. She shivered at the thought. It was unsettling to think that just having normal conversation could give her away. She would have to watch herself more carefully when she reached Mettain. Andrus and Jaqlai knew her secret, but it was imperative that no one else learn where she was from.

"Let's not look for any more spots, right?" Jaqlai teased, attempting to cheer her up. "No more calling up krakens from the deep."

Thinking of the patrel made Aja shudder again. "No more *Listening* to the ocean," she agreed. Who knew what *else* lay hiding deep under the waves? *The world is far bigger and more dangerous than I can possibly imagine,* she realized. And her heart ached with longing for home. What would they say if she tried to tell them about her experiences out here? Would any of them believe her?

Emrin would, she thought, a smile breaking across her face. She wondered what face he would make, if she told him about how a patrel came up to his brother's ship to say "hello."

Mettain

It was the eleventh day since they set out from Port Anatya, and Andrus had guided the ship out of the current to draw closer to land. Aja could see it on the left side of the ship—the larboard, as the sailors called it—though they weren't close enough to make out any details. It was a dark, bumpy line on the horizon where seabirds would come from. They would swoop around the ship looking for easy food, and after making a bunch of racket, perching on all the rails and sails, and leaving droppings for the crew to clean up, they would fly back to land before night fell.

Andrus had said they would be arriving in Mettain either today or tomorrow, so Aja was up on deck leaning against the railing, watching the land growing near as Andrus steered the ship in closer. *Soon I'll be where I'm supposed to be,* she thought, nervous with anticipation. *Will I be able to find Vedlyr? Will Andrus stay docked long enough for me to find Vedlyr and return?* She didn't know if he would be willing to bring her *back* to Port Anatya, but she intended to ask before they reached land.

"Ah, so here you are," Jaqlai said, walking up beside her. He leaned against the railing to her right, offering her a somewhat nervous smile. "I was wondering if I could talk to you for a bit."

"Of course," Aja answered. *He's not rethinking our deal, is he?* She turned to face him, worry flashing across her face. "You'll keep your promise?" she asked. "You won't mention—"

"I'll keep my promise," Jaqlai said gravely. "I will tell them the Zyphans plan on attacking from the Uliah River, but I won't mention the valley. I promise."

She let out a sigh of relief, relaxing her shoulders. She hadn't realized they had tensed just then. "What is it, then? Is everything alright?"

He offered a short, wry laugh. "No, not nearly," he admitted. "Truthfully, I would rather not say anything at all, but I don't think I can avoid it, because it's going to affect you." He glanced out across the sea toward the land, sighing. "My nation... won't be happy to see me. In fact, they were so relieved I went missing that they already pronounced me dead. When we make landfall, there's a chance they may be harsh with you just because I brought you."

Aja was shocked to hear him say this, especially since both Cait and Mikail had been on good terms with him. "Why would they want you dead?" she asked. "That doesn't make any sense."

He grimaced, not meeting her eyes. "It's not for anything I've done personally," he insisted. "Rather... it's because of who my family is."

"Your family?" Aja asked. She could tell there was a story he wasn't sharing, and she found herself so curious that she couldn't leave it at that. "What happened? Are you allowed to tell me?"

Jaqlai clasped his hands, hunched over the railing with a nervous posture. His tail twitched erratically behind him. "I'm *allowed* to," he said slowly. "It's just not a pleasant story to tell."

"Will you tell me?" Aja asked, her voice quiet. She wanted to know, but more than that, she could sense that it was bothering him. *Maybe it would help for him to share it with a friend*, she thought.

He was silent for a moment, staring out at the water, and Aja waited patiently beside him. At length, he let out another sigh. "Why not?" he asked, shooting her a half-hearted smile. "Just... bear with me. I've never told anyone else about it. Never had to, because everyone always *knew*." He inhaled deeply and let his breath out slowly. "About six years ago, Mettain was part of war of secession. The island of Jeinu wanted independence from Queria, and while they were excellent at defending their island with magic, they didn't have a large army. So, they were petitioning other nations   . Zypha, Kirilian, Scoria, and Mettain."

Aja remembered seeing Jeinu Island on the map Andrus showed her. She had often gone back to look at it, curious to learn more about the continent she lived on.

"At the time, Mettain was allied only with Kirilian," Jaqlai continued. "But after careful consideration of the facts and the reasons Jeinu wanted to secede, our king decided that he would send aid to the island so that it could have its independence." He paused, glancing at Aja as if checking to see whether she was listening. "Mettain is exceedingly careful about who we fight against, and who we ally with," he said gravely. "A small amount of Influence can turn the tide of a battle. And an army full of people who can use Influence is enough to determine the outcome of a war. We sided with Kirilian when they had a conflict with Zypha and won. We sided with Jeinu Island against Queria and won. And after that war ended, Queria was anxious to get on our good side and sought an alliance with us."

"Influence is that powerful?" she asked, and then thought about Slyen. His Influence had kept her from getting killed several times over, and it would be able to stop a war entirely if she managed to find Vedlyr in time. "Never mind, I think I understand," she added, before he could reply.

He smiled wryly. "Anyway, six years ago, during the war of secession, there was a very powerful Vedlyran fighter named Jaquel Videlle in the army. Most Vedlyrans have tan fur with black tips, like I do. But Jaquel's fur was a deep black. He was the only one in history to be born with all black fur. He was exceptionally gifted at Influence, and he could use it in ways no one else could even dream about. At the start of a battle, he would wrap himself in a cloud of Influence he called his 'Shroud of Death.' It caused people to perceive him as more terrible, more powerful, and more vicious than anything they could dream of. His Influence pressured others to feel despair when they saw him, and enemy soldiers would flee when he got close."

For some reason, Aja's dream of red skies and death came to her mind. If it was true that Moglians could turn the sky red with their anger using Influence, then she could picture just how terrifying that fighter's Influence would be. *How horrible,* she thought with a shiver. *What a cruel way to win.*

"The problem was that Jaquel wasn't satisfied with causing the enemy to flee," Jaqlai continued, his face grim as he told his tale. "Jaquel loved to fight. He loved violence, killing, and crushing his enemies—even the ones that surrendered. He became known as the Black Death, and whenever he joined a battle, he would always win." He paused, and his ears angled backwards with displeasure. "On the last battle of the war, Jaquel shrouded himself with his Influence and destroyed the entire Querian army single-handedly. It was a grim victory, if it can even be called that, for as soon as he got done killing the enemy, he decided that he hadn't had enough. He slaughtered our own soldiers until there were none left on the battlefield."

Aja's face drained of color, and she could see the distress in Jaqlai's face as he recounted the battle. *He killed his own people?* she thought. *What kind of person would do something like that?*

Jaqlai turned, leaning his back against the railing and gazing up at the sky. "The war ended that day, because neither side could bear to fight any longer. Our army tried Jaquel in court and sentenced him to death for his crimes, but he shrouded himself in his Influence and fled, killing anyone who got in his way. He was never seen again." He paused, tilting his head and giving Aja a sidelong glance. "The reason my country is so harsh toward me is because of him."

She frowned, opening her mouth to ask why, but he answered her question before she could.

"Jaquel Videlle is my older brother."

Aja's stomach tightened. She stood there looking at him without knowing what to say.

"I am not my brother," Jaqlai said dryly. "His crimes are not mine. But when other Vedlyrans look at me, they compare me to him. That's why I was sent alone to Scoria to find information about the war. They can't just kill me because I've done nothing wrong, and they can't discharge me because I'm one of the best Scouts in the military. So, they have been sending me on difficult jobs in the hopes that I die."

Yet here he was, alive because of Aja, and bringing back critical information about the war. Aja reached out a hand and placed it on his arm. "You're nothing like him," she said firmly. "You're a kind and honorable man, and I'm lucky to know you."

"Thanks," he smiled faintly. "It's encouraging to hear you say that." His smile faded, and he looked down at the deck with concern written on his features. "They won't be happy to see me alive, and they may try to hinder me from relaying my information out of spite. I expect them to give you a hard time too, because you're with me. So, I just… wanted to warn you."

"I appreciate the warning," Aja said. Her excitement and anticipation for reaching Mettain now felt soured by the prospect of the reception they would receive. *There's a chance Mettain won't listen to Andrus either, just because he brought Jaqlai home,* she realized. And it filled her with frustration. *It's not fair. Not fair to Jaqlai, or Andrus, or me.*

But what could *she* do about it?

"No matter what happens," Jaqlai said, placing a hand on her shoulder, "I'll look out for you. I'll set you up in an inn near the military compound in Venecalle Fief, and make sure you have funds for food. But it will be up to you to accomplish your own goals."

"I'll find Vedlyr," Aja said firmly, more to psych herself up than to convince Jaqlai.

He patted her shoulder with a sympathetic smile. "Riiight. Sure."

She narrowed her eyes at him. "Vedlyr is real," she insisted. "And when I find him, I'll prove it to you."

"Sure," he said again, the corners of his mouth twisting upward further. No matter what she said, it was clear he wasn't going to believe her.

I'll show him, Aja thought, indignant. *I **will** find Vedlyr, and I'll make sure they meet before I return home.*

"Thanks," Jaqlai said quietly, and Aja's frustration melted into confusion. When he saw her expression, Jaqlai turned away awkwardly. "For not acting differently around me, now that you know about Jaquel. I thought you'd become afraid of me if I told you."

"I've had plenty of time to get to know you," Aja encouraged, shaking her head. "I'm shocked to hear something so horrible, and I'm sorry that you've had to deal with the ire of your own people. But I'm not so fickle that I'd change my opinion of you based on something someone else did."

"You're a good friend," Jaqlai offered a half smile. "Thank you for saying that."

"I meant it," Aja smiled back. She might have said more, but at that moment a sailor up in the crow's nest called out in a loud voice.

"Three ships approaching on the larboard!"

Jaqlai turned around, gazing out at the ocean. He squinted his eyes, then pointed with one finger. "See the white triangles?" he asked. "Those are the sails. It's probably the military."

"Vedlyran!" Andrus called from the helm. "I'll need you front and center!"

"You should get below," Jaqlai said. "Wait for us to negotiate with them." He turned and dashed up the steps to the helm to stand by the captain. Aja could see his mouth moving, but she couldn't hear what he was saying.

Glancing out at the horizon, she noticed the white sails getting steadily larger and felt an uneasiness wash over her. Considering what he had learned about Jaqlai's brother, she was worried that they wouldn't let them dock. *They'll let us,* she thought, walking swiftly for the stairs and heading down into the belly of the ship. She went to her cabin and closed the door, lying down on her bunk.

They had a letter from the embassy. They would let them dock.

They have to, she thought anxiously.

All she could do was wait.

———✸———

"I want to talk to you before you disembark," Andrus said, pulling Aja aside by the arm. They had finally come to port this morning, escorted by the three military ships that had come out to meet them.

Aja was feeling nervous. Even though the talk between Jaqlai, Andrus, and the military officers who boarded the ship had gone well, she still felt like anything could go wrong. "I want to talk to you, too," she said.

"Let's talk in my cabin, then," Andrus nodded. He exchanged a look with Jaqlai, who was standing by the gangplank, and nodded once. Jaqlai's ears angled backwards slightly, but he nodded in return. He looked toward Aja, his gaze questioning.

"I'll be right there," she called to him. And with a nervous smile, she followed Andrus into the captain's cabin.

Andrus closed the door, letting out a sigh. "Listen," he said seriously. "I've been told I'll be allowed to meet with the Duke of Venecalle, but my meeting isn't for three days." He leveled a glare at her that seemed almost worried. "Can you finish whatever you have to accomplish in that time? I'm not sure how long they will allow me to stay here after my meeting is concluded. They didn't want to let me stay at all, but they're willing to meet with me because I'm coming as a representative of our nation."

"Three days isn't a lot of time, but I'll see what I can do," Aja said, her worry increasing. Would she be able to find Vedlyr in that time? "I was going to ask if you'd be willing to wait for me, so I could return to Port Anatya with you."

"I'm willing, but it's not up to me," Andrus grimaced. He leaned against the door with his arms crossed, studying her with a serious look. "I'll do my best," he promised. "Even if it weren't for Emrin's sake, I would still look out for you. You're one of us."

He thinks of me as a Zyphan, she thought, smiling faintly. *Even though they've only been staying with us for seven months. Is it because of Slyen's Influence, or are they just that kind of people?* She couldn't help feeling grateful he thought of her that way. "I'll try my best, too," she said, despite the doubt she felt. "But if you have to leave before I'm done here, don't worry about it. I'll find another way back to Slyenials."

Andrus nodded, though he didn't look so sure. Pushing away from the door, he turned and put his hand on the knob, hesitating a moment. "Your friend, the Vedlyran," he said awkwardly. "Are the two of you…?"

It took a minute for Aja to realize what he was asking, and then she flushed. "No, we aren't. We're just friends."

"Does *he* feel that way?" Andrus asked dryly. His face told her that he didn't believe her.

"I'm certain of it," Aja insisted. Jaqlai was kind to her and looked out for her, but she had never sensed the kind of attention that indicated he felt more. He thought of her only as a friend, she was sure of it.

"If you say so," Andrus said, and he opened the door. "Come on, your *friend* is waiting."

"Yes, my friend is waiting," Aja stressed, wanting to roll her eyes, though she resisted. I don't get why it matters to him, but I'm definitely not interested in Jaqlai. Grateful to him, yes. But not interested. It was at that moment that she recalled Emrin's interest in her, and she suddenly realized why Andrus was asking at all. "You can't say anything to Emrin, remember?" she demanded. "Don't mention my being here, or anything about Jaqlai!"

"I'm not going to say anything," he answered, a smirk spreading across his face at her reaction. He held the door open for her and gestured with his hand. "After you."

Aja stifled her frustration as she walked past him. Her steps were confident as she strode out of the cabin onto the deck and made her way to where Jaqlai was waiting for her. Turning at the gangplank, she shot one last look at Andrus and the *North Wind*. Though she had only spent twelve days onboard, she felt a burst of affection. Abruptly, she hurried back to Andrus and threw her arms around him in a hug. "I forgot to say it but thank you. Thank you for everything, Andrus." She pulled back, offering him a faint smile. "And remember, you can't tell your brother *anything*."

"It's confidential, I get it," Andrus smiled back at her with a twinkle in his eye. He patted her on the shoulder before waving his hand toward Jaqlai. "Now go on, you've got a job to do, and so do I."

"Goodbye Andrus," Aja said, stepping backwards. "I hope your meeting goes well. And with luck, I'll see you again soon."

He nodded, still waving her off as though he felt too awkward to respond. So, Aja turned, making her way toward the gangplank once more. This time she crossed it, with Jaqlai following her, until she stood on the worn wooden pier. It surprised her to find that her sense of balance was off now that she was off the ship. The ground seemed to sway back and forth, and she stumbled side to side trying to catch her balance.

"Sea legs," Jaqlai said with a chuckle. He seemed perfectly fine, largely due to his tail, Aja thought. It was swaying back and forth behind him, helping him to remain steady. "You'll adjust, don't worry. For now, hold my arm." He offered it to her.

Grateful, Aja held onto it with one hand and walked beside him as they headed up the dock for solid ground. "Where are we going?" she asked. She studied the city with interest, noticing that it was different than all the ones she had seen before.

Buildings of many different shapes and sizes were nestled tightly together inside a stone wall, like a bundle of colorful vegetables inside a square box. They were built out of wood and cobblestone, with large square windows and tall, angled roofs. Ivy grew along many of the walls, and there were trees scattered throughout the city on every street. The roads were paved with carefully lain, rust-colored bricks, so seamlessly packed that they seemed like smooth red rivers, dividing the city into rectangular blocks. Many of the buildings were accented with painted, wooden beams, and all of the roofs had dark-colored shingles. The city was colorful, and all of the colors worked together.

"To an inn," Jaqlai said, leading the way confidently up one street and down another. Unlike Port Anatya, this city was not built on a hill. It was fairly flat ground, tucked up against the tree-covered foothills of tall mountains. "We'll stop in there to lock up our belongings and get something to eat. Then, I'll head to the compound to give my report."

Aja's stomach growled at the prospect of food. She had been too restless to eat earlier that morning when they pulled into dock. *It won't be hard tack, potato soup, or pickles,* she thought hungrily. She'd be glad if she never had to eat any of those things again. "What is this city called?" she asked, looking up at Jaqlai curiously.

"This is Port Umber, in Venecalle Fief," Jaqlai answered. "There are seven fiefs in Mettain, all of them ruled by a duke or duchess. And over all the fiefs, the King rules."

"Where I live, we have five villages," Aja said, "and each village is governed by a village elder. Is it like that?"

"Who rules over the village elders?" Jaqlai asked. "Is there anyone like that?"

Aja shook her head. "They are all equal, so that power is balanced. When decisions have to be made, all the elders meet and come to an agreement together." There had not been time for such a meeting when the Zyphans first arrived. But when the elder of Northbank Village welcomed the Zyphans, all the other elders supported his decision. That was just how the people of Slyenials were.

"That's sort of how it works here," Jaqlai smiled, his ears perked upward with interest. "The seven fiefs keep a balance of power, and the King presides over them all as a check for them. However, the King does not have absolute authority; any decision he makes has to be voted on and approved by the dukes and duchesses."

"So, whether or not Mettain goes to war, that's something that all the fiefs have to support?" she asked, considering what he told her seriously. If Mettain joined the war, their Influence could ensure that the side they supported won. *What a frightening responsibility,* she thought.

"Yes," Jaqlai nodded gravely. "But I don't think Mettain will go to war this time. The conflict between Zypha and Queria is regarding their sea trade and has nothing to do with us. They need to resolve this on their own."

And I need to stop it from happening altogether, Aja thought. She asked nothing else as Jaqlai took her through the city, and her thoughts turned toward a breakfast that wouldn't be hard, stale bread or watery potato soup. Her mouth watered as they walked through the door of the inn Jaqlai chose. She could smell fresh bread, as well as other delicious smells she was less familiar with. *I'm so hungry,* she thought, pressing a hand against her stomach. She shifted the bag hanging from her shoulder, adjusting its weight. It was only carrying her clothes and cloak, but it was starting to feel so heavy that she was anxious to put it down.

A Vedlyran woman came towards them from a room in the back, wiping flour from her hands onto her apron. Her ears lifted curiously when she saw Aja standing beside Jaqlai. "How can I help you?" she asked.

"We'd like two secure rooms," Jaqlai answered. "And something to eat. Can you tell me how much that will be?"

"Two sterling a night, and food comes with the room," the woman smiled brightly. "We don't get many humans visiting us. Where are you from, dear?"

It was the first time that Aja was asked so directly, instead of her origins being assumed. She answered the only thing she could think of. "I'm Zyphan," she smiled, "and I'm just visiting for a short while. Thank you for the room and food."

"That's what we're here for," the woman said, gesturing with her hand. "My name is Katie, I'm one of the owners here. You must have come in on the ship that just pulled in! Everyone's been talking about it. Port has been closed for weeks, and you're the first ship to be allowed through."

"Nice to meet you, Katie," Jaqlai answered quickly, clearly determined to guide the conversation away from the ship and its purpose. "What's for breakfast?"

"Porridge and sliced apples, with some fresh bread on the side," Katie responded. She led them to a flight of stairs and headed up to a wide hallway lined with closed doors. Taking out a ring of keys from her pocket, she unlocked two of the rooms and unhooked the keys from the ring, giving both to Jaqlai. "Why don't you get settled first, and when you come down to the dining room, I'll have your breakfast waiting for you."

"Thank you," Jaqlai smiled warmly. After Katie had retreated down the stairs, he tested the keys in the locks to see which was which, then handed one to Aja. "Here, this can be your room," he said, gesturing to the one on the left. "I'll have the one next to it."

"Alright," Aja answered. She took the key, glancing in the door curiously. From here, she could see that it was a small room with a bed and a chest of drawers, and a window looking out toward the sea. The bedding was colorful, a bright blue and white quilt with red roses embroidered along the edges. There was an unlit oil lamp on the chest of drawers. "Strange that a room like this only costs two sterling when my jacket cost four," she murmured.

Jaqlai looked at her quizzically, before he started with realization. "You don't know how our money works," he said quietly. Then, glancing quickly toward the stairs, he gestured to Aja's room. "Come in, I'll show you," he said.

Aja followed him into her room, waiting by the window as he closed the door. When he pulled out his pouch of money, he began to spread the coins and paper bills on the mattress.

"This right here is a sterling," he said, lifting a copper-colored coin like the ones Aja had used to pay for her jacket. It was as wide as two of her fingers. "This is a half-sterling," Jaqlai continued, lifting up a bronze-colored coin that was about half the size of the sterling. "One sterling is worth 100 stones." He held up a dull, silver-colored coin that was smaller than the half-sterling. "For a frame of reference, a single meal in Mettain costs about 20 stones."

"Why are they called stones if they're coins?" Aja asked, coming toward the bed to get a closer look. She picked up the coins to compare them, intrigued.

"Because our money is based on the Kirilian value scale," he explained. "They use semi-precious and precious stones as currency, and they have value based on their weight. Our coins are easier to keep track of, but we can still trade with Kirilian using them."

"What are these?" Aja picked up the paper bills, looking through them. They had numbers written on them, as well as an intricately printed design of the Mettain Crest—the crown on a shield surrounded by a rose vine with seven roses.

"They are slips of paper that represent higher values," Jaqlai answered, pointing to the numbers on the bills. "This is a 10-sterling bill, and this is a 50. I don't get paid enough to show you a 100-sterling bill."

"Is there anything above sterling?" Aja asked.

"Sort of," Jaqlai shrugged. "One precious stone is worth 100 sterling. Such as diamond, kirilite, or beryl. But we don't have coins that represents those."

"I understand the concept." Aja turned over the coins in her hand, frowning. "I guess what I don't understand is the *value* of things. Why is it two sterling for two rooms and food for both of us, when it cost four sterling for my rain jacket?"

"Rain jackets are made from a very rare synthetic fabric," Jaqlai scooped up his coins and bills, sliding them back into his money pouch. "Some of them can cost up to nine sterling. Four sterling is a fair price for something that difficult to make."

"Oh," Aja said, touching the jacket with her fingers. She was wearing it right now, and it had been invaluable to her while on the ship. Thanks to this jacket, she stayed mostly dry even when the waves were high, and the wind was wet. "Then... is two sterling a night a fair price?"

"It's fair right now, since the port is closed off and prices are higher with less trade and fewer customers coming in," Jaqlai gave her a wry smile. He tucked the pouch into his pocket. "But it's a bit high. One sterling would be fairer, any other time." He gestured toward the door with a nod of his head. "Let's go get something to eat. We've got a long day ahead of us, and I don't want to wait too long to get to the compound."

"I'm hungry too," Aja agreed. She left her bag in the bottom drawer of the chest in her room and locked the door on her way out. Jaqlai did the same. Then, they walked down the stairs together.

"There you are!" Katie called from the dining room, which was just to the left of the stairs from the entryway. "Come get your food while it's hot."

Aja gratefully made her way to a wooden table near a window, where Katie had placed two bowls of porridge, along with a plate of fruit and bread to share. The porridge seemed to be made from cooked oats, seasoned with cinnamon and honey, and it smelled heavenly. It wasn't until she and Jaqlai had sat down and begun eating that she recalled something he had said. "You said 'we've got a long day ahead of us.' What did you mean by that?"

"Right, I forgot to tell you," Jaqlai paused, a spoonful of porridge halfway to his mouth. "You'll have to come with me to the military compound when I give my report. It was the only way I could get permission for you to disembark the ship. You're the informant with a firsthand account of the Zyphan's plan to travel up the Uliah."

That was true, but it was intimidating to think she might let the wrong information slip. What was she supposed to tell them? She'd already called herself a Zyphan. Would the Zyphans reveal their plans to Mettain at all? "I feel like I'd be betraying them by saying anything," she sighed. "But if that's the only way…"

"Tell them you saw the Zyphan ships head up the river, and nothing else," Jaqlai said quietly. "Tell them you only shared it with me because we had a deal. I'm going to tell them that you were captured like I was, and we escaped together. Captain Andrus has been appointed as a representative of Zypha, and he's got the documents to prove it. If you say you both came with the purpose of sharing information with Mettain, they will believe it."

"Then will I be free to look for Vedlyr?" Aja asked, overwhelmed. What if the Vedlyrans asked too many questions? Should she just tell them she wasn't authorized to say anything else? *I'm an eyewitness that can back up what Jaqlai wants to tell them, and that's all I have to do. It will be alright,* she thought. She ate a slice of apple with a grimace. Somehow, she didn't feel reassured.

"You'll have three days," Jaqlai predicted. "After Andrus meets with Duke Jermain, he'll have to leave. And I expect they'll want you to leave with him."

"Three days," Aja murmured, resignation weighing heavily on her. That wasn't much time, and she didn't know the first place to start looking. Mettain was a very large nation, and they were only in one tiny part of it. What if Vedlyr was not in Venecalle Fief?

"Good luck," Jaqlai said, in a somewhat patronizing tone. As far as he was concerned, Vedlyr didn't exist.

"I'll find him," Aja retorted. "You'll see." She picked up her spoon and began to eat her porridge as swiftly as she could stomach. The sooner they finished the meal, the sooner they could go to the compound.

And the sooner she could attempt to find Vedlyr.

The Search

The military compound was like a small city within the city. There were many buildings, wide open fields where soldiers were training, a stable for horses, and Vedlyrans everywhere Aja looked. Jaqlai brought her though the main gate, which was heavily guarded, and led the way to one of the larger buildings on the far side of the compound. Here, the two of them waited for nearly half an hour before a soldier came and told them they could see "the General."

Aja was nervous. Her heart was racing, and her palms were sweaty. She followed Jaqlai through a simple wooden door to a wide office filled with cabinets. Behind a desk opposite the door sat an older Vedlyran man wearing a crisp khaki-brown uniform with gold and red accents. There were several medals pinned to the front of his jacket. He was sitting when they entered, and Jaqlai came to a halt in front of the desk, saluting him.

"Jaqlai Videlle, reporting from reconnaissance," Jaqlai said, his voice firm but polite.

"At ease," the general said, scowling. "I thought you were pronounced dead."

"That seems to be a mistake, sir," Jaqlai answered politely, though his ear twitched, angling back slightly. "I'd like to have it corrected and my name re-instated."

"Hmmm." The general's scowl deepened, and his mustache moved when he pursed his lips. Aja noticed that his ears were angled back, too. "Show me your report," he snapped.

Jaqlai pulled a bundle of notes out of his pocket, the same bundle that Aja had seen him pack in his bag before they boarded Andrus's ship, and stepped forward to hand it to him. He returned to Aja's side, standing stiffly with his legs at shoulder width apart, his hands clasped behind his back, and his head held high.

"And who is this?" the general snapped, gesturing toward Aja with one of the notes. Aja noticed a nameplate on his desk—Gen. Marcus Freed—and she was relieved to know what to call him.

"It's in my report, sir," Jaqlai responded. "She is the eyewitness who was willing to share information with me."

General Freed shot him a glare, returning to the notes in his hand. He read each one, and a tense silence filled the room while they waited for him to finish. Then he tossed them down on his desk and glared at Jaqlai. "So," he said, his tone sharp as he looked directly at Aja. "You are a Zyphan?"

"Yes, sir," Aja responded, finding her mouth dry.

"And you witnessed the Zyphan navy sending ships up the Uliah?" Marcus demanded. She nodded, and he rose to his feet. "Thank you, that will be all. Please step outside and wait while I speak with Scout Videlle."

Aja bowed her head nervously and walked toward the door. She barely had her hand on the knob when she felt an uncomfortable pressure of Influence behind her. She cast a look at Jaqlai over her shoulder, confused until she realized he wasn't the one using it. The general was, and he was glaring at Jaqlai.

What is he mad about? she thought apprehensively, slipping out into the entryway where she and Jaqlai had waited. Settling into a chair, she realized she could hear the general yelling inside the office. Her worry for Jaqlai rising, she opened her senses and *Listened*, anxious to know what the general was saying.

"You're telling me you got yourself *captured* by Scorians, and then made a deal with that Zyphan?" General Marcus roared. "THAT'S how you got your information? How am I supposed to trust what one woman says? Did you even go to the Uliah to verify her account? And all this about Querian navy ships at Port Anatya. How did you get *that* information?"

"I verified her story with Influence," Jaqlai answered respectfully. "And I scouted the information about Queria's navy myself."

"This information is worthless," Marcus snapped, slamming his hand on his desk loudly. Aja flinched at the sound. "We sent you out for crucial information, not sloppy eyewitness accounts!"

"Sir, I believe this information *is* crucial," Jaqlai said crisply. "The Zyphans are not going to attack from the west, they plan to travel through Moglian territory to attack Queria directly. What happens when they incite the wrath of the Moglians?"

"I didn't give you permission to speak," the general hissed between his teeth, his tone furious. But after that he was silent, and Aja heard the sound of his chair scooting backwards on the stone floor. Eventually, Marcus spoke again. "The ship that docked. It's a Zyphan ship?"

"Yes, sir." Jaqlai's voice was flat, and though it was carefully emotionless, Aja thought she could sense the anger and frustration he was feeling. Like a peculiar timbre that only she could hear.

Was *Listening* able to detect emotions, too? Or was that her own interpretation of what was happening?

"Then the Zyphans have ships masquerading as Querian, most likely for espionage," Marcus grumbled. "At least *that* is useful information. Ah! I see your mouth, don't speak while I'm thinking!"

Jaqlai said nothing, but the frustration Aja thought she could sense seemed to grow heavier.

"This has been a recurring problem with you," Marcus sneered. "Cursed Videlle! Always bringing information we can't use, wasting our time and money. It would have been better if you *had* died, instead of bringing back this—I don't even know what to call it. You were supposed to bring vital information, not a *woman*. How dare you waste our limited military budget with your dalliances!"

Here, Jaqlai couldn't hold his tongue. *"Dalliances?"* he asked angrily.

"I said silence!" Marcus yelled, slamming his fist onto his desk again. "This is the last time we let you get away with sloppy work and wasteful spending. I'll see you dishonorably discharged!"

"Sir, I—"

"Dismissed!" the general roared.

Aja hastily pulled in her senses, and realized she was sitting so stiffly in her chair that her neck and shoulders were hurting. She looked up as Jaqlai stormed out of the office, his face was clouded with fury. *Because it wasn't fair,* she thought unhappily. *None of that was fair.*

"Let's go," Jaqlai said under his breath as he approached her. She stood up and walked beside him as they left the building together. It wasn't until they were halfway across the compound that he spoke again. "Were you *Listening*?" he asked.

"Yes," Aja admitted, glancing back over her shoulder. She saw two soldiers whisper to each other and saw that they were glaring in Jaqlai's direction. *He wasn't exaggerating when he said they would rather he died,* she thought, and she felt angry on his behalf.

Jaqlai exhaled loudly, his ears angling backwards. "To my face, he's completely disregarding all the information I brought, but I already know he's going to present it to his superiors as if he got it himself. Why does everyone I report to have to be so stubborn? Why can't they just acknowledge that I did a good job? Dishonorably discharged? For exceeding expectations and coming back alive against the odds? How is that fair?"

"It isn't," Aja said, wishing she could help. But her being here was part of what had caused him to get in trouble. "What are you going to do now?" she asked.

He crossed his arms, tail flicking side to side agitatedly as he walked. "I'll have to wait," he said. "Wait for them to re-activate my identification to show that I'm no longer dead and wait for them to discharge me. They've been threatening to do it ever since my brother escaped. I guess now they can say I blew my last chance."

"I'm sorry," Aja said quietly. She placed a hand on his arm, wanting to comfort him.

The bitterness on his face lessened, some. "Thanks."

They were quiet for the rest of their trip back to the inn.

That night, Aja slept fitfully. And the following morning, she woke up feeling like she had dreamt something important, only she couldn't remember what it was. All she could do was get up and get ready for the day, and hope that it would come back to her eventually.

Today, she wore her Slyen clothes, tired of the gray and garnet Scorian ones. She braided her hair in one long braid that came down over her left shoulder, noticing that it was getting a bit long for her tastes. When she came out of her room to head downstairs for breakfast, she knocked on Jaqlai's door, but didn't hear a response. Not wanting to disturb him, she headed down the stairs and walked into the dining room. She was hungry, after all.

"Good morning!" Katie announced, coming out of the back the moment she heard someone enter the room. She had a charming smile as she beckoned Aja over to one of the empty tables. Three other tables in the room had other Vedlyran guests seated at them, drinking tea and eating. None of them so much as looked in Aja's direction as she took a seat. "Would you like breakfast?"

"Yes, thank you," Aja replied. "Have you seen…?"

She didn't have a chance to finish her question before Katie was already answering. "Ah, yes, he left early this morning for the compound, asked me to pass the message along when you woke up. He asked me to give you directions to wherever you want to go, if you need them."

I hope whatever he's doing goes well, Aja thought, feeling sorry for him. But she was glad that she didn't have to go back there. The Vedlyran general was intimidating and unpleasant, to say the least. As for where Aja wanted to go, there were a couple things she needed to do. The first was to buy new shoes. Her canvas ones were so worn that she was certain they wouldn't survive the return journey to Slyenials. And the second was the most important—she needed to find Vedlyr as soon as possible.

"I was hoping to buy new shoes," Aja said, glancing up at Katie with a polite smile. "Can you direct me where to go for that?"

"There's a market district a little way south from here," Katie responded cheerfully. "Once you exit the inn, turn right and head down 5th Avenue until you reach Elm Street, then take a left. You'll see lots of lovely little shops on that road, and I'm sure you can find what you're looking for."

There was a beam of sunlight coming in from the window, just low enough that it was shining in Aja's eyes. She held up a hand for shade, contemplating the directions worriedly. She could only assume that 5th Avenue and Elm Street were the names of the roads, reasoning that they were probably written on signs if she was expected to find them. "Thanks," she murmured.

Contemplating finding Vedlyr, she began to feel discouraged. It was one thing to find a shop to buy shoes, and another to search a whole country for one person.

"I'll be right back with your breakfast," Katie said, heading off for the back rooms once more.

After she was gone, Aja felt like she was being watched, and turning her head, she saw a Vedlyran woman sitting at the table behind her, watching her with interest. When their eyes met, the woman flushed and looked away at once, embarrassed to have been caught.

In a country full of Vedlyrans, I suppose it's strange to see a human, Aja thought, feeling awkward as she turned back toward her table. It was uncomfortable to be stared at, but she didn't think trying to talk to the woman would be a good idea. What would she say?

Katie returned promptly, carrying a plate of sliced fresh bread, sliced cheese, and fruit. "You just let me know if you need anything else," Katie said cheerfully. She set the plate down and returned to the back, leaving Aja alone to eat.

Aware that she was being watched again, but not wanting to turn around, Aja ate her breakfast nervously. The bread and cheese were tasty, and the fruit was tart and sweet. She finished them off swiftly and then rose to her feet, casting a glance over her shoulder at the woman who was watching her. Again, the Vedlyran looked away rapidly, seeming embarrassed to have been caught. *Just don't stare,* Aja thought, managing not to frown as she carried her empty plate toward the back rooms.

It was a Vedlyran man, not Katie, who came out to meet her when she approached. Aja could see that there was a short hallway leading to four rooms, one of which was a kitchen. The man took the plate from her hands with a smile. "You could have left it on the table," he said. "We'll always come get it."

"I didn't know," Aja admitted. When the man turned and went back into the kitchen, she hurriedly made her way for the door.

Once outside, it was cold, the air brisk with the nearing of winter. Aja hesitated for a moment before ultimately rushing back in and heading up to her room for her cloak. She came back out again wearing it and was much relieved when it prevented the wind from blowing right through her clothes.

As it turned out, Katie's directions were easy to follow. The street names were clearly printed on rectangular signs, and the shops on Elm Street had large display windows which showed the products one could find inside. In a short matter of time, Aja was able to find not one, but two shops that made shoes, and she chose the one with sturdier options to pick from.

The cobbler was an elder Vedlyran man with a hunched back, and before she even had a chance to tell him what she wanted, he cleared his throat and spoke up with a grumpy tone to his voice. "Sit down. No, not there, there!" He pointed to a stool beside his counter, and she hastily went to sit on it, afraid she had done something wrong. But then he walked over and knelt down, taking out a ruler from his back pocket.

At once he began to measure her feet, grumbling under his breath about her shoes being worn through.

Aja waited patiently for him to finish, worried about upsetting him with her questions. But at last, he straightened and began rummaging through his shelves of shoes. "I'm looking to buy new shoes," she began, but he answered her before she could specify what kind.

"Well of course you are," he complained. "Or you wouldn't have visited a cobbler." He turned to glance at her over his shoulder, frowning. "Are you Querian?"

"Zyphan," Aja corrected at once.

"Hmph." He looked back at his shoes, moving down the shelves until he found a pair. "Never liked the Querians," he grumbled. "We accepted their proposal of alliance too easily."

Aja didn't know what to say to that. "I was hoping to find a pair of shoes similar to the ones I have now," she answered. "Do you have anything like that?"

"You mean like this?" he said, coming back toward her with a pair of leather flats similar to her own. "Try them on," he said, setting them on the floor before her. "They will be a little large for you, but I'll measure how to adjust them. Should be ready for pickup tomorrow."

That was fast, Aja thought, impressed. He knew what she wanted even before she had asked. Slipping off her worn canvas shoes, she slid her feet into the leather ones and was impressed by how comfortable they were, if a little large for her. He knelt down and took several measurements before instructing her to take them off, and she put her own shoes on again with a smile. "What time should I come by tomorrow?" she asked. "And how much are they?"

"Two sterling," he said. "And don't try bargaining, we don't do that here. Either you pay or you get out."

"Do I pay now or tomorrow?" Aja responded, eyeing the shoes thoughtfully. They were very pretty, a dark leather that would complement her Slyen clothes, and not look out of place with her Scorian ones. *If he adjusts them to fit my feet perfectly, then walking through the desert on the way back will be a lot easier.*

The Vedlyran fingered his beard, considering. "Tomorrow," he said at length. "I should have them ready in the morning."

"Alright, I'll be back, then," Aja smiled warmly at him. She rose to her feet and headed for the door, pausing as a thought occurred to her. She still needed to find Vedlyr, but she didn't know the first place to start looking. If Slyen lived in the wild forest of Slyenials, maybe Vedlyr lived in the wilderness, too. "Is it far to the edge of the city?" she asked.

"Eh? What do you want outside the city, Zyphan?" the man snapped.

"I live near a forest, back home," she responded gently. "I just wanted to take a walk."

He frowned, but something about her face must have persuaded him because he grumbled a little and waved his hand toward the north. "There's the forest at the edge of the city," he said. "Don't go far, there are wild animals in there. The mountain lions will hunt you once dusk approaches."

"I'll keep that in mind. Thank you, mister…?" she tilted her head, waiting for a name.

"Thomas," he said, clearing his throat. He went into the back with the chosen pair of shoes before she was even out the door.

He was an odd, grumpy old man, Aja thought, retreating from the cobbler's to the street outside. She looked around until she spied the mountain foothills to the north and began to walk towards them. *I couldn't tell if he was pleased I came or if he was upset by me. But I suppose, he sold me the shoes in the end.*

The wind was brisk as Aja walked through the city, but her cloak was warm enough to protect her from the worst of it. The only thing she wished for was a hat for her ears. Yet despite how cold it was outside, the city was alive with people, and many of them stopped and stared at her as she walked by. She heard many of them whispering about her, and sometimes, the wind died down enough for her to hear their words.

"Querian, here?"

"Mama, is that a human?"

"Shouldn't let humans just wander around the city like this."

"Did she come on the ship?"

"Her cloak looks warmer than my coat."

Eventually, as Aja's walk took her closer and closer to the city's edge, the number of people nearby decreased, until at last, she was walking down an empty road toward the forest. She could see tall evergreens ahead of her, and the sight of them filled her with such excitement and homesickness that she walked faster and faster.

She missed tall trees, the scent of pine needles, and the sound of wind blowing through their branches. She longed to be surrounded by mountains and forest, to work in her garden cultivating vegetables during the day and relaxing during the night. She wanted to be home.

Breaking into a run, she dashed the final rest of the way out of the city into the forest, through the sparse trees, until she entered the thick of it. The trunks and branches helped to break the wind, and she laughed with delight when the ground became soft and covered in needles.

I missed this, she thought, tearing up. *I missed this so much!*

She only stopped running through the trees when it occurred to her that she could get lost. Not wanting to risk that, she turned to face the direction she had come from and sat down on the ground, leaning her back against a tree trunk. Here, she decided, would be just fine.

Aja closed her eyes, opened her senses, and *Listened.*

Wind. Pine needles. Swaying branches and echoing footsteps. She acknowledged these things and continued stretching her hearing as far as it could reach. Then she could hear the clip-clop of a horse's hooves on paved roads, the calls of birds, and the soft thud of pinecones falling to the ground from the evergreens. The forest was as silent and lively as her own, as foreign as it was similar.

It was distracting, when she didn't know what she should be *listening* for.

But I can do more than Listen, she reminded herself. She inhaled deeply and reached out with her senses. *Vedlyr,* she called. *Are you here?*

She waited, her heart pounding with anticipation as she *Listened* for a response. Several minutes passed, but unlike the time she had called the patrel, there was no response. Not even the hint of one.

Vedlyr, she called again, forcing all of her strength into the call. *Vedlyr please come, I need you!*

Again, she waited, sweat trickling down her forehead. She felt dizzy and exhausted, yet all she had done was call out with her energy. Was that all it took to drain her? Why was this time so different, when she had been able to call the patrel by accident?

Unless, the patrel had just been so strong that his senses were always active?

Vedlyr! Aja tried again. She opened her mouth, inhaled deeply, and called as loudly as she could. "VEDLYR!"

Her voice echoed through the trees, dampened by their trunks, until it was swallowed by the forest. She waited for several minutes, her head splitting, for something to happen. While she was still waiting, exhaustion fell over her, and she lapsed into unconsciousness.

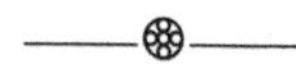

"—ja? Aja!"

Aja's eyes snapped open, and she sat up abruptly, searching for the voice that had called her from a sleep she hadn't been aware of falling into. She found herself alone in the woods, the sky growing dark and the wind colder than ever. She shivered, rubbing her arms with her hands under the cloak as she looked around. Who had called her?

There was no one here.

"I need to get back," she whispered, pulling herself to her feet. She swayed as she stood, leaned against the tree for balance, and put a hand to her head with a wince. Her head was aching with sharp pains, and she could feel her pulse pounding in her temples. Would she even be able to find her way back like this?

The wind blew through her clothes, causing her to shiver, and she gritted her teeth and forced herself to walk. She was pointed in the right direction; so as long as she could just keep moving forward, she would find her way to the city again.

The forest was even more silent than before, a place of danger now that dusk had fallen. She was keenly aware of this as she moved, and she felt an acute urgency to get back to safety. Ignoring her headache as best she could, she picked up her pace and traveled swiftly through the forest toward the city. It was a relief when she caught sight of buildings ahead of her, and she darted right up to the closest street.

I made it back, she thought, casting a glance over her shoulder toward the forest. She couldn't see any wild animals, but perhaps she wouldn't. Mountain lions might be as dangerous as forest jaguars. *I got extremely lucky,* she acknowledged. *Now if only I could figure out who was speaking to me back there.*

She walked swiftly back the way she had come, essentially in a straight line through the city toward Elm Street. There were far fewer Vedlyrans wandering at this time of night, and they only seemed to be walking about in groups of three and up. So, when she saw one Vedlyran pacing back and forth ahead of her, she was surprised.

The Vedlyran paused when he heard her footsteps, turning in her direction. It was too dark to make out his face from where she stood, and she slowed to a stop as he stiffened. *Who is he?* she thought, recalling the last time she had been wandering around a city at night. A guard had become suspicious of her in Port Anatya, and if Jaqlai had not been at the embassy when they entered, she was sure something bad would have happened.

What would she do now, if it was a Vedlyran guard? Would they be upset at her and escort her back to the ship?

"—ja?" his voice called, breaking through her thoughts. "Aja!" He broke into a run straight for her.

And Aja's fear evaporated into relief. *Jaqlai,* she realized, staying where she was as he came skidding to a stop in front of her with his ears perked high and his tail whipping side to side with anxiety. *It was his voice,* she realized. *His voice woke me from my sleep. I heard it before it happened.*

"Aja, what in Mog's name are you *doing* out here?" Jaqlai demanded. "Do you have any idea how long I've been looking for you? Mountain lions are common in this area!"

"I'm sorry," she said, smiling despite herself, she was so relieved to see him. "I was looking for Vedlyr in the forest, and I lost track of time."

"In the forest?" Jaqlai demanded, anger flashing across his face. He looked over her shoulder as though searching for danger, before taking a light hold of her elbow and tugging her along with him. He began to lead her down 5th Avenue toward the inn. "I don't even know why I'm surprised," he huffed. "Just… promise me you won't do anything that foolish again. You got lucky *this* time, but you can't count on luck. Sooner or later, it will run out, and the cost will be your life."

"I know," Aja said softly, rubbing her forehead lightly. Her head was splitting worse than before, and her stomach was grumbling incessantly. She couldn't wait to get back to the inn to eat more of Katie's delicious food and sleep in the comfortable bed in her room. "But I have to find him, Jaqlai. If I don't find him before I'm forced to leave, then everything will have been pointless. I can't come this far only to go back empty-handed."

Jaqlai sighed, shaking his head. For a few moments he was silent, his tail swishing agitatedly behind him as they walked. But when they sighted the inn, he spoke. "I was discharged, today," he said quietly. "They couldn't dishonorably discharge me, because of the information I brought back. But they would have if they could have gotten away with it."

"I'm sorry," Aja said, and she was. From the moment they had met, he had been working against all odds to return home with valuable information for his country. Yet the reward he had received was a scolding and a discharge. She didn't know what she could say to something like that.

"I don't really know what I should do with myself now," he continued, grimacing. "I can't work the only job I've ever known, and I can't return to Armons Fief because my home was seized when I was pronounced dead. I *could* go visit my parents, but it feels like giving up if I go back to them without some kind of plan."

"Your parents are your parents," Aja answered him, baffled at his reasoning. "They wouldn't care that you don't have a plan, they probably would just be happy to hear you're *alive.*"

Jaqlai paused by the door to the inn, looking at her in surprise. Then he glanced away, his expression conflicted. "I suppose you're right," he said.

"Then you know what to do," Aja said, and she opened the door. She was eager to get out of the cold and get something to eat. "I guess this means you and I will be parting ways." The relief she felt to enter a warm building was soured by the prospect of saying goodbye. Jaqlai had become such a stalwart friend that it was sad to realize she might never see him again. *Not "might,"* she corrected herself glumly. *I won't ever see him again, after I return to Slyenials.*

"I can always go home," Jaqlai said quietly. He entered after her, closing the door swiftly to shut out the chill. "But you're only here for two more days. I would rather stay and help you search."

"I thought you didn't believe Vedlyr was real," Aja said, growing hopeful at his words.

"I don't," he smiled wryly. "But I might as well stick around until it's time for you to leave."

She smiled back at him. "Why not make another deal with me?" she suggested. "If Vedlyr is real, then you'll admit that I was right, and you were wrong. Then you can buy me a nice warm hat for my return journey."

"Why stop there?" Jaqlai asked playfully. "If he's real, I'll make the return journey with you and escort you safely back to your home. I have nothing better to do, anyway." He glanced toward the door, chuckling, "And if you need a hat, I'll just buy you one."

"Hmm." Aja touched a hand to her chin thoughtfully. "Alright, it's a deal."

"We didn't discuss what I get if you're wrong," Jaqlai said. He realized he was still holding her arm, and he let go of it swiftly.

At that moment, Katie stepped out from the back, looking relieved when she saw them. "Ah, there you are," she said. "Would you like to take dinner in the dining room?"

"Yes please," Jaqlai responded. He led the way there, and Aja fell into step beside him.

"What do you want?" she asked, after the two of them took a seat at a table in the corner. No one else was in the dining room at this time. Aja assumed the other guests had eaten earlier.

"A promise," Jaqlai responded. He looked at her straight in the eyes, his expression serious. "No more *Listening* when you're on the ship. No calling up krakens, or sharks, or whales, or anything else that might be lurking about in the water."

"Done," Aja said with a shiver. She was certain that was a promise she would keep whether she found Vedlyr or not.

"Then we have a deal," Jaqlai grinned. He offered his hand, and Aja shook it.

Vedlyr

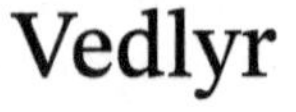

"Two sterling is a good price for leather shoes," Jaqlai said, holding the door to the cobbler's open for Aja as they both exited. They had stopped there first and after trying on and paying for the shoes, the two were headed out to the forest Aja had visited the day before.

"Is it?" she asked, stepping through with a shiver as she adjusted to the chill of the late autumn air. "I suppose leather is more valuable than canvas?" She had to admit, the shoes were warm and perfectly fitted around her feet, and the soles were sturdy and cushioned. They were a little stiff around the balls of her feet, but that sort of thing would go away as she broke them in.

"Leather shoes always fit best and last the longest," Jaqlai assured her. "And it takes a skilled craftsman to make them. I wouldn't have been surprised if he charged you four sterling."

"Then he gave me a discount?" Aja asked, thinking about their conversation from the day before. He had been cranky and gruff, but he must not have disliked her if his price was so fair. *I wonder if it's because I said I was Zyphan instead of Querian,* she thought curiously.

"You probably left a good impression," Jaqlai chuckled. "That, and you're a pretty young woman who dearly needed a new pair of shoes. I'm sure he had a soft spot for someone like you."

"Not *that* pretty," Aja laughed.

Jaqlai narrowed his eyes, one eyebrow arched. "Are you making a joke?" he asked.

Aja looked at him, not understanding his question. Feeling awkward without knowing why, she hastily changed the subject. "So, the forest," she began. "I was thinking we should go deeper this time. I had to walk two hours into the woods in Slyenials before I found Slyen, so it stands to reason that Vedlyr would be deeper in the wilderness, too."

"Well," Jaqlai shrugged, "*if* Vedlyr were a real Moglian, then your logic is sound. Moglians dislike populated areas and are notorious for being hard to find. But Mettain is a vast nation divided into seven fiefs," he shook his head. "There's no guarantee that even if he *was* real, you'd be able to find him." He frowned, looked ahead of them to the north where the tree line waited. "Not that I'm saying he exists. No Moglian would suffer their lands to be governed and ruled by others who would take their lands and do what they want with them. Moglians hate mining, logging, manufacturing… anything that the humans brought to this world. And those are all things that we do in Mettain."

"Maybe Vedlyr is different from other Moglians," Aja suggested.

"You don't know Moglians very well, do you?" Jaqlai asked wryly. "They are as possessive of their lands as a wild bear, and they'll fight to protect what's theirs. It's not their nature to approve of anything that would drastically change the landscape of their territories."

Aja thought of the changes that the Zyphans were bringing to the valley, and how Slyen was against that. She couldn't disagree with what Jaqlai was saying, but neither could she agree that he must be right. "Slyen told me Vedlyr is real, that Mettain is his land, and the Vedlyrans are his people," she said firmly. "He sent me across the whole continent to find him, so he *must* be real. That's what I choose to believe."

"You aren't going to find him," Jaqlai said, his expression pitying. "But I'll help you try. I have nothing better to do."

"You could visit your parents," Aja said, her tone defiant. She didn't want his pity, she wanted to prove him wrong.

"Later," Jaqlai said, stuffing his hands in the pockets of his jacket. "They live in Armons, which is two weeks away by carriage. You only have one more day here in Mettain before you'll have to leave with Captain Andrus. I will go see them, but I'll wait until you're gone."

"Aren't you forgetting our deal?" Aja asked playfully. "You said you'd come with me back to Slyenials."

"You're assuming you're going to find a non-existent Moglian in one tiny section of a large country," Jaqlai laughed. "When you don't find him, you'll have to leave. I might as well spend the rest of your time here *with* you, since I may never see you again."

Aja's smile faltered, and she looked down at the bricks below her feet as she walked. She didn't want to think about leaving empty handed. Didn't want to think that she would never see Jaqlai again. But he was right, wasn't he? After tomorrow, she would have to say goodbye.

Taking a deep breath, she lifted her chin and forced a confident smile. "We'll see," she said.

She sensed his smile, and the pity behind it. He didn't believe in Vedlyr or in her.

They walked for a couple of hours before Aja was satisfied with their distance from the city. She wanted to try calling with her *Listening* again, but she didn't want to attract unwanted attention. Jaqlai was not overly thrilled with how deep into the woods they had come, but he didn't argue for stopping sooner. He picked up a branch from the ground while they were walking and drew lines in the dirt, so that they could easily determine the way back.

At last, coming to a stop on the slope of the foothills, Aja took a seat on the ground with her back to a tree, facing the direction they had come from. It was colder up here than it was down in the city, and she was glad for her cloak and the warmth it provided.

"So, what now?" Jaqlai asked, drawing an arrow in the dirt with his branch. He tossed it aside and took a seat next to her, leaning back against the tree and giving her a sidelong glance. "We just sit here and wait?"

"Now, we *Listen*," she said.

"That's it?" he asked, smirking. "Seems a bit passive, if your goal is to find someone."

"Who was it that called up a patrel by *Listening*?" Aja asked, touching a finger to her chin with a thoughtful expression.

Jaqlai's smirk faded, replaced with a look of genuine worry. "Please *don't* call anything like that out here," he blurted.

"Are there any patrels in Mettain?" Aja asked, stiffening.

"Krakens only live in water," Jaqlai said, looking concerned. "Though there's no telling whether something just as dangerous lives in these woods. They're the foothills to the Rivian Range, which is the longest mountain range on the continent. Anything could live here."

"Including… Vedlyr?" Aja asked, feigning surprise.

Jaqlai flicked a pinch of pine needles at her. "Just do your *Listening*," he smirked again. "Teach me how it works. Maybe I can help."

"Alright," Aja said, brushing the needles off her cloak. "When I do it, I find it's easier if I close my eyes so I don't get distracted. Then… I just…" she struggled to put what she did into words that made sense. "It's like, listening very hard," she said, grimacing. "It feels like my skin becomes awake, and my ears open wider. I can hear things farther and farther away the longer I keep at it."

"I'll give it a try," Jaqlai said, and he closed his eyes. Aja saw his ears lift, swiveling left and right as he attempted to *Listen*.

I need to be Listening, too, she reminded herself, and closed her eyes so she wouldn't get distracted. With a deep breath in and out, she opened her senses and stretched her hearing out as far as she could. Her headache from yesterday hadn't fully gone away this morning, and it pinched painfully when she began to *Listen* as intently as she could. Grimacing unhappily, she shoved her headache to the back of her mind and focused on what she could hear.

Branches rustling in the wind, pine needles falling to the soil, the calls of birds overhead as they flew north to warmer climates. She could hear Jaqlai's quiet breathing, and the swish of his tail against the ground. And stretching her hearing further, she heard small critters skittering about in the upper branches of the evergreens.

Vedlyr, where are you? she called, wincing when trying to reach for him sent a jab of pain through her skull.

"Oh," Jaqlai started, his shoulders stiffening. "Was that you?"

"What did it sound like?"

"Nothing," he said thoughtfully. "I couldn't hear it. But I sensed something like… it's hard to say. There was a pressure in my ears that made them pop, just now."

"Interesting," Aja murmured, keeping her eyes closed. "Can you tell what I'm doing?"

"It feels a little like Influence," Jaqlai admitted. "It's familiar, at any rate. I think I can try something like it." He lapsed into silence, and Aja felt the pressure of his Influence all around her. She couldn't tell what he was trying to do, but she could certainly feel it.

Focusing again, she tried once more to call for Vedlyr. *Where are you?* she called, stretching her *Listening* out as far as she could through the trees. *Vedlyr, come here! I need to talk to you!*

Sounds from far away seemed to draw closer the longer she *Listened*. A twig snapped under a deer's hoof, startling it, and it sprinted up the hill further into the trees. A branch cracked and fell from the bowers, landing with a soft thud onto the needle-covered earth.

Vedlyr! she called, wincing as the pain in her head began to ache tremendously. This was difficult. She wasn't sure how much longer she could keep it up.

"Do that again," Jaqlai whispered. "I'm going to try something."

She felt his Influence press tightly around her, and with a nod, she tried once more. *Vedlyr, where are you?* she called. This time, she heard a quiet rumble like an earthquake emanating out from the two of them, making small echoes as the sound wave knocked against the trunks of the trees around them. It kept going, and going, further and further out in a circle.

Aja's mouth popped open, a shiver traveling down her spine. "Oh," she whispered.

"Did you feel that?" Jaqlai asked, and it sounded like he was grinning.

"I felt it," she nodded, keeping her eyes closed. "Let's do that again!"

"Okay," he said, and lifted a hand to wipe his forehead. "This is hard work."

"Yes," she agreed, but her excitement echoed his own. This was something new, something that brought his Influence and her *Listening* together. They were creating sound waves out of her call, strengthening them with Influence so that they would carry.

Taking a deep breath, Aja called again. And again. Over and over, calling Vedlyr's name. Each time, Jaqlai's Influence carried the call further, until both of them were pale from the effort. It was hard to believe that they could become so worn out while they were simply sitting down. Yet Aja was certain she had never worked for something as hard as she was working right now.

Her strength couldn't last, and soon she had to cease trying. "I need a break," she gasped, opening her eyes and turning to look at Jaqlai. It surprised her to find that the light had changed, indicating the sun had moved lower in the sky. How long had they been out here like this? Had so much time truly passed since they started?

"I get it," Jaqlai murmured, leaning with his head back against the trunk of the tree. He had a look of wonder on his face, his eyes closed tightly, and his ears raised high. "Influence… it's not as simple as we've always believed it to be. It can do so much more than just change perceptions. I can use it to strengthen things, too. My own senses, my hearing… your call. How does it work? *Why* does it work?"

Aja watched him curiously, rubbing her forehead as pain seemed to stab right through her eye. "I don't know," she said. "But I can't do what you just did."

"When you're ready, let's try again," he said, grinning. "I want to see what else I can do."

"I need a break," she said again, wincing. "My head is…"

Her words died off as a strange feeling began to wash over her. Like the swell of an ocean wave, a bewildering sensation swept over her. It began in her lower back, moving up her spine, over her shoulders, down her arms. Then it rose higher, spreading through her scalp to the very top of her head. A tingling so intense that she shuddered. It was like every single hair on her body was standing on end, screaming at her that she was being watched. A pair of eyes were now fixed directly on her, and deep in her chest, she felt a soundless rumbling like a deep purr.

I see you.

Aja's lips parted, a shiver shaking her body as she weathered the incredible sensation she had no name for. Even now, the feeling was only growing stronger. Whatever it was, it was growing closer, and the pressure of its gaze felt like the full force of the summer sun beating down on her.

I'm coming.

"Jaqlai," she said, a smile breaking across her face.

He opened his eyes, looking at her curiously. "What is it?" he asked, straightening when he saw her face.

She grinned, unable to help herself. "You should write to your parents," she said. "Tell them you won't be seeing them for a little while longer."

He frowned, ears angling suspiciously. "What do you mean?" he demanded.

"Oh, nothing," she said innocently. "Just thinking you should tell them you're about to leave Mettain for a little while."

"That's funny," Jaqlai said dryly. "Because last I checked, there were just the two of us here. I don't see any Moglians around, do you?"

Aja shrugged, closing her eyes and leaning her head against the tree behind her. "I have the feeling he'll show up," she said. "Call it a hunch."

She could still feel Vedlyr's eyes on her, like a beacon had been dropped on top of her. It was a wonder Jaqlai couldn't sense it himself. When the wind blew a gust in their faces, she shivered with the feeling of goosebumps up and down her skin all over again. *Someone* was coming, and she was certain it was Vedlyr.

"What, so that's it?" he asked, sounding disappointed. "You're not going to keep calling?"

"No, I'm done," she answered. Her skin tingled with another swell from the base of her spine to the top of her head.

"And you're just going to wait here till the supposed Moglian shows up?" he pressed.

Aja looked over at him, studying his scowl. "Would you rather I kept calling, not knowing what *else* might hear and come looking?" she asked.

He sighed, shaking his head. "No, I guess when you put it like that." He glanced up at the sky. "We can wait another hour, but after that we have to start heading back. I don't want to be out here when dusk falls."

Mountain lions, Aja reminded herself, and she was forced to agree that was for the best. "I don't think it will take too long," she said hopefully. "I can feel his gaze, even from here."

"That sounds ominous," Jaqlai frowned. "Are you *certain* it's the Moglian? And not... something else more dangerous?"

"Is that what you would prefer?" she asked coyly, and he shot her a disapproving look. "I'm sure," she said placatingly. "It's hard to say why, but it reminds me of the time Slyen called me out to speak to him. Back then, it felt like the forest was watching me, and I couldn't turn away from it. This time, it feels just like that, except less paralyzing."

"I suppose we'll find out," he remarked dryly.

The two of them waited in silence, the tingling feeling in Aja's skin only growing, until the hour had passed. Then, with a sigh, Jaqlai rose to his feet and offered his hand, pulling Aja up alongside him.

"That's as long as I'm willing to wait," he said firmly. "Let's get going."

Aja was disappointed that Vedlyr hadn't shown up, but as she could still feel the pressure of his beacon on her, she wasn't overly worried. She walked beside Jaqlai down the hill, following the lines he had drawn in the dirt. Neither of them said anything, but Aja didn't feel the need for conversation at the moment. She was anticipating Vedlyr's arrival with growing excitement, and she couldn't think of anything else.

Jaqlai, on the other hand, seemed to grow more and more worried as the minutes ticked by. He kept looking around them, glancing up at the sky to see how low the sun was. His tail swished agitatedly behind him, his ears were angled backwards, and he wore a concerned scowl on his face. Aja could feel the pressure of his Influence around them, but it was so small in comparison to the beacon that she hardly noticed it.

They were silent for the next hour and a half as they made their way back to the city. They were just getting close enough to see the buildings when suddenly, both of them turned around and stared back into the forest at the same time. Aja turned because she felt another wave of tingling wash over her, stronger than all the others. And Jaqlai turned with fear on his face, drawing a dagger from his belt and holding it out with tense muscles.

Something was running towards them on all fours.

"I want one that matches my clothes," Aja said, breaking the tense silence that had been their companion for the past hour and a half.

"What?" Jaqlai blurted, putting himself between Aja and the beast racing towards them.

"The hat," Aja said. "I want one that matches my clothes."

The sprinting cat stopped several paces from them, before straightening and standing upright like a person. Then, with a relaxed gait, he began to come towards them. Aja saw that he had tan fur with black stripes, pointed ears like Jaqlai's, and a black-tipped tail as long as he was tall. He was wearing a buttoned-up coat with a large collar and two tails in the back, and trousers that came to a stop at his knees. His eyes were yellow, and his expression was curious.

"Relax," he said, a purr to his words as he gestured with one paw toward Jaqlai's knife. "I mean you no harm."

Jaqlai did not move. His body was tense and still, his eyes wide, as he gazed at the Moglian across from them without reply. Aja wasn't even sure if he was breathing. Seeing that he was frozen in place, she stepped cautiously around him and met the Moglian's questioning gaze.

"Hello Vedlyr," she said politely. "My name is Aja, I'm here on Slyen's behalf."

"I thought that was his Influence I sensed," Vedlyr responded, coming towards her with a smile breaking across his face. "Ah, yes. I can sense it better now. What a peculiar blessing he's put on you. He always was very creative with Influence."

Here, Jaqlai's lungs protested his lack of breathing, and he sucked in a breath of air with a gasp. Grabbing Aja's wrist with one hand, he yanked her back and put himself between the two of them again. "You're no Moglian," he blurted, ears lying flat against his head. His tail had puffed up twice its normal size.

"What do you mean?" Aja asked. "How is he not a Moglian?"

Vedlyr didn't look upset in the slightest, rather his eyes shone with amusement. "My appearance?" he guessed, gesturing toward his pointed ears and long tail.

Jaqlai nodded, his eyes narrowed. "Moglians have round ears and bobbed tails," he accused.

"That is true," Vedlyr answered, folding his paws behind his back with a gentle smile. "But I am half Raelynx, and I bear the features of my mother."

"What is a Raelynx?" Aja asked, glancing between the two of them. She was certain that this was Vedlyr, and she found Jaqlai's suspicion baffling. *I'm not being tricked, am I? Is this another being like the patrel?*

Jaqlai hesitated, his knife lowering slightly. "Raelynxes are a race of cat-people like the Moglians," he said with a frown. "But they live up on Silvanus."

"Here or there makes little difference to our kind. Silvanus is the Zyphan name for Northern Moglia," Vedlyr remarked, tilting his head. "Although when I was born, Northern Moglia and Southern Moglia were still one land, and the Falling Sea had not yet fallen." He looked down at Jaqlai's knife. "I have not come here to threaten you, my son. I am simply answering your call."

"Then you *are* Vedlyr," Aja said, pulling her wrist out of Jaqlai's hand. "Aren't you?"

"Yes, I am Vedlyr," he answered, and placed a paw over his chest. He bowed at the waist, his ears flicking twice. "Greetings, Child of Slyen. To what do I owe the pleasure of your company in my lands?"

"I've come to find you at Slyen's bidding," Aja said, her heart beginning to race. She had finally done it. She had found Vedlyr and could finally accomplish what she had set out from the beginning to do. She was so relieved to be speaking to him that she found herself speaking rapidly, her words coming out in a rushed tumble. "He sent me to find you because he needs your help. There's a war starting—or actually, there's a war he wants to *stop* from happening, but he can't—or it's not just about the war, it's about Influence. He needs your help to—"

"Relax, my dear," Vedlyr chuckled. "There's no rush. The mountain lions will not hunt when I am near, so we have plenty of time."

Aja took a deep breath, her cheeks flushing with embarrassment. Why was it so hard just to say what she needed to say? "Vedlyr," she tried again. "Slyen sent me to ask for your help. He wants me to bring you back to Slyenials with me, so that the two of you can send the Zyphans out of our valley and stop the war from happening."

"Is that so?" Vedlyr asked, raising his brow. "That's rather a tall order for merely two Moglians. He should know better than anyone that I don't get involved in human wars. Neither does he."

"If the war isn't stopped, something terrible will happen," Aja insisted.

"Naturally, war is a terrible thing," Vedlyr agreed, his expression turning compassionate. "Nevertheless, I cannot get involved. I made a promise that I would never join a war, even to save lives."

"But you *wouldn't* be joining, you would be preventing one!" Aja insisted, growing frustrated. "Slyen needs your help, Vedlyr. I can't go back without you!"

"My dear…" Vedlyr sighed. "I'm afraid I cannot compromise. Even to help my brother."

"It's not a compromise," Aja insisted. "Don't you get it? He just needs your Influence to make the Zyphans leave the valley, that's all. You don't have to get involved in a war."

Vedlyr gave her a pitying look without replying.

Jaqlai had been listening and watching their conversation without moving, but at this moment he sheathed his dagger and stepped in. "Vedlyr," he said slowly. Vedlyr turned to look at him, his expression curious. "Are you familiar with human magic?"

Vedlyr's ears lifted curiously. "Somewhat," he remarked.

"Then you know that some of them have visions of the future," Jaqlai said. He turned to Aja, a conflicted expression on his face. "Tell him what you told me—about your dream."

Aja had forgotten about the conversation she and Jaqlai had shared in the desert, when she had foolishly told him all about her valley and learned that the Moglians had been the ones to cause red skies when they attempted a genocide against humanity. She shivered, her face paling. "I had a dream after I met with Slyen," she said gravely. "The skies were red, and there was a horrible sound of anger in the air. Everyone in my valley was dead, Slyens and Zyphans alike. It was because of that dream—which I had more than once—that I decided to come here in search of you."

"Aja didn't know about the past," Jaqlai said, looking towards Vedlyr. "She had never heard about the genocide that nearly wiped the humans out. I was the one who told her about it, about what the Moglians almost accomplished. If she truly does have Clairvoyance, and I personally believe she does, then there is more at risk than just a human war."

"Red skies can mean anything," Vedlyr grimaced. "It doesn't mean that the Moglians will go to war again."

"And what will happen if the Zyphans attack Queria through the forests of Moglia?" Jaqlai asked, gesturing northward with his hand. "If the forest suffers because of their war, what then? Will the Moglians be content to leave things be, or will they rise up to defend their lands?"

Vedlyr stiffened, his whiskers adjusting as he considered this.

"Please, Vedlyr," Aja said. She was grateful for Jaqlai's assistance, especially since it hadn't occurred to her to mention her dreams. "Only you can help Slyen. Only you can stop this war from happening. Won't you come with me? I only have until winter to stop them, or else they will go to war in the spring."

The half-Raelynx sighed, his shoulders slumping in defeat. "I will consider it," he said quietly. "These lands are my territory, mine to protect and watch over. If I leave, then I leave them at risk."

"Funny," Jaqlai said tersely, "I thought these were *our* lands."

Vedlyr smiled almost sadly at him. "They *are* your lands," he said, his voice gentle. "From the moment you became my children. Not once in my lifetime have these lands ever been invaded, thanks to my Influence. Or did you think it was coincidence that the only wars Mettain faces are the ones they *choose* to participate in?"

Jaqlai stiffened, his tail flicking behind him agitatedly. He said nothing in reply, as though he didn't know what he could say.

"Return to your dwellings," Vedlyr waved his paw tiredly. "I have much to consider. Tomorrow, I will give you my answer."

"Tomorrow, I have to leave," Aja said. "On the *North Wind* docked at the pier."

"You will have my answer before you go," Vedlyr promised. He turned and walked deeper into the trees.

"Wait," Aja blurted. "I have so many questions to…" her words faltered, seeming to drop off as her mind drifted. The next thing she knew, she was standing in the city at the tree line, blinking her eyes and wondering how she got there. "What happened?" she asked.

Jaqlai stood beside her with a dazed look in his eyes, his tail still puffed up twice its normal size. "He didn't want to talk anymore," he said, as though that explained everything. It didn't, but Aja was too tired to press him for a better explanation.

"I'm hungry," she said instead, and rubbed her aching forehead with one hand. She shivered when the wind blew through the open sides of her cloak.

Jaqlai blinked, glancing at her. "Me too," he admitted, before offering a wry half-smile. "Tomorrow, before you get on the ship, I'll buy you any hat you want."

"Don't forget to write your parents," she quipped, smiling back at him.

He laughed quietly under his breath. "Right," he said, leading the way back to the inn. "I'll do that."

Letters

————————⊛————————

Aja was discouraged. She waited throughout the whole next day for Vedlyr to show up, but the only thing that came for her was a notice from the city ordering her to leave on the *North Wind* with the tide. She was expected to stay the night on the ship so that they could set out first thing in the morning. After fretting and waiting the whole day, rehearsing what more she would say to Vedlyr when he showed up, an officer came by the inn to escort her to the ship. That was what brought her to the docks, where the *North Wind* waited.

"He never came," Aja said to Jaqlai, who had accompanied her to the dock. She stared dejectedly out at the city, part of her still hoping that he would show up at the last second. Her pack was slung over one shoulder, holding her clothing, and she wore her cloak over her Slyen outfit, her new leather shoes on her feet. On her head was a brand-new, wine-colored knit cap, complete with little triangles for a Vedlyran's ears to fit into. They were empty on her, of course, but it gave the impression that the cat ears were there. "I guess I have his answer."

"He may still show up," Jaqlai replied. He looked up at the ship, sliding a hand into his coat pocket where he kept his coin pouch. "For now, let's get on board and let Captain Andrus know we're heading back with him."

"You're coming?" Aja asked, glancing at him in surprise. "But I thought… since Vedlyr never showed up…"

"We had a deal, right?" he smiled kindly at her. "And anyway, I'll feel better about escorting you back to Port Anatya. Someone has to make sure you don't call up any more krakens."

She smiled back at him, chuckling. "I'm sure Andrus will be glad to hear it," she replied, turning to face the ship. She began to walk up the gangplank and heard one of the sailors calling for Andrus to let him know she had returned. *Another long trip over the sea,* she thought, sighing. She would be glad if this one were uneventful.

Captain Andrus was waiting for them once they came aboard, his arms crossed, and his eyebrows raised. "Didn't realize we'd be bringing a Vedlyran *back* with us," he said, his tone stern.

"I have money for you this time," Jaqlai answered, and Aja felt the slight pressure of his Influence around them. "I just want to make sure she gets back safely, and I'll be spending some time in Port Anatya. You won't have to worry about bringing me back here."

"Huh." Andrus scowled, glancing between Aja and Jaqlai sharply. When Jaqlai handed him a pouch of money, Andrus took it and counted it. He took half of the coins, handing the rest back. "Don't let it be said that a Zyphan swindled a Vedlyran in his own port," he complained.

Jaqlai smiled, his expression amused. "I'd never dream of it," he answered. "Thank you."

Andrus waved his hand. "I'll expect you to bunk with the crew again," he said firmly. "And you'll work if you want to eat."

"I'm fine with that."

"You, get below," he pointed to Jaqlai. Then he turned to Aja. "You, come with me a moment. I want to talk to you."

Aja nodded, shooting Jaqlai a curious glance as they parted ways. Jaqlai's smile was reassuring as he headed for the stairs and went below. *I am grateful he's coming,* she thought. *I can trust Andrus, but I feel better having a friend nearby.* She dutifully followed Andrus to his cabin, shivering as she stepped out of the cold.

He closed the door behind them, still scowling as he came toward Aja. "Getting all nice and cozy with your *boyfriend*?" he asked, an irritated tone to his words.

"He's not my boyfriend," Aja reminded. "He's just a friend."

"Does *he* know that?" Andrus accused. He walked toward her, pinching one of the pointed ears on her hat. "You're even trying to look like him, now."

"I needed a hat, and they didn't have any human ones," Aja said, frustrated by his tone. Why was he being so antagonistic? She'd only just gotten here! "Vedlyran hats all have ear sleeves sewn into them. What's wrong with you?" A thought occurred to her as she recalled his meeting with the Duke of Venecalle Fief, and some of her frustration faded. "Did your talk with the Duke go poorly?" she asked.

"It went fine," Andrus said flatly. "We presented our side of the story with proof to back it up. Since we weren't asking Mettain to join the fight, they accepted our testimony and sent us on our way."

"But you're upset," she insisted. "And it's not about my hat. What's wrong?"

Andrus sighed, folding his arms and walking across the room. He pulled something out of a drawer in his writing desk, returning at once. He held out a folded piece of very thin paper. "Read that," he said sternly.

Aja unfolded the paper, amazed at the tiny letters printed in perfect handwriting upon it. Her eyes widened as she scanned it, her stomach twinging with dread. It was a letter from Emrin.

Andrus,

This might be the last letter I ever write, but there's no getting around that. Where I'm going, the tree-cover is so dense it will be difficult to send messages by satellite. Forgive me, brother, but this is important.

Aja's gone missing, we think into the forest. The General gave up looking for her, and the men are saying she was probably eaten by a jaguar. I can't just sit by and do nothing while she's all alone out there. She was so upset about the war, and when she tried to talk to me about it, I shot her down. This is my fault, and I can't bear to think that something's happened to her because of me.

I'm going out to look for her. If you never hear from me again... then at least, I'll have disappeared to the same place she went. Stay safe on the seas.

Emrin

Aja felt light-headed reading his words, unsure whether it was distress or frustration she felt. "Emrin," she whispered, sinking down to sit in the nearest chair. How could he have been so foolish? The forest was dangerous! Aja would never have gone into it if Slyen hadn't called her out there!

"Have you read it?" Andrus asked, his tone sharp.

"I've read it," she said gravely. She lifted her gaze, staring at his frown, the anger in his eyes, and she understood. *His brother went out there because of me. That's why he's so upset.*

"If I had messaged him to tell him I met you, he never would have left," Andrus accused.

Aja nodded, feeling sick to her stomach.

"You're not going to say anything?" he demanded.

She moistened her lips, glancing down at the letter again. "What is satellite?" she asked.

Andrus looked away, re-crossing his arms. "Never mind," he said tersely. "It's not important."

"He didn't know where I was going because I didn't tell him," she said, her heart beating rapidly as anxiety rose inside her. What would he do when he couldn't find her? Would Slyen be aware of him? Would jaguars kill him? Would he get in trouble with the General for leaving? "I couldn't tell him."

"Your mission had better be important, Aja," Andrus said, raising his voice. "Because from here, it looks like you ran off to spend time with your Vedlyran boyfriend while my brother is going out and getting himself *killed* because of you!"

Aja flinched, gripping the letter tightly in her hands. "He's *not* my boyfriend," she said quietly. "He's just a friend."

"And what about Emrin?" Andrus demanded angrily. "Is he just a *friend* to you too? Did you ever *tell* him you weren't interested in him?"

"We never talked about anything like that!" Aja snapped back at him, feeling defensive. "We were friends, and I enjoyed spending time with him. He never told me he *was* interested!" All she had were her mother's words, telling her that he was probably interested in her.

Andrus seemed like he might have yelled some more, but he bit down on his words and started pacing instead, a vein bulging in his forehead. After a moment, he replied. "I know my brother," he said angrily. "And from where I'm standing, his life is in danger because of you. Because I didn't say anything when I had the chance."

Aja stared down at her hands, fighting the urge to cry. The weight of Andrus's judgment and Emrin's life was painful. Another failure, along with her inability to convince Vedlyr to come with her. *Everything was pointless,* she thought miserably. *I came down here for nothing. And now, Emrin...* she stared at the letter, at his regretful words about how Aja leaving was somehow his fault. Why on earth would he think something like that?

"What is satellite?" she asked again, her voice strained by her effort not to cry.

"I can't tell you," Andrus muttered.

"Because it's a secret, or because you don't want to?" Aja accused. She lifted her eyes, looking at him. "Is it something I can do to write back to him?"

Andrus hesitated, eyeing the letter in her hands with a conflicted expression. "It's a secret," he said slowly. "But... it *is* something you can use to write to him."

"Then I want to write to him," she said. "Please."

Andrus sighed, some of his tension relaxing. "Here," he said, returning to his writing desk. He brought a slip of paper and an ink pen to her at the table. "Write what you want to say, and I'll send it to him. I can't show you how it's done, but I will make sure it's sent to his receiver."

"Thank you," Aja said quietly. She took the pen and stared at the paper, thinking for a long time about what she could say. Finally, when the words were settled in her mind, she wrote.

Emrin,

I didn't leave because of something you said or didn't say. I left because I had something I needed to do, something important. I'm on my way back right now, so please get out of the forest before you get in trouble. Somehow, I think General Ryder's anger might be more fearsome than a jaguar. I'll be upset if you aren't there to greet me when I return.

Aja
P.S. Ask your brother to tell you about the patrel sometime.

She set the pen aside when she finished, handing the letter to Andrus. When he finished reading it, he cracked a faint smile despite himself. "Is that good enough?" she asked.

"It as much as tells him you're here with me," Andrus warned, glancing at her. "Are you sure you're okay with telling him that?"

"I'll tell him anything if it means he'll stop being foolish and leave the forest," she replied wryly. "Just… if he responds… let me read it before you reply to him, won't you?"

"You have my word," Andrus said gravely. He held the page carefully, so that his thumb didn't rub the drying ink. "For now, go back out to your cabin for the evening. I'll make sure this is sent, and I'll be sure to tell you if he replies."

"When did you receive his letter?" she asked.

"This morning," Andrus said with a grimace. "I was at the Duke's so I didn't see it until a few hours ago. But by then, it was too late to stop him."

She nodded, her stomach twisting with worry. *He's been in there since this morning. It's evening now, and the sun has already set. Dusk has come and gone. If the jaguars were to hunt him, it would have already happened.* Rising to her feet, she walked toward the door with her pulse racing. She felt sick. Why hadn't she left behind a letter or something with her mother? *Who else might have tried to come looking for me?* She wondered. Her friend Seila? Her sister?

Why hadn't she asked Slyen to watch over them for her?

"We leave before the sun rises," Andrus called to her. He remained where he was, beside the table, Aja's letter in his hand.

"Alright," she answered. She slipped out of his cabin and headed across the deck to the larboard side and leaned her arms against the railing. She gazed out across the city, feeling discouraged.

All of that travel, all of her efforts, all of the danger she had lived through—all for nothing. Tomorrow morning, they would leave Mettain. And she would have to return to Slyen empty-handed. *If I came home to find Emrin was dead, too...* her eyes filled with tears, and she buried her face in her arms so she could cry silently.

It was too painful to think about.

"There, there," a gentle voice soothed. "What's wrong, child?"

Aja sucked in a breath of air, trying to stifle her sobs. She didn't know which sailor was talking to her, but she didn't feel up for conversation right now. *Should have gone down to my room,* she thought. "Nothing," she said miserably. "Please, just... leave me alone. I don't want to talk."

There was no reply, and when she lifted her head, she saw that she was alone. Relief washed over her, and before anyone could have the chance to talk to her again, she hastily left the railing and made her way down to her small cabin that she had used on the trip down here. After closing the door and dropping her bag to the floor, she climbed into her bunk and cried herself to sleep.

They were already far from the shore and on their way northward when Aja woke up the next day. She was surprised that she hadn't had any dreams, but grateful all the same. Knowing that tragedy might be waiting for her when she returned home was almost more than she could bear, and she remained in her bunk for several hours without moving.

At length, the grumbling of her stomach prompted her to get up, so she exited her little cabin and made her way to the kitchen. *Hard tack, potato soup, and bitter tea,* she thought unhappily. She wasn't looking forward to a whole two weeks of ship meals, that was for sure.

After eating some tack and drinking a mug of tea, she went upstairs to the deck, swaying a little on her feet. She would have to adjust to being at sea all over again.

"There you are," Andrus called loudly from the helm. She looked up to see him grinning at her, which was a far cry from his anger last night. "Meet me at my cabin, I want to show you something."

Please let it be good news, she thought, making her way to his door as Andrus passed off the helm to someone else. *I don't think I can handle more bad news right now.* She was barely through the door when Andrus strode in after her, and she jumped when he slammed the door with more enthusiasm than she would have expected.

"What's wrong?" she asked.

Andrus chuckled, walking past her to his writing desk. He came back with a whole stack of papers, handing them over to her. "Read those," he said. "They're in order of when they were sent."

Curiously, and hoping for good news from Emrin, she read through the stack of letters. There were dozens of them, some only a single word or two long.

ANDRUS! EXPLAIN!

Is Aja with you?

Andrus answer me!

IS AJA WITH YOU?

Aja, if you're there with Andrus... setting aside how insane that is, we'll talk about it later... Why did you leave? Where did you go? Why are you with Andrus? And Andrus, if this is just you trying to keep me out of the forest, I swear I'll string you up by your ears next time I see you!

Why haven't you answered me?

What was that about a patrel? What patrel!?

ANDRUS.

TALK TO ME!

By the time she got to the last one, she found herself smiling in amusement. She could practically hear his voice in her mind, his exasperation at not being answered, and his impatience that caused him to send message after message trying to get a reply. "Have you written back?" she asked.

"I was waiting for you," Andrus admitted. "The good news is, I think we got him back to safety thanks to your letter. Now it's up to you to determine how much you want to tell him."

"May I write a reply?" she asked. She heard a strange beeping noise coming from his desk, and she tilted her head curiously. There was a whirring sound, a *clink, clink* of tiny metal pegs moving in rapid succession, and then another beep. "What was that?" she asked.

Andrus glanced at his desk, opened a secret panel in the side of it, and tore out another sheet of thin paper. "Another one from Emrin," he said, smirking faintly. "This one just says, 'I want to talk to Aja.'" He handed her a blank sheet of paper as well as his pen. "Go ahead, write your reply."

"Thank you," Aja murmured, taking both from him. Taking a seat at his dining table, she began to script a reply.

Emrin,
It's really me. Don't go into the forest, I'll be home in a few weeks. Will you wait for me?
Aja.

She handed it over to Andrus, relief spreading through her as she realized that one crisis at least was averted. Emrin had *not* gone to his death. "How soon will he get it?"

"The satellite has already passed, so it will be another 90 minutes," he said, taking the paper and setting it on his desk. "I'll have to ask you to leave while I'm sending it."

Nodding, Aja rose to her feet and headed for the door. "Tell me if he sends a reply, won't you?" she asked hopefully.

Andrus nodded once. "I'll do that. But we should try to limit messages to about once a day. If you spam the satellite multiple times like Emrin is doing, you'll get a slap on the wrist for misusing government property."

She wasn't sure what the satellite was, but she could understand that it was a closely guarded secret. She knew better than to ask him to explain it to her. Shooting him a faint smile, she slipped out of his cabin and walked back to the stern of the ship, looking out across the waves, and studying the line of mountains and land to the starboard.

That was where Jaqlai found her, a few minutes later.

"You're awake at last," he said, his voice wry. When she looked over at him, she saw that his ears were flat against his head, and his tail was puffed up again. It really was a comical sight, and she had to stifle the urge to touch his tail. She might have asked him what was wrong, but he started speaking before she could. "I figure we'll travel through Scoria the same way we came," he said, his voice low. "Do you know how to get back into your valley from there?"

"Not really," Aja admitted, her mood deteriorating. She leaned against the railing dejectedly. "I guess that's just one more thing I'll fail at. Wouldn't surprise me if I get all the way there only to get lost trying to find the canyon."

"I'm sure we'll find it," Jaqlai said, worry flashing across his face. "You said it's a canyon? That shouldn't be too hard to find."

"I thought you were staying in the port when we got there," Aja said, growing hopeful at the thought he might travel with her. She hated the idea of facing the desert alone.

"I did agree to travel with you," he answered, cracking a faint smile. "And a deal is a deal."

"Except that I failed my mission," Aja said miserably. "I couldn't convince Vedlyr to come, and now the Zyphans will go to war and the skies will be darkened with red and anger. Everything I love will perish."

"About that," Jaqlai said, his voice dry.

Someone cleared their throat softly on Aja's other side, and she whipped her head around to see that she and Jaqlai were not alone. Standing directly beside her with one arm resting on the railing was Vedlyr himself. She hadn't even sensed he was there.

"Feeling a little better than last night?" he asked, his voice gentle.

Aja's face flushed when she realized that *he* was the one who had spoken to her last night, when she was crying. "That was you?" she blurted. Then suddenly a more important question popped into her mind. "Wait, you're *here*?" she asked. "When did you… *how* did you…?"

Vedlyr chuckled, his tail arching elegantly behind him. "I arrived the same time you did, naturally. I had some arrangements to make—had to make sure the ship was provided with extra rations and water, most importantly. I apologize that I didn't get the chance to speak with you before boarding, but once I'd made up my mind I simply acted. I'm not used to interacting with others much these days."

"You decided to come?" Aja asked, hope and emotion surging through her so strongly that her eyes watered. *Then I haven't failed. Vedlyr is coming with us!*

"Something occurred to me last night," Vedlyr said thoughtfully, gazing out across the water toward Mettain. "I have been alive for a very long time, and not once since my brother and I parted ways has either of us tried to visit or contact the other. Your coming here was the first time I've heard from Slyen in hundreds of years. If I ignore his request to come to his aid… I may never get the chance to see him at all before…" his voice trailed off and he cleared his throat.

"Before Aja's dream has a chance of coming true?" Jaqlai asked.

"Something like that, yes," Vedlyr answered vaguely.

"Well… have you told Andrus that you're here?" Aja asked, looking around the deck. She saw Andrus at the helm again, and several sailors going about their duties. None of them so much as looked in her direction.

"It's better if they don't know I'm here," Vedlyr said, shaking his head. "My Influence directs their gaze elsewhere, so they aren't even aware of this conversation."

Aja thought of Jaqlai's Influence that had caused Cairon and Leila to freeze in the Scorian prison. "It really is fascinating what Influence can do," she said carefully. She shivered when she realized she couldn't feel Vedlyr's Influence at work. She couldn't sense it at all.

"Influence is the Seed of Ascendance that exists in all of my children," Vedlyr said, though he looked at Jaqlai as he spoke. "But only some of them are capable of Ascension. What one can do with it depends on how far they can grow."

Jaqlai narrowed his eyes. "Does that mean that some of us can learn to use Influence like the Moglians do?" he asked. "To change how plants grow, or…" he faltered, looking for another example.

"Or convince a nation of people not to go to war?" Vedlyr finished for him, sighing. "You are limiting yourself if you think of specific uses. Influence is more abstract than that. Have you ever used it to accomplish something you weren't aware Influence could do?"

Aja thought of the time they spent out in the woods, calling Vedlyr. She thought of the blessing Slyen had put on her, and of the time they escaped from Scoria. Without really understanding how it worked, it seemed to her like Influence could do just about everything. *Or is that what he's saying?* she wondered. *That what limits Jaqlai is his imagination?*

"Do I have the capability to Ascend?" Jaqlai asked quietly. There was a grim look on his face, as though he was remembering something unpleasant. "Is Ascension how my brother was able to…" he grimaced and fell quiet, shaking his head.

Vedlyr's ears angled forward curiously. "Your brother?" he asked.

Jaqlai shook his head again, firmly. "Never mind," he said quickly. "Let's change the subject."

The half-Raelynx nodded obligingly, his tail swishing as he considered what to say. "You have the capability," he remarked. "Rather, I believe you have already begun to Ascend. That is partially why I decided to come along."

"Because of me?" Jaqlai raised his eyebrows.

Vedlyr nodded. "You have come farther than anyone else, pushed yourself harder than any other. I have sensed a seed blossoming in recent years, and then quite suddenly it disappeared from my lands. I was very disappointed over it, until three days ago when it reappeared. Imagine my delight when I realized it was you," he smiled at Jaqlai. "You have been working very hard, haven't you? Pushing your Influence past its limits time and time again. It shows."

Jaqlai looked doubtful, though his ears lifted slightly at the praise. "You're sure it's me and not… someone else?" he asked, and Aja wondered if he was thinking of his brother again.

"Of course," Vedlyr chuckled. "My senses are very attuned to this sort of thing. I am something of a scholar when it comes to Influence, myself." He turned to Aja, leaning forward and gazing into her eyes thoughtfully. "I shall have to ask my brother how he came up with this blessing," he murmured. "It's quite beautifully done."

"Which blessing?" Jaqlai asked, glancing curiously between them.

"Slyen gave it to me," she said. "He said that anyone who looks in my eyes will decide not to kill me, whether they're an animal or a person."

"So that's why," Jaqlai straightened, "when the kraken came…"

"That's why," she smiled wryly.

Vedlyr touched a paw to his chin, gazing out at the waves. "I'd rather not tangle with a kraken," he said, ears angling backwards slightly. "I shall have to put a shield around the ship."

"A shield?" Aja asked, picturing the kind that could be worn on the arm. The Zyphans had ones that popped out of their gauntlets to cover half their body. Emrin had tried to explain the mechanism to her once, and she had found it fascinating.

"Something to deter any eyes from looking at us," Veldyr nodded. "Just a bit of Influence. So long as I get enough to eat, I'll have no trouble maintaining it. And we won't have to worry about any deep-sea beasts coming to check us out."

"Now that," Jaqlai said with a wry smile, "is the best news I've heard all day."

"Very good, then," Vedlyr purred. "I shall find somewhere to sit in solitude. I don't talk much with others, so I'm finding myself very tired. Farewell for now."

Before Aja had a chance to reply to him, he had suddenly disappeared. When she looked around, she couldn't find him anywhere. "It's weird," she said, shivering. "Impressive, but weird."

"Not so weird to me," Jaqlai admitted, glancing over his shoulder. "I do that too when I want to be alone."

She recalled him disappearing from sight in Scoria, when they escaped, and nodded her head in understanding. "How long will it take to reach Port Anatya?" she asked, her stomach twisting with anticipation when she thought about traveling through the desert again. Hopefully, it would be much easier   with Vedlyr.

"Roughly two weeks," Jaqlai answered. "We don't have the current with us, so it's a little slower going back." He glanced at her, his eyes drifting toward the hat she wore, and the empty triangles sewn into the cap for cat ears that she didn't have. "Is the hat warm enough?"

"Yes," she said. She was embarrassed about the cat ears, after Andrus' comments about them, but she liked how warm the knit cap was. The wine color perfectly matched her gray and garnet clothes, and it complemented her Slyen outfit as well.

"Are you still worried about finding the way back to Slyenials?" Jaqlai asked. "I don't think you need to worry. We'll have Vedlyr with us, so if you can't find the way, I'm sure he can."

"I hope you're right," Aja said. She was beginning to believe everything would work out well after all. Vedlyr was here, Emrin was safe, and they were on their way home.

I'm succeeding, she thought firmly. *I'm not a failure.*

She felt like she could face any journey, now. Even a return trip through the cold, empty desert of Scoria.

Asfarnil

A deep, vast forest of evergreens beckoned, like gravity pulling Aja inward. *Come home,* it said, filling her with longing so strong she could barely breathe. *Come home. I am waiting.*

Aja awoke with a gasp, bolting upright in bed. She forgot for a moment where she was, until she recalled everything that had happened last night. They had arrived at Port Anatya, purchased supplies for traveling in the desert, and stayed at the Vedlyran Embassy for the night. They would be heading out into Scoria today.

I dreamed of home, she thought, touching a hand to her chest and shivering. She could still feel it calling to her, as strongly as it had the day she had first gone to the clearing and met Slyen. *He's calling me home,* she realized. *I know where to go.* It was a relief to feel the tug of his call, and she felt a calm in her heart when she realized… there was no way she could get lost. She knew the way home, because Slyen was calling her there. *I'm coming,* she thought, gazing out her window. *I'll be there soon.*

She was quick to get dressed and pack up her things, few as they were. She lightly brushed her hands over her stack of letters from Emrin and smiled faintly. Andrus had let her keep them, every single one. They had written to each other once a day during the trip north, and though Aja didn't tell him anything about her quest, they talked about almost everything else.

Emrin told her how everyone was doing at home. Kyra, Aja's sister, was pregnant. Seila was courting Loran, from Nettledown. The Zyphans had stopped building new facilities and were focusing on training now that winter was on their doorstep. And Emrin talked about his work, maintaining their equipment and machinery. The most interesting letter he had sent was when he talked about his journey into the forest.

I wandered for the whole day, trying to go deeper, following my compass to the southwest. But at one point, it stopped working entirely. The strangest thing happened then, that I can't explain. While I was lost, unable to reach the satellite to check my bearings or send any messages, I became aware that I wasn't alone. When I looked up, there was a great big jaguar in front of me.

You know that saying you have, "by the time you see the spots"? I was really feeling that then, and I was sure it was the end for me. The jaguar began to walk toward me, and I started retreating from it. They say you should never take your eyes off of them, so I didn't. I just kept walking backwards. It kept following, and it stalked me for hours, never letting me go any direction but back.

*Then suddenly, before I knew it, I was stumbling out of the forest into the outskirts of Northbank. The jaguar didn't follow me out, and I got the strongest sense that I should **not** go back in. That's when I got the message from you, that you were on Andrus's ship. It felt like a sign, like you were the one who had shown me the way out of the woods.*

Aja was greatly comforted by that message, and she knew that Slyen must have been the one to guide the jaguar, to keep it from hunting him, so that Emrin would make his way safely back. *I'll have to thank Slyen when I see him,* she thought, smiling.

When she headed downstairs, Jaqlai was waiting for her. Vedlyr was nowhere in sight, but she was not surprised.

She was sure he was nearby, waiting to follow along with them as they headed out into the desert.

"Ready?" Jaqlai asked, handing her a pastry stuffed with cheese and mushrooms.

She took it, nodding. "Yes," she replied. She was wearing her cloak and long-sleeved dress, new leather shoes, and wine-colored cap. She would not be too cold out there, even with winter on their doorstep. Cait was glaring at her from the desk, but she ignored it and headed for the door.

Even though it would be the last time she saw the embassy, she didn't feel like saying goodbye.

The desert was cold, day and night, though it was colder at night. The first three days were miserable for Aja, despite her warm cloak and hat. She found herself gaining a new hatred of sand, and she regretted not buying a scarf when she had the chance. The wind was cold in her face, and the sand it threw got in her eyes and mouth. And while it was nice that the three of them came into the desert with supplies this time, she was weary from carrying two bags. She couldn't complain about it though, because the other two carried two bags as well.

It was the fourth day since they had come out into Scoria, and the sun was glaring off the sand directly into Aja's eyes. She stumbled forward with a lethargic gait, wearily putting one foot in front of the other with her mind wandering and her heart longing for home. The closer she got to Slyenials, the stronger she felt the sensation of being called. Slyen was beckoning to her unceasingly and it was becoming so unbearable to be away from home that she wanted to cry.

She missed writing to Emrin every day, reading his replies to her questions about home, enjoying his stories, and regaling him with her own. She had told him briefly about the patrel coming up to the ship while they were headed south to Mettain, and he was horrified that she and his brother had come that close to death. When he asked her about Mettain, she only said that she arranged a way for Andrus to tell Mettain their side of the conflict with Queria. He had been impressed, and when she said she couldn't talk about it further, he had let it drop without issue.

I want to tell him about my whole journey, she thought, thinking of how bizarre her trip had been. From getting captured by the Scorians to rescuing Jaqlai, even meeting Andrus and getting a ship to Mettain. All of it was surreal to think about. *I can't believe I've done all this,* she thought. *I wonder if anyone back home will believe me?*

A sharp sense of foreboding broke through her wandering thoughts, spreading through her body in a swelling wave. It crawled through her stomach like a mass of spiders, and goosebumps spread across her skin all the way down her back and arms.

Something was wrong.

"Do you feel that?" she asked, speaking loudly over the wind. Jaqlai and Vedlyr both walked ahead of her a few paces, so she almost had to shout for them to hear her.

"Feel what?" Jaqlai asked, stopping and turning around to face her. "Do you need a break?" he asked, compassion flashing across his face. They had to stop often for Aja, to make sure she had enough to eat and drink, and because she was not as physically fit as they were.

"No, I think... I think something's wrong," Aja stammered, frowning as she tried to put into words just *how wrong* it felt. Alarm was growing in her mind, and her body was reacting with dread. Stopping in place, she closed her eyes and opened her ears, stretching her senses out around her. "Something's..."

And then she heard it, like a deep rumble, too low for her ears to pick up the sound, yet it reverberated through her bones. It was surging upward from deep underground, coming toward them fast.

"Move!" Vedlyr suddenly yelled, and he grabbed both Jaqlai and Aja by the arms and sprinted, dragging them to the side. He threw them down to the ground and rolled, his fur puffed up across his whole body. His eyes were wide, the pupils narrowed to mere slits.

Aja tumbled and rolled, sliding down a slight dune before picking herself up, and she looked over just in time to see the sand swirling and sinking where they had once been standing. A wide oblong section of the desert was roiling and churning as something massive rose up underneath it, and the sand ran off to fill the space it left behind.

The first thing she saw were two massive pincers, then eight legs wriggling up through the sand. Finally, as its bulk burst upward, towering over them so large it was three times her size, a huge tail sprang up and curved over its body. There was a thick, sharp point at the end of its tail, the spike as long as Aja's arm, yet as thin as her pinky finger at its tapered tip.

Jaqlai grabbed her by the shoulders and hoisted her up, dragging her backwards away from the beast. "Don't stop!" he yelled.

"What is that?" Aja blurted, shuddering with an instinctual fear she couldn't shake. Yet all she could do as she stumbled backwards was stare, wide-eyed, at its massive form. Its exoskeleton was a deep brown, almost black, and it had fierce black eyes that seemed to follow her as Jaqlai dragged her backwards.

"It's a scorpion," he answered, his voice unsure. "But I've never seen one this big, before."

"This is no scorpion," Vedlyr said gravely, positioning himself between them and the arthropod.

The beast hissed, and Aja   as an overwhelming sense of anger emanated through the air. "Mine," it rumbled, its voice deep and whispery all at once. "How dare you steal what is MINE!"

Its massive tail came darting downward, stabbing right at Jaqlai. He shoved Aja to his left as he dove to his right, barely avoiding getting speared by the long spike. Again and again, the tail came charging down, chasing Jaqlai each time he rolled and sprinted out of the way.

"Thief!" the scorpion shrieked.

Vedlyr came darting in on all fours, sending a blast of power with a swing of his long tail. Aja could feel the force of it even though she was far away, like a gust of very strong wind. The scorpion recoiled, its pincers snapping angrily as it moved sideways, glaring at Vedlyr accusingly. "Hold!" Vedlyr called. "We come in peace. We are only passing through."

"Peacsssse?" the scorpion hissed, its tail circling in the air as its eyes fixed on Jaqlai. "*Peacsssse?*" it demanded again. "That beast stole my citizen. He stole what is *mine*."

Vedlyr looked over his shoulder at Jaqlai, who lay half-sprawled in the sand, his chest heaving as he breathed rapidly. Jaqlai's fur was puffed up too, his eyes wide and his ears laid back across his head. "Is that true?" Vedlyr asked.

"No," Jaqlai blurted. "I didn't steal anything! What are you talking about?"

A feeling of dread and understanding stole over Aja as she listened. *She* was the citizen that had been stolen, and that would make the scorpion… She swallowed, pulling herself to her feet. "Guardian!" she called loudly.

The scorpion turned its body so it could eye her, and it beckoned with its claw. "Come," it insisted, with its whispery voice barely audible over the wind. "I will take you down into the deep. You will be safe."

"I'm sorry," Aja shook her head. "I can't go back with you. I have to go back to Slyenials."

"No, come," the scorpion insisted, trying to step toward her, but Vedlyr compelled it backwards with another swing of his tail. The great arthropod made an enraged hissing sound, and once more its tail came darting downward, this time at Vedlyr.

Vedlyr sidestepped it expertly, scowling. "I understand now," he said firmly, eyeing the beast with a sharp glare. "But I'm afraid this one cannot return with you. She must go to her original home, in the Slyen Mountains."

"You *dare* steal what is mine?" the scorpion demanded.

"We are not stealing," Vedlyr said, and Aja felt pressure in the air that made her ears pop. She could only assume it was Influence. "We must escort her home."

"I will not let you!" With a cry of rage, the scorpion launched itself at Vedlyr and Jaqlai, attempting to snap both of them up in its pincers. It let out a shriek when Vedlyr sidestepped it, and Jaqlai rolled out of the way. Then it dove at them at a speed so blinding, Aja could scarcely follow its movement.

Sand sprayed everywhere as the arachnid's legs skittered across it. Its tail swung in wide circles, only to stab downward again and again. It snapped and sliced with its great pincered arms, trying to clutch at them with all of its strength. And its body exuded a horrible feeling of pressure that made Aja sick to her stomach. She was unable to remain standing as she watched, and when the ground rocked and sand moved in landslides away from the turmoil, she fell backwards, and scrambled away so that she wouldn't get caught up in the thick of it.

Despite how terrified she was, she couldn't bring herself to look away. She watched with dread and horror as it lashed out at her companions over and over, fighting to stay on her feet as the sand slid out from under her toward the struggle.

The scorpion snapped its claws toward Jaqlai, and he jumped into the air, twisting his body to avoid it. He pulled his knife from its sheath, slicing the arthropod's arm and cutting through its hard exoskeleton. It shrieked in anger and skittered sideways away from his blade.

Vedlyr sent another blast of power towards the beast, the pressure so strong that when he swung his tail, the scorpion staggered and fell backwards. Its legs flailing, it hastily gathered itself back to its feet and threw itself into the fray. As it continued to stab at them with its tail and snap at them with its pincers, a realization came over Aja.

The Guardian was trying to kill them, but they were only trying to drive it away.

Jaqlai dodged another swipe of its claws, leaping out of the way, but didn't quite make it. The claws grazed his leg, and with a cry of pain, he rolled in the sand and hacked at the pincer with his knife desperately. The scorpion hissed, drew its claw back, and stabbed downward with its tail. Jaqlai was unable to roll out of the way this time, and Aja's stomach tightened with horror when she realized that it would strike him.

It was then that Vedlyr rushed in, grasping Jaqlai with both paws and tossing him out of the way. The scorpion's tail came down, and sand sprayed into the air, obscuring Aja's view.

I can't see what's happening, she thought, her heart pounding with dread and adrenaline. *And I don't know if I want to. What do we do? How do we stop this thing? If this continues, they'll both die!*

Vedlyr had said it wasn't a scorpion. But he didn't say what it *was*. How was she supposed to help when she didn't even know what she was dealing with? And yet… could she afford to do nothing?

Her companions weren't fighting to kill, but to *survive*. And if this went on, they would both die.

This is my fault, she thought, swallowing in terror as the struggle continued. Seconds seemed to take ages, and each time the scorpion's tail stabbed downward, she feared the worst. *This wouldn't have happened if not for me. But what… what can I possibly do?*

Could she try to stop this raving beast, after it had already begun to attack them? Would her blessing work on it, even though she wasn't the one it was trying to kill?

Pulling herself upright, Aja took a step toward the battle, but then her legs froze as fear took over her. She couldn't move, all she could do was stand there. "Hey," she called, her voice dying on the wind. She sucked in a breath of air, coughed when sand got in her mouth, and then screamed. "HEY! LISTEN TO ME!" She forced all of her strength into those words, letting her energy billow out of her the way she had done when she was calling for Vedlyr with Jaqlai.

This time, her words carried. The scorpion turned, leaping toward her, and at the same time Vedlyr sprinted for her on all fours. He snatched her up in his arms and twisted his body, pulling her sideways before the arthropod could snatch her up in its pincers.

"You won't take her!" Vedlyr shouted, his words so full of authority and Influence that Aja shuddered. "She is not yours to take."

"You will release what is mine," the beast hissed, "or I will kill you all."

"You'll kill the girl?" Vedlyr demanded, scowling as he planted himself between her and the scorpion. "The very girl you came to 'rescue'?"

"If I cannot have her, then neither can you," it snarled.

Jaqlai came crawling toward them, breathing hard. There was a slash on his leg where the scorpion's claws had swiped him, but he ignored it as he pulled himself upright beside Vedlyr. "What kind of guardian does that make you?" he accused, his breath short. "Why do you even want her if you're also prepared to kill her?"

"She is mine," it insisted, pulling itself upright to its full height, tail swirling menacingly in the air. "I chose to let her live when her life was already mine. I chose to accept her gift to me in exchange for the sacrifice of *your* life. Then you stole her from me and took her far away."

"That doesn't answer the question," Jaqlai insisted. He stood as straight and tall as he could, placing one hand on Aja's shoulder. "Killing her defeats the purpose of coming out here to take her back."

"It's his pride," Vedlyr sighed, speaking under his breath. He was breathing unsteadily, and the arm he held around the small of Aja's back was trembling. He was exhausted.

This will go right back to how it was, Aja thought, prying herself from Vedlyr's grip. She stepped forward, so full of fear that her legs were shaking. But she couldn't afford to back down, now. "Look at me!" she yelled. She glared up at the scorpion's eyes, willing it to look back at her. "I was grateful to you for letting me live," she said, her voice wavering with emotion. "I believed you were benevolent, that's why I gave you something that was precious to me, so that Jaqlai could live. When I left, it was because I had to. And now, I go to my home because I have to. Don't you get it? I don't belong to you. I never did, and I never can! I *must* go home before it's too late!"

"Garnet Eagle is your home, now," the scorpion insisted, anger in its tone. "Come."

"No," Aja said. "I won't come. And if you try to hurt us one more time, I'll never, never forgive you!" She didn't have any retribution she could rain down on it. There was nothing she could have done to prevent it from taking her and killing her companions. But it didn't stop her from speaking her mind, from glaring up at the great beast despite her fear and trembling and staring it down with all her might.

It was like facing down the patrel, all over again. She felt impossibly small and weak, pathetic compared to its strength and anger.

"Come," the scorpion ordered again, digging its pincers into the ground.

"No," Aja said firmly.

"You will come," it argued. Its body pressed down against the sand, legs shifting across the ground as it nestled downward.

"I won't," she insisted, holding its gaze. They were almost eye-level now, glaring at each other, each with their own anger and defiance. But Aja could feel the pressure of Influence behind her, some of it subtle and convincing, the rest harsh and empowering. Vedlyr and Jaqlai were lending their power to her words.

"You belong to me," the scorpion hissed.

"I belong to the mountains," Aja waved her hand toward the horizon, to the northeast where her home beckoned to her even now.

The scorpion let out an enraged shriek, its body wriggling side to side as it began to bury itself under the sand. "I wanted to keep you," its voice rumbled through the earth, angry and begrudging. "I wanted more gifts of power to devour."

So that's what he did with my bag? she thought, a pang of loss flickering through her. She felt the loss of the bag that Slyen had made for her keenly. But there was no question that Jaqlai's life was more valuable. "I gave you the only power I had," she said. "And you gave me Jaqlai's life in return. Our debts to one another are paid."

"I will not forget this," the scorpion promised.

"Neither will I," Aja snapped back at it. "You are not the Guardian I thought you were."

It seemed surprised at this, and shuddering in anger, it finally had no more arguments left to make. With a rumble of power, it buried itself under the sand, delving deeper and deeper until it was so far down that they could no longer see sand swirling and pooling into place after it.

An uneasy quiet stretched around them, as they all waited breathlessly to see if it would return. And then, with a long exhale, Aja dropped down to her knees. *It's gone,* she thought with a shudder. *It's finally gone.*

Jaqlai groaned, slumping over until he was laying on his back. "You have… a terrible knack for drawing giant creatures out of the deep," he said, his heart racing so fast that he was having difficulty breathing. After a second of lying there in relief, he pulled himself up and observed his leg. "Thank goodness it's just a scratch," he added. "Those claws could have taken my whole leg off."

Vedlyr sank down to the sand, exhaustion flashing across his furry face. "I need to rest," he said quietly. "How long… till we reach your home?"

"At least a day before we enter the canyon," Aja said regretfully. "And then it's another two to three day's walk to reach my village of Northbank."

"We won't be entering your village, I think," Vedlyr dropped his head down into his paw, eyes closed with weariness. "It would be best for us to stay with Slyen."

Aja had never considered that, but now that he said it, she understood why. Showing up out of the blue with a Vedlyran and a Moglian was a surefire way to cause chaos. "Three or four days till we reach Slyen," she said. "But we can rest longer and stretch it out another day if we need to." She hoped they wouldn't need it. Being this close to home and having to prolong getting there by another day seemed like a travesty.

"We'll just rest for a little bit, and then keep going," Jaqlai said, looking across the sand in search of his bags. He spied them off in the distance and sighed in relief, grunting as he pulled himself to his feet. "I need to dress my wound."

"I won't rest long," Vedlyr said, his voice grave. "The sooner I reach my brother, the better."

Aja found herself anxious at his tone. "Are you okay?" she asked, studying him closely. He was still trembling slightly, as though the mad dash of avoiding the claws and tail of the beast had taken more out of him than he could spare. Had he been injured in the fight? Or was he just weary? She couldn't see any blood, but then, his body was covered in fur.

"I'm a lot older than I used to be," he laughed quietly. "Don't mind me. You did well, talking him down like that. That Asfarnil is older than I am, and he has pride as fearsome as his tail."

"I couldn't have done anything without Slyen's blessing, or your Influence," she shook her head. "I felt you helping me, and I'm sure it's the only reason that worked."

"I don't think you give yourself enough credit," Vedlyr said, smiling gently.

Aja didn't argue, though she felt that the only thing she really contributed was her foolish determination, and her uncanny luck. "What is Asfarnil?" she asked, changing the subject.

"A being like me," Vedlyr gestured vaguely with his paw. "Ascendant, and powerful. I do not know the name of this one, but I could sense his strength was greater than mine. He has grown lazy, which is why we are still alive. But my Influence could not have compelled him without your words."

"I'm glad he's gone," Aja shivered.

"Your words have their own power, Aja," Vedlyr said gravely. "I believe we will need them again, before all of this is over." He sighed, closed his eyes, and grew quiet.

Jaqlai rinsed his wound with some of his limited water, and bandaged it up as best he could, lamenting that there was no way to escape the sand. Then, they rested a while longer so that Vedlyr could regain his strength. At last, after munching on some of their travel rations, which were not overly tasty but well preserved, they gathered themselves and their belongings and began to head northeast once more.

Aja could not shake the shock and unease she felt at how close they had come to death. Even now, as they walked wearily but victoriously away from the scene of the fight, she felt the weight of it bearing down on her.

A heavy cloud of dread hung over her, for what reason, she didn't know, but she felt in her heart that something bad was coming, something they would not be able to avoid, no matter how lucky she was, or how persuasive her words could be.

Transference

———————⊛———————

Aja found the canyon completely by accident. It looked like any other part of the rocky slopes at the foot of the mountains, and she had passed right by it as though it weren't there. Yet after she had gone several paces, she found herself coming to an abrupt halt, unable to move her legs further. Baffled and tired, she was frustrated with herself for several seconds as she fought the invisible force holding her in place. And then suddenly, it was familiar to her.

She turned around, and immediately the feeling of being frozen faded.

We're close, she thought, and she walked until her legs froze again. Only then did she turn and face directly toward the mountain, *Listening* with all of her senses. Like a mirage being burned away by the desert sun, the mouth of the canyon appeared before her, and she inhaled excitedly. "This way," she said, and strode forward with a burst of energy.

It didn't matter that they were all three exhausted from their trip, the discovery of the canyon was like a breath of fresh air. They hurried into it, relieved to get out of the wind. Their mood lifted, and for the rest of the day, they walked quicker than before.

Since the encounter with the Asfarnil, Vedlyr had been doing poorly. He trembled and couldn't get warm, even with his fur coat. His gait was unsteady, and several times he asked them to stop so he could rest a while. But now, as they walked on firm ground towards the temperate climate of the valley, he seemed to find new energy that he hadn't had before. They rested less frequently, following the winding crevice through the mountains toward the forest.

That night they slept huddled together in a cleft of rock, Vedlyr between Aja and Jaqlai so that they could help keep him warm. Aja's dreams were troubled, vague and undefined except for one moment. One dreary moment when she saw Slyen weeping. When she woke, she felt unsettled in her heart, and she didn't know why. *Why was he crying?* she thought, burdened by her dreams. *Does he not know we're coming?*

Vedlyr was stiff and lethargic in the morning, and when they gathered up their belongings to keep going, he was unable to carry his bags. "I'm sorry," he said wearily. "I fear this journey has been harder on me than I expected."

"We'll carry them," Jaqlai said, his face full of worry. He took both of Vedlyr's bags, which were nearly empty of supplies anyhow, so that Aja didn't have to carry them. After walking for a while, Jaqlai caught up to Aja who was leading the two of them. He lowered his voice to a whisper, glancing over his shoulder with worry. "I think he was injured," he said quietly. "Back there when the scorpion was attacking us."

"Injured how?" Aja asked, anxiety rising inside her. "I didn't see any blood. Should we try to treat the wound?"

"I tried to ask him about it while you were sleeping, but he told me to leave it alone," Jaqlai sighed. "He said Moglians heal best when left alone... but I'm not convinced. He's getting worse, not better."

"Because we're traveling?" Aja asked. She looked ahead of them, longing to see the trees of her forest. They still had at least an hour before they exited the canyon. "Poor Vedlyr... what should we do?" She again felt the weight of dread hanging over her and thought of her dream where Slyen was weeping. *I have a bad feeling,* she thought, her shoulders tensing.

"I don't know," Jaqlai shook his head. "I suppose reaching his brother is the best thing we can do for him. Maybe he can help him."

Aja nodded, but she didn't feel so sure. The two of them lapsed into silence, walking with a heavy mood as they traversed the rest of the canyon.

The moment they entered the trees, it was like a weight lifted from Aja's shoulders. She felt peace in the air around her, calm in trees, and a welcoming feeling in the wind. *Welcome home,* the forest seemed to say, and she cried with relief when she sensed it. "I'm home," she said, and she rushed forward with renewed energy. Behind her, the others quickened their pace, though they slowed when Aja came to an abrupt stop.

There, standing before her amidst the trees, was Slyen.

His furry face was full of worry, his eyes shining with relief to see her. Aja shivered as a sense of joy rippled through her nerves, and then she ran forward and threw her arms around him in a hug. He stiffened with surprise, relaxing with a faint chuckle a few seconds later. "Welcome home," he said, and when he patted her awkwardly on the back, she released him. "You're thinner than when you left," he said, his voice full of concern. "The journey must have been hard for you."

As his eyes shifted to gaze past her shoulder, Aja pulled back and gestured toward the two behind her. "This is Jaqlai," she said. "Without him I never would have made it. And this is Vedlyr." Her conversation with Jaqlai sprang to her mind, and she found herself speaking before she could check her words. "I think he's injured. Can you help him?"

"Injured?" Slyen's rounded ears perked upwards in alarm. He stepped past her toward his brother, his nose and whiskers wrinkling as he sniffed. Then he flinched, taking a step backwards. "Venom?" he asked. "Vedlyr, what…?"

Vedlyr sighed, leaning against the nearest tree wearily. "There was an Asfarnil in the desert," he said gravely. "I was not quite fast enough to avoid his tail." He glanced at Aja, smiling wryly. "Seems I didn't do a very good job of keeping it hidden."

"Can you help him?" Jaqlai asked. Unlike when he had met Vedlyr, his tail had not puffed up upon meeting Slyen. There was just something so peaceful about the forest that there was no need for alarm.

"I will try," Slyen said gravely. He placed a paw on Vedlyr's shoulder, closing his eyes. Aja couldn't sense any Influence being used, but she could tell that he was concentrating very hard. At length he sighed, dropping his arm. His face was grave. "Let us travel northward," he said quietly. "There is more Influence in my grove. You may find healing there, given enough time."

"How far?" Vedlyr asked tiredly.

"Less than a day's walk," Slyen replied. He grimaced, sadness in his eyes. "If I had known…"

"You could not have known," Vedlyr shook his head. "I am still glad I came, if only to see your face again. How long has it been?"

"Too long," Slyen smiled wryly. "Far too long. Come, I will care for you in my grove as best I can." Here he turned to Jaqlai, and offering a polite bow, he said, "My name is Slyen. I welcome you to my valley, child of Vedlyr. And I thank you for caring for my child on her journey. You have my gratitude."

Jaqlai bowed awkwardly in reply, as though he wasn't sure what to do with himself. He glanced at Vedlyr questioningly. "Should we leave now, or do you want to rest?" he asked.

"Come now," Slyen said, sliding an arm around Vedlyr's shoulders to support him. "While you still can." He concentrated, closing his eyes a moment, and then turned to look to his left. Out of the woods, a large jaguar came bounding toward them, so large that Aja froze in terror. But all it did was run up to Slyen, where it waited patiently by his side. "Fear not," Slyen said, glancing toward Aja and Jaqlai in amusement. "This one is here to help."

Slyen helped Vedlyr climb onto the jaguar's back and stood by his side as they began to walk. He led the way at a brisk pace, and the four of them traveled through the forest northward. It was quiet, even with the sounds of birds and insects, and wind blowing through the branches overhead. Several hours passed as they walked, yet not once did they have to stop and rest. The air was revitalizing, and even Vedlyr seemed to improve the longer they were in the woods.

When they reached the clearing, it was evening. Slyen brought his brother to the center of it and made him lie down on the cushy moss. The jaguar who had carried him purred as it rubbed up against Slyen's side, and then, just as quickly as it had appeared, it bounded away into the trees. "Rest now," Slyen said quietly. "You'll need your strength."

Vedlyr gave a short, wry laugh. "I came all this way," he said wearily, "and I may not be able to help you after all."

"You don't know that," Slyen said, worry flashing across his face. His whiskers bristled as he grimaced, and he placed a paw on his brother's shoulder. "I need you, Vedlyr. There's no one else."

"What is it you need?" Jaqlai asked, coming forward. "If it's Influence… maybe I can help."

Slyen scowled, looking at him sharply. "Your Influence is not nearly strong enough," he scolded. "No, I don't think you can help me."

"You won't even let me try?" Jaqlai asked, crossing his arms. His tail jerked side to side erratically. "This forest is *filled* with Influence. If I use mine to join with it, I'm sure I could help you convince the Zyphans not to start the war."

"Your heart may have the determination needed," Slyen sighed, shaking his head. "But it is not your heart that is lacking, it is your strength. And I'm not trying to stop the humans' war. My goal is for the Zyphans to leave the valley, and not use it *in* their war. Trying to prevent it entirely would be futile."

Aja felt a clenching in her stomach as frustration bubbled up inside her. "But we *have* to stop the war!" she insisted. "If we don't, the Moglians will try to finish what they started. Everyone will die—not just the Zyphans, but the people of Slyenials too."

Slyen looked astounded at her words and tone, his eyes widening as he stared at her. "Good gracious," he exclaimed. "How on earth did you learn about that? Not from me, certainly." He sighed, shaking his head. "You needn't fear such a thing happening, it would take a very serious grievance for Moglians to band together for war. We are fiercely individual, and trying to unite territorial recluses like us is like… well, herding *cats*."

Despite the humorous picture his words painted, Aja felt only dread in her heart. "I don't know *how* it will happen, but I am certain it will. I saw it in a dream." Her face twisted with a grimace. "And my dreams come true."

At Slyen's baffled face, Jaqlai cleared his throat and explained. "Have you heard of Clairvoyance?" he asked. "It's human magic—the ability to see things before they happen. I believe Aja has it."

Slyen glanced between the two, frowning thoughtfully. "I'm aware that Aja has *nightmares,* but nightmares are not truth."

Vedlyr lifted his paw, placing it on Slyen's arm. "There is cause for concern," he said gravely. "And it's the reason I came at all. This war they intend to start… the Zyphans plan to attack Queria through Moglia."

"I was aware of that," Slyen frowned. "And I have observed their plans while they were unaware of my presence. They will take their ships eastward up the Uliah, then make landfall outside the mountains. Then they will travel south and infiltrate Queria. The northern cities are not well fortified, because they would never expect to be hit from the north. Zypha plans to take control of many cities, and then they will leave when Queria meets their demands. It will not be a drawn-out war."

"You think that the Moglians will be content with humans marching through their territory?" Vedlyr asked, shaking his head. "And what if Queria does something unpredictable? Do not forget that it was Queria who incited the Moglians to band together in the first place."

"I have not forgotten, but I do not think it will be an issue," Slyen insisted. "They will be traveling right up against my mountains, which is still part of my territory."

"I know what I saw in my dream," Aja cut in. "It was red skies, and all of us were dead. I could feel anger in the air."

Slyen hesitated, eyeing her thoughtfully. But at length, he sighed and took a seat beside his brother. "I do not believe the Moglians will band together over this war. It will not last longer than a year, I'm sure of it. Zypha does not fight for conquest."

"But," Aja began, filled with frustration.

Slyen cut her off with a shake of his head. "I will not discuss it further," he said. "The goal is to make the Zyphans leave the valley and not use it in their war. That is all." He turned to his brother, his face softening with worry. "Are you sure you can't manage even that?"

Vedlyr looked up at him with a sad smile that said more than words could. It was full of resignation and apology. "I am fading, brother," he said quietly. "I made it here, but that is all I had strength for. I'm sorry."

Jaqlai came forward, kneeling on the moss beside him. His ears drooped against the sides of his head as he reached a hand out and placed it on Vedlyr's shoulder. "I'm sorry," he said grimly. "It's my fault you were struck by the scorpion's tail."

"You could not have predicted the Asfarnil's appearance," Vedlyr shook his head. "Fret not, my son."

"I want to help," Jaqlai said. He lifted his head, turning to Slyen. "Please, it's my fault this happened. Let me at least *try* to help you."

"There is *one* way you may be able to help," Vedlyr said, a thoughtful expression crossing his face. He pulled himself upright with a grunt, exhaling tiredly when he was sitting up beside Slyen. "And I fear... it is something I must do anyway. Mettain needs a guardian. It has been my territory to watch over, given to me by our father before he passed. And now that I am faced with my own end, I realize that I have no descendant to pass its protection to."

"Your death is not certain," Slyen said quickly, tensing at Vedlyr's words. "You may still recover."

"And I may not," Vedlyr said. "Either way, here I must remain until I die or survive. And Mettain needs a protector." He looked into Jaqlai's face, his gaze searching. "Are you willing to be that person?"

Jaqlai's ears shot up in surprise, and he glanced quickly from Vedlyr's intense gaze to Slyen's anxious one. "Me?" he blurted. "What do you mean? What kind of guardian?"

"One who will use his Influence to ward away ill intent," Vedlyr said, his words calm. "Who will convince other nations to not invade or attack. Who will put pressure on the hearts of Mettain's leaders, to hold them accountable for their deeds and encourage them to seek peace and rule justly. Someone who will use their Influence to remind other Moglians that Mettain is guarded, and they may not come and claim territory there."

"I can't do those things," Jaqlai grimaced. "I'm not a Moglian."

"No," Vedlyr smiled faintly. "But you *are* ascended. You have broken through the barrier of your kind, pushed your Influence past its limits. All you lack is strength, which will come to you as years pass. Or…"

"Vedlyr," Slyen said, his voice grieved.

"Or," Vedlyr continued firmly, "it can be given to you. The only question is whether you will accept it, and the responsibility that comes with it." He offered a weak smile, his ears twitching to the side. "Are you willing, Jaqlai? Willing to become my successor, and protect my lands as I have done?"

"For how long?" Jaqlai asked. "And what happens after I die? Do I need to find a successor, too?"

Slyen looked him up and down, eyes narrowed slightly as he considered him. "Hmm," he said thoughtfully, touching a paw to his chin. "I see."

See what? Aja wondered. She was standing a few paces away, listening with worry and awe. She didn't have anything to contribute to the conversation and felt like an outsider watching the situation unfold. Would Vedlyr truly die? *It was my fault he got injured,* she thought miserably. *Not Jaqlai's, mine. I wish I could help him. But what can I do? I'm useless now.*

She had done her part, and now the rest was up to them. So why did she feel so restless? Why did she feel like there was something more she should do?

"Yes," Vedlyr said, to whatever it was Slyen had observed. But then, for Aja and Jaqlai's sake, he explained. "You see, Jaqlai," he reached out and took Jaqlai's hand. "You have already ascended, which has expanded the years of your life. And if you accept my strength and ascend again, your years will extend further. You will live for many, many years, growing stronger and stronger."

"You mean I'll live as long as a Moglian?" Jaqlai asked, looking alarmed.

"Yes," Vedlyr nodded. "You would anyway, I think. Your affinity for Influence is very strong, and you push yourself past your limits carefully. You are wise in how you use your strength, and it makes me very proud."

"Then, I can help?" Jaqlai asked, glancing between the brothers hopefully. "If I become the guardian for you—until you are well enough to return—will I be able to help you make the Zyphans leave?"

"Theoretically, yes," Slyen sighed. "With Vedlyr's strength, you would be able to help. Though I suspect I'll have to guide you."

"Then I accept," Jaqlai looked at Vedlyr firmly, squeezing his paw. "I will become the guardian until you return."

"I may never return," Vedlyr warned, sadness filling his eyes. "I may stay here until I perish."

"I'll wait for you," Jaqlai insisted, shaking his head. "So, you have to hold on, Vedlyr. Hold on, and don't give up."

Aja walked forward, taking a seat beside Slyen, her chest aching with concern. *I don't want him to die,* she thought. *I wish there was something I could do for him.* She began to search her thoughts and memories, trying to find some way she could help him. Her people had medicinal plants and poultices they could make, some of them good for insect bites and stings. Perhaps they could be used to draw out the venom and fight any infection left behind. *It's worth finding out,* she thought. *I'll have to ask my mother what she recommends.*

"Thank you," Vedlyr smiled warmly. "Now, lean your head forward." Jaqlai obliged, and Vedlyr placed a paw on top of his head. Then, closing his eyes, Vedlyr inhaled deeply, held his breath for a long time, and then exhaled on Jaqlai.

A strange sensation rippled through the air, causing the hair on Aja's arms to stand on end. The air felt tight and electrified, her ears popped, and she sensed something like a current of wind flowing from Vedlyr into Jaqlai. She watched with amazement, yet she could see nothing happening. They just sat perfectly still, and if she hadn't been able to feel the change happening, she would not have known it was happening at all.

At last, the sensation faded. Vedlyr dropped his arm, letting out a tired sigh. Now that his strength had been passed on, a change came over him that Aja could not quite place. His color had not changed, yet he seemed faded and desaturated. His height had not changed, yet he seemed somewhat smaller than before. A presence of strength and authority that he had once carried effortlessly now seemed to have evaporated, leaving him nothing more than a tired, frail-looking cat.

She felt grieved in her heart at the change and had to fight to keep tears from rolling down her face. *It's my fault,* she thought again.

Jaqlai sat very still after the transfer. His fur was puffed up, his eyes wide, and he was holding his breath. When he could no longer hold it, he inhaled deeply and began to shudder, lifting a hand and placing it over his heart. "I feel," he whispered, blinking. He didn't finish his sentence, as though he didn't know how.

Slyen stood, nodding. "It was successful," he said gravely. "I did not expect that."

Jaqlai's eyes snapped up to meet his, and he rose to his feet as well. "I can help," he said.

"Yes," Slyen agreed. "I'll instruct you on what to do when the time is right. But first," he turned to Aja, offering his paw. When she reached up to take it, he pulled her up beside him. "Our Influence will be persuasive and compelling," he explained, looking into her face with a grave expression. "But it will work best with a catalyst. You are that catalyst, Aja."

She stared at him questioningly, her heart beginning to race. *I knew there was something more I could do,* she thought, hope stirring inside her.

"I need someone to speak for me," Slyen said. "Someone to represent my will to the Zyphans. You will be my right paw, and you will bring this message to the Zyphans: Leave my valley as it used to be, and do not use this place for your war. Those who wish to stay may only do so if they follow the Tenets of my people. And do not speak of this valley to anyone, or my wrath will follow you."

"That's all?" Aja asked, disappointed. She was still frustrated that he didn't care about stopping the war, and in her heart, she knew that she would not rest until she had tried her best to stop it. *I have to believe my dreams,* she thought. *I will never make the mistake of ignoring them again.*

"That's all," Slyen nodded. "Your words will be the catalyst, and our Influence will compel them to listen and follow them. It cannot happen without you, Aja."

Aja's resolve solidified in her heart. "Alright," she said. "I will go and speak to them."

She knew where to start. All she had to do was go home and see the General.

"Good," Slyen smiled warmly, patting her shoulder twice. "You have grown bolder on your journey, Aja. I'm proud of you."

It made her heart clench with emotion to hear him say that. She had worked so hard, doing things she wasn't good at, never giving up until she completed her mission. Now she was back, and it meant the world to her to hear him praise her.

Now, it was time to return to her home, to pass on Slyen's message, and to finish her task.

I can't wait to tell my mom everything, she thought, smiling brightly at Slyen. She hugged him tightly, filled with anticipation of what was to come. "I'll give the General your message," she promised, releasing him and stepping back. "And I'll convince them to leave."

She would convince them not to go to war, too.

"Good luck," Slyen smiled at her. "My Influence will be with you."

"And mine too," Jaqlai promised, and he grinned at her playfully. "Put that luck of yours to good use, Aja. And try not to get *too* distracted by your sweetheart."

Aja flushed, surprised to hear him tease her about Emrin. She hadn't talked about him to Jaqlai, so how did he know? Or was it obvious that she was thinking about him?

Perhaps he had seen her reading through Emrin's letters every night. "I won't get distracted," she said indignantly.

"When the Zyphans leave," Slyen said, raising an eyebrow at their banter, "I want you to return here once more. I would like to speak to you when it's over."

"Alright," Aja promised. She looked toward the edge of the clearing, anxiety beginning to grow inside her. As much as she longed to go home, she was afraid. What would they say when she walked in? Would the General listen to her? Would she be able to say what she needed to say without faltering?

"Our intentions are with you," Vedlyr said. She turned to look at him, and saw that while he was lying down again, resting, his eyes were open and fixed on her face. "You will not fail."

"Alright," Aja said, smiling faintly. Weeks ago, before she had set out on her journey, she had been upset because no one spoke up to the Zyphans to get them to leave or give up their war. Now, it was her chance, her *responsibility*, to be the one to speak to them.

I won't fail, she repeated to herself. She turned her back to the others and walked toward her home. The sooner she left, the sooner she could return with help for Vedlyr.

Catspaw

It was surreal, stepping out of the trees into the clearing, and seeing her home after all this time. The sun had set by the time Aja came to Northbank, and the only lights came from inside the buildings and houses. It was too cold for people to be spending time outside, so she encountered no one as she walked briskly toward the village and headed for her house.

The garden had been tended to while she was away. As she came up beside the fence, she saw that all the fall vegetables had been harvested, and the beds were ready to rest during the coming winter. Smiling gratefully, Aja faced the door of her house, walking up the short steps and pushing open the door. *I'm home,* she thought, turning her head to the left as she entered. There was the mirror, showing a thinner woman than the one who had left, with knotted hair tied loosely in a frazzled braid, wearing her Scorian clothing and cloak, and her cat-eared hat atop her head. Aja closed the door behind her, sliding off her shoes and stepping into the sitting room.

She had scarcely taken one step before the General came storming out of his room, demanding, "Who's barging into the house uninvited?" But as he turned the corner and stared at her, his anger evaporated, astonishment filling his face. "Aja?" he blurted.

A smile spread across Aja's face. She had not expected the rush of emotions that went through her when she saw his face, and she had to struggle not to cry. "I'm home," she said.

Delia came hurrying out of the kitchen, wiping flour from her hands on an apron tied around her waist. Then she ran forward and threw her arms around her daughter, her breath catching in her throat. "Aja," she said, her voice wavering. "I was so worried."

"I'm sorry," Aja hugged her back, tears filling her eyes. She couldn't help it when they slid down her cheeks. "I had to go."

"I know," Delia murmured. She released her daughter after a moment, staring searchingly into her face for a while. Then she smiled wryly. "Don't ever go again."

Aja laughed, wiping her eyes.

"Where did you go?" General Ryder asked, coming towards them with relief and emotion in his eyes. "I don't understand. We searched for you—searched for weeks! We were devastated when we couldn't find you. I thought..." his voice trailed off, and he placed a hand on her shoulder, giving it a squeeze. It was clear he thought she had died, but he didn't want to say the words. "I'm so glad," he said, his voice tight. "That you've returned."

She was touched by his concern, reminded of her dream all those weeks ago. He had not wanted to give up on her, even when he knew it was foolish. "I left Slyenials," Aja said, surprised by how calm she felt as she spoke. Even though it was daunting to tell the Zyphans Slyen's message, she felt no fear. She was emboldened by the safety she felt in her own home, and she knew that Slyen and Jaqlai were supporting her, using their Influence to make her words more persuasive.

"You left the valley?" Ryder asked, astounded. "How on earth did you do that?"

"I went through the mountains," Aja said, not wanting to tell him about the canyon. Somehow, she had the sense that Slyen wouldn't want her to tell him.

"What on earth for?" Ryder asked, now looking alarmed. He turned toward Delia, eyebrows raised. "She looks half starved," he began.

Delia nodded, a mothering look entering her eyes. "Come and sit down," she told Aja, taking her hand and pulling her toward the dining table. "I'll get you something to eat."

I've missed mother's cooking, Aja thought, her stomach grumbling at the thought. She allowed herself to be pulled to the table, and smiled when the General pulled the chair back for her to take a seat. "I missed you," she said to them. "I missed you both so much."

The General cleared his throat, standing awkwardly beside the table. "We missed you too," he admitted, and he twisted the end of his mustache between his fingers absently.

They didn't question her again until she had eaten a healthy portion of soup and bread, and when she had finished eating, her mother gave her a mug of honey tea. Then Delia and Ryder both sat at the table with her, studying her with worried glances.

"Where did you go?" Ryder asked softly, and there was no accusation in his words. Only concern, and relief that she had returned. "Why did you go? Is it because you were upset?"

"I suppose that's part of it," Aja admitted, warming her hands by holding her mug between them. "But I left because I had to." She stared into his eyes with calm determination. "I was sent by the guardian of Slyenials."

"The... guardian of Slyenials?" the General asked, frowning.

Aja nodded. "Slyen," she said. "The Moglian."

Fear filled Ryder's eyes, and he tensed at once. For a moment he just sat there, gazing intently into her eyes as though trying to see if she was serious. Then he let out a breath of air, leaning back against his chair. "Slyen mountains... Slyenials..." he said with an almost weary tone. "The naming should have given it away. Of course, they belong to a Moglian. That's why no one has ever heard of this place."

Lifting her mug of tea, Aja took a sip and studied him, wondering at the resignation in his face. *It seems like he already understands what I'm about to tell him,* she thought. *He knows that Slyen wants him to leave.* "Slyen sent me to Mettain," she said. "So that I could bring his brother up here. I did what he asked, and now I have a message from him for you."

"Now there's two of them here?" Ryder asked, stiffening. He rubbed his face with one hand, sweat beading on his forehead. "Tell me the message," he said, his voice grave.

It was clear that he had no doubt toward Aja or her words. He believed her.

"Slyen said, 'Leave my valley as it used to be, and do not use this place for your war. Those who wish to stay may only do so if they follow the Tenets of my people. And do not speak of this valley to anyone, or my wrath will follow you.'" The words came to her easily, as though Slyen had placed them in her mind so that she wouldn't forget them. Perhaps that was his Influence at work.

"Is that all?" Ryder asked, skepticism in his tone. "No threats or punishment for us being here?"

"Of course not," Aja said, shaking her head. "Our people welcomed you. And you are welcome, just not your war, and not the changes you want to bring."

"He won't even allow us to bring your people electricity and plumbing?" Ryder asked in frustration. He leaned forward, folding his hands and resting them on the table as he considered her words.

Aja waited for a moment, unsure how to answer him. But then her heart prompted her to speak, and she breathed deeply. "I have one other message," she said. "Not from Slyen, but from me. From my journey to Mettain and back."

The General grimaced, and he gave her a weary look. "Can it wait till tomorrow?" he asked gravely. "I... need time to think. It's late, and I'm troubled by this news. I promise you that I'll listen to you tomorrow."

Aja wanted to talk to him now, but she recognized that it might not be the best time. Reluctantly, she nodded her head. *Perhaps it's better this way,* she thought. *Influence might have a better chance to work on him if I give it some time.* "Alright," she answered.

General Ryder rose to his feet, scooting his chair backwards. He came around the table and patted Aja on the shoulder a couple times. "I'm glad you're back, and that you're alright," he said genuinely. "And thank you, for bringing Slyen's message to me. I will consider it seriously." He glanced toward Delia, giving her a nod. "I'll see you in the morning," he told them both.

"Good night," Delia nodded back.

Ryder walked out of the room, his face clouded with worry and dread as he headed down the short hallway for his room. When his door was closed, Delia leaned across the table, placing a hand on her daughter's arm.

"I missed you," Aja said, swallowing. "I missed you so much."

"I worried for you every day," Delia said, squeezing her arm. "But I believed in you. I believed you would return to us safely."

Aja placed her hand over her mother's. The mention of safety brought Vedlyr's condition to mind, and she looked at Delia urgently. "The Moglian I brought up from Mettain," she said quickly. "He was stung by a giant scorpion, and he might be dying. Is there anything we can do to help him?"

"Scorpion?" Delia asked, frowning slightly. "I'm not sure what that is."

"It was a giant insect with eight legs," Aja explained. "It had sharp pincers and a long tail that carries venom."

"An insect sting," Delia said thoughtfully. She let go of Aja's arm and leaned back, considering. "Yes, we could make a poultice I suppose. And there's tea we can brew that will help him fight infection." She tilted her head, her eyes brightening as a thought occurred to her. "The Zyphans have advanced medicines that might be more helpful. Perhaps tomorrow you could ask for some."

"I'd rather go to him tonight," Aja said, thinking of how frail he had looked when she had left. "He needs help as soon as possible."

"It is too late now," Delia shook her head. "I need time to prepare everything. Besides, sleep is necessary for healing, and interrupted sleep can make an injury worse. Wait until morning, and I'll have something ready that you can take to him."

Aja's face pinched with worry, but she saw the logic in her mother's words, and she herself was so tired she was unsure she could make another journey out to the clearing tonight. "First thing in the morning," she said.

"First thing," her mother agreed. "Now, come get ready for bed."

It was a relief to be able to brush her hair, bathe herself, and dress in clean nightclothes before climbing into her own bed. She was so comforted by the familiarity of home that she fell asleep the moment her head touched her pillow.

The next morning, after Aja dressed herself and came out to the kitchen, she helped her mother make a poultice for Vedlyr, while Delia made medicinal tea and stored it in a bottle that could be closed and carried. They were just finishing when there was a knock at the door.

General Ryder came out of his room, dressed in his uniform and grumbling under his breath. When he saw Aja, he came to an abrupt stop with his eyebrows raised, and astonishment filled his eyes. "You're back!" he declared. "Of course, last night you..." he paused when another knock sounded at the door, and his face twisted with irritation. "Right, well, since you're back, *you* can deal with him."

Aja glanced toward the door questioningly. "Him?" she asked.

"He's been showing up here every week," Ryder sighed. He went into the kitchen, found the kettle already hot, and began to prepare himself his morning coffee. "Go on," he waved his hand. "Go get the door."

Aja's heart fluttered as she walked toward the front door, anticipating who would be on the other side. She hesitated with her hand on the handle, wondering what face he would make when she opened the door. Smiling nervously, she pulled it open and gazed out toward the soldier who was standing on the front steps.

It was Emrin. She had known it would be him.

Emrin's handsome face filled with disbelief when he saw her, and then he reached out, grabbing hold of her hand with his own. He inhaled sharply when he squeezed it. "You're real," he blurted. "You're really... home?"

Aja felt a pounding in her heart as she looked at him, and she realized that she had been longing to see his face and hear his voice for so long, that she hardly knew what to do with herself. She smiled nervously. "I'm home," she confirmed.

"Invite him in," Delia called from the kitchen.

"May I?" Emrin asked, unable to take his eyes away from her face. His eyes were worried as he studied her. "I've been coming by to help out during my off days."

"Help out?" Aja asked, stepping backwards to allow him into the house.

"You know, since you weren't around," Emrin said, a little awkwardly. He offered a meek smile. "I couldn't let your garden go untended."

"You were the one who harvested the vegetables?" Aja asked, surprised. "I didn't realize you could garden."

"Well, I had help," he laughed as he stepped into the house. Aja noticed that he took his shoes off at the door and smiled gratefully. He didn't even glance at the mirror beside him. "When did you get back?" he asked.

"Last night," Aja said. She glanced toward the General and saw that he was standing in the sitting room, arms crossed, watching them. Nervously, she let go of Emrin's hand.

"I'd like to speak with you," Ryder told her, his voice grave, "about what we discussed last night. Will you come to my office at the barracks?"

Aja thought of Vedlyr, and worry clutched at her heart. "One of my traveling companions was injured," she said. "I need to take medicine to him."

"Can it wait?" Ryder asked. "I need to speak to you right away."

"No, I don't think it can," Aja insisted. "He was stung by a scorpion, and he's dying."

Ryder's face filled with surprise. "A scorpion?" he asked, baffled.

"We came up through Scoria," she explained.

Understanding passed through his eyes. "We have medicine for that kind of thing," he said, his voice softening with compassion. "If you wait until after our meeting, I'll get some for you."

Emrin stepped forward, saluting the General. "Sir," he said politely. "Perhaps I could get the medicine and take it to her travel companion?" He glanced at Aja with a concerned expression. "Then you could meet with the General and not have to worry about your friend."

"Would you really?" Aja asked. She felt the pressure of urgency, both to help Vedlyr, and to speak to Ryder about the war. And if Emrin was willing to go… "We made a poultice and some tea," she said. "If you could bring that and your medicine into the forest, that would mean the world to me."

"Sir?" Emrin asked, looking toward the General with a hopeful expression.

Ryder nodded once. "It's your off day," he said. "Just be back before dusk."

Emrin smiled gratefully. "I'll take them," he told Aja. "Which way do I go?"

"There's a large clearing to the southwest," Aja explained. "It will take you a couple hours to reach it, and I'm worried about you getting lost. But… if you call out for Slyen by name, perhaps he will guide you there like he guided me."

"Slyen?" Emrin asked.

"He's a Moglian," Aja said, smiling faintly when he jolted and gave her an alarmed look. "Don't worry," she added. "He's peaceful. This is his valley, and it takes after him."

"I'll… take your word on it," Emrin said nervously. He seemed reluctant to leave her side, but after a moment he walked toward Delia and took the tea and poultice from her. "I won't rest until I find him," he promised. "So please… still be here when I get back."

"I'll be here," Aja said.

He smiled, relief filling his face. With a final salute to the General, he put his shoes back on and walked out of the house, heading first for the barracks.

Ryder waited until he was gone to speak again. "I would prefer if you don't tell anyone else about the Moglian, for now," he said quietly. "Until we're done with our discussion, I'd like to consider it confidential."

"Alright," Aja replied.

"You said you had more to speak to me about," he continued. "And I'd like to hear it all. Please come with me to the barracks." He walked toward the door, pausing beside the mirror to fix his uniform, and then walked outside. He waited for her on the path as she slipped on her leather shoes, put on her Vedlyran hat, and donned her warm Scorian cloak. When she stepped out beside him, he looked at her hat with a raised eyebrow.

"I went to Mettain," she reminded him.

He nodded, cleared his throat, and began to walk. It was a short trip to the barracks, and when they entered, Aja was surprised by how warm it was inside. The building was well designed to have improved air flow, but it wasn't heated by wood-fired stoves like the Slyen houses were. The Zyphans had built the barracks to run on electricity created by a steam-powered generator. Aja remembered the General describing it proudly to her, though she hadn't paid much attention to that particular soliloquy. Now as she considered how nice the temperature was in the building, she wished she had.

Aja felt the eyes of several soldiers as she and the General headed toward his office, and she heard several hushed comments as they passed by.

"She's back?" one blurted.

"I thought she died," another remarked.

"Someone should tell Emrin," another snickered.

Aja flushed at the last one, thinking of Emrin and how warm his hand had felt when he held hers. *I'm glad he was willing to take medicine to Vedlyr,* she thought. *But I wish I could have gone with him.* Maybe after her meeting, she should go into the forest after him… just to make sure he made it. Her *Listening* would help her find him.

When they reached the General's office at the back of the first floor, he instructed his officers not to disturb them and closed the door. Then he gestured to a chair opposite his desk, waiting until Aja was seated before he sat down himself.

"Thank you for coming," he said. "I've been thinking about what you told me last night, about the Moglian and his message for us." He gave her a wry look, folding his hands on the surface of his desk. "For what it's worth, I believe you. Somehow, at the back of my mind, I think I always knew that these lands belonged to a Moglian. It was too secluded, too perfectly situated, and the fact that no one in the world knew it was here seemed like a miracle."

"Then about his message," Aja said, leaning forward. "What are you going to do about it?"

"That's the question, isn't it?" he commented soberly. "He asked for four things—leave the valley as it used to be, don't involve Slyenials in the war, follow the Tenets of your people, and keep the valley secret from the world. It doesn't seem like a lot at first glance, but I don't know how easily I'll be able to implement it. Even I have people I answer to, and they may not take the message well."

"There's more that I haven't told you yet," Aja said seriously. "And I think once you hear it, you might find it easier to follow Slyen's request."

Ryder grimaced. "Let's hear it then," he said.

Aja took a deep breath, hoping that Slyen's and Jaqlai's Influence was still with her. She couldn't sense it being used, but then, she had not been able to sense Slyen's Influence very well to begin with. Perhaps now that Jaqlai was stronger, his Influence had become subtler, too.

"Continuing what I mentioned last night," she began, "I went on a journey to find Vedlyr, the brother of Slyen, and bring him up to Slyenials. I went through Scoria to Port Anatya and took a ship down to Mettain. While I was traveling, I learned many things I hadn't known. The reason Zypha is going to war against Queria, for example."

Ryder nodded, listening with a resigned expression on his face. "Do you know the reason we kept it secret from your people?" he asked. "It was to protect you. Your people are peaceful, and they welcomed us warmly instead of taking up arms against us, even though we came in as invaders thinking this was a Querian settlement. Somehow, it felt wrong to involve you in our dispute, so we planned to keep the valley secret, and protect you from the turmoil found outside this quiet valley."

"I understand," Aja admitted. "I understand a lot of things now, that I didn't before. Like the reason you want to stand up against Queria and not let them get away with what they've been doing. It makes sense to me, but I still think that war is not the right answer." She gave him a grave look, preparing herself for her argument. "There's something you don't know. Something important, and I fear what will happen if I don't tell you."

"Then tell me," Ryder said. "I will hear it."

She nodded. "Have you heard of Clairvoyance?"

A scowl flashed across his face, and skepticism filled his eyes. "I've heard of it," he said hesitantly.

"Long ago," Aja said, hoping he would continue to listen, "my people were led to this valley because of a dream one man had. He dreamed about disaster coming to the world, and he told everyone he could about the danger. Those that listened followed him, and they settled in this valley and founded the five villages and wrote the Tenets of our people. As it turns out, the dream he had protected my ancestors from dying in the genocide caused by the Moglians."

Ryder straightened with astonishment, and worry stole into his eyes. "How do you know about that?" he asked. "It happened hundreds of years ago—it's not something people talk about."

"I know because I had a dream too," Aja said. "I've always had dreams that show me things before they happen. Usually it's bad things, and if I ignore my dreams, they come true." Her face grew pale as she recalled her dream of red skies, of the bodies of Zyphans and Slyens alike, lying dead in the valley. "The dream is why I left the valley at Slyen's request."

"What dream?" Ryder demanded.

She met his eyes with a resolute stare. "I dreamt of that same genocide happening a second time. Zyphans and Slyens were dead, and the sky was red with the sound of anger. The Moglians were angry with us. Although, I didn't know it was Moglians at the time, I learned about them later. I know without a shadow of a doubt that they will band together once more if Zypha and Queria go to war. And this time, we won't be spared."

Ryder leaned back in his chair, studying her face intently. Then, rubbing his face with one hand, he let out a sigh. He was quiet for a long time, considering her words. He said nothing, just sat there with his eyes unfocused, staring at nothing.

"I know why you want to fight," Aja said grimly. "And I feel the same things you must feel. The injustice of being pirated, the frustration of being lied to, and the determination to not let them get away with what they've done. I am Slyen, but in my heart I am also Zyphan. I think of your people as our people."

The General's expression softened at her words, and when his eyes focused again, he looked at her thoughtfully. "We think of your people as our people too," he said quietly.

"Trust me," Aja urged. "I understand why it's important to Zypha. But you *must not* go to war. Not through Moglia, not from our valley. Not at all. I know it's hard, but please trust me. All of us will *die* if you go through with your plans."

General Ryder rose from his chair, walked toward the window, and gazed out across the village with a dreary expression on his face. For a time, he was quiet, thinking. And then, with a sigh, he spoke. "Most of the world may have forgotten what happened," he said, in the tone that implied he would be speaking for a while. "But Zypha remembers. We remember, because we made a promise—a promise that we would *never* be the cause for this world to reject humanity again. That dream you had… it's the red skies that makes me believe you. You could not have known about it, because the sky was not red everywhere. It was only red in the place where the genocide began."

Aja turned in her chair to face him, listening to him as intently as he had listened to her.

"You see," the General continued, gazing off into the distance, "the sky was not red because of the Moglians' anger. It was red because their forest was on fire. It's not clear how the fire started. Some say it was intentional, some say it was an accident. But the fire could not be controlled, and it swept through Moglian territory, destroying ancient forests that had been around longer than humanity had been on the planet." He paused, glancing toward her. "Yes, humanity is not from this world, originally. We found a home here long ago, and at first, we were welcomed. But on that day, when the whole of Moglia was burning, the Moglians regretted that we had been allowed to stay."

"Where did humanity come from?" Aja asked, unable to help her curiosity.

"Another world, far, far away," Ryder answered vaguely. "It doesn't matter anymore. What matters is that, when humanity was nearly wiped out, the Moglians decided to let a few survivors live. It was on that day that Zypha made a promise, that we would never forget what had happened, and that we would teach our children these truths—that humanity are guests to this world, that it was our fault the Moglians' wrath was incited, and that we must never allow our knowledge or technology to advance the world further than it would naturally advance."

"When I was on Captain Andrus's ship," Aja said thoughtfully, "he mentioned something called satellite."

"Yes," Ryder smiled thinly. "It's human technology, a metal machine that orbits this planet, and allows us to send messages to each other. It's secret because of our promise. A relic from the time before the genocide. We have not added more satellites, though we know how, because we are determined to keep to our promise. That said, we do use the one that is still up there."

"And the electricity and steam powered ships?" Aja asked. "Are those advanced technologies too?"

"Yes," he admitted with a laugh, turning to face her. He walked back to his desk and leaned against it. "I will admit, we do use technology that is more advanced than the rest of the world, but we have used Mettain as a guideline for what we are allowed to utilize outside of our island. They use swords and archery, so we used swords and archery. They recently designed pistols using magnetic technology they picked up in Kirilian, so we can now use pistols, too. And like us, the Querians copy any tech they can get their hands on. They don't have the knowledge we have, since we still have the original spacecraft that carried us to this planet. And that is part of why they pirate our ships."

"Then, if Zypha is determined not to cause another genocide," Aja said firmly, "there's a chance they will listen if you bring word that another one is going to occur."

"I can't promise that," he shook his head. "But it is my responsibility to bring that risk to my superiors." He lifted a hand, touching the badges on his uniform. "I am one of five generals that can direct the course of our nation," he explained. It was something Jaqlai had told Aja once before, so she nodded to show she understood. "If I bring a compelling argument, then I have the authority to call for a vote—one that could stop us from going to war. I'll have to get one anyway, to convince them to obey the Moglian's message you gave me."

"Then if you have to have one anyway, you should tell them about my dream," Aja insisted. "Can't you see how your plans are a threat? Traveling through Moglia, taking Querian cities… even if you manage to pull it off, what kind of response will Queria make? Can you predict it, or prevent it? I dreamed of red skies. How much of the forest will burn this time, if the Querians choose to fight with fire?"

Ryder started, looking at her in disbelief. "How do you know all of that?" he demanded. "Who told it to you?"

"Slyen," Aja stared back at him evenly. "The Moglian."

Ryder sighed, his alarm fading. "Of course," he said blandly. "I suppose I should have guessed."

"Can't you see the problem?" she pleaded.

"I can see it," Ryder answered wryly. "Perhaps better than you can. I know what kinds of things Queria might do, and how the situation might turn. It was something we considered long before we launched this campaign, and it was deemed an unnecessary concern. We planned to rush in, take a few cities and hold them until Queria acquiesced to our demands. Then we would leave, and the war would be over."

"It won't work that way," Aja said. "Please, General Ryder. You must believe me."

She could feel a strength behind her words, a flow of energy that made the hair stand up on her back and arms. *Their Influence is with me,* she thought excitedly. *I can't fail.*

Ryder stood up again, pacing back and forth in his office. After a moment, he came to a stop and faced her. "You said that there are *two* Moglians here in Slyenials right now?" he asked. She nodded. "That might be enough."

"Enough for what?" she asked. She didn't want to tell him that one of them was dying.

"Enough for me to convince the others that the Moglians are watching this conflict, and that we risk their wrath," Ryder said. He lifted his hand and twisted the end of his mustache, his expression thoughtful. "Yes… Moglians don't normally like being near one another. If two have gathered, then it stands to reason that more might join them."

"So, you believe me?" she asked hopefully.

"I never doubted you," he gave her a weary smile. "The problem was whether *they* would believe *me*."

Aja nodded, her face grave. Ryder would not have the Influence of Slyen and Jaqlai backing his words, when he went back to Zypha. *Oh,* she realized, sadness rising inside her. *That's right. Ryder… is going to leave. And not just him… all the Zyphans. Even Emrin.*

It hadn't occurred to her until that moment, if the Zyphans obeyed Slyen's request, they would all leave and the valley would go back to how it used to be. Her heart clenched with grief inside her, and she placed a hand over it with a shiver. It was only now, faced with the reality of the situation, that she realized the truth.

She didn't want them to go.

"It's going to take time," Ryder said, his voice cutting into her thoughts. "But I will follow Slyen's request. Our forces will be moved back to Zypha, we will cease development of the valley, and we will keep the valley secret from the rest of the world."

"Do you… *all* have to go?" Aja asked, looking up at him with a sadness she couldn't hide. "Slyen never said you weren't welcome… he said only that those who remain must follow our Tenets."

"I remember," Ryder said, smiling faintly. He came toward her and patted her shoulder. "And I suspect that many of my men would rather stay here than return home. I've been approached by several of them, asking to be stationed here long-term. The problem is that they are soldiers sworn to service. They must go where they are ordered to—including Daly."

It took a second for Aja to remember that all the Zyphans referred to each other by their last names. *He means Emrin,* she thought, her ears turning red with embarrassment. She glanced away nervously. "Even you have to go?" she asked, wanting to turn the conversation away from her and Emrin.

"Especially me," Ryder chuckled. He let go of her shoulder and walked to his desk, taking a seat. "I'll send word by satellite first, of course. It is within my authority to postpone launching the attack if I judge it necessary, though I will have to report the situation and my reasoning. It is my plan to inform them of the Moglian development and request a vote regarding the war. At the very least, I'll make sure Slyenials is left out of it, and that the bulk of our forces move out in the spring."

Aja nodded, both relieved and saddened to hear it.

"I suspect you are going to return to Slyen to tell him about our discussion?" Ryder asked, raising both eyebrows questioningly. He took a slip of paper out of his desk drawer, took up his ink pen, and began to write.

"Yes," Aja said, thinking of Emrin and Vedlyr.

"Then please take my answer with you," Ryder said. He finished writing on the paper, blew on it to dry the ink, and then folded it up. She took it when he handed it to her. "Ask him if the people of Zypha will still be welcome here, if they come to visit or to live here."

"I will ask," Aja promised.

"Good." He rose to his feet. "Then this meeting is adjourned. I must make my report to my superiors at once."

Aja understood that he meant for her to leave, and she rose and nodded her head quickly. "I'll go right now," she promised.

Ryder smiled faintly at her. "You have become much bolder than before," he said gently. "It must have been a hard journey to make on your own. If going meant you were able to bring me this message, then I'm glad you went. Gladder you returned safely."

I almost didn't, she thought, recalling all the close calls she had managed to slip through. Being captured by Scorians, the walk through the desert, the patrel while she was on Andrus' ship, and the great scorpion on their way back. All she said was, "Thank you."

As she stepped out of his office and headed out of the barracks, she slipped the letter under her cloak into her pocket. Then, she headed straight for the edge of the forest and entered it at a swift pace. After walking a short distance, she closed her eyes and opened her senses, *Listening* to the forest around her. It didn't take long for her to hear the crunching of twigs and pine needles, the echo of footsteps that had passed recently through.

This way, she thought, and she headed in the direction Emrin had gone.

The Final Meeting

Aja stepped into the mossy clearing, her senses exhausted from *Listening* to the echoes of Emrin's footsteps. At first, she was concerned that she had missed him in the woods somewhere, but when she cast her gaze around the wide-open space, she saw that he was here. He was kneeling beside Vedlyr, speaking to him in a soft tone, though she could hear nervousness in his voice. Relieved, she walked forward to join him.

Slyen stood by Vedlyr's side, arms crossed and his face scowling, as he observed Emrin tending to his brother. But when he sensed Aja approach, he looked up at her. "Well?" he asked. "What happened?"

With a proud smile, Aja handed over the folded letter that Ryder had given her. "He agreed," she said. "It was surprisingly easy to convince him."

"Easy?" Slyen blurted, his brow furrowing and his whiskers twitching.

To Aja's left, she heard a wry laugh. When she turned, she saw Jaqlai lying on his back on the moss, drenched in sweat and pale in the face. "That's because *we* did all the work," he complained. His eyes were closed, and he lay perfectly still aside from a twitch or two from his tail.

"Thank you," Aja smiled in amusement. *It must have been difficult,* she thought.

Slyen unfolded the letter Aja had given him, shooting Jaqlai a glance. "If you weren't wasting so much energy trying to *force* the results, you wouldn't be so exhausted. Influence works best when it's subtle."

"I know that," Jaqlai said dryly, "but it's hard to tell what's subtle when you have this much strength to work with. It was like trying to shave with a claymore when all you need is a razor."

"It's all about intention and focus," Slyen said sternly. "You must internalize the goal first, and then let your Influence follow the flow." He glanced down at the letter and scowled. "Aja," he said flatly. "Did you read this?"

"No, why?" Aja couldn't tell whether he was irritated or disappointed. Either way, his reaction wasn't good. *What did he write?* she wondered curiously.

Slyen handed her the letter, his whiskers twitching and his eyes narrow.

She opened the folded page, glancing down at the words. "Come meet me in person," it said. And that was all. "That's… not what I expected," she admitted, smiling despite Slyen's annoyance.

He crossed his arms, glaring at the edge of the clearing in the direction of Northbank. "How dare he make a demand like that. Meet him in person? I need do *no* such thing. I sent you, my representative. If he's not willing to listen to you, then he's already lost my favor."

"But he *was* willing to listen to you," Aja insisted, surprised by his anger. Was it really such a difficult thing to ask for? "He already told me that he plans to follow all of your requests. If he's asking to meet with you, then it must be for a good reason." Her voice turned firm as she spoke, determination filling her as she defended General Ryder. "I trust him, Slyen."

Emrin lifted his head, glancing toward her with a faint smile. He said nothing, only continued to treat Vedlyr's hidden wound, but Aja could sense his appreciation.

"I do not need to speak with him in person to get my message across," Slyen said, lifting his chin defiantly.

"No, you don't," Aja agreed. "Just as I did not have to go to Mettain to find your brother. But I went anyway, because it was the right thing to do."

"This is different," Slyen shook his head, though by the changed expression on his face, it was clear he was thinking about her words. "I shouldn't have to leave my forest for him to take his people and go."

"You don't have to," Aja said, her voice gentle. "But if you went, it would mean a lot to *me*. I believe in General Ryder, and I know he wouldn't have asked without a good reason. But I also believe in you, that you care about everyone in this valley. Even the Zyphans."

Slyen frowned, though he said nothing. His ear twitched and he avoided her gaze.

"It was you who kept Emrin safe in the forest, both times he entered," Aja said knowingly, one corner of her mouth lifting slightly. "And even though you could have turned this whole forest against them if you wanted to, you didn't. Instead, you sent me to find Vedlyr so you could convince them to leave peacefully. Won't you show one last kindness before they go? For me, if nothing else?"

"I suppose if you're going to be that adamant about it," Slyen complained, letting out a tired sigh. He shook his head, though his expression softened. "Very well, I will meet with General Ryder tomorrow. Go and tell him to expect me at noon."

"I'll tell him," Aja smiled, stepping towards him. She leaned in and kissed him on the cheek and was surprised by how soft his fur was. "Thank you, Slyen."

He waved her off, seeming embarrassed, but the expression in his eyes was warmer than before.

Aja went to Vedlyr next, kneeling on the moss by Emrin's side. The half-Raelynx looked up at her with a tired smile, lifted a paw and touching her arm. "You did well," he told her. "I knew you would."

Sadness colored Aja's thoughts as she gazed down at him. She placed a hand over his paw, her eyes moistening. "I'm sorry," she said. "You came all this way because of me, but... because of me, you were injured. Because of me..." she couldn't bring herself to say the words she feared the most. Even though she knew he might be dying, she didn't want to admit it out loud.

Vedlyr chuckled lightly, shaking his head. "Because of you, I made a journey I should have made a long time ago," he corrected. "It is a comfort to me, to spend my twilight days with my brother. And it was my honor, to protect not only a promising child of Mettain, but my brother's precious child as well. It is the duty of the old to protect and empower the young. I have no regrets."

"Vedlyr," Aja said, tears spilling down her cheeks.

"Do not weep for me," he insisted. "I do not think I will perish. Not with the help of Slyen's Influence, and the kindness you and this young man have shown me."

"I wish I could do more," Emrin said regretfully.

"You've done enough," Vedlyr murmured. He closed his eyes, dropping his arm by his side. "Now, I would sleep, if you would be so kind."

Aja nodded, wiping her face with her sleeve as she rose to her feet.

Slyen cleared his throat. "You two should head back before it gets dark," he said, glancing first at Aja, then at Emrin. "And you," he walked over to where Jaqlai was lying on the moss. "You and I have some more training to do."

"Ugh," Jaqlai groaned. "Aja, use your magic words and convince him to give me a break."

Aja smiled innocently. "Don't work too hard," she said.

Jaqlai opened his eyes, ears twisting backwards. "And I thought we were friends," he said.

Emrin glanced between them, his brow furrowing slightly. He rose to his feet and hung a bag on his shoulder, which he had used to carry the medicinal supplies. "Do you know the way back?" he asked quietly. "Because I don't."

"Yes," she said. She peered around him to where Vedlyr was lying, eyes closed, breathing evenly. "Will he be alright?" she asked worriedly.

"I've done what I can, and I'm leaving the supplies with them," Emrin answered. "He drank some of the tea, and his wound has been cleaned and disinfected. I'm afraid of offering any antibiotics though—cats have such a different metabolism than humans, it might kill him if I gave him something."

"Rest in this clearing will do as much good as your medicine," Slyen assured them. "For now, what he needs is time."

"Alright," Aja said, worried and encouraged simultaneously. As she left the clearing behind, she cast one last look over her shoulder to see Slyen sitting beside his brother, and Jaqlai pulling himself to his knees across from him. *He'll be alright,* she told herself. *And I'll see them tomorrow.*

When they had walked for a while, Emrin broke the silence by clearing his throat. "So," he said, glancing over his shoulder. "That Jaqlai fellow that you traveled with…"

"He's just a friend," Aja said quickly, not wanting to have the same kind of discussion she had had with Andrus.

"Right," Emrin cracked a smile. "I was actually wondering, what was he doing that was so exhausting?"

"Oh," Aja said, flushing with embarrassment. *I guess he wasn't asking if I liked him.* "He was using Influence. Vedlyr would have done it, but he was injured. So Jaqlai stepped up to help Slyen in his place."

"What sort of Influence were they using?" Emrin asked. "Should I be worried?"

"I don't think so," Aja said, turning her head to look at him. She wondered if he would be hurt by Slyen's purpose when he heard it. "Slyen was using Influence to make General Ryder listen to me when I brought his request. He wants the Zyphans to leave the valley as it was, and not use it in the war, because these are his lands. And he used Influence to persuade Ryder because he is peaceful."

"Hard to imagine a peaceful Moglian," Emrin admitted nervously. "But… there's no arguing with the evidence. They say a Moglian's lands reflect what sort of person they are. And there's no place more peaceful than Slyenials."

Aja smiled warmly, encouraged by his words. "I'm glad you found the clearing alright," she said, her thoughts turning to Vedlyr, and how grateful she was that he was willing to come. "It means a lot to me that you came to help Slyen's brother."

"Actually, it's a funny story," Emrin said, raising his eyebrows a little as he spoke of it. "Do you remember what I told you about the first time I came into these woods?"

"A jaguar made you leave," she nodded. She almost admitted that she still had all of his letters but lost her nerve at the last second.

"Right," he nodded. "Well, wouldn't you know it, a jaguar came to me this time, too. I was only ten minutes into the forest when it just leapt down from the branches behind me. When I tell you… my heart was in my throat, and I thought for sure I was going to die." He laughed, shaking his head. "But just like before, it walked toward me while I walked backwards, until suddenly my back came up against a tree and I was frozen in place."

Aja shivered, understanding just how terrifying that must have been.

"But then," Emrin continued, "it walked right past me. It stopped a few paces away, turned its head, and *looked* at me so intently, I thought for sure it must be intelligent. I had the strangest sense that it wanted me to follow it. And…" he smiled at her, reaching for her hand.

Aja looked at it, then lifted her gaze to meet his. She reached out and took his outstretched hand, her heart fluttering in her chest. They continued walking side by side.

"And I thought of you," Emrin said. "I believed in you, that you wouldn't have led me astray. So, I pushed myself away from the tree and started following it. Sure enough, the jaguar began to walk ahead of me, checking every now and then to see that I was following. Eventually, I reached the clearing. That's when the Moglian—the one who wasn't injured—spoke to me." He chuckled, shaking his head. "He said, 'There you are, Emrin.' I was so shocked to hear my name that I just stood there with my mouth open like a fool. 'There you are, Emrin,' he said. 'I gather that Aja sent you. What is your purpose for coming here?'"

Hearing Emrin tell the story was as entertaining as reading his letters, and Aja listened in rapt silence. She could feel a rapid pulse between their hands, and she wasn't sure if it was his or hers.

"Well, I told them I came to help someone who had been stung by a scorpion," Emrin continued. "I had no idea it was the other Moglian who was injured. You could have warned me."

"I didn't think of it," she admitted.

"Well, it's alright now," he said, his voice warm. "It was very interesting, I have to admit. Tending to one Moglian while listening to the other talk about Influence. The way he talked almost had me believing *I* could do it, too. It wasn't long before you arrived, too." He squeezed her hand, turning to look at her with a searching gaze. "I didn't get to say it before, so I'll say it now. I missed you, Aja. Every day that you were gone, I missed you."

"I... missed you too," she admitted. "Not at first. In the beginning, I just missed *home*. But soon I realized that when I thought about home, I thought about you, too. Getting to write letters to you every day made riding on the ship bearable."

"Not fond of ships?" he teased. But then his grin softened. "Writing to you made waiting for you bearable. I was visiting your mother every week, since the day you went missing. I know you said I couldn't tell anyone where you were, but I ended up telling her that I was writing to you. I just felt like it was the right thing to do."

"I'm glad you told her," Aja said. She thought of home, of her mother, of Ryder, and longing filled her chest. She couldn't wait to return to all of them. "Would you like to stay for dinner tonight?" she asked, feeling nervous. She hadn't asked ahead of time, but she didn't want to just wish him farewell once they exited the woods. Getting to spend more time with him sounded nice.

"I'd love to," Emrin beamed.

They held hands all through their walk through the forest, talking about Aja's journey and all the places she had seen.

——— ✦ ———

It was noon the following day, and all of the Zyphans had been assembled outside the barracks. General Ryder stood atop a raised platform, looking over the men and women standing at attention before him. Beside him was one of his lieutenants, who was transcribing everything that occurred on a notepad with a firm, wooden back. On the side, watching the soldiers curiously, were the people of Northbank. They had come when they saw the soldiers gathering, as though they could sense something important was happening.

Ryder had asked Aja to come stand next to him on the platform as they waited for Slyen to appear, and her nervousness was so great that her stomach felt sick.

The General cleared his throat loudly and began to speak. "I have called this assembly for a very important reason," he said, his voice carrying across the field. He was so loud that Aja flinched when he first started speaking. "Today, I will be meeting with the guardian and owner of Slyenials—the Moglian Slyen."

A sensation of shock and alarm passed through the soldiers, many of their faces transforming with fear at these words. But they didn't break control, standing firm at attention and listening intently to their general. Not one of them said a word.

"Many of you will recall Aja Sorinsa," Ryder continued, "who went missing several weeks back. This was because she was sent as the Moglian's emissary to call *another* Moglian to these lands." He clasped his hands behind his back, looking at all of the soldiers gravely. "She returned bearing this message from Slyen: 'Leave these lands as they were, do not involve Slyenials in the war, and those who choose to remain must abide by the Tenets of his people. Do not speak of this valley to anyone, or his wrath will follow us."

The tension amongst the soldiers grew stronger, and Aja saw many of them cast glances at each other, a few whispering under their breath to one another. She caught sight of Emrin in the crowd, and saw that it was her he was watching, rather than Ryder. Her cheeks warmed, but she felt braver seeing him.

"I have called for Slyen to come here in person," General Ryder announced. "To come to an agreement regarding his terms. And I ask that all of you bear witness, for we *will* abide by the demands he has made."

Aja felt a prickling in her nerves, a sense of awareness and pressure, and she turned her head to see Slyen himself walking onto the platform, though she would not have noticed him if she couldn't sense him. He must be using Influence, not to make himself invisible to their eyes, but to lower their awareness of him. He met her eyes, nodding his head once, and he came to stand beside her.

"Well," Slyen declared, and though he didn't raise his voice, it carried so that everyone could hear him. "Here I am."

As soon as they became aware of him, the Zyphans began to speak to one another in fear.

"A Moglian," someone whispered.

"It's really true!" another gasped.

General Ryder straightened, lifting his chin and calling out, "Attention!"

At once, the soldiers fell silent, their grim faces pointed at their leader. But among the Slyens, there arose a murmur of amazement. They whispered to one another, some with excitement, and others with disbelief. They had heard the same stories Sorin used to tell Aja. The story of their history, and of the Guardian who had welcomed them.

Ryder nodded, turning to face Slyen. "I thank you for coming," he said, inclining his head in a show of respect. "I wanted to meet like this so that our words can be recorded. If I am to honor your request faithfully, I must follow the guidelines our nation has set in place."

"Yes, very well," Slyen remarked, a little gruffly, though his demeanor was calm. "What is it you wish to discuss."

"You have asked us to leave the valley as it was," Ryder smiled gratefully. "Am I to understand this means, you do not want us to develop the valley?"

"Correct," Slyen said. "I do not wish for this to become a commercial or military establishment."

"Does that mean we cannot bring better plumbing to the buildings here?" Ryder continued. "What about electricity?"

Slyen scowled, glancing toward the new buildings that the Zyphans had erected in the months they had been here. "Let the elders of the five villages determine what they will allow. I believe they understand the way of the valley, and what I will tolerate."

"I understand," Ryder nodded, and moved on. "You have instructed us to not include the valley in our war. Does this mean you do not wish our soldiers to stop here, even for rest or supplies?"

"That is correct," Slyen said, drawing himself up to his full height. He was much smaller in stature than the general, who was tall and broad, but with the added aura of his Influence, Slyen seemed much more imposing. "You must take your soldiers and leave the moment winter has ended, and do not ever bring your military here again."

"We will pack up and leave when spring returns," Ryder promised, a grave expression on his face. "Zypha has always proudly remained neutral with the Moglians and respected their territories. We did not know these were your lands when we landed here."

"I know you didn't," Slyen said, his tension easing when he had the General's agreement. "Had you shown hostility to my people, or refused to listen to my request, we would be having a very different discussion."

Ryder smiled uneasily. "You have also requested us to keep the valley a secret and not mention it to anyone. This is something we have already been doing, and it is not difficult to continue. You have my word."

"Thank you," Slyen said, his whiskers flexing when he offered a faint smile.

"Lastly, there is the matter of those who choose to remain," Ryder continued. "Those of us who are here are soldiers, we serve our nation for a length of time that we have sworn to complete. We cannot simply choose to remain behind. But I wonder… does this mean that some of us may return to stay here when our time is served?"

"I will allow only those who will swear to the Tenets, and live the way my people live," Slyen said firmly.

"And what about Zyphan citizens who are not soldiers?" Ryder asked. "Are people welcome to come here to live, if they abide by the Tenets?"

"Just how many people are you thinking?" Slyen's fur bristled. "I do not want these lands overrun by people. There isn't that much space here."

"Then what if people came here temporarily?" Ryder asked gently. "As a vacation destination? Then, those who wish to stay may apply through our nation, and we can have a representative come to get your approval on who can come."

"This all sounds very tedious," Slyen sighed, rubbing his forehead with one paw. "I suppose if people came temporarily—and not too many at once—I would allow it."

"And those who wish to stay?" Ryder lifted his eyebrows questioningly.

"Let the village elders decide who and how many may come," Slyen waved his paw. "They understand the burden on the land each new resident will cause, so they will know how many is too many."

"It is gracious of you, to allow any of our people in your lands," Ryder acknowledged with a smile. "I am grateful to you. We will miss this valley and its people. They welcomed us with open arms, and we in turn have welcomed them. Slyenials will always be a part of us, a place we would cherish and protect as our own."

"Just so long as you remember that it is *not* yours, it is mine," Slyen reminded dryly.

"Yes," General Ryder said quickly, offering a somewhat nervous smile. "Of course."

Slyen nodded, crossing his arms. "Then if there is nothing more to discuss, I will take my leave. I will hold you to your word, General. And should Zypha break it, then you will face my wrath."

"Right," Ryder cleared his throat. He glanced at his lieutenant who was transcribing the meeting and nodded gravely. The lieutenant nodded back. "Well then," Ryder declared, "thank you for coming to meet with me, Slyen. And for sending your representative, Aja, to give us your message."

"Indeed," Slyen replied evenly. He glanced at Aja, his face softening with a smile. "Farewell." He bowed his head to the people of Northbank, many of whom bowed back to him. Then, before their eyes, he disappeared.

A murmur went up amongst the soldiers and the Slyens, marveling about what they had heard and seen. And as Aja looked around her, trying to determine where he had gone, she heard a whisper in her ear.

"Come back to my clearing," Slyen said softly. "And come alone."

She turned, looking for him, but could find no trace of him. *He left as mysteriously as he came,* she thought, and her heart squeezed in her chest. *And I'm the only one who gets to speak with him more.*

As Ryder turned to address his soldiers, re-affirming what they had heard and instructing them that they would be returning to Zypha in the spring, she stepped off the platform and slipped away, heading for the edge of the forest. The sooner she caught up with Slyen, the better.

She didn't encounter him on the way to the clearing, even though she hurried there. And when she arrived, she saw Slyen and Jaqlai sitting down near the edge, waiting for her.

"Come, sit," Slyen said, gesturing for her to join them. "Let's talk away from Vedlyr, so that he can sleep."

Aja dropped down to sit beside him, folding her legs and leaning her elbows on her knees. "Thank you for meeting with Ryder," she said. After what she had seen and heard today, she was glad that she wasn't made to be an errand girl between the two of them. She would have had to make several back-and-forth trips just to discuss Zyphans coming to live in Slyenials.

"You did well," Slyen praised, resting a paw on her shoulder. Then he glanced at Jaqlai and cleared his throat. "You *both* did well," he amended.

Jaqlai's ear twitched, a smile spreading across his face. "I was glad to help," he said, glancing toward Vedlyr. His smile faded, concern now taking its place.

"I suppose we should get right into it," Slyen nodded, and he dropped his paw from Aja's shoulder, turning to face her. "There's a reason I asked you to come out here. I'm afraid Jaqlai must leave at once—I'm to take him to the canyon in just a few minutes."

"Leave?" Aja blurted, alarm shooting through her. "But why? You only just got here," she said, facing him. "I wanted to show you around my village, introduce you to my mother, my sister…"

"I'm sorry," Jaqlai grimaced. "Winter is coming, and I don't want to get stuck here. Vedlyr…" he sighed, looking at the sleeping half-Raelynx sadly. "Before he fell asleep, he begged me to return to Mettain immediately. If I don't, another Moglian may try to claim those lands as theirs, or worse, the fiefs may vote to go to war. I'm supposed to Influence them to stay out of it."

"Do you know how?" Aja asked, worried and upset. "And what about the Asfarnil in the desert? What if he comes back to finish what he started?"

"I know how in theory," Jaqlai said, gesturing toward Slyen with one hand. "It will just take practice, and I can't do that without being there in person. As for the scorpion, I don't think he will appear again."

"I have given Jaqlai the same blessing that I gave you," Slyen said. "As thanks for escorting you to Mettain and back. He will not come to harm."

Aja chewed her lower lip, still anxious, but unable to find reasons to convince him to stay. If it really was at Vedlyr's request—possibly his *last* request—then how could she argue? "Then… you're leaving right away?" she asked.

He nodded, rising to his feet. The other two followed his lead, and there they stood a moment, silently regarding each other. Jaqlai lifted his bags, which had been sitting beside him on the moss. They were full, and Aja wondered if he had consolidated the supplies from all the bags into the two he carried. Would he have enough food for the journey?

"Do you have enough?" she asked. "Food, I mean."

"There were rations left over," Jaqlai nodded. "Enough to get one person to Port Anatya. I'll be fine." He hesitated, glancing at the sky.

It was time. Past time, if they wanted to reach the canyon by nightfall.

"I owe you more than I can ever repay," Aja said with a melancholy smile. It was difficult to be cheerful, when at the back of her mind, she knew she might never see him again. Her mind drifted to the journey they had taken together, all the times that he had been there for her, and a thought struck her. "Oh, wait, I almost forgot!" Fishing into her dress pocket, she brought out the pouch of coins and bills that he had once given her, handing it over. "You should take this back. I won't need them, here."

"Right," Jaqlai answered, taking the pouch a little hesitantly. His face fell, his ears drooping slightly. "I'll miss you," he admitted.

"Then come visit me again someday," Aja said, not wanting to say goodbye for good. "You know the way."

"I guess I do," he laughed. He glanced toward Vedlyr's sleeping form and his expression turned thoughtful. "Maybe someday," he said. "If I ever need to come back and get advice. Since I'm the temporary guardian of Mettain, I'm sure I have a lot to learn."

"I'm sure Slyen would be happy to teach you whatever you need to know," Aja offered, smiling playfully when she saw Slyen straighten with surprise.

"Don't promise things on *my* behalf," he scowled, though his expression softened slightly. "But yes... I suppose, I *should* help if you need it. You are my brother's chosen successor."

"I'll remember that," Jaqlai smiled.

"Well then," Slyen brushed a few stray pine needles off his fur and looked across the clearing. "Let's go while we still have light."

"Be safe," Aja said. And then, as an afterthought, she hastily added, "I'll miss you too."

Jaqlai's tail flicked side to side, and he offered her a teasing smirk as he began to walk across the clearing. "Good luck with your sweetheart," he said. "He seems nice."

Aja's ears turned red, though she managed to keep a blush from spreading across her face. "Good luck with yours," she retorted. "I'm sure Cait will be thrilled to see you again."

"Cait?" Jaqlai blurted, looking baffled. "What are you on about?"

"Keep your voice down," Slyen scolded, his whiskers bristling. "You'll wake Vedlyr." He walked soundlessly across the moss and disappeared between the trees.

Jaqlai paused before following him, then returned to Aja and pulled her into a hug. She hugged him back, unexpectedly overcome with emotion. She had to struggle to keep tears from falling. "Goodbye," he said, and without waiting for a reply, he turned and sprinted across the clearing after Slyen.

Aja lifted her hand and waved, and finally her tears fell. *I'll never forget him,* she thought. And then, with hope, *I* will *see him again, someday.* She left the quiet clearing, heading back through the woods for her home.

Epilogue

It was an early spring morning, and the wind was chill blowing up the sides of the cliffs from the raging river Uliah. Aja stood near the cliff's edge, watching General Ryder yell commands at his men as they loaded cargo onto the three steam ships that were anchored on the shore. They had been turned to face the west, so that when it was time to leave, they could simply push off from the bank into the current, and let it carry them out to the ocean. They would be leaving any day, now. Their preparations and packing were almost complete.

These cliffs always seem to take things from me, Aja thought, her mood dreary as she gazed down at the shore. They had taken her father when she was young. And now, in a few short days, they would take the man that she hadn't realized she viewed as a father until now.

It had been such a delight to be home, to spend time with her family and tell them all about her journey. To watch with amusement as Ryder cheerfully complemented himself in the mirror before he left for work in the mornings. To have him and Emrin spend so much time with her and Delia. Now, they were leaving. And it was with a heavy heart that she realized she might never see them again.

I don't want them to go, she thought, and laughed to herself. Months ago, she had been wishing they would leave. And now that they were, she wished they weren't.

"You're laughing," Emrin said, walking up the stone steps from the shore. "Is that a good thing, or do we look that ridiculous down there?"

"I was just laughing at irony," she said, and didn't feel like explaining. "Aren't you supposed to be working with the others?"

He stepped up behind her, wrapping his arms around her waist and pulling her against his chest. "I'm on break," he said, walking her a few steps away from the edge of the cliff, as though it made him nervous.

"Oh well, in that case," Aja said, leaning her head back against his shoulder. "I suppose it's fine."

"You suppose?" he chuckled.

Aja smiled, though she found it difficult to be cheerful, even in Emrin's presence. He would be gone soon, too. "I wish you didn't have to leave," she admitted quietly.

Emrin nodded, his face grave. "I still have two years left in the military. But after that, I plan to retire. I won't make that much money, retiring early, but… I won't need the money if I'm going to come live here. Right?"

"You're coming back?" Aja asked hopefully.

"Of course I am," he said, his arms squeezing her gently. "I want to be wherever you are. Although it's more than that. It's… this place… it feels like home to me."

It filled her with warmth to hear him say it, and Aja's heart filled with hope. She *would* see him again. It was definite. She just had to wait two more years.

"I'll wait for you," Aja said, and she meant it. She wouldn't have access to satellite, so she wouldn't be able to write letters to him. But she would wait for him to return. She would wait ten or twenty years, if she had to.

Emrin turned her to face him, taking both her hands in his. She could see his love for her shining in his eyes, alongside a boldness that sprang up in response to her words. "Marry me," he said with a smile. "Marry me and come to Zypha, Aja. We could live there while I finish my service, I could show you the place I grew up, introduce you to my family. Then, when my time in the military is over, we'll move back here and build a house in Northbank. One with a big garden out back, and you could teach me how to tend it with you."

The more he spoke the more earnest he became, his face lighting up as he painted the picture of what their life could be like. He squeezed her hands tightly, hope filling his features. Aja listened with a smile on her face, first in amusement, and then with curiosity.

She loved him. She wanted to spend the rest of her life with him, here in Slyenials where her heart was at home. And yet, as he spoke of his home, of the life they could have and the prospect of seeing a new place, she felt excitement growing inside her. She *wanted* to see Zypha, meet his parents, see Andrus again. But most of all, she just wanted to be with him.

"You'd love Zypha," Emrin continued, still trying to win her over without knowing he'd already succeeded. "It's right on the equator, so it's warm all year round. There's a volcanic island in the center of a large inland sea, and on the south side is a jungle where our coffee and cacao plants thrive. There's ocean, rivers, jungle, mountains… it's beautiful there, Aja. I'd love to show it to you."

"Alright," Aja said, a smile spreading across her face. "I'd like that."

"The sunsets are spectacular, and from my hometown, you can see the volcano on the—" he paused, blinking. "What was that?"

"Alright," Aja said again, her voice amused. "Let's go."

His face filled with amazement. "You mean it?" he asked. "You'll marry me?"

"Yes," Aja said, and her heart fluttered in her chest. She had never imagined a day would come when she would say that to someone, and here she was. *Mother knew before I did,* she thought, amused. *When I tell her, she won't even be surprised.*

Emrin grinned, lifting her in the air by the waist and spinning her around in excitement. When he set her down, he pulled her close and kissed her. "I love you," he said, leaning his forehead against hers.

Aja's face warmed. "I love you too," she said.

The End

Afterword

————————⊛————————

Cat's paw (Catspaw): definition
> *Noun: A person used to serve the purpose of another;*
> *a tool or pawn.*
> *Nautical: a light breeze that ruffles the surface of the*
> *water over a small area.*

The pawn is the weakest piece on the chess board. It can only move forward, one space at a time. And forward it must go, sometimes to sacrifice itself, and other times to make it across the board to the other side. But the pawn is more versatile than it seems. It can still attack diagonally, and when it reaches the other side of the board, it can become anything, restoring something important that has been lost.

In my life, I have often felt like a pawn; weak and insignificant, only able to move forward one step at a time. Yet even though the journey of life is difficult, and there are some days when it's a battle just to get out of bed, I've learned that every step of this journey is worth it. My goals may not be as lofty as a rook's, or as impressive as a bishop's, but like the pawn, I have worth even in simple steps. And when I reach the goal, I know that I too will be transformed for the better, and even things that are lost may be restored.

I wrote Catspaw many years ago, when I was still young, and my head was full of imagination and adventure. The story was much different back then, though the important parts are still the same. Aja left Slyenials to travel to Mettain, rescuing Jaqlai from captivity, getting stuck in Scoria, and heading back to Slyenials in victory at the end. But I was unhappy with it, and like me, the story itself was immature. I needed time to grow, to learn things in my life, to improve, before I could reshape it. And now, having written it as I wanted to at last, I am encouraged by the result.

Compared to others like Slyen and Jaqlai, Aja might seem like little more than a light breeze in a world much bigger than she has ever known. But even a light breeze can ruffle the water, causing ripples of change that spread in all directions. She was a pawn in a game between kings and knights, yet she was able to reach her goal, and found herself changed for the better in the process.

It is my hope that my readers will, likewise, not give up. Even when each day is harder than the last, the journey is worth it, and the right words have the power to make things possible. May you hold fast to your dreams, which will someday cause their own ripples. And may you find lost joy restored to you.

About the Author

Nia Jean

Reading and writing have been Nia's obsession since she first learned to write the word "cat". Greatly inspired by works such as L.E. Modesitt Jr.'s Recluse Series, Tolkien's Lord of the Rings, and Brian Jacques's Redwall Series, she gained a profound love for world building and book series. From a young age she began crafting worlds, characters, and adventures, and has always wanted to share the worlds she created with others. Now at last, she is beginning to publish the stories she has spent her whole life developing.

Catspaw takes place in a world she built along with her brother, and it is a world both authors intend to write many more books about.